I0654215

The Naughty Chocolatier

Ana'Gia Wright

Published by Penned In Blue, LLC, 2022.

This is a work of fiction. Similarities to real people, places, or events are entirely coincidental.

THE NAUGHTY CHOCOLATIER

First edition. December 1, 2022.

Copyright © 2022 Ana'Gia Wright.

ISBN: 978-1735727790

Written by Ana'Gia Wright.

Also by Ana'Gia Wright

A Guatreaux Family Saga
The Agency: Reviving Resurrection

Standalone
Doubletake
The Naughty Chocolatier

Watch for more at www.anagiawright.com.

Chapter One

Soliel stared out the window as the driver followed the driveway up to an unassuming home perched atop a gentle incline of a manicured lawn. Okay, so maybe among the other homes in this neighborhood Yaddi's house was unassuming. From the bottom of the hill, the old farm-style house with the wrap around porch seemed like an image out of one of those country television shows, the brick-front single-story abode out of place compared to the two- and three-story mansions they'd passed once entering the gated community. It gave the impression of this house being an original construction, quite possibly the only structure tucked away in the woods; a private lake front sanctuary of years gone by.

Like with everything else though, progress crept in. Plots of land sold off until the world outside the surrounding wall of trees encroached on the tranquility, albeit a structured and calculated intrusion for those with funds enough to snap up acreage and build their dreams.

Our vehicle pulled into the turn-around and the man in a black suit and tie rushed around to the rear passenger door to help me out of the plush SUV. I'd opted for a real car service forgoing a regular ride share considering the four suitcases and trunk I traveled with. My entire life packed in the bags as I sought a new beginning from a crumbled past.

I shooed the driver on to the task of unloading my life from the back of his vehicle. Slinging the carryon bag of immediacies over my shoulder, I started the trek over the brick walkway to the entryway of the house.

The front door swung open as I approached, my best-friend, Yaddi, bouncing from foot to foot, her fro bobbing in time as she waited for me to pass the last rocking chair before dashing out the door and engulfing me in one of those old big-momma hugs I'd so missed.

A hefty woman who always held her own, Yaddi knew what she wanted in life and went after it. Damn what others thought. With a warm smile and boisterous personality, she could brighten up any room or make a person feel minuscule with a flick of the wrist.

"Hey girl!" Yaddi exclaimed a little too close to my ear, her arm full of bangles cool against my bare back.

I leaned out of the hug, though I didn't really want too, as I struggled to maintain my composure. I was on the verge of tears; the Georgia heat did little for my asthma. I needed to get into the air conditioning and fast. I offered a questionable smile, the kind that said I'm trying to save face and failing miserably.

"Let's get you situated."

"But..."

Yaddi waved off my protest ushering me into the house with the driver on our heels toting two bags. We rounded the corner, a tall shirtless and shoeless brown skinned guy in grey sweatpants, ladies y'all know what that means, cut his eyes in our direction as he leaned casually against the island.

Embarrassed, for more than one reason, I said, "My bad. I didn't know you had company."

The man crossed his muscular arms, giving me the once over, his tongue rolling across his teeth beneath his lips like he liked what he saw.

"Who Dwayne? Girl Dwayne is a lot of things. But company, ain't one of them."

With a hitchhiker's jerk of her thumb, Yaddi directed Dwayne to assist the driver with the rest of my things as she guided me to a door next to the single step up that led to another entrance and a hallway to the back of the house.

"I thought you might like your own space, so the in-law suite is all yours."

We descended the staircase, which to my surprise, didn't lead to a damp dark dungeon basement. It really was a total in-law suite furnished with black leather movie theater seating, giant television hung from the wall, private bedroom, bathroom, and full kitchen.

"Wow." My jaw dropped as I took it all in. The wall of sliding glass doors led out to an in-ground pool, grassy yard with a trampoline and... "Wait, is the lake actually this close?"

"Really Soliel? When have you known me not to have lakefront with immediate access? And heads up, the pool is saltwater."

Yaddi was right, even when she resided in the heart of the hustle and bustle of New York City she kept a condo on Myrtle beach. Something about always needing to reconnect with the sea.

Still in awe, I crossed the room taking in the sea green of the pool water. "Looks like you are living it up."

'And now," Yaddi stepped to the side allowing Dwayne to make his way down the stairs, "so are you."

"I won't be in your hair long."

"Take all the time you need. It'll be nice to have someone else here. I don't know what I was thinking when I bought this big ass house."

"Big? If this is a big ass house, then what do you call what you neighbors have?"

She laughed, "Obnoxious."

I joined in Yaddi's merriment, just for a second though as my thoughts drifted back to the ever-growing list of to-do's vying for the shining top spot.

"You mind opening the gate? I'd rather not try to lug that trunk down these stairs."

The deep rumble of Dwayne's voice sent a shiver up my spine. I steadied my hand as I reached for the latch and opened the sliding glass door. Yaddi moved up behind me, the creaking of the stairs indicating Dwayne's retreat.

I felt her hesitation, that motherly alarm system of hers blaring, "You, okay?" she asked in a gentle tone.

My arms circled her body, gaze lingering on a white spot out on the lake, "I will be."

"I'm here when you're ready to talk."

Yaddi gave me a quick hug before disappearing around the side of the house to open the gate. We did need to talk. So many secrets I needed to purge, and not just about the demise of my marriage. Checking the time, I rushed back to her new kitchen where I'd dropped my bag, the alarm on my phone indicating it was time to start the next leg of my daily pill party.

After retrieving my carryon bag, I slipped into the bathroom and secured the door behind me. The bathroom was almost as large as the bedroom, with a full walk-in closet, separate makeup vanity, immaculate tiled steam shower, and dual sinks. Whoever designed the place tended to every detail from matching stainless-steel handles to the funky designed chandelier in the closet. It all fit together nicely against the black and white marble with a splash of red trim.

On to the ritual. I lined the orange bottles with white tops up on the vanity counter in order of number of pills. Two, two, two, one, one. I was down to five different medications from sixteen, a manageable enough number to start a pill pack service to not have to lung around a boat load of bottles or torture myself once a week dividing the pills into containers for travel.

Not that I traveled much as of late. The discovery of my husband's infidelity led to my reclusiveness. The decision wreaked havoc on my already struggling immune system. What was the point? Why care about anything? The illness. The meds. Hell, life itself. That was until Yaddi showed up on my doorstep furious at being ignored and avoided. I understood her worry, her mind probably in as much of a dark space as I'd felt. I was slowly killing myself, and Yaddi had thought I was dead.

She'd nursed me for a week where I'd spilled my guts about Daniel leaving me for some healthy highbrow hussy. While I kept the specifics to a minimum sooner or later, I planned for her to hear the full story. Luckily, I'd managed to hide my sickness then, Yaddi attributing my weakness and discomfort to stress. However, private space or not, I won't be able to do the same living under her roof.

I plucked a tissue from the box in the corner, dividing out the pills and taking them with the last of the water from the bottle from the plane. For the first time in months, I looked at myself in the mirror. The long curly lace-front wig. Splash of demure pink lipstick. Airbrush foundation and golden eyeshadow professionally applied before my departure. It was all wrong. All Celestial Soliel Divine Brodie and I was sick of it.

I flung the bathroom door open with newfound commitment to wash away the façade and again walk in my truth. I'd become a person I no longer desired to be under the watchful eyes of Daniel Brodie and I was done with that. I no longer had any ties to the man aside from the next ten years of alimony payments, full medical coverage, and the seven-figure chunk of change Yaddi's attorney friend had convinced Daniel it was in his best interest to fork over. Before we married, I warned him Yaddi wasn't one to be played with and attempting to screw over her friend was like a sheep prancing into a lioness den. It would not end well.

I found Yaddi perched on one of the dinette table bar stools scrolling through her phone acting like she wasn't waiting on me to come out and spill my guts.

"You ready to talk yet?" She said not bothering to advert her eyes from the glowing screen.

"Not yet. And not here."

That made her lower the phone, "What do you have in mind?"

"Girl's night?" Even I heard the devilishness in my voice.

"I'm game if you are?"

I scanned the room, mentally inventorying the bags to determine which ones I needed to rummage through. "Give me a couple of hours to settled in. "

"No problem. I'm sure I can find entertainment to my liking...until then." And up the stairs she went.

Chapter Two

Barely five, our driver pulled into the driveway. Excited out of our wits as we dashed out the door leaving Dwayne to his own devices, or quite possibly passed out from exhaustion, I slid into the rear passenger door held open by the driver with Yaddi's wide hips and thick thighs competing with my own forcing me over to the other side of the seat. Our driver closed the door, rounding the vehicle from the rear before easing back into the driver's seat. He offered soda, sparkling water, chocolate of which we declined before introducing himself and pulling out of the driveway.

"Why are you staring at me like I've grown another head?" I leaned into the soft leather seats of the Genesis G90 taking in the confusion on Yaddi's face. Our driver, a perky Black guy named Armond who kept glancing back at us in the rearview mirror flashing a chipped front tooth smile, took the highway headed north on I-75 towards downtown.

Yaddi did her classic Southern Belle hand over her cleavage in surprise move, "I'm just still in awe."

"Of what? I haven't forgotten when I came from."

"Could have fooled me," she quipped, eye roll included.

"Okay now. You really want to go there with me."

Yaddi's hand drifted across the seat, fingers running up the side of my thigh as she bit her bottom lip. Her voice dropped, and I felt Armond's eyes on us, "Now you know I wouldn't mind...."

I slapped her hand away, "I didn't mean that."

She snickered, a little on the hey-I'm-just-testing-the-waters side before shifting in her seat to gawk at me.

"Seriously though," her fingers tucked part of my oversized puff behind my ear sliding the rhinestone bobby pin back to keep it in what she deemed to be a more acceptable place. "When's the last time I've seen your real hair? And wait," she grabbed my arm easing the silver cuffed bracelet off, "Is this new ink?"

6

I'd forgotten about the tattoo. Our girl's nights fell few and far between after my marriage and ultimate move seven hundred miles away. And when Yaddi visited we did these dinner dates in fancy restaurants. Daniel loathed my tattoos, so I tended to cover them with makeup. The one on my wrist was only a couple of years old. A three-dimensional gimbal. If she was impressed by this one, she was gonna flip over the Phoenix on my back that played the chorus of Erykah Badu's *Next Lifetime* with a special app on my phone.

"It's a few years old."

"Can't be." Her brow furrowed as she studied the image closer by twisting my arm in an uncomfortable position. "I don't remember seeing it the last time I came up."

"Now you know Daniel..." She cut me off before I finished the thought. We'd agreed, no ex talk tonight.

Relinquishing my arm she said, "any others?"

"Maybe." I teased, scooting closer to the door on my side to stare at the Atlanta streets as we wove our way down College Ave.

Armond dropped us in our old stomping grounds. A strip of homes converted into restaurants, trendy shops, and a yoga studio on the main street. The side streets remained residential though the signage indicated not all of the neighbors were keen on the mixed transformation. A MARTA train roared by as we entered the brick front restaurant with old school charm and the glorious scent of fresh ground coffee permeating from the front counter.

Since Yaddi made reservations, I meandered over to check out the desserts in the display case deciding that before I left, I needed to fully indulge in a slice of triple chocolate mousse cake. When we were seated, I waved off the offered menu knowing exactly what I wanted.

"Shrimp and grits. Hot Chocolate, and a slice of that chocolate mousse cake. You can bring dessert first."

The auburn-haired girl with dark eyeliner and freckles scribbled my order on her little notepad and by the time she completed the task, Yaddi rambled off something about salmon as I took in the surroundings. Sun in My Belly was just as I remembered it. A quaint little café with the best food and best service. We'd sneak over here around this time after class to grab a snack before hitting the clubs or parties for the night. So many great memories.

"I'm glad this place is still here," I said my eyes drifting to the artwork hung from the interior brick walls. I often wonder what the place was like before it was converted into a restaurant. Had it always been a storefront, maybe a pharmacy or grocery? Or maybe a family once inhabited these cozy rooms.

"Me too. I occasionally meet clients here. Mostly small business owners without corporate boardrooms."

Good. Start out with something other than why I'd really asked to come back to the A and squat at her house for an undisclosed amount of time. "How is business?"

'Maddening. Especially with these newfound calls for diversity. But you know how I roll. Put up and implement or don't waste your time calling. I have more business than I know what to do with. I can get you in on it if you want to learn. You been around this circus as long as I have and the system I use is not that complicated."

Yaddi worked as a diversity consultant. One of the best in the business. Her reputation for lasting change preceded her and anyone even remotely considering her services knew two things for sure: she didn't come cheap, and she didn't half-ass do the job. She expected fifty percent of her negotiated fee up front and staggered payments due upon each complete implementation stage. If a client didn't follow through, then they went to the bottom of her waitlist which gave them roughly a year to get their shit together and get serious or opt to discontinue her services. At $400 - $600 an hour Yaddi knew her worth and in the current climate she had corporate bigwigs rolling out all the stops just to get on her radar as a potential client.

"I'll think about it," I said as our server returned with my hot chocolate and cake and Yaddi's wine.

When the woman scampered away Yaddi asked, "Not drinking?"

"I should eat first. I've had a long day. Stagnant recycled airplane air and all."

Accepting my explanation, she took a sip of wine, "I'm serious about the job though. I typically turn down the smaller clients just because I feel like I can make a bigger impact with the Fortune 500s."

"Not to mention the dollars."

"Ain't no shame over here. But in all seriousness, you could start out with the smaller clients vying for my attention. You're my girl and I got you."

"That you do. I never thanked you for your attorney recommendation."

Her face turned cold, "I thought we weren't going to talk about the ex."

"I'm not. I just wanted to thank you for the bank account." We laughed at the implication. While Yaddi didn't know exactly how much her attorney friend rang out of Daniel, she knew it was enough that if I played my cards right, I'd never 'have' to work again.

She raised her glass, "Happy to oblige."

Instead of delving into deep drama we spent our time catching up on inconsequential topics, avoiding men of course. Assuming I was going back to the me she'd known from our college days, Yaddi grilled me on what I planned to do with my hair. And of course, she just had to know if we need a shopping trip for a new wardrobe or if one of my suitcases harbored a secret stash of eclectic wares.

"Maybe I'll start sewing again," I said before shoveling the last spoonful of grits into my mouth.

"Uh oh. Are we going to do Bohemian Chic again?"

I gave her a seated hips sway dance as I said, "Me taw't chu like de Boho Chica?"

"See, this is why I can't with you."

I allowed Yaddi to pick up the tab as I waited for Armond to circle back around. In the meantime, I scrolled through my phone checking the weather and dismissing the four missed calls from my ex. I hadn't told anyone he'd started calling again and oddly he never left a message, just the incessant back-to-back calls that I ignored.

A quick trip back through downtown and Armond dropped us off at one of those fancy rooftop lounges Yaddi found so intriguing. I will admit I liked this one. Open air. Blue illuminated glass shielding encircling the edges to keep too- tipsy patrons from accidently plummeting to their demise. And the mojitos were to die for.

"Slow down," Yaddi warned as I ordered round three.

I'd eaten good, nothing wrong with a drink or two...or three. To divert her attention away from my spiraling descent into lush-dom I asked, "What's the deal with you and Dwayne."

"I thought we weren't discussing men tonight," she countered.

"Oh, I'm sorry, you misunderstood. We aren't discussing my men. Your men are fair game." I leaned in, flashing cleavage she took note of, as I rested my chin on my hand. "Now spill it sister."

Yaddi took a slow sip of her second Martini gawking at me over the rim of the glass before she lost the battle with the smile tugging at the corner of her lips. "Not much to tell. You know how I do. He came down for a long weekend." She lingered on the word 'long'. "He'll be on a plane back to New York Sunday evening."

"Ah, so he came down for a fix?"

"Among other things. Dwayne's a chiropractor and massage therapist. He can do wonder with those hands." Her eyelids lowered in that seductive remembrance way, "Dwayne is thorough and utterly generous, in case you ever need an," she paused for dramatic effect and to allow a Cheshire cat smile to cross her face, "adjustment." Double entendre duly noted. Not that I hadn't started down this road with flashing my tits in her direction.

One thing about Yaddi, she owned her sexuality. She flitted from lover to lover with what most would consider to be reckless abandonment, but scantily clad determine woman with a full-lipped bright smile knew what she wanted and where she stood in the world and anyone not with the program could kiss her big Black behind.

As far back as I could remember she never hid her preference for men and women alike. Yaddi did have a type for each gender, preferring average but perky breasted women who were bottom heavy. Though she kept one or two men under 5'9' due to other special skills they brought to the table, most of the men in her self-proclaimed harem stood over six feet, dark chocolate with a little to hold on to around the middle. Like myself Yaddi didn't go for the overly fit physique. The buff guys spent way too much time in the gym, and we liked our food. All layered in sweet syrupy chocolaty goodness and fried to beyond inches of its life.

And like others who drifted into Yaddi's gravitational pull, I'd succumbed to the intoxicating energy about her that made a person feel safe enough to test the waters and explore uncharted territory. Yaddi was an all-encompassing judgement free zone who never asked for commitment. In fact, that was rule number one when it came to sexual rendezvous. Yaddi made it clear to her partners she enjoyed sex and sexuality, but she was not looking to settle down with one lover.

Of course, there had been one run in with a certain man who'd assured her he didn't mind physically sharing her. I believe Stanley loved her. I think he was just naïve to believe in immunity to jealousy. And when it reared its ugly head Yaddi saw the writing on the wall. Even now, she kept a close eye on her partners, anyone turning clingy received walking papers. None had succeeded in taming the lioness.

My rapidly glazing over eyes caught movement to our right, a brown-skin man in slacks, a green button-down shirt and sports coat holding a Corona making his way to us. And yes, I noticed the big feet and the way he commanded attention as the other women studied his approach. Our eyes locked and he offered a straight smile I convinced myself was genetics and not years of professional dental work.

"Ladies."

My lady parts tingled at his greetings. I stared up at this tall drink of water as my nana used to say.

He lowered his drink to our table, offering a hand to me. "Hope you don't mind if I steal your friend away for a dance?"

It was a question, a cautionary one like he was trying to get a feel for not only my interest in his offer but men in general. I suppose in this day and age, with society finally getting over its bullshit gender norms and more same sex couples saying screw it we're going to do us, I understood the approach and kind of appreciated it.

Yaddi tossed back the rest of her drink as she gave this guy the once over before leaning over and whispering in my ear, "If you don't want him, I'd gladly take him off your hands. He looks real flexible. I could toss him around and bend him like a fresh rolled pretzel."

I couldn't hold the laughter, my head lowering, hand covering my face in embarrassment. When I regained enough composure to allow a straight face to fall into place, I tossed her my handbag and took the gentleman's hand.

Chapter Three

G *ood morning sunshine!*
That's what the sun said to me as it beamed through the open bedroom door. I dared to crack my eyes, head pounding as I recalled the five Mojito's I'd downed last night in a flashback to my college years that I immediately regretted. What was I thinking?

I tried to move, but the piercing pain shooting through my limbs zapped every ounce of energy and motivation. Tears welled in my eyes.

No. No. No. Not today.

I knew I'd taken a risk, alcohol being one of the triggers to exacerbate my medical condition. But for the first time in a long time, I didn't want to think about being sick, so I'd thrown caution to the wind and indulged and now here I lay utterly immobilized. I tried again. Maybe if I could just inch my way up to the head of the bed and the nightstand, I could reach the pain meds. I breathed my way through each thought before garnering enough courage to just do it.

My teeth gritted as I threw my all into one futile attempt to move; The floor and I shared an intimate kiss as I miscalculated and rolled off the end of the bed. At least I was facing the right direction now. And I was clothed so that would save me from carpet burn as I contemplated my next move. Still too far from the nightstand, I decided to just rest for a moment.

I must have drifted off because the next thing I knew, a hand grabbed my ankle, and I wailed so loud the flock of geese that congregated around the pond shrieked and took flight.

"Oh, my goodness," Yaddi immediately dropped my ankle. "Are you hurt?"

Hurt was putting it lightly. I heard the fear in her voice suspecting she thought I'd injured myself falling out of bed. I couldn't talk yet, the pain radiating all over my body. All I could do was lay there and cry as she crawled up to my head.

"What's wrong Soliel? Oh, my Goddess. Do I need to call 9-1-1?'

Way to panic Yaddi. I stopped her jabbering with a grunt. She leaned down to put her ear near my mouth to hear my faint whisper.

"Nightstand.... meds." I muttered through concentrated sobs. It even hurt to cry. I didn't want to move any more than I had to, so I closed my eyes and listened as she slid open the drawer and gasped.

Before heading out last night, I'd organized the drawer of medication for easy access. Two big boxes of pill packs and the five daily bottles. Plus, the two white bottles of powerful painkillers that I only took in times of desperation. And believe you me, I was desperate.

She scooped up every bottle, plopping down in front of me. "Which ones?"

Good. She'd calmed down and taken a more analytical approach to the situation instead of her initial fight or flight instinct. Yaddi was good that way. Give her something to focus on and she'd think things through instead of panicking.

"White bottles." I said wanting to roll up in the fetal position but sure it would hurt too much so I dismissed the natural desire and homed in on my breathing.

Yaddi's feet disappeared for a minute, and I heard the sound of pills being shaken out of the bottles followed by the fridge opening and closing. To my surprise, when she reappeared, she thrust a straw into my mouth. "Drink and I'll give you the pills one at a time."

I sucked a mouth full of water as she forced the first pill between my lips and gave me a minute to swallow. We repeated the process for the next two pills before I was beyond spent. So long as I didn't move, I could tolerate the slow aching pain. I'd used everything I had to get to this position and all I could do now was wait until the meds kicked in.

When I finally woke from my drug-induced stupor, hours later I suspected by the change of the sun's light, fear still reigned supreme. The aching was gone but it could just be a trick of my mind, so I just laid there for a minute watching as Yaddi picked up one of the pill bottles and started typing something into her phone.

Crap. Yaddi had camped out in the corner giving her a view of me but allowing her to rest her back comfortably against the wall. She'd dragged one of the Yoga pillows from the exercise room I'd seen upon my initial inspection of my new living arrangements.

Cat was out the bag now. I dared to wiggle a finger. Start small I told myself. Test the waters before diving into the deep end. No pain. I secretly danced inside before rolling my head. The crook in my neck from the awkward position annoyed me but nothing like the excruciating pain from before. If I made it through this test, I'd stretch it out first.

Yaddi's eyes came to rest on me as I worked to roll over onto my side.

"How ya feeling?" She asked, returning the pill bottle to the pile as she placed her phone on the nightstand.

"I'll live." Everything still hurt. Or maybe just my pride.

She claimed her feet, padding closer to me. "Need some help?"

"Yeah."

We managed to get me into an upright position opting for the theater seating in the open living space over the bed. I'd seen enough of it to know that I'd rather sit in something with more support. Yaddi thrust a full bottle of water towards me.

"Drink. You're dehydrated."

Among other things. I was glad she hadn't chosen hungover. I obliged, pressing the button on the side of the seat to raise the legs.

"You should have told me."

My eyes darted to my friend, "Are you going to lecture me now?"

"I should. You could have died."

I shrugged, "But I didn't."

'What is wrong with you?"

Everything and nothing. While her question might have had two meanings, I knew she wasn't referring to what physically ailed me. She wanted to know what was going through my mind and right now I was a blank slate waiting for the entity in dark billowy robes wielding a scythe to be like Calgon and take me away.

My life was a wreck. Though the average person wouldn't think so. But the money meant nothing when life itself meant so little. As the saying goes, money can't buy happiness.

"I need to eat," I finally said, closing my eyes.

"Oh. So, you're just not going to answer my question."

"Not on an empty stomach." I peeked an eye to gauge her reaction. "And possibly not at all. Either way, food comes first."

Yaddi huffed, sulking while she stalked around the room. I just laid there like a toad on a stool waiting on a juicy fly to appear. Eventually she stormed upstairs slamming cabinets and rattling pots and pans until the aroma of sautéed veggies and bacon hooked me. So easily manipulated.

I took inventory of my fridge. Couple of my favorite yogurts, bottled water, and blueberries. This would never do, though I silently thanked Yaddi for at least thinking of a quick something to grab and letting me shop on my own.

By the time I showered and changed out of last night's clothes, Yaddi was plating the food for herself and Dwayne. She handed him a plate, and he strategically excused himself daring not intrude upon girl talk. When he disappeared around the corner to the hallway leading to the bedrooms, I plopped down on one of the bar stools.

"You know I'm livid with you," Yaddi said scooping potatoes onto a plate for me.

"Yes mother."

"This is serious Soliel. You half scared me to death."

"Welcome to my new life. That's why I said I wouldn't be in your hair long. Almost dying all the time is rough on others. I don't want to put you through that."

"Put me through that? What the hell are you talking about?"

I gestured for her to finish putting the food together. "You might want to sit down for this."

She rounded the counter placing a plate before me piled high with skillet bacon still dripping in grease, potatoes scattered with bell pepper and onions, and eggs, just how I liked them fried hard. "See, if I keep eating like this, I'm gonna have a heart attack."

Yaddi chose the seat at the other end of the bar, the slinky yellow robe trimmed in lace she adorned left little to the imagination. She focused on her food. "Is that a change of subject?"

"Look. A lot has happened."

"Hmm. Are you saying, I should just be thankful you called me out the blue when you needed an attorney?"

"That's not fair Yaddi."

"Pot and kettle." She tossed her fork onto her plate. Appetite spent. "I get it Soliel. You have secrets. I have secrets."

"It wasn't always this way. Remember when we were staying in that shit-hole apartment in the bluff. And the guys downstairs used to come up to make us play truth or dare to see which one of us would spill the dirt on the other's kinky behavior?"

Undeterred, Yaddi just stared silently at her plate.

"Fine." Though I did need to eat, I slid the plate away from me and swivel to face her. "I saw you checking the meds."

"What is it?" She tried to keep the quiver out of her voice but failed. "Cancer?"

"No. That would be a more definitive diagnosis. I don't have nearly as many options as cancer patients."

She turned to face me then. "What? What is it then?"

"The medical term is Trypanosoma Cruzi." The words rolled off my tongue with ease at this point. I'd said them a million times to hundreds of doctors in search of an apparently nonexistent cure. "It's commonly known as Chagas disease. I'm a giant experiment."

"I don't understand?"

Her genuine concern forced me to press on. "I shouldn't be going through what I'm going through. Or at least, not right now. What the doctors are seeing usually doesn't show up for decades in people who've been exposed."

"But what is it?"

"It starts out as a parasitic infection. I must have gotten it on one of our trips to South America. You know I'm a country girl and I don't mind roughing it, so we'd opt for jungle cabanas instead of lush hotels. A couple months after one of those trips Danny noticed lesions on my arm and back. I'd had on and off headaches since we'd returned and fever that refused to break. I chalked it up to the heat and stress. Then one of my eyelids started to swell and it was all downhill from there."

"Wow."

"Yeah. None of the doctors seemed to know what was going on. I was talking to one of the cleaning ladies who'd apparently been watching my descent into illness. She knew we traveled to South and Central America a lot and suggested I might want to get checked for Chagas. She said in the smaller towns it can be easily transmitted. Since we ventured into jungle instead of staying in the more touristy sections it made sense."

"What's the prognosis? I mean there has to be a cure."

"Like I said, I'm one big experiment. Because it took so long to identify the cause there was no guarantee the anti-parasitic drugs would work. I'm on to the chronic phase. For most patients that doesn't start for decades. Here I am a year and a half down the road, and they are already seeing signs of an enlarged heart."

Yaddi moved to the empty seat between us, resting a hand over mine her robe falling open to reveal her lack of bosom support. "I'm guessing Danny didn't take the news too well."

I huffed. "Bastard." It was the only word I could use to describe him. "First, he started missing my appointments. When I was hospitalized, I'd barely see him. I mean he was in surgery, and I tried to dismiss it as work obligations. Then some chick started playing on my phone. Sending me random detailed texted messages. Next came the photos of them cuddled up. Instead of him sticking by my side, he started seeing this nineteen-year-old. By the time I had the strength to confront him, the girl was knocked up."

Yaddi gawked at me, mouth wide open in disbelief. I hadn't told her the full story because I was tired of it. Just like I was tired of the shitload of pills and the watching what I ate and what I did. I was basically tired of life and was over it all.

"Um," I reached out, hand propped under her chin, "You can close your mouth now."

She was on her feet, "That trifling, sleazy no-good son of a bitch. I'll kill him."

"See." I waved a finger at her, "This is exactly why I didn't tell you. Don't worry. He got what he deserved and then some."

"Oh please," I swear I could see the devil horns rising out of her head, flaming pitchfork and all, "what you got out of him wasn't nearly enough."

'Ah that's just it. Thanks to your attorney, I'm set for life. Money. Medical care. Life insurance. I'm in a good spot. However, his floozie gave him more than just the gift of life."

Intrigued, she eased back onto the vacant barstool. "Do tell."

"Let's just say, she gave him a couple of gifts that just keep on giving. He'll be popping more pills than a hot Vegas hooker in July for the rest of his life. And he had to give up a lot more than me. No more sunny beach vacations. No more chocolate. And at the top of his trigger list," I couldn't help but enjoy this one. "Red meat. I've never been more thankful we'd stopped having sex when this sick thing started with me."

"Damn.... Karma is a bitch."

"A hormonal bitch in the peak of personal summer menopause." We shared a much-needed laugh. A long coming one. Ashamed of my behavior my chin tilted down, "I'm sorry I didn't tell you."

In typical Yaddi fashion she pulled me into a big girl hug that made the world right. "And I'm sorry I wasn't there. I should have known something was up. I'm slipping."

"Are you two done?"

I pulled out of Yaddi's embrace catching Dwayne's eye over my shoulder. He was still half dressed though the fresh scent of lavender wafted off his smooth, glistening skin. There went my lady parts again. Yaddi might be right. I might need to get laid.

"Not that it's any of your business," Yaddi replied, "but yes, we're done. And I have a job for you, so run along and I'll be there in a moment."

Dwayne's gaze never left mine as he dropped his plate in the sink and backed out of the kitchen with a swipe of his tongue over those luscious pink lips. I wouldn't mind that tongue swiping over my lips, and not the ones still glistening with bacon grease.

When he broke the spell and turned to continue down the hall, his firm, sexy behind taunting me with each step. A hand sliding up my thigh pulled me back to Yaddi.

"You sure you don't want to join us. Dwayne isn't a tease. He means what his eyes were saying."

I considered the offer, then remembered I was in no shape to take a romp in the hay with anyone at the moment, so I gracefully declined.

"Suit yourself," she said regaining her feet. "We'll try not to be too loud."

I stopped her when she reached the hallway, "Um, one question."

"Yes, ma'am?"

"Does he ever wear a shirt?"

"Now why would he do that?" When she'd reached the point where her back was to me, I'd watched her untie the flimsy strip of cloth failing to keep her robe semi-closed. Yaddi was never a fan of undergarments. "Actually, this modesty is all a show for you. We usually don't wear any clothes at all. They tended to," she stopped to consider her word choice, "get in the way."

Her devilish laughter trickled down the hall as I grabbed my food and retreated downstairs.

Chapter Four

I danced from one foot to another silently rushing the microwave to finish the reheat cycle before the two above my head ventured down their tunnel of naughty. When it finally finished, I retrieved my plate, snatched my headphones from the couch and gathered my tablet on a mad dash out the doors onto the patio.

It was quiet out. The empty bird feeders swaying in the wind on the edges of the tree lines. Even at this hour the sweet aroma of bourbon BBQ wafted through the woods from the neighbor's house.

"Noise canceling my ass," I muttered as I turned the volume up on my headphones beyond what the manufacturer listed as the optimal level to ensure safety. It still wasn't enough to drawn out Yaddi's wails of pleasure, so I moved further into the woods finding a quiet spot by the lake.

To my surprise, the Wi-Fi reached out this far, I shoveled food into my mouth while making a grocery list then searching Groupon for an activity to get me out of the house. I wasn't ready to begin the task of finding a place to live and I knew once this long weekend came to an end Yaddi would hop on a plane to her next destination for three to five days working with her clientele.

My daddy taught me well. Although I received a good chunk of change in my divorce with alimony covering me for the foreseeable future, shopping for discounts and deals was my specialty, both for the charities I once volunteered for and the side businesses I occasionally ran to pass the time. When I stumbled across a chocolate making class I jumped on the deal. And luckily for me they had an opening for their class tomorrow afternoon which left the rest of the day for shopping and pretending to unpack.

Yaddi joined me after her tryst, the sweet scent of her honeysuckle body spray reaching me on the gentle breeze before she plopped down in the chair a step from mine.

"I see you're still walking. Is Dwayne slipping on his job?" I teased sliding the headphones off.

"Au contraire. I am quite sated. He's a masseuse, remember. And those magic hands work wonders after play time. What are you up to?"

"Minding my business." She rolled her eyes, her head bobbing in a dramatic fashion at my attempted humor. I continued when she held her tongue. "I need to make a grocery run."

"Are you up for it? If you have a list, I can send Dwayne. Or better yet have it delivered."

"I'm not an invalid. And living life while managing the pain has become my new normal. Besides, I feel like roaming around a store. Might find a sale or two to splurge on."

Yaddi laid back in the chaise, her eyes drifting closed. "Don't get sucked in by those clearance aisles."

"And why not? I sold just about everything I owned. I need to start planning for my new place."

"You don't have to leave. Hell, I'm gone most of the time anyway. I don't mind having you here. Sickness and all."

"Sounds to me like you want to keep an eye on me."

Silence hung between us, and I could see Yaddi struggling to decide what she wanted to tell me and what she wanted to keep close to her heart. "I miss my friend," she finally admitted.

"I've missed you too."

"And we've both been too pig headed to reach out to the other. Why are we so stupid?"

Yaddi and I started to see the world differently the last four or five years. A big part of that was the physical distance between us. The semi-north I called home in the Virginia and DC area was much different than the South. Not to mention Yaddi's line of work, spending her days in corporations claiming they wanted to address lack of representation and diversity in their ranks but had done so poorly because they'd hired the least diverse teams to address the problem.

I could see her exhaustion, the beating the dead horse and repetition with each new venture. And yet her spark for the work continued. I no longer held the mental capacity for the fight, or at least not on the level she did. I'd had a mental break down the year before meeting my husband, the layering of micro-aggressions related to my very existence and the constant need to have my guard up because I was a woman and therefore a potential target for criminals or even a man having a bad day and not able to accept an 'I'm not interested.'

We'd had the lessons growing up. You're safer in crowds and yet those very crowds masked potential perpetrators. Always keep your keys in your hands the longest poking between two fingers so if you have to punch someone in the eye the key will strike. The years of hyper vigilance led to isolation until one day I was just over it all and considered leaving life behind.

"Not stupid," I replied. "The response is purely reactive. A product of our childhood, of being told to be seen and not heard. It stifles the learning process of having a conversation to resolve issues."

"You going all shrink on me?"

"Gotta put my Transpersonal Psychology degree to work sometimes."

We shared a much-needed laugh, bringing up old times, the tension falling away. Just like old times.

"In all seriousness though," Yaddi sat up, her attention squarely on me. "Are you going to tell me what I need to look out for with your new condition. I don't want to hurt you again like I did earlier."

I studied her expression, the twitch of her lips as she tried to maintain eye contact, "Why do I feel like you have an ulterior motive?"

"Because you know me so well. I promise its nothing bad. Just a potential friend who could occupy some of this free time you all of a sudden have."

Chapter Five

"Chocolate people. Where is my white chocolate?" Ellis gathered the individual flourless tortes arranging them on the copper platter before dropping three fresh raspberries atop each. "White chocolate!" he bellowed once more beyond annoyed with the chaos in the kitchen. His voice boomed over the clacking of pots and pans as the waitstaff danced around the cooks collecting their dishes to save the others a few steps.

"Ellis?"

"What? I don't have time for chit chat. Where! Is! My! Chocolate!" Ellis reached for the whipped chocolate mousse, folding it over a few times in the stainless-steel bowl with a spatula. This was the first time he was serving this version. He'd spent the last week perfecting the recipe to get the texture just right.

They'd been slammed all night. A wedding rehearsal party. Steady stream of club hoppers. Reservations out the wazoo. Ellis wasn't complaining per se. Good business was good business especially in an industry where every dollar counted. Still, he needed a minute to breathe but right now he needed to get these desserts to the bride and groom to be.

"Ellis!"

Something crashed to the floor and an ominous silence descended upon the kitchen staff. As everyone stopped to gawk at the mess on the counter. It only lasted a second before the hustle and bustle resumed and a looming presence at his back drew Ellis's attention.

"What do you need? I'm a little busy here." Before he returned to his rampage, a double boiler filled with melted white chocolate appeared next to him. A thin brown arm with a red, white, and blue potholder released the handle and moved away.

"You're needed out front."

Frustrated, Ellis reached for the handle, nearly toppling the boiler when a searing pain raced up his fingers. "Dammit." He snatched his hand away from the scalding handle, grabbing a dry dish rag to wrap around it before pouring the liquid into the funnel he held in his other hand to decorate the tortes. "What am I paying you for?"

"I wouldn't be asking if it wasn't important. Just come out here." The man turned as Ellis escaped to the other side of the kitchen bobbing through the room to run cold water over his hand.

After allowing cold water to temporarily sooth his skin, Ellis removed his chef hat depositing it on the table at the door with the others and shimmying out of his coat to hang it on the empty hook. He exited the kitchen stopping at the edge of the bar to scan the crowd. The place was packed. Wall to wall tables filled with tipsy diners enjoying the special for the night. Italian lamb stew.

He leaned on the side of the bar, waiting for Yusef, the bartender to finish pouring a shot for a portly man with a scruffy beard and sleepy eyes. The man lounged against the wood-grained bar railing running his hands through thinning grey hair. After settling the man's tab, Yusef gestured from Ellis to join him on that end of the bar.

"Now, what's so important?"

"Don't make a scene," Yusef grumbled under his breath. "But look at table six. By the window."

To not draw suspicion, Ellis busied his hands clearing empty glasses left by three women finally getting their table. He watched the tense exchange between a brown-skinned woman with a beautiful bouncy afro and a clean-cut well-dressed man who kept making advances the lady obviously found uncomfortable. She kept looking around, like she was plotting an escape plan.

"How long has that been going on?"

"Not sure. Charity brought it to my attention five minutes ago. She delayed their food in case you wanted to intervene."

The woman reached for her water glass then snatched her hand away when the man attempted to grab it. She tucked it beneath the table fidgeting with the purse resting on her lap. There was something vaguely familiar about the woman, but Ellis couldn't place it. And from this angle, he couldn't see her face.

"Bathroom?" He finally said, anger flaring as he watched the man try again to reach for the woman, this time beneath the table.

Yusef waved their waitress, Charity, over.

"You see it too?" She said. Charity dropped a tray of empty glasses on the edge of the bar and Yusef excused himself to take care of a group at the other end of the bar.

"See if you can get her to the restroom." Ellis said, growing more concerned by the minute. "Make sure she's ok. Let her know if she's uncomfortable we have a place for her, and we'll make sure she's safe."

"Got it."

Charity turned on her heel, making a beeline not for the table, but the hostess station. She made a few erratic moves, enough to draw the woman at the table's attention. Charity did a little kid potty dance pointing toward the restroom and stayed in place as the woman excused herself from the table and headed toward the lady's room.

Ellis watched the woman's hips sway in the blue dress tapered at the waist and covered in sunflowers. She held her head high, her purse securely in her grasped as she wove through the tables towards the restroom. She physically relaxed the further from the table she got, more comfortable and confident now that there was space between her and her date. And there was that inkling again, it gnawed at Ellis's psyche but refused to fully form.

He waited for Charity to join the woman before turning his attention back to the man at the table. Ellis burned the man's face into his memory. The salt and pepper groomed goatee. The prominent nose, disproportionate to his other features like it may have been broken a time or two and the swelling never completely abated. And mole over the man's left eye. If for some reason they needed to identify the woman's date, Ellis was fairly sure he'd be able to pick the man in the striped button-down shirt, creased grey pants and soft brown loafers out in a line up.

"Keep me posted," Ellis said as he returned to the kitchen.

STUPID. STUPID. STUPID. "Come on Yaddi. Answer the phone." I dialed for the third time sure after the back-to-back calls she'd get the clue I needed to talk to her and answer the phone. And for the third time the answering service picked up. I hung up, less dramatic than old school. I do miss slamming the receiver down. Pressing an end button just didn't have the same effect.

I knew better than to trust her judgment. She wanted one thing and that was to get me laid. But I could only be angry with myself. I'd walked into her widow's web willing prey. Regardless of how much I reminded her of my disinterest in a roll in the hay to get over the situation with my ex, when Yaddi formed a plan, she stuck to it. I loved and hated her for it.

At least the restaurant staff gave me a reprieve. I'd definitely give this place a five-star rating. Besides the appetizers being absolutely delicious, identifying when patrons needed unconventional intervention was something I wasn't accustomed to. Not that I'd frequented places or found myself in scenarios where I needed others to bail me out. The forethought necessary to consider the possibilities from a customer's point of view and then have staff with enough ingenuity to pull off an exit strategy without making a scene, this is definitely the kind of establishment deserving of my patronage.

Charity's assurance that I could take all the time I needed offered comfort after the stressful encounter and I appreciated the care she showed me.

The office she'd deposited me in was nice, the walls covered in pictures of a man I assumed was the Italian owner with patrons over the years. I recognized a handful of celebrities; their signatures scrawled across the snapshots in colorful script. It made me sad in a way. With new technology I wondered how long before the traditional of adding to the wall of images fell by the wayside either due to printing expense or lack of importance.

Not wanting to pry, I hunkered down in my seat, scrolling through my library app to find a book to read. After making my selection, I chose ambient music to play before losing myself in a little bit of smut while waiting on the night to pass me by.

THE LAST HOURS OF THE night passed quickly. When Ellis was satisfied, he had enough desserts prepared for the orders made and the few that might trickle in in the next thirty minutes, he took a leave of absence from the kitchen to get some air. Diving into work took his mind of the mysterious woman and the inkling that he'd crossed paths with her before. He hadn't even taken a breather to check back with Charity to see if the woman had made it out ok. That actually bothered him, though he couldn't figure out why.

It wasn't like they didn't have protocols for these scenarios. He and a few of the other business owners in this strip of converted houses put a process in place with their staff that if they saw something that looked suspicious to notify management. The bartenders tended to chat up single women coming in and if they found out the woman was there to meet a blind date, they'd slip them a card to order a specific drink or dessert to tip the waitstaff off that they needed help.

As a community, they conducted meetings. Drills. Role played with their staff to identify a patron in distress. And it wasn't just the women. Sometimes cougars brought their dates to fancy restaurants to impress the impressionable or as part of their sugar daddy/sugar baby agreements. Sometimes they just wanted to be seen with a younger man to make their husbands jealous. Ellis had pretty much seen it all over the years and didn't put anything past anyone.

Curiosity getting the best of him, he decided to track down Charity. He found her at the bar, propped up on the stool at the corner counting out her tips. Only one couple remained in the dining room, and they were handing over the black case to the hostess to pay for their meal.

"Good night?" Ellis asked as he approached.

She smiled her head bobbing, eyes dancing with glee. "Yes. That wedding party left a two-hundred-dollar tip."

"And I bet they made you earn every dime of it."

"Oh, they weren't too bad. I think they could tell we were overwhelmed and a little shorthanded." She handed a stack of credit card receipts to Yusef to verify.

"Did you notice how long before that guy left?"

"Not long. He quickly figured out he'd made the wrong move and she wasn't coming back."

Hmm. "And the woman?"

"Her name is Soliel. And she's still in the office. I checked in on her a couple of times. Brought her the food she'd ordered and water. I supposed I owe you for a torte. I gave her one on the house. Told her she was welcome to stay until close. I hope that's ok. She was really shaken."

"Yeah. Thanks. Both of you. For being observant."

"It's what we do." Yusef responded. "Gotta keep the patrons happy. And safe."

"I apologize for snapping at you earlier." Ellis said to Yusef, the well-groomed bartender who always captured the attention of every single lady in the place with his dimpled smile. "I appreciate your push."

Yusef waived off the apology; gathering his till, he started his closeout process.

"I'm going to check on her. See if she needs us to call a ride or walk her to her car."

"I'll come with you," Charity slid from the barstool.

Charity knocked on the door when they reached the office down the hall, sticking her head in first. "We're closing up for the night. I brought the manager back with me." When the woman nodded, Charity entered with Ellis in tow.

The minute Ellis rounded the corner and his eyes locked on the woman sitting on the couch it all clicked into place. She appeared surprised to see him, but not in the way he expected. She paused the music playing from her phone as she stood to greet them.

"Thank you so much," she said, extending her hand as if greeting him for the first time.

He offered a warm smile grasping her hand. He held on for a little longer than necessary to see if she showed any sign of recognition. When she didn't, he said, "I hope you don't mind our intervention."

She drew her hand away, busying herself with gathering her purse and the containers for her leftovers. "Not at all. Charity was a life saver."

"Do you need someone to escort you to your car?"

Ellis circled the desk, giving her space while Charity eyed him suspiciously from her spot by the door.

"The guy left hours ago," Charity said.

"I'd still appreciate it. You look busy." She gestured to the stack of papers on the desk, "I'll get out of your hair."

Ellis glanced at the disarray littering the desk. Piles of unprocessed invoices, stacks of inventory sheets, a half made up schedule. Paperwork taunting him at every moment.

"You need to find someone to help you with that."

Ellis shot Charity a hard glare. She turned away, embarrassed. Apparently forgetting they had company.

"Are you looking for help?" The woman asked Ellis.

"You're a guest in my restaurant."

"I have restaurant experience. And I suddenly find myself with more free time than I know what to do with. Paperwork is a breeze for me."

"I can't ask..."

"I'm the one asking." Soliel stated in a matter-of-fact authoritative motherly tone. "Consider it my thank you for your gracious hospitality."

Not daring to challenge a woman clear in her mission, Ellis conceded. "We could use the help."

"Then its settled. What time would you like for me to come in tomorrow?"

Soliel's phone dinged as they negotiated the time of her arrival. She glanced down at the screen, "My ride's here."

"Then I'll walk you out." They headed to the front of the restaurant, Charity breaking off towards the kitchen as they entered the dining room. When they reached the door, Ellis paused, surprised by the black luxury vehicle parked at the curb, a driver dressed in black with a white shirt standing at the rear door. "Your ride?" He asked as he burned the man's face into his memory.

"Yep. So, I'll see you in the morning?"

Ellis trailed her down the steps to the curb, making sure she made it into the car safely. "I'll be here." He waited for the car to drive away before trudging back up the stairs. "Well done, Universe. Well done," he muttered as he reached the door.

"What'd you say?"

Ellis looked up to find Yusef standing in the doorway. "Nothing."

"No, you said something. And why did that woman look familiar?"

"Think long and hard," Ellis said patting his friend on the shoulder, "and when you finally figure it out, you're going to kick yourself."

Chapter Six

"One day I'm going to learn to trust my gut instead of you when it comes to blind dates." I said as I claimed the seat next to Yaddi at the breakfast bar. She'd dismissed Dwayne half an hour ago, leaving us to finish off the French toast and eggs benedict he'd tediously prepared to her liking.

"You didn't give him a chance."

"I gave him plenty of chances of which he took full advantage in the wrong way." I sopped up the yolk from my egg with the edge of my French toast.

"Just nasty," Yaddi remarked.

"Then quit watching me eat. And why didn't you answer the phone when I called last night. I could have been stranded on the side of the road in need of rescue and you just ignored my calls."

"First of all," she stuffed French toast into her mouth, her way of stalling, "if you had signal enough to ring my phone, you had signal enough to call a car service."

Wow. Did I mean so little to her? Had I been gone so long she no longer felt I needed saving? Yaddi'd designated herself my personal savior in college, steering me away from the bad boys towards the nerds. Little did she know, the dates she chose for me were far from the wholesome nerds she pegged them to be behind closed doors. I allowed her to maintain her illusion of being a great judge of character even now.

The scowl on my lips and valley girl eye roll indicated my annoyance with her dismissing me under the dire circumstances she'd forced upon me. "I guess."

"You guess?" She turned on me, eyes narrowed, scrutinizing every bat of an eye. "What's that supposed to mean?"

"Never mind. Besides, the restaurant staff rescued me."

"You didn't need rescuing."

31

"Now who's being naive. You have no idea how uncomfortable your suitor made me feel."

I waited for her to protest, not sure if she'd spoken with Rodney since I'd abandoned him at the table last night. Her lack of comment assured me she had, and the picture he'd painted of me had been none too pleasing. If she wanted to hear my side of the story, then I'd be more than happy to oblige.

"He was handsy and you know I am uncomfortable with strangers touching me."

"Nothing wrong with a little human contact."

"There's plenty wrong with it when both parties aren't in agreement," I snapped. "You might crave the contact of others. I've watched you work a room. The way your hand brushes over the arms of men and women alike. You make them comfortable. Your caresses innocent. Rodney's your type, not mine."

Yaddi studied her plate like a scolded toddler. "I'm sorry," she finally muttered.

My hand came to rest on her arm, a small gesture to offer my assurance. She meant well. She'd always meant well but sometimes she went about things in a way that didn't work for others. Though we remained close friends over the course of my marriage, the last year, when I was sick, I'd withdrawn. The neglect from my husband sent me into hiding affording me time to evaluate my life and choices. I'd come to the conclusion that for the first time in my life I was putting me first. In the end, I really was all I had.

I willed away the tears threatening to fall. The hurt on her face cutting at my resolve. Still, I remained in my truth and this time, when I let Yaddi back into my life it would be on my new terms. "I get it Yaddi. I know you want what you think is best for me. You always have and I love you for that. You've always been true to you, not letting anyone else deter you from your beliefs whether about your sexuality, your size. Your voice. I've looked up to you since you took me under your wing back in college."

"But?"

"No but."

"Liar."

"Seriously. No but. However, comma, space..."

"I knew there was more." Yaddi sighed heavily. "Lay it on me."

"I've grown since our college years. The Goddess knows I've cheated death. I'm more resilient than I've ever been. Don't get me wrong Yaddi I need your support. This entire process would be so much harder if I had to worry about a roof over my head."

It was her turn to offer support. She elbowed me in the side, that cocky schoolgirl half smile tugging at the corner of her lips. "Now you know I got you. You're my girl. Through thick and thin."

"Glad to hear." And just like that, it was over. I finished my food, gathering my plate as I circled the island to the sink. "Last night wasn't a total bust."

Her fork scraped across her plate, the screeching sending a shiver up my spine. "Holding out on me?"

"Something like that." I took my time washing my plate, glass, fork, and knife. I felt her eyes boring into my back as she waited for me to spill the tea.

"If I didn't know any better, I'd think you enjoyed torturing me."

I shrugged as I dried the dishes, satisfied I'd ruffled her delicate, controlling feathers. Eventually I gave her the answer she'd waited anxiously for. "I might have found a job."

Yaddi nearly spit out her orange juice. She'd managed to hold it in only for the liquid to travel down the wrong pipe sending her into a coughing fit. I rushed to her aid, rubbing her back as she struggled to simultaneously hack up the offending liquid and wipe her mouth.

She eventually pulled it together enough to stutter, "A job. Are you serious?"

I reclaimed the seat next to hers. "Well, not a nine to five. Just something to occupy this excess time I now have on my hands."

"Um, what excess time? You do have my party to plan and coordinate. That should keep you hella busy."

"It will," I assured her, "And I still have my calligraphy business, not to mention the ladies I game with. But I need something more productive. Besides, it's only temporary. Maybe a few weeks tops. The restaurant owner's business manager left abruptly. They're in a bit of a bind. I haven't done bookkeeping in a while, and this is a great opportunity to get back into the swing of things."

"Are you worried about money? You know I could always use an assistant. I mean, I pay the firm that handles my consultations and engagements top dollar. I'm sure I can get you in."

"This isn't about money. Danny paid well for his abandonment and infidelity. Very well," I said with a devilish grin. Though Yaddi wasn't privy to the specifics she'd recommend the divorce attorney I'd used and apparently the woman's reputation preceded her.

"I'm sure he did," she chided chomping on the last morsel of her French toast. Her fork clanked against the expensive China when she dropped it.

"I need more in my life though. Substance. A challenge."

"A man."

"Yaddi," I warned.

"Or a woman." She shrugged as she observed my expression from the corner of her eye.

"I'm not jumping into another relationship. Is that clear?"

"Relationship? Who's talking about a relationship? I'm merely suggesting..."

"Stop. Stop right there. Mind your business." I stood, "I mean it. No more blind dates. No hookups. Not even a snide remark about me joining you for a roll in the hay with Dwayne or any of your other bedmates."

"Uh. You suck the fun out of everything."

"It's what I do. Now I have to get ready for work." The declaration sounded strange to my ears. I'd hadn't gone to work in at least eight years. That's not to say I hadn't been a contributing member to society. Between the charity work with the women at the hospital where my ex-husband still worked and my lucrative side hustles, I filled my days with running to and fro or buried beneath stacks of invitations hunched over a magnifier with a calligraphy pen in hand.

"And where exactly is this job of yours," Yaddi shouted over her shoulder as she sipped her mimosa.

I'd made it to the stairwell leading to the basement apartment where I now resided. I considered answering her query but opted to play my hand close. "Wouldn't you like to know."

Chapter Seven

The sweetest of smells met me at the rear door of Angelo's along with, to my surprise, Charity's bright smile.

"Good morning," she greeted stepping to the side to let me enter.

"Morning," I responded. "I didn't expect to see you this early."

She secured the door, leading me down the hallway towards the office. "Ellis thought you might be more comfortable with a woman's presence on your first day."

"How sweet?"

Charity chuckled. "He means well. He's quite the gentleman once you get to know him." She moved closer, her hand cupped over the side of her mouth as she whispered, "a big ole teddy bear. He's a push over once you get beyond the businessman persona."

The office door opened as she reached for the handle, startling us both as my gaze rested on the man in jeans and a graphic tee-shirt, I couldn't quite make out beneath an apron stained with chocolate and what I suspected was powdered sugar. The sweet scent of cinnamon laced with I believe nutmeg wrapped around me. He smelled simply divine.

"Sorry," he moved to let us pass. "Phone was ringing."

"This early?" Charity asked.

"Unfortunately. Or maybe I should say fortunately. A quiet phone puts us all on the unemployment line."

Charity bumped his shoulder with her own, a snicker shared between them like brother and sister sharing an inside joke. "You'd never let that happen."

Ellis turned his attention my way giving my attire the once over as he untied the apron. I suddenly felt overdressed in my navy pencil skirt, white shirt, and jacket. Not quite full-on suit but far from the casual dress of both Ellis and Charity in her knee-length rainbow print tee she passed off as a dress, complementing purple leggings, and low-heeled ankle boots. At least the bottom of them appeared to be slip proof. Not ideal for seating customers but acceptable for roaming restaurant kitchen floors.

"A bit formal, don't you think," Ellis said, giving me a once over.

"How so?" I retrieved a copy of my resume from the bag slung over my shoulder thrusting it out in his direction. "I know I volunteered to help but the least I could do was make a professional impression my first day on the job."

Charity stifled a laugh, "oh that is rich. I'm headed to prep tables. You know where to find me if you need me." She made herself scarce.

I steadied my breathing as we stood in the office entry. Ellis perused my resume as I took a seat, his expression relaxed as if it was a formality. Under the circumstances I suppose it was. At the very least I wanted to make sure he knew I was qualified to review his books. I might need time to get up to speed on the specific program the restaurant used but that wouldn't be a problem. Between online video tutorials and the notes he said the previous manager left, I knew I could handle the task. And if not, I'd make some calls and find a suitable replacement.

"Wow."

"Pardon?"

"That is some name."

I cringed, annoyed with myself for not cleaning it up. Though I'd kept the work history up to date, choosing a functional format instead of a chronological one, I'd neglected to remove my married name from the top on the few copies I kept on hand. I realized he waited for my response, so I said, "My mother was a very spiritual woman. Hence the Celestial Soliel Divine. I use it for legal purposes but prefer to be called Soliel."

"Soliel it is," Ellis snapped the paper gesturing me to take a seat at the desk. "This all seems to be in order."

"Now who's being formal."

"I'm just playing to the room."

Was that a joke? "Oh really."

No longer hiding his smile he reached around me to power on the laptop positioned between two stacks of papers. "Seriously though, I don't expect you to dress up. It's pretty informal around here. And especially with you volunteering to help. Wear whatever is comfortable." He paused, reconsidering the blanket statement before adding, "within reason."

"Oh?" I chided playfully, "You mean no lingerie on the job?" His eyes widened, mouth dropping as he gawked at me. Then his gaze narrowed, one eyebrow rising as if he was imagining me in lingerie. "Just kidding. And for the record, I'd never. I'm actually comfortable in what most people refer to as 'real clothes.'"

"They fit you well."

I thanked him, then we started our crash course on what was where. The business basics appeared to be well organized. The necessary bills already paid for the month. Linda, the previous business manager, had been a stickler for details leaving a notebook of step-by-step instructions for first of the month, mid-month, and end-of month items that needed to be addressed.

"If I ever meet Linda, remind me to thank her for the notes. This is over the top even by my standards."

"Are you saying you are just as anal when it comes to your workspace?"

"You make having things in order sound like a bad thing."

"Maybe not bad. Just trying to gage if I need to stay out of your way while you're working. We had a special sign made for Linda to hang on the door when she was in here. It was more of a warning for us to avoid the office or at least tread lightly if we needed to retrieve anything."

"Tough cookie. Huh?"

"But she was good at what she did, so I overlooked her quirks and worked around her schedule. If I needed to get anything from the office I'd plan to come in stupid early, grab it during her lunch hour, or wait till she left."

"Hmm." I tapped my cheek, contemplating if I wanted to be that level of pain in the ass.

"Uh oh. Here it comes." When I didn't comment, he said, "what are your demands?"

I considered asking for something outrageous like filet mignon and scallops on the days I came into the office. And chocolate tortes. Lots and lots of chocolate tortes. I'd fallen in love with the one from last night. I'd never tasted anything so divine and that said a lot coming from someone with a stint or two under her belt as a professional baker.

"You've done enough," I finally said. "I volunteered for this, remember. You giving me the opportunity to return the favor is enough."

"Well, the least I can do is offer you lunch," he stood, scooting around the far side of the desk to keep me from having to move. "I have desserts to make. When you need a break feel free to come find me. Charity is around if you have any other questions."

I watched him leave; my gaze fixated on the roll of the muscles in his back. I wonder if the strength came from working with fondant. I shook the tantalizing thoughts from my head staring at the screen then the stacks we'd rearranged together so that I could tackle what I deemed most pressing first.

The work kept me occupied for two hours, the sound of the others arriving and the prepping for the late afternoon opening of the restaurant reminding me that I hadn't eaten anything since breakfast at Yaddi's. I glanced at my watch realizing I'd been so engrossed in the tasks at hand that I'd totally ignored the alarm reminders for my medication.

"Hmm, that's not good." I stretched my legs screaming for reprieve as I'd been sitting in the same position for hours without so much as a shift in the chair, which was unbelievably comfortable. I walked the room, giving my legs time to adjust to the new position before venturing out.

The clanking of dishes and aroma of spices met me on the other side of the door, my stomach protesting at having been ignored for so long. As the first patrons took their seats, I waved Charity over. She hadn't changed making me question if she planned to stay. Another woman with unnaturally dark hair dressed in a starched white shirt, black pants, and black shoes met the now seated couple at their table while a guy I pegged to be no older than mid-twenties greeted three men dressed in business attire near the front door.

"I was wondering when you were going to come up for air," Charity said ushering me towards a swinging door. My mouth watered at the aroma permeating from the kitchen. Few words were spoken among the handful of people prepping salads, stirring the contents of bubbling pots on the stove, and shuffling freshly baked rolls into napkin-lined wire baskets.

"We'd hoped to introduce you to everyone before brunch but when you didn't emerge Ellis thought it best to leave you be. I'm guessing you're famished by now."

"To say the least." I scanned the kitchen for Ellis.

Charity must have noticed, "he made a chocolate run."

"He does seem to like chocolate."

"In more ways than you know."

She quickly ushered me out the doorway leaving it free for the servers to perform their duties uninterrupted. I stood in a designated corner as she grabbed one of the servers and instructed him to make me a salad. "Soup work for you? Its Italian wedding."

"Definitely."

Chapter Eight

The numbers on the computer screen swirled as I attempted to reconcile the inventory pattern from the prior year with the numbers Charity provided. I wasn't sure which set frustrated me more, the well-organized spreadsheet left by Linda, or the handwritten numbers scribbled on the paper Charity had handed to me.

Maybe neither worried me. Maybe I was tired and needed a break. I tried to shift gears, moving from the desk with the computer to the little dinette in the corner I'd used last night. Still, I couldn't make any of it make sense. I eventually conceded, my attention drawn to the photos on the wall again. I'd only glanced at them before, trying to see if I recognized any of the famous faces. However, as I took my time roaming the space taking in each picture, I noticed the aging of the man I assumed must have been the previous owner of the establishment.

A handful of the pictures featured the man with two younger versions of himself along with whom I assumed was a patron, doner, or long-time friend. I completed the half circle, my attention drawn to three photographs I'd hadn't paid attention to previously. One was of Ellis with the previous owner in his later years, the man with a jovial smile, arm swung around Ellis's shoulder as they posed in front of the restaurant. I wondered of the significance of the moment if it was the celebratory or just the type of relationship the two shared.

The next photo was of Ellis with a woman. He held a boy he favored, maybe six or seven, in his arms as the sun set behind them. The silver scribbling on the bottom corner read Panola Mountain. I'd heard of it. It wasn't popular in my college years. I'd only learned of its existence from our classmates who like to explore the local trails. Assuming the woman was his wife and the child his son I moved to the last photo. This one of Ellis and Yusef. Both men donned tuxedos, a glass of champagne raised in a toast. The photographer captured the joy of the moment perfectly.

"How's it going?"

I turned at the voice from behind. So engrossed in the happiness behind Ellis's eyes in the picture I hadn't heard the door open. "My brain is fried."

"You hung around much longer than I expected." He held out a white box twice the size of my petite hands. "I hoped you'd be around when I returned. I brought you back something."

I accepted the box peeking through the cellophane window on the top to discover four different chocolate confections ranging from white to dark chocolate. "If I didn't know any better, I'd think you assume I had a sweet tooth."

"Charity told me about your fondness for the tortes. Figured I'd switch it up this time." His eyes flickered between me and the photos I'd been perusing. "Are you calling it a day?"

"I think I need to. The numbers are swimming, and I haven't had to focus on one task since an all-night gaming competition over a year ago."

"Gamer huh?"

"I know my way around a joystick," I shot him a devilish grin, "and game pad. I'm not big on computer gaming. I'm a console girl."

Ellis eased down on the edge of the desk, that half smile I'd started to become fond of tugging at the corner of his luscious lips. Lips that I found myself engrossed in.

"I'd love to see you play sometime."

It was my turn to gaze into those deep brown pools to that soul of his. I could feel his eyes drawing me in, beckoning me to close the distance between us and...I caught myself before my mind ventured down a path I wasn't prepared to travel. I'd just exited a bad marriage and I wasn't ready to jump into a relationship. And why the hell was I even thinking about this? He obviously already had a family of his own.

"One day. Maybe."

Ellis perused the mail as I collected my things, that smile I'd grown to expect falling away when he reached the last envelope in the stack. He'd opened the others one by one, placing some in the in box to be reviewed. I assumed they were invoices. This last letter though. I watched as he'd considered dropping it in the trash can. It hovered over the bin, barely clinging to fingertips before he balled it in his fist and tossed it across the room.

Not knowing what to say I headed towards the door. "I'll look at those invoices in the morning. I can come in for a couple of hours. Now that I know where everything is, and I have a better idea of what needs to be addressed, if it works for you, we can discuss a schedule that works for us both."

He hadn't heard me, his mind obviously still engrossed in thoughts of whatever that envelope contained. I considered touching his arm or snapping my fingers in front of his face, but I wasn't sure how he felt about personal contact and, well, the snapping was just rude. Instead, I exited the office heading to the front of the restaurant to call a ride.

I'd barely made it to the place where the hallway converged with the other two leading to the restrooms and main restaurant when the walls around me shook. Charity rounded the corner nearly running me over in the process as she raced to see the origin of the ruckus.

"Oh, sorry," she managed as we danced around each other.

I eventually stopped, granting her the opportunity to choose which side she wanted to pass on. Instead, she stopped her advance. "Was that Ellis?"

I glanced over my shoulder, the light from the open office door illuminating the area down the hall. I couldn't see much past the office, but I assumed Ellis had exited out the back security doors. "I'm guessing so."

"Is he alright?"

"I can't say. He was perusing the mail when I left."

"You're heading out?"

She seemed anxious, like she wanted to ask if Ellis and I had had a disagreement. "Yes. It's been a long day and I'm exhausted."

"I can have one of the guys walk you to your car."

I held up my hand stopping her before she got ahead of herself. "That's not necessary. I'm not driving. I'm just going to order a drink while I wait on my ride." I stepped to the side making the choice for her as I continued into the restaurant.

I claimed a seat at the bar, the bartender, a woman I estimated to be in her thirties with straight black hair she'd arranged in a tight bun at the nape of her neck greeting me as she placed a napkin in front of me.

"What can I get for you?"

I knew I shouldn't be drinking but I needed something stronger than my usual virgin margarita. "White Russian."

An eyebrow rose at my declaration. I suspected she'd expected me to request a cosmopolitan or mojito. Yaddi once said a woman's drink told a story about her. I wonder what a white Russian said about me. I sent Yaddi a text letting her know I was headed back and to ping me if she wanted me to bring food. Then I opened the ride-share app and arranged my transportation home.

I low-key hoped to catch one more glimpse of Ellis before heading out. It was still early, and I really didn't need to hurry. Yet, his mood swing caught me off guard. I reminded myself that he was obviously spoken for and although my volunteer status meant he wasn't exactly my boss, if I continued to work on his books in a longer-term capacity then getting involved with the person I'd see each day crossed the professional line amounting to trouble in paradise.

I downed the last of my drink, siding fifteen dollars towards the bartender and telling her to keep the change. My ride rounded the corner as I stepped out the door. I felt a few eyes turn in my direction as the car rolled to a stop and the driver got out, rushing around to open the door for me. Busy street or not I paid extra for good service and this driver obviously understood the expectations of his clientele.

The driver delivered me to Yaddi's driveway an hour later his fingers wrapping around the twenty-dollar cash tip I slid his way. I could have kicked myself for not grabbing food. I was not in the mood to cook. The front door swung open, Yaddi stepping out onto the porch with a glass full of lemon iced tea.

"I thought I heard a car," she said claiming a seat on the swing. She glared at me over the rim of her glass. Her glossy lips covering the straw as she took a sip.

"What?"

"I didn't say anything."

She tried to play innocent. I read through the act. "Is there something I can do for you?"

"Why, I don't rightly know." She leaned back in all her sensual glory the thin cloth of her dress struggling to hold her amble bosom in check. And that added southern drawl told me all I needed to know.

Movement at the corner of my eye caught my attention and I knew then they'd been plotting for my return. Not today. I was not falling for this one. "It's been a long day. And I need to eat. So, if you two will excuse me I'll leave you to your devices." Not trusting Dwayne to not make a play I opted to take the long way around through the azalea path leading to the side gate and private entrance to the basement apartment.

I ignored the two new bottles of cherry wine strategically placed on the center of the counter as I made a b-line to the stairwell door and locked it. Yaddi probably had a key but the fact that I'd made a point to secure it would let her know I was not to be disturbed. If she wanted her party planned properly then I needed to work around this new schedule to make that happen.

Chapter Nine

I failed miserably at sleeping in late. I woke before everyone else in the house. Or maybe it was just as they'd drifted off to sleep. My head throbbed, the white Russian from yesterday catching up with me. Alcohol was the enemy I reminded myself as I padded my way into the kitchen to retrieve a glass of water. The boxes still piled in the middle of my living area stared back at me accusingly as if I'd intentionally crowded the area as a makeshift fortress to keep others out.

Turning my back to them I collected a Mason jar of raspberries from the fridge and claimed a seat at the bar. Too early to venture out, or eat heavy food for that matter, I opened the laptop I'd left on the counter to charge and perused my email.

The house remained silent for another hour, long enough for the sky to brighten and the cardinals to begin their morning ritual of spreading birdseeds over the ground for their feathered friends to enjoy. The dominant male made a point to defend his self-proclaimed ownership of said bird feeders. No others could directly partake of its spoils, sans the brown female strutting about the edges daring him to question her boldness.

A crash from above sent me racing up the stairs without thought as to what I might find. This was after all Yaddi's house.

"Stop!"

I skidded to a halt at the command, my eyebrow rising at the giggling coming from my friend. One look and I knew she was still wasted. "Really Yaddi."

I dared not cross the threshold; the sharp edges of shattered porcelain scattered about. I hoped the vase wasn't expensive, not that Yaddi didn't have the money to replace it. She stumbled, this time the couch catching her, and she fell into hysterics.

"Yaddi?"

First her fingers, then her head inched slowly over the edge of the sofa like a kid playing hide and seek scoping out the scene. She tried to stifle another laugh but failed sorely. And where the hell was Dwayne?

I refused to cut up my feet, so I told her, "Stay there."

She nodded understanding, and I hope she maintained enough wits about herself to not attempt to clean up the mess or worse, follow me down the stairs. I donned a pair of thick sole shoes, needing more protection than my fuzzy slippers afforded, and I returned to the main level to discover Yaddi still in place passed out.

She was too old for this. Hell, I was too old for this. I cleaned the mess collecting the pieces of the vase in a bag that I left on the dining room table. Yaddi liked re-purposing items. Maybe she'd create a mosaic tabletop for the garden, or a porcelain portrait. Enough larger pieces remained to even be converted into coasters. All they needed was a little polishing and rounding around the edges.

I considered bailing on my volunteer position today wondering if my roomie and her bedmate needed a supervisor. Then I remembered the way they attempted to corrupt me upon my return yesterday and thought better of it. One of us needed to be an adult today and it appeared that needed to be me.

Yusef let me into the front door of Angelo's two hours later. It was close to the time most of the cooks arrived to start prepping for the brunch crowd. He offered a welcoming smile taking in my attire apparently pleased with the patchwork ankle-length jean skirt and emerald-green puffy sleeved shirt I donned. Charity must have told him about my professional attire yesterday and how they made it clear that the stiff clothing wasn't necessary in my role.

"Glad we didn't scare you off," he chided as the lock clicked behind me.

"Is that what happened to Linda?" Yusef was one of the more chipper employees. I suppose the others have their moments, but I hadn't officially been introduced to anyone other than Charity.

"Quick wit too. You'll fit in nicely around here."

I followed him towards the hallway, but he diverted me to the kitchen. "Don't get used to me being around," I said. "I'm just paying off my debt."

"Hmm. I don't know about this debt you speak of."

The clanking of plates and the knock of knives chopping drowned out my snide remark which I suspected was the point.

"Hey everyone," Yusef yelled over the ruckus to get everyone's attention. "I just wanted you all to meet Soliel. If you see her around, she belongs. "

"Hi," I said, making eye contact with the three cooks and two servers. Each person gave me a nod then turned their attention back to their tasks.

We left them to their responsibilities, Yusef rounding the bar as I headed down the hallway to the office where I'd set up shop for the next few hours. I'd expected Ellis to be around and almost returned to the front to find out when he'd be in. We needed to talk about my schedule and how long he thought he might need me.

I worked on the invoices from yesterday, entering the necessary data into the system. Over the top of the laptop the white of the envelope from yesterday caught my attention. *Not my business.* I reminded myself. I was here to work on the books and get things in order so when the time came, Ellis could take over or until he found a suitable replacement.

An hour and a half passed as I leafed through the manual of the software and watched video tutorials to see if the current processes could be streamlined. The possibilities kept my mind occupied and off the speck of white goading me. I'd even resorted to lowering the chair so that I would have to make a special effort to look over the rim of the screen. The ruse worked for another ten minutes before the torture of curiosity hooked me and I stood.

The balled-up paper lay right where Ellis had thrown it which meant he hadn't bothered to retrieve it. I almost wondered if he'd left it there intentionally for me to find. Was this a test? Did he want to see if I would invade his privacy. I stopped in the middle of the room scanning the wall and ceiling. There was a lone security camera in the corner opposite the desk. From that vantage point the video captured the only way in and out as well as the desk. So maybe someone was watching. Not that it mattered to me.

I retrieved the envelope, straightening it as much as I could on my thigh before glancing at the type on the front. The word attorney caught my attention and immediately I slid the envelope under the corner of the inbox on the desk.

Not getting involved. I told myself and not just because of the camera. I was here as a volunteer. If I needed to bail at any moment, I was free to do so. Everything I'd seen so far appeared to be on the up and up so even if I somehow got sucked into a legal matter my hands were basically clean.

The mail for the day arrived just as I'd planned to figure out food. The scents from the kitchen tempting me even behind the closed office door. Unable to deny the demands of my stomach I ventured out. I found Yusef behind the bar, clipboard in hand as he inventoried the bottles on the shelf.

"Hey," he looked up at me in the mirror but didn't turn around.

"What can I help you with?"

"Is Mr. Alexander coming in?"

"Probably not until this evening."

I checked my watch wondering if I wanted to wait it out or call it a day. There wasn't much left for me to do at the moment. The schedule Linda left indicated that Monday was inventory and order day for the Thursday delivery. The order had been placed before I started, and it was only Tuesday. I could watch more videos to see if I could streamline any of the ordering or inventory processes, but I really needed to speak with Ellis before proposing changes that he might not be in the mindset to hear.

"Thanks." I sounded disappointed, even to myself. I'd come today with a plan to hash out a schedule and get a better understanding of my temporary role here and I'd only been met with disappointment. Secretly I was also concerned about the way Ellis had stormed out yesterday. And curious about the letter leading to the reaction.

I considered my options, marking food on the top of that list. Deciding I needed to take my mind off the nagging of my conscience to open the envelope sitting on the edge of the desk I grabbed Mika, one of the servers I'd been introduced to earlier and asked her to bring me a to-go plate to the office when she got a free moment. The crowd was growing but it was still early enough to be manageable. She assured me she would, and I accepted the stack of mail and inventory sheet Yusef held out to me.

"Mind leaving that in the office for Ellis. He'll be able to pull the additional bottles I need when he gets in."

Something about the way he looked at me made me think he wanted to say something else. Or maybe ask me a question. "Is there something on your mind?"

His face fell to a neutral expression. "Nothing at all." He busied himself wiping the counter on the other side of the bar, as far away from me as possible without blatantly walking into the kitchen using the 'out' door.

I left the inventory sheet on top of the computer as I stacked the mail next to it. The envelope on top caught my attention, the name of the supplier, The Naughty Chocolatier sketched across the white envelope in chocolate colored script. Must be the place that supplied the chocolate Ellis used in his desserts. I opted not to open the envelope though, we hadn't spoken about opening mail, so I added that to the list of topics to discuss with Ellis whenever we crossed paths again.

My food arrived and satisfied in my contributions for the day, I gathered my things and took my leave.

"THIS IS THE LAST ONE," Yusef said as he hauled the last of the boxes from the back of the pickup Ellis drove.

"Let me pull into a spot and we can sort." Ellis climbed back into his truck backing it into his usual spot across from the back door of Angelo's. Four designated spots in the back of the building were reserved for the staff though being on the bus-line and paying generously only two were typically in use at any given time. They allowed the delivery drivers to use the spots during the day and when special guest arrived and the lot and street parking was full, he'd allow the spaces to be utilized for their purposes.

Ellis paused as he reached the office from the back door, expecting to find Soliel with her head buried in paperwork or camped out at the dinette partaking in lunch. His watch read four thirty. She usually hung around until he popped in to check on her or until the evening rush hour subsided even if she used the time for her own projects.

"Did Soliel come in today," Ellis asked, meeting Yusef next to the temperature-controlled storage area where they stashed the bars of chocolates from The Naughty Chocolatier.

"Yeah. You just missed her. I was wondering what was taking you so long. I expected you to be here when I came in."

Damn. He'd tried to rush back but the extra stop at the chocolate shop to pick up what he needed for a large dessert catering order delayed his return. She must have come in right after he left.

"Don't worry. She did ask about you," Yusef chided as he tossed a box at Ellis.

Ellis popped the top of the box, rifling through the bars of white chocolate. He put the box aside and moved on to the next one Yusef passed his way. "Oh, we got jokes."

"Only when they're at your expense. She'll be back tomorrow; I suppose."

"You suppose? Do I need to worry?"

"So easily baited. No, nothing for you to worry about. She hunkered down in the office for a few hours, took her lunch, and grabbed a drink before she bounced. It was all on the up and up. I do think she lingered just to see if she could catch you but must have had other pressing matters to tend to."

They finished stocking the chocolate in silence, Ellis keeping one more box of dark chocolate out to start on the order. The kitchen was in full swing, orders moving in and out as the clashing aromas of onion, garlic, and cheeses vied for attention. Ellis's stomach growled, reminding him that in his haste to return before Soliel departed, he'd failed to eat.

"Can I holla at you for a minute?"

Ellis cut his eye at Yusef mid-ladle. "About?"

Yusef scanned the room shaking his head in the process, "A bit loud in here don't you think."

Catching the hint, Ellis responded as he grated fresh parmesan over his pasta. "Let me get my food and I'll meet you in the office." Yusef departed as Ellis topped his food off with a few turns of a pepper grinder and helped himself to a bite-sized loaf of bread.

He found Yusef stretched out on the couch in the office, feet propped up on the armrest with his fingers clasped behind his head.

"Comfortable?"

"Very. Thanks for asking."

After a moment of contemplation, Ellis used an elbow to slide the laptop and paperwork to the side before resting his plate on the desk. With his hands free he slid the paperwork into the drawer and dug into his food. He ate, waiting patiently for Yusef to say what's on his mind.

"I know you aren't napping over there," Ellis finally said, breaking the silence.

"Nope."

Yusef's response was so nonchalant it was actually disturbing. "Well?"

"You really not going to address the white elephant."

"I have no idea what you're talking about." Suddenly the pasta on the plate in front of Ellis became exceptionally intriguing.

When he didn't comment further, Yusef swung his legs around to face Ellis. "Has she said anything?"

"Not a word."

A smile tugged at the corner of Yusef's lips. "That sounds like your feelings are hurt that she doesn't remember you."

"She was beyond wasted," Ellis shrugged, "It's probably better that she doesn't remember."

"Are you going to say something?"

"Not if she doesn't."

"And," Yusef urged.

Ellis rose rounding the desk and squatting. Ignoring his friend's question, Ellis rolled up the corner of the rug pushing it out the way revealing a door in the floor. Sliding open the panel, he entered the code. The latch released and he raised the door.

"Go back to your food. I got it." Yusef elbowed Ellis out the way.

As instructed, Ellis returned to the desk, his mind whirling. He'd been anxious to see Soliel again which is why he'd rushed back. He thought back to that night when she'd appeared in his restaurant on a date and the memory alone gnawed at him in the back of his mind. He'd intended to get her phone number that night at the club when they'd met but she'd been too liquored up by the night's end and while being chivalrous, he hadn't thought to give his to her or her friend.

Then fate stepped in, dangling the prize before him again and this time he refused to let the second chance go to waste.

Yusef emerged with a bottle of Chateau Elon Duncan Creek Red. Ellis tossed him the corkscrew he kept stashed in the desk. Not only did the office hide an underground wine cellar, but also a bar behind a panel of pictures. Ellis had once asked Mr. Angelo, the previous owner, about the compartments of which the man replied, some questions are best left unanswered.

While Yusef prepared their drinks, Ellis contemplated his answer to his comrade's query. With glass in hand, he twirled the red liquid around before inhaling its aroma and taking a sip. He leaned back in the executive chair, rocking gently as he savored the liquid playing on his palette.

Eventually Ellis gave in, "I haven't decided."

Yusef almost spit out the wine. "Bullshit."

"Her volunteering to work here complicates matters."

"How so?"

"Mixing business and pleasure," Ellis eyed Yusef over the rim of his glass. He held it up to the light observing the clarity of the red.

"Soliel is not Janice."

"How can you be so sure? Janice didn't show her true colors until it was too late."

"Actually, if I recall correctly," Yusef leaned forward, arms resting on his thighs, "I did try to warn you about Janice. And not just because of the business/pleasure thing."

Yusef was right. He had tried to warn him, but she'd already injected her love serum and he'd been hooked.

"Besides," Yusef continued, pulling Ellis back into the present, "She doesn't exactly work here. And I'm not going to lie, everyone sees something blooming between you two."

"She's been here what, three or four days?"

"Doesn't matter. We've all noticed you've taking a liking to Soliel. The others think its new, even Charity is plotting to get you two together."

Ellis sighed, finishing off the last of the wine in his glass. "If only they knew the truth."

"You look at her the same way you did that night at the club. She intrigues you."

"That's putting it lightly. But..."

"No buts."

"Actually," Ellis interjected, "there is."

"Alright. What am I missing?"

"She's only recently stopped wearing a wedding ring. Or at least a ring on her wedding finger."

Now that revelation sent Yusef leaning back against the couch again. He too finished his drink reaching behind him to refill his glass. He offered the bottle to Ellis who declined.

"You might want to slow down on that. Aren't you holding down the bar tonight?"

Yusef looked longingly from his glass to the bottle, then back to his glass. He opted to put them both onto the hidden bar counter. "How do you know?"

"Tan line."

"Dang, you saw all that in the bad lighting at the club."

"No. Here. "

"Hmm. Well man," Yusef stood checking the time on the clock on the wall. "You'd better make a decision. And soon. You ain't hear it from me but she has piqued the interest of at least one other member of your staff."

"Who?" Ellis demanded.

Yusef only smiled at the reaction. "I got work to do."

Chapter Ten

"I feel like shit," Yaddi whispered as she buried her face in folded arms resting against my cool countertop.

"Let's see. I do recall a declaration from her majesty of our younger years as she cradled the porcelain throne: alcohol is the enemy." I offered the little comfort I could muster. Considering she'd made her own bed; it was time she reckoned with the consequences of her recklessness.

She groaned, peering at me through bloodshot eyes, "Can we do this later?"

"Not if you want this party to go off without a hitch."

"Coffee?" She perked up for half a second before reality crashed down upon her.

I thrust a glass of room temperature alkaline water in her direction. "Caffeine will only dehydrate you more. Now drink."

I retrieved the binder of potential vendors. Once Yaddi chose, I'd transfer the details for each vendor along with a backup to my tracking software. "Where do you want to start?"

"Bed."

"Yaddi," I said with a warning tone, "the quicker we get this done the sooner you can wallow in your alcoholic sorrows and leave me in peace."

"Fine."

I waited for her to add an explicative that never came. We were making progress. We started with the basics: headcount. When she settled on twenty-five max, including the plus ones, we moved on to location.

"It'll be here."

The confident declaration caught me by surprise. "Do you have room inside for all these people?"

"Not inside," she retorted refilling her glass with the rest of the bottled water. "The garden and patio."

"Okay, is this the hangover talking? You do realize Yule is the middle of winter?" Yaddi's parties alternated between Samhain and Yule depending upon her mood. I hadn't attended one in nearly five years. She always invited me, but Yaddi's party circle wasn't exactly my crowd. Especially since I was married and my then husband was a stick in the mud.

"I have nine patio heaters. The heat from the pool permeates through the deck covering, and before you ask of course its heated. Add the awning and a tent if necessary and the cold is a non-issue. Besides, this is the south. Might still be eighty degrees in December."

"Well then. I guess you've thought of everything."

"Far from it."

The playfulness returned to her voice. The Tylenol she'd popped when she first ventured downstairs must be kicking in. Between that and the water she'd be on the mend in no time.

"Very well. Theme."

"All-white masquerade."

"Didn't you do that already?" Yaddi never, and I mean never, repeated a theme.

"Not all white. And the last masquerade occurred five years ago for Samhain. You know, the first time you missed my big party of the year."

"Yeah. Yeah, don't remind me."

"You never told me why you passed. Your absence hurt me deeply."

I studied Yaddi, trying to determine if she told the truth or toyed with my emotions. She appeared genuinely hurt I'd opted out. Even when we weren't on the best of terms, I typically called a truce for the party. I thoroughly enjoyed the events. The food. The drinks. And in most cases the company. The year before that change in plan she'd done the party differently. While it was her party and she was free to do with it as she pleased, I clearly saw a change in both attendees and motives.

As a married woman who preferred monogamy over plural or partner switching relationships, I was no longer comfortable with the direction of the guest list and the underlying theme, for Yaddi to determine her designated partners for the year. I love Yaddi for who she is. However, I wasn't in the space to filter through the bull that came with constantly reminding partygoers that not only was I off the market, but I didn't share the same lifestyle as my best friend.

"You know you're my girl and all."

"Here it comes. But?"

"Are you going to let me explain or not because you know I'm not one to waste my breath."

She huffed and slid the now empty glass from one hand to another across the counter before conceding, "Yes. Please continue."

"Those last couple of years were," I paused searching for the right word, "I'll just say, uncomfortable. You know I love you and I've always enjoyed your parties but," I didn't want to hurt her feelings. I also didn't want to alienate guest who might be on the list this year either.

"Did something happen?"

"No. No, nothing like that." The words came out too quick and I could tell she didn't believe me. "Look, I was married, and you and your guest were single and living your best lives and..."

"Who did it?" she demanded slamming the glass against the counter. She checked the bottom for chips then turned to place it in the sink behind her before she broke it.

When she reached for one of the bottles of cherry wine, I rounded the island and snatched it away. Like a mother silently ordering her tween to have a seat before a lecture I pointed to the stool I'd vacated on the other side. She glared back at me in a silent challenge but eventually, as my foot tapped in impatience, she sat.

I ignored the scowl and eyeroll that followed opting to continue my explanation. "Now that you're done acting like an indignant adolescent, I'll finish. Like I said, nothing happened per se. It just wasn't my scene anymore. The parties became less about celebrating the season and more about...well..." I shrugged, resigned to speak my truth, and let the cards fall where they may, "you."

I'd prepared for her to protest. Instead, she appeared almost relieved.

"You could have said something. I would have scaled it back."

"I couldn't have asked that of you. Yaddi you are who you are, and I know these parties aren't just about us as friends. Or about the rituals we'd established. You were growing into your own role. Just as I was as a married woman."

"Daniel?"

"Had absolutely no influence over my decision. You and I were in different places in our lives. Trying new experiences and determining what we needed to keep and what we needed to release."

She tore a sheet of paper from the legal pad I'd tucked into the binder pocket. "Where were we?"

How quickly she moved on. I watched her scribble on the paper as I typed in the web address of the florist from the top of my list. The reviews were impeccable, praise given for both professionalism and design. "I liked this one best."

We discussed the flower arrangements, gathering ideas from the site of The Glenwood Florist. Yaddi provided enough information to setup the initial appointment with the florist to at least select flowers and place an order. Though short notice, Yaddi paid well. An extra couple hundred dollars went a long way to convince a vendor to go the extra mile in a crunch.

Yaddi yawned. I was losing her fast. "That just leaves the names for the guest list and food. I've completed the invitation design as per your specifications. I just need names and addresses for the envelopes and reply cards." I passed the mock-up to her.

Her finger traced the calligraphy as she admired my penmanship. "That was quick."

"Now you know I've been doing this forever. While calligraphy is art, there is a science to the organization. And I know how you like things done. Makes the process easier. Typically, the hardest part from my perspective is having the client select a style of font appropriate for the occasion. I don't have to do that with you. You trust my judgment."

"You sound sure of yourself?"

"Well, you're looking at what will be the final product. Is it to your liking or not?"

She flipped the card over, making a show of checking for smudges or ink seeping through. Of course, none existed, my card stock choice depending heavily on its ability to absorb the amount of ink necessary in the calligraphy process. "Beautiful. Not that I expected any less from you."

"Good. Now that we've settled that, do you have it in you to discuss food?"

"Uh, no."

"Okay, how about type. We can discuss specifics later. But are you thinking Greek? French? Italian?"

"Italian."

I hid my smile. She'd just made food easy. While I knew a couple of Greek restaurants in the area and at least one French place Daniel and I had visited the last time we'd traveled to Atlanta I was sure I could convince Ellis to cater Yaddi's party. He wouldn't even have to serve. I could hire a company to provide wait staff or maybe we could do buffet style.

Yaddi's eyes glazed over as the hangover and meds dragged her into a state of lethargy. "Go get some rest. I have what I need for now."

"Trust me, you don't have to tell me twice." She managed to make it to the stairs without falling flat on her face. "By the way, I've booked consultations next week, so I'll be gone all week."

"And Dwayne?" I asked, not sure I wanted to be left here alone with him roaming the main house. I'd crash at a hotel for the week if I needed to.

"He's leaving Friday instead of Sunday. And it can't get here fast enough."

When she chuckled, I questioned whether she really meant that last part. I hadn't asked the specifics of her current boy toy's obligations to earn his keep in her reverse harem. Truth be told I didn't think I wanted to know.

"Oh, before I forget," Yaddi paused on the first step, "the old who-ride is in the garage. Keys are in the last kitchen counter drawer."

"You seriously still have that thing?"

"Can't believe you think I don't. I meant what I said, I will keep it until the symbols fall off. Hasn't happened yet. I still get folks flagging me down asking if it's for sale."

"Big fat no huh."

"You know it. So be prepared if you decide to take her for a spin. She still purrs like a kitten."

"I bet she does."

Chapter Eleven

Ellis and I missed each other by minutes. Or at least according to Charity. Not that it mattered, I brought the calligraphy set, card stock, and my portable magnification light with me. I could wait him out. It only took me an hour to handle the set of paperwork I'd designated for the day, so I hunkered down at the dinette in the corner of the office and perfected the letter structure I wanted to use to address the party invitation.

Unfortunately, my plan came crashing down when Charity knocked on the office door.

I held up a finger, glad she saw it as I made a final loop in the name Tunde. I hated wasting card stock yeah oh and of course Yaddi's would be the most expensive in the bunch. The knot in my back tightened when I leaned back against the chair. I'd been hunched over for too long.

"Looks like you could use a break."

"Yeah." I stood, painstakingly slow as my right knee popped. "Pray your joints don't turn against you when you get my age." Truth be told, I was in excellent shape considering my medical condition. I made sure to get in as much exercise as possible on the good days because when the bad days came, they dug their claws in with a vengeance. The only thought is drugs and sleep.

"You sound like an old woman. You probably only have me by a couple of years."

"I'm sure I have you by more than you think." The shoulder rolls loosened my neck and after a few more stretches of my head from side to side and arms in the air my body ceased its infernal creaking.

"What are you working on?" Charity asked taking in the magnifying light and funky tipped pens.

"I do calligraphy on the side."

"Do you mind?" She gestured to the full sheet of paper I'd written the letters of the alphabet out on in upper and lowercase letters as my reference.

"Go ahead. I'm going to do a pass in the hall real quick. Get the blood circulating in my legs again."

I found Charity straddled over the chair across from mine at the dinette upon my return. She examined one of my pens, handling it with care as she tried to determine how the ink flowed from the metal tip with the split up the middle.

"Fountain pen type," I said as I claimed my seat. "I can change the ink cartridges to whatever color I like."

"The lines in the letters are different sizes." She pointed to the letter 'c' on the page. "How?"

"Practice. Lots and lots of practice. The pressure on the tip, angle, and position play a role in the shape the tip maintains and the ink flow."

"Is it hard?"

In that moment I realized how young Charity must really be. She looked so innocent, inquisitive, like a child waiting for the magician to show her how he pulled the coin from behind her ear. I'd pegged her in her late twenties by the way she spoke and handle unruly customers. But in this moment, she appeared much younger.

"It takes loads of patience. And a steady hand. They have markers now with different tips sizes for different styles. I assume they are much easier to navigate than the fountain or dip pens like these. And I wouldn't fathom trying the brush style."

"How did you even get into this?"

I pointed at myself, "nerd. I'm a gamer too. But shh don't tell anybody."

We shared a laugh, something I'd found myself doing more since hanging out at Angelo's. "Calligraphy is good money, especially once you build a client base. You can do it from just about anywhere. I've heard it called a dying art; but I'm not convinced. It does have a specialized market and exclusivity has its perks."

"The good money part huh."

"Yep. But I don't think you came in here to talk about calligraphy. What's up?"

She toyed with her ponytail removing the tie from the bottom and proceeding to unbraid it. "I just wanted to check in with you. See how you like it here."

That sounded like a fishing question. But I liked Charity, so I played along. "I think it's a good place to spend all this free time I suddenly have."

"I meant to ask you about that. I saw the Baltimore address on your resume. Recently relocated?"

I caught her looking at my ring finger. I busied my hands stacking the dried cards. "Coming home. I went to college here. I needed a change of scenery and Atlanta is still near and dear to my heart. Is that all?"

"Am I being that obvious?" She wrapped her hair around in a bun using the tie to secure it.

Charity was easy to talk to. And she had been the one to come to my rescue after all. We'd bonded over that moment and while I didn't befriend people easily, I think we both wanted to learn more about one another even if it was just as a networking opportunity.

"A little," I admitted. "I've noticed a couple of employees eyeing me."

"I should have known you'd catch on. It's just."

I held up a hand, "let me stop you right there. I'm not here to ruffle anyone's feathers or stake a claim. I'm just finding my way and trying to help where I feel called."

Charity blushed, "I didn't mean it like that."

"Hun, I've been around long enough to know how all of this goes. Besides, it's a moot point. Linda did her job well. The books are very much in order. I think the biggest struggle is having someone to keep up with the invoices and details. You all have more than enough on your plates, and I suspect Ellis does as well. I was going to offer to assist in finding a permanent replacement. I can make sure the new person is up to speed before I graciously bow out."

"Really?" Her surprise caught me off guard. "I thought if we made a good impression you'd stick around. You've brought a ray of sunshine in this place that's been missing for a while."

Her mood turned somber. "You all must miss Linda then."

She looked away, her gaze falling on the pictures of Ellis and his family.

I changed the subject, "May I ask you a question?"

Her head swiftly turned in my direction. I almost expected the bun to loosen, sending stray strands of hair over her shoulder. It held, not a rebellious strand in sight. She hesitated as if anticipating my question.

I gestured to the letter on the edge of the desk, though it wasn't in the same place I'd left it, it still balanced just close enough to the edge to be noticeable compared to the envelopes placed in the trashcan or inbox. "I was going to ask Ellis about it. He balled it up when it first arrived without even opening it."

Charity reached for the envelope, scowling as she read the attorney's name on the front. "They're at it again."

She tossed the envelope onto the desk, rolling her eyes in the process. "Mr. Angelo's sons. They've been stirring up trouble ever since they discovered he left the restaurant to Ellis instead of them. They didn't even want the place and made as much known to their father over the years. Not until the reading of the will did Angelo's become important."

"So, the restaurant was bequeathed to Ellis?"

"Yes, along with the family recipes. I think the recipes are what they really want." She stood, turning the chair to face the right direction. "Don't worry about it. We've handled them before." Her eyes flicked to the envelope again, the scowl now replaced with a strained sense of worry, though she tried her best to hide it.

Charity headed towards the door as I gathered the rest of the calligraphy supplies, "Ellis isn't coming back today so if you were hanging around to catch him don't waste your time."

That was two days in a row we'd missed one another. Was he avoiding me? "Thanks. I think I am pretty much done."

She sighed as she took one last look over her shoulder at the discarded letter then left me to my devices.

Chapter Twelve

I typed The Naughty Chocolatier into the browser URL bar. While taking note of the direct website, I first waded through a few articles and reviews. The place received glowing reviews from patrons for everything from their chocolate selection to the holiday classes and workshops. They even did community demonstrations and events at local libraries to educate people on the chocolate making processes, how the cocoa is sourced, as well as health benefits and overall fun with confections.

Struck with an idea for the party, I retracted my descent down the Internet rabbit hole finding my way to the actual company site. Though not right off the highway, I passed the location on my daily commute to Angelo's. The Naughty Chocolatier rested in the center of a brick building with a bookstore and cafe on one side and a braid shop on the other. The store occupied the area of three storefronts while the bookstore and cafe took up two on that side with the hair shop filling the end slot.

I scrolled through the site reviewing the chocolate offerings, cakes, and cupcakes. It wasn't just a chocolate shop; they sold an assortment of items to fulfill anyone's sweet tooth. I homed in on the bulk order form, adding the information to my notes to run by Yaddi for the party. While we'd discussed food, dessert didn't always fall into that same category. And Yaddi had a mad sweet tooth.

I clicked the link to the classes as the door at the top of the stairs open.

"Soliel?" Came Yaddi's voice. She sounded close, like she might have already started her descent.

"Yeah, I'm here." Yaddi stepped into the room, the baby blue pants suit catching me by surprise. She'd pulled her hair up, securing it in three intricate braids that formed a topper on top of her head. "I don't remember the last time I saw you in that many clothes."

"Ha ha. Funny."

I continued to scroll, the Yule log class catching my attention.

"What are you up to?" Yaddi asked over my shoulder.

The subtle undertones of passion fruit and mango from her perfume tickled my nose. "Do you mind?"

Taking the hint, she stepped back to lean against the counter. "How are the plans? Have you talked to your people about the food?"

"Not yet. The owner and I have been missing each other."

"Ah. So that's where you've been heading to every day."

Dang-it. I forgot I was trying to keep my new employment details to myself. I love Yaddi to death, but the woman was nosey and right now I needed a place and a situation just about me. I already felt the pressure of squatting in Yaddi's house regardless of her rent refusal and continuous assurance that she was good with the living situation.

'Let me have this Yaddi. Please"

Yaddi raised her hands in surrender. "You're a grown woman. I'm confident you can handle your business."

The last part seemed like a trap, but I chose not to take the bait. "I was just checking this place out for dessert. Or maybe a chocolate demonstration. You know, give your guest an opportunity to participate in the process of making the gifts they take home."

I scribbled gift bags on my notepad. One more item they needed to address soon to make sure any customized gifts were ordered in time. I slid the computer to the side giving Yaddi plenty room for a closer look.

"I hadn't thought about that." She scrolled through the gallery taking in the chocolate sculptures, pointing out the white chocolate doves perched on dark chocolate branches. "That's cute."

"I think I'm going to check out the Yule log class. They have one Sunday after next."

"I'd go with you, but I think I'm flying out that day. That's the weekend of a rescheduled client. I haven't been to Maryland in a minute and there are a couple of seafood spots I want to check out before I dive into playing nice with the ..."

"Don't say it."

"What?" Yaddi said feigning innocence. "I was just going to say clients."

"Sure, you were." I bookmarked the page, "I think I can swing this class on my own."

"Isn't this usually a couple's thing? I mean chocolate making."

"No." I said pointing to a group of women in sashes reading bride to be, bridesmaid, and maid of honor slung over their shoulders as they held up the items they'd made.

Yaddi sucked her teeth retreating to the spot she'd vacated. She suddenly found her nails interesting as she responded, "date night. Group activity. It's all the same. Doesn't look like something people do alone."

And there it was. The jab at my independence. "I don't mind dating myself. I've been going to movies and restaurants by myself for years. Even when I was married. You must have forgotten the crazy hours Daniel worked. And when he was promoted, they got even crazier. Believe me Yaddi, I'll be fine."

"Whatever you say. Anyway, are there any other details we need to discuss related to the party?"

"You still haven't given me a budget. Am I working with the usual? Do you want to spend more or less?"

"I don't rightly care. You know my level of expectation."

"And you know I'm an expert negotiator." To my surprise, she hugged me. Not quite the big bear hug from the day I'd arrived but the kind of hug signifying absolute trust.

"I know you won't send me to the poor house."

"Of course not. Where would I live?"

We shared a laugh, two old friends reliving times long past, and we both felt it. "So..."

She released me and I eyed her suspiciously. "Uh oh. Here we go again. I knew you wanted something."

Yaddi crossed her arms awkwardly, like she couldn't decide whether her arms should rest above, at, or below her ample bosom. "I have a business proposition for you."

"My hands are already full."

"They aren't that full if you have time to go to a class."

"Am I not allowed free time?"

"At least hear me out." I sighed heavily before agreeing. "Fine. What you got for me?"

Yaddi swiped a bottle of Cherry wine from the counter. "Cake?"

"Hmm. For the party?"

"Yes and no." Yaddi opened the last cabinet. Her height giving her a greater advantage than me. She plucked a glass jar from the top corner of the cabinet and placed it on the counter next to me.

I frowned. "Fifty dollars a pop. And you supplying the good liquor."

"I always do."

I sighed again knowing there was no way to escape this surprise development, "How many?"

"That my friend," Yaddi's grin widened as I took the bait, "Is always negotiable."

Chapter Thirteen

To my surprise, Ellis beat me to the restaurant the next morning. We hadn't seen each other in a couple of days, the timing off just enough that he arrived after my departure, or it was his day off. While Yusef greeted me at the back door, I heard Ellis's voice booming around the restaurant. Good thing it was early. The language was far from appropriate for customers.

"I see someone is having a bad day," I bemused, sliding past Yusef into the office where I dropped my bag into the dinette chair. The office lay in a state of disarray: papers tossed around, a shattered coffee mug, the executive chair toppled in the corner. Whatever had triggered Ellis's current tirade probably originated here.

"What happened?" I asked, feeling Yusef at my back though he hadn't entered the office.

"Wish I knew. He's been on a warpath since I arrived. No one else is here yet."

"Probably a good thing."

"I concur." With a curt lift of the chin, he turned to exit. "I'll leave you to get this place in order."

"Um. Excuse me?" I glared at him; hands placed firmly on hips. "I'm no one's maid."

Yusef stopped in his tracks. I waited for a response. Instead, the man turned his head ever so slowly, an approving smirk on his lips. He moved to the side, allowing me to precede him down the hall.

"You sure you're ready for this?" He finally asked as we stopped in front of the swinging kitchen door marked 'in'.

His question gave me pause. "You sound like I'm a rabbit about to intrude upon a lion's den."

"Ellis can be, shall I say, brash when he's like this."

I rounded on Yusef, "and how often does he get like this?"

69

For the first time I felt like I was seeing the real Ellis. Not the one I found charming. The Ellis working to stay in my good graces. I wasn't entirely blind. I felt the attraction we shared but like I'd told Charity, the last thing I wanted was a rebound, or to step on the toes of another suitor. And I had definitely seen the competition for his favor. Not that it mattered, I reminded myself. Ellis was a married man, and I don't do married men.

"Let's just say, it's been a few good weeks."

So, Ellis had anger issues.

"Let me qualify this. He isn't usually on a tirade. At least not to the point of ransacking the office or kitchen. But there are things you don't know about him."

"Like?"

Yusef pinched the bridge of his nose his eyes shut tight like he struggled to decide how much to share. The tension in his shoulders releasing when he sighed. "Not for me to say. Or at least that part. I will say this, and he's probably going to kill me for it but he's really into you. I haven't seen this light in him in a long time. He's been through some shit."

"I'm gonna stop you right there. I don't do married men."

Yusef's brows crashed together as he took me in. "What gave you the impression he's married?"

I crossed my arms glowering at him. "That smiling family picture in the office."

Yusef stifled a laugh, "The woman in that picture is a former employee and longtime family friend. And I don't think her wife would appreciate your assumption."

The revelation caught me off guard making me hesitate even more. Did I really want to try to pursue something more than this working relationship with the man on the other side of the door?

"Fuck!"

We raced into the kitchen just as a knife clanked to the floor. Neither of us turned at the sight of blood dripping from the side of Ellis's hand. Yusef met Ellis at the hand-washing station steading his friend's bleeding appendage to get a closer look at the damage.

"That's gonna need stitches," Yusef said.

"Is it bad? Do I need to call an ambulance?"

Ellis stared at me as Yusef checked the hand further. He didn't say a word he just watched as my worry escalated.

"No," Yusef responded after careful consideration. "Bring me the first aid kit."

I retrieved it from the shelf on the counter by the door, placing it on the cart next to where the two men stood. I flipped it open tearing the corner of an antibiotic swab before handing it to Yusef while I gathered gauze and tape.

"I have to apply pressure," Yusef said. Ellis didn't respond. We worked together to patch the hand as best we could with the supplies available. "You need to go to the hospital."

"Yeah, that's not happening," were the first words Ellis had spoken since we'd entered the room. He admired Yusef's handy work. The binding secure but leaving his fingers free. "I have work to do."

"Seriously," I said in that mother bear tone. "At least get it looked at."

"I don't have hours to spend in an emergency room."

"What if I can get you seen quickly. And I promise it won't cost an arm and a leg."

"I'd take the lady up on her offer," Yusef commented as Ellis eyed me suspiciously.

"Can't drive like this. I'm in the car." Ellis moved each finger and his thumb. At least he hadn't cut off a digit. When he finally looked up, he added, "it's a stick," for my sake.

I shot him an intentionally over-dramatic eye roll with a side of neck swing. "Let me get my purse."

We met in the hallway, Yusef trailed behind as Ellis pouted. The shift in mood implied the pair had had an intense conversation in my absence and Ellis lost. After assuring Yusef I could handle Ellis's car, and Ellis, I backed out the parking spot and headed for the highway.

"I do have a license you know," I said to break the ice. Ellis stared out the window until I hit the highway. I ignored his occasional glance my way as I effortlessly shifted gears to merge and keep up with the flow of traffic.

"Then why use a car service?"

"Why not?" I retorted. I exited at Lenox and followed the other drivers to make a left turn.

"Most people prefer public transportation or their own vehicles."

How condescending. I thought. "Well up until I started volunteering at Angelo's," I hoped he heard the emphasis on volunteering, "I had little need for a vehicle. And in the grand scheme of things, I still don't. I've been trying to connect with you to discuss my hours. Things are in order now," *or at least they were until he ransacked the office, but I wasn't going there.* "I don't need to be there every day. And I was going to talk to you about finding a permanent replacement."

"You're leaving?" He sat at attention, his words coming out quickly as if my decision worried him.

Interesting. I turned into the lot of an office park pressing the button on the parking machine. When I removed the slip, the arm on the gate rose and I pulled through. I lucked up on a spot in a sparsely used row pulling in next to a Honda and the wall.

"Come on," I said reaching for the car door prepared to exit. His fingers catching my arm stopped me.

"You didn't answer my question."

A smile tugged at the corner of my lips as my heart beat a thousand beats per minute. His light brown eye drew me in, the fear and concern readily apparent. Eyes that told a story. Eyes screaming for me not to leave him. He looked lost, like a wounded puppy and I hated it.

"Come on. We'll talk about it after your hand is taken care of."

Chapter Fourteen

*S**he was leaving.* Ellis thought. Just like that she'd walked back into his life, and she was about to walk right back out without so much as a thought. He'd forgotten about his hand. The sharp pain was minute compared to the knife twisting in his heart.

"Mrs. Brodie," the woman at the desk dressed in a green blouse and wearing at least six layers of make-up exclaimed. Ellis wondered why women felt the need to paint a face on. He didn't get it. He preferred his women natural. Soliel's natural beauty drew him in the moment he'd laid eyes on her in the club. The giant afro. The tinge of lip gloss. The row of freckles dotted across her nose and forehead.

"Hi Helen. How have you been?" Soliel said a little sheepishly, "And its Boudreaux now."

The woman's eyes flicked to Ellis. He'd stayed a few steps behind allowing Soliel to make the necessary introductions. Her scrutiny meant nothing. He was there to get his hand stitched. Nothing more. Nothing less.

"Is Fatimah in? My friend has a nasty cut that probably needs stitches."

Helen again gave Ellis the once over, whispering, "friend huh."

Soliel only shook her head, "My boss actually. Now, about Fatimah."

"Yes, she's in. You're lucky you got here when you did. I think she was about to head over to the hospital to make rounds." Helen shooed them away as she grabbed the phone.

Ellis sat in the seat next to Soliel the hand throbbing again.

"How is it?" She asked.

"Hurts like hell. My own damn fault."

"What upset you so?"

He just shook his head. The last thing he wanted to do was burden her with his problems. She'd been so kind helping out now that Linda was gone. He didn't have the heart to drag her further into is drama filled business world.

Soliel busied her hands scrolling through the emails on her phone. "You're worrying your staff," she muttered, eyes strategically locked on the screen, "You might actually feel better if you talk about it."

"No need to concern yourself with my problems."

"And what if I want to?"

Now that gave him pause. Not that she could do anything to help. The entire situation with Angelo's sons was hopeless. Or at least he thought it was. And then there was the anniversary coming up. Ellis pushed the thoughts from his mind before the rage returned. He was embarrassed enough Soliel had seen him losing his cool. He didn't want a repeat of the situation.

"Well look what the cat dragged in."

The pair looked up in unison as Fatimah stood in the doorway waving them over.

"Come on," Soliel said to him. "My girl will have you patched up in no time."

She was right. They were in and out in forty minutes. The cut had been clean. Fatimah had commented that it must have been made by a well-crafted knife, not like some flesh torn jagged cuts she was accustomed to repairing.

Ellis tested his fingers again reveling in the new freedom. The side of the hand was still numb, but he could still feel his fingers. The bandage only covered the side giving him just about the full range of motion though he dared not try to close the fingers into a fist. Busting stitches didn't bode well.

"I can drive if you like," Ellis said as they exited the building. "I at least owe you lunch."

Soliel handed him the keys. "We can eat at the restaurant."

"Come on. Let me do something nice for you. Besides, I'm over Italian food and once I get back, I have sixteen pans of chocolate truffles to make. I'm probably gonna be there all night."

They climbed in. "Any preference?"

"You're gonna laugh," Soliel said sheepishly.

"Try me."

"Varsity?"

He didn't laugh, "Gut full of grease it is."

They passed through the line at The Varsity, collecting their food and ascending to the upper deck where the couple perched in the back of Ellis's Subaru. It was a beautiful day in Atlanta. The calendar read October, but this was the south and while some years this was sweater weather, today's sun warmed the city to a comfortable eighty degrees.

"My knees are going to be screaming at me when I finally try to stand," Soliel said as she gathered fingers full of grease dripping onion rings.

Ellis moved to allow her to stretch out if she so chose. He'd perched on the end of the half a piece of bumper the hatchback sported. "We can grab a table if you'd be more comfortable."

"Nope. All part of the nostalgia. We used to come here after exams and football games and eat till our heart's content. It was tradition."

"We?"

"Me and my girls. College days when I could scarf this stuff down without a thought of the pounds it would add to my stomach and thighs."

"I think you're beautiful. Every form fitting curve." He'd watched as she'd walked up the stairs ahead of him admiring the view but trying to remain discrete. She'd caught him ogling and insisted they walk side by side to the car. It didn't matter he'd already committed her curves to memory.

She blushed, her shiny lips wrapping around the straw to take a sip. He imagined those same lips wrapping around each finger...

"Are you listening to me?"

"Huh? Oh, sorry. I spaced out for a second. Must be the blood loss." He waved the stitched hand quickly digging into the red and white stripped boat of flimsy French fries he'd slathered in ketchup. "What were you saying?"

"I was asking about earlier. About the...you know..."

"It's nothing to concern yourself with. I was just having a bad day."

"Oh, is that what bad days look like."

He turned away. Embarrassed. "I don't make a habit of almost severing a digit if that's what you mean."

Her hand came to rest on his shoulder, drawing his attention back her way. "Talking about it helps."

"This can't be helped. I just..."

"Need to let someone in."

Ellis's gaze narrowed. Soliel inched away at the scrutiny. "Someone's been telling my business."

"I didn't say that. I did, however, see the letter, and before you again jump to conclusions, I didn't read it. But letters from attorney offices are usually bad news."

Why did he want to spill his guts to her? To catch her up on all the drama and trauma preceding her arrival in his life. Yusef had dragged him to the club that night hoping to get thoughts of Angelo's sons out of his head before he crossed a line and screwed them all. And there she was, a beacon of light shining through the dark only to slip through his fingers. And now she'd returned drawing him back into her warmth.

"I don't want to burden you."

"I'm not asking you to. I'm just offering to be a sounding board. No judgement. Maybe you just need to speak your truth. Get it off your chest so you can approach the matter with a clearer head and open heart."

He took a bite of his chili cheese slaw dog, catching the escaping onions in the wax paper before they stained his shirt with chili grease. "You sound like Charity."

"She gives good advice."

He was glad when she allowed him time to consider her offer. They enjoyed their food as a bus full of teenagers unloaded and raced inside vying to be the first in line. A few of the young girls giggled and whispered as they stole glances at Ellis and his car until they notice Soliel inside.

"Looks like you've attracted their attention," Soliel said.

A smile tugged at the corner of his mouth. "I'm old enough to be their daddy."

"Speaking of. The little boy in the picture in your office."

"My son."

"Hmm. Well, I don't see a ring. And according to my sources you aren't married."

"Divorced."

"Ah."

He nodded at her now empty ring finger, "You?"

"It's only been final a few months. But it was a long time coming. We'd been separated over a year. I suppose he was waiting on me. He made no move to file and when I did, he gave me what I asked for and sent me on my way."

"So, you're starting over."

"Yes and no." Soliel gathered her trash securing her used napkins and now empty cup in the box before passing it to Ellis.

He shoved their discards into the bag and offered a hand which Soliel took. She gave him a half dip and he almost dropped the bag in his attempt to keep her from falling if her legs gave way.

"Got ya," she chided giving him a little shimmy as she rounded the passenger side.

"Touché. Let me toss this and we can finish our conversation on the way back."

Chapter Fifteen

I enjoyed our conversation because neither of us vied for attention. The banter and sharing flowed naturally, like old friends instead of new acquaintances getting to know each other. Unfortunately, I still allowed Ellis to do exactly what I'd wanted to avoid, which was dance around the subject of the trigger event of the day.

Refusing to allow him to continue to avoid the situation, I cornered him so to speak when we reached Angelo's. "I'm going to tell you like I told Yusef, I'm nobody's maid." His brow furrowed as if he was trying to figure out what I was talking about. "The office?" Still, he just stared at me like a deer in semi headlights.

I climbed out the passenger seat, beating him to the door as I waited for him to unlock it. When we reached the office door, I kindly pointed at the mess he'd left.

"Oh. That. I don't expect you to clean this up."

"I know," I pointed to his hand, "however, since you're injured, I'll be willing to help only if," I paused. Maybe for dramatic effect, or maybe I wanted to toy with him further. He could easily opt to complete the job without my help. His hand wasn't that much a hindrance since being stitched up. Still, I secretly wanted to be with him, to finish our conversation and get to the bottom of the mystery that sent him over the deep end earlier.

"If?" Ellis finally said when I didn't continue. He'd entered the office making a b-line for the personal photographs splayed over the floor.

"You tell me about," I waved my hand at the mess as he faced me, 'this."

While I suspected the reason based on the information Charity dropped in my lap the other night and the black and white photos pinned to the walls all around, I needed to hear the full story from him. It was for my benefit, and his.

"They're throwing every trick in the book at me to make me give up the restaurant."

I started with the papers strewn about, gathering them together first. I'd work on arranging them after we cleared the floor. "Do they have a leg to stand on?"

"I don't think so. There have been other letters," Ellis said as he up righted the overturned office chair, "the first ones were handwritten."

"Threats?"

"Depends on how you look at them. I've known Angelo's sons since I was a teenager. We were friends when I first started. When I wasn't working or helping Mr. Angelo out, we played in the branches of the oak out back. We practically spent our last couple of years of high school together."

"Then what happened?"

"They had me by a couple of years. They went away to college, and I was, well, still here. Cooking. Cleaning. Doing maintenance. By then Mr. Angelo had taken me under his wing. He'd seen my love of cooking and taught me everything he knew. He even let me experiment with the sweets bringing my grandmother's southern flare to his traditional Italian desserts."

"That doesn't sound so bad. I mean, isn't that what's supposed to happen. Kids grow up. They go off to their own lives."

"Yeah, but I think they always expected to get the restaurant. I was the one here working side by side with their father for the next eight years. The boys came home for the holidays, but they'd pop in, spend a couple of hours with their dad, and bounce to hang with their friends in the city."

I plopped into the chair starting the process of organizing the paperwork. The task helped me focus and kept me from attempting to soothe the sadness creeping into Ellis's voice.

"I suppose their lack of enthusiasm cut their old man deep. I don't think they realized how much he just wanted to spend time with them. Instead, he invested the time in me, telling me stories about when they were kids and how they'd follow him around the kitchen, wielding their own spoons and pots trying to 'help'. I think he'd always planned to bring them into the business."

"What stopped him?"

"They did." Ellis sat on the couch his now bandaged hand resting on his leg. His expression strained against the pain.

"I've got Tylenol if your hand is bothering you."

He shook his head before resting it on the back of the couch and closing his eyes. "Its fine."

Unable to maintain the distance between us, I join him, though I sat on the opposite side, one leg tucked beneath me. "What did they do?"

Ellis cracked an eye before shutting it again. "Broke his heart. It was the Christmas after their mother passed. They started hounding Mr. Angelo for the recipes, something about they belonged to them. That he'd gotten them from their mother's family, and she wanted them to have them. They'd all but threatened to ruin him if he didn't hand the recipe over."

"Wow."

"Yeah. His own flesh and blood." His head rocked from side to side in disbelief. "While the oldest was on the up-and-up and about his business, that young one was a lot like me. Or like I was when I first started out here. Lost. Alone, doing what I wanted to do to get by without a care in the world about who I hurt in the process."

I filed that last comment away. While we'd gotten to know one another better on the drive over he hadn't mentioned anything about being a troubled youth. Everyone had a past. We all fought demons and celebrated victories as well as learned from the defeats. Ellis becoming a successful entrepreneur took courage, tenacity, and a knack for business. While I observed inefficiencies in a couple office procedures, for the most part Angelo's ran in the black.

"Do you think this is an organized front?"

"I think they are getting more organized. Getting lawyers involved. I don't have money to burn on litigation."

"And you think they do?"

Silence hung between us, and for a moment, I questioned if he'd answer.

"I have a suspicion. They may not have the money upfront and might even be using a friend to see if I'd bite based on the letters."

My interest piqued, I asked, "and the suspicion?"

"I'm not ready to say."

I considered pushing, but he'd opened up enough today and I didn't want to come across overly eager. "Well," I stood, "I'll let you get back to your order." He didn't move though he did open his eyes.

"Are we going to discuss your replacement.?"

"It's not pressing, though I need a couple of days off. I'll leave them on a post-it on the desk. And I have a business proposal for you as well but, again, it's not a pressing matter." Well actually it was pressing considering the party was a couple of months out and during peak holiday season. Still, whatever this was growing between us gave me confidence that he'd make the food for the party happen, even if just to impress.

"I appreciate the heads up." He rocked in the sofa, gaining enough momentum to stand without the use of the bad hand. "I'll finish cleaning this mess when I'm done. Have a good evening."

I watched him leave. He didn't close the door behind him, the noise from the dining room and kitchen swallowing his footsteps. I'd half expected him to take the letter. He'd divulged enough detail to placate me and yet he didn't go out of his way to keep me from reading it myself.

Picking the letter up from the top of the stack of organized papers, I skimmed the contents, frowning in the process.

"I heard I missed the fireworks."

Charity peered at me over the edge of the paper. "I don't know about fireworks."

"You don't consider a chef nearly severing a finger fireworks? Man, what world did you grow up in?"

"Can I help you with something Charity?" She was fishing, just like she'd baited me with a tidbit here and there about Ellis.

"Was just stopping in to say good afternoon. And by that smile on Ellis's face, he definitely had a good afternoon."

Chapter Sixteen

I examined the tightly sealed glass jar containing pitted prunes, currants, gold and black raisins, soaking in what I was sure was cherry wine and a dark spiced rum. "Do I want to know how long this has been soaking?"

Yaddi busied her hands chopping a fresh batch of prunes before dividing them into the six glass jars they'd lined up on the counter. She wiped her hands on the black apron she'd tide over her blue and green tie-dye jumpsuit. "Long enough."

We'd risen early, one because Yaddi wanted to make sure Dwayne made his departure on schedule and two because I had agreed to make a few black cakes for the party and to sell. In traditional Yaddi fashion a grocery order appeared with every ingredient for both the cake I'd make today, and the preparations needed for the fruit for the cakes I'd do first week of December.

I suspected Yaddi had prepped a batch early for a trial run to get a couple of cakes to snack on before December.

"Seriously?' I said, popping the top and inhaling the intoxicating aroma of the fermented fruit. "When did you start this?"

"Uh. June."

Okay, June wasn't bad. Black cake fruit 101, the longer it sits the better it gets. "And what kind of alcohol."

Yaddi feigned genuine hurt, "now you know it's the good stuff."

"Um hmm."

As Yaddi prepped the jars, I floated around the kitchen gathering the orange, lemon, and lime peel we'd chopped earlier. When they'd been spread into an even layer on a parchment lined baking sheet, I slid them into the oven.

"We haven't done this in forever," I said, buzzing around like a worker bee organizing and gathering ingredients for the cake batter.

"Remember the parties."

"You mean the assembly line?' I lined the ingredients up one next to the other making a show out of the proper order of mixing and to account for everything needed to prep this cake. "Tada!"

"Girl you are a hot mess."

I hmphed as I measured the sugar to make browning, "I am not. And you forgot the aromatic bitters."

The mood in the kitchen changed; like the air had been sucked out the room. It felt heavy, even with the sweet smells surrounding us. Yaddi suddenly quieted and I got the impression she wanted to ask a question.

"Okay, Yaddi. What's on your mind?"

"It's nothing."

I regarded her fiercely, "ding ding ding. That is a lie. Now spill it."

"I said it's no big deal. Just, you seem really happy." Yaddi continued to chop, her gaze fixed on the knife and fruit.

"What's wrong with me being happy. Last time I checked you were going out of your way to make sure I wasn't sitting around here moping over Daniel."

"True. Still, I am happy for you. I mean look at you, already found a job. Your side hustles are flourishing. I don't think I could have bounced back so easily."

"Where is this coming from?" I asked, genuinely concerned.

Yaddi shook her head. She scooped the next cupful into jar in front of her before returning to the chopping task.

"Aren't you happy for me?"

"I'm cautiously optimistic."

"I'm not jumping into anything, Unlike the hookups you set me up with."

"Hey, those were no strings attached."

It was my turn to focus on the task at hand. I didn't want Yaddi to witness my fury. "And you know I don't roll like that."

Silence again. Neither of us was ready to admit the truth. We were different but that was okay. We'd been different people our entire friendship. Yaddi was the busy bee buzzing around the scene like the extrovert she was. She thrived in a crowd, feeding from the energy of others in her element. I, on the other hand, was the friend burdened with the purses. Or maybe burdened wasn't the right word. Charged. Yes, I was the one charged with keeping the purses and acting as the designated driver. The responsible one in our group of friends. Or the disapproving mother bear as I'd been called once before.

I didn't pretend to not enjoy the role, preferring to living vicariously through others. Let them contend with the dangers. Face the heart breaks. Experience life as they saw fit while I did the same.

"How have you been feeling lately?" Yaddi asked, the task of chopping and dividing the fruit now complete, she rinsed off her knife and left it in the sink. She poured a glass of the cherry wine.

"Isn't it a little early to be drinking?" I waved a finger at her. "And that's for the cake."

"Are you going to answer my question?"

"I'm fine Yaddi. I know my limits and what steps to take to keep my disease under control."

"And this new light in your life?"

"You'll meet him soon enough. If it's alright with you I wanted to bring him by before you leave. That way you two can work through the menu and any details."

"Sure. I have a few things to take care of before I fly out Monday morning. Sunday works best."

"I think I can arrange that. It's usually slow until the after-church crowd trickles in. I'll see if I can grab a few dishes for you to try tomorrow."

"What? No work at all today."

"Um, hello." I gestured around the room, "You know these cakes take all damn day; right. And where are the tins?"

We spent the next two hours prepping, mixing, and almost burning the house down trying not to get burned from making browning.

"See, this is why people purchase this stuff premade," Yaddi murmured under her breath but not quiet enough that I couldn't hear the snide remark.

"And again, you know I don't roll like that. I could purchase mixed peel too, but you know if I'm going to do something I'm gonna go all in or go home."

"If you say so. So, are you really going to make me wait to meet this new man?"

"Sure am."

"Dang, a sista can't even get his name."

"Nope. I know you. Anyway, now that Dwayne has made his exit, what are you going to do with yourself when you return from your consultant visit."

"Are you calling me a hussy?"

"Did you hear that word come out of my mouth?"

I continued to mix my cake batter, adding in the spoonful of the fermented fruit as I stirred. My shoulder ached with each rotation, but I preferred to fold in then stir so a mixer just wouldn't do.

"I was hoping to spend some time with my girl. I've been preoccupied and now that you have work."

"I'm a volunteer. Remember. If you want to hang out just let me know. Besides, I've already hinted that now that I've learned the system and have a feel for how the place is run, I wanted to help them find a permanent replacement."

"Bailing already? What? You don't think they'd pay you?"

"I'm not bailing. But I don't want to tie myself down. I'm not ready to take on the responsibilities of working for someone else, or at least not in an 'I'm obligated to be on site x number of hours on x days per week. Been there. Done that. Like I said I got what I deserve from Daniel. My health care is covered. I have my alimony checks, the rent money from the remaining condo, and my investments. Not to mention the calligraphy work. Hell, you keep dropping money in my lap too."

"And your living arrangements?"

My phone pinged, saving me from having to answer Yaddi's question. And just in the nick of time. Though I hadn't yet started looking for a place, eventually, I wanted to move out of Yaddi's house to a home of my own. Not that I didn't have it good here. Aside from the sexcapades, life in Yaddi's house wasn't bad at all. Beautiful scenery, pool, fresh herbs, and veggies all year round. Even if I managed to get a place of my own, I was sure I'd spend a good chunk of time here. Might even suggest using the place as my office that way if I needed a change of scenery I could come and camp out by the lake.

"We'll have to finish this later. I need to return this call. The batter is done. Do you mind pouring and sticking them in the oven? I've already lined the tins with parchment and the oven is set to the proper temp. Just set the timer for fifty minutes. I'll come up and check them.

Yaddi shooed me away and I graciously took the reprieve.

Chapter Seventeen

Bounding down the stairs I pressed the phone button in the messaging app. Ellis answered as I hit the last step and rushed into the bedroom to throw something on. "Hey, is something wrong?"

"Why would you think that?" Ellis replied calmly.

I stopped in my tracks, the panic dissipating as I eased down on the corner of the bed. "I wasn't sure. Your message caught me off guard. How did you even get this number?"

"It's on the front of your beautifully printed resume."

I'd forgotten about giving him one, not that he'd asked for it. But if there was no emergency, why was he ringing my phone on my day off? I'd requested the day to prep the first Black cake, testing out Yaddi's alcohol to fruit ratio. My girl loves her liquor and tends to be heavy handed. Black cake required a delicate balance, especially during the fermenting stage.

"Is there something you need? I can come in if necessary."

"No, no. Nothing like that. Though there is a small request."

I tucked a leg beneath me rolling back on the bed to collect the notepad and pen I kept on the nightstand. Pen poised over the paper I asked, "What's up?"

"How would you like to go on a real date with me?"

Phone still pinned to my ear with my shoulder, I froze. Was he really asking me out? Like on a date date?

"Soliel?"

My name snapped me back to reality, "I. I'm not sure." Silence from the other end. "I mean. I'm not sure it's a good idea. You know, mixing business and pleasure."

"Well then, you're fired. But seriously, since technically you don't work for me." He let the rest speak for itself. When I didn't respond he dropped a few more encouraging words, "No pressure, okay. I just had a good time with you at lunch the other day and I'd just like to get to know you better outside of the work environment. But only if it's something you might want too."

I couldn't hide my smile; glad this was a phone call, and he hadn't asked me face to face. No way would I have been able to hide my excitement. "I'd like that," I said nonchalantly.

"Good to hear. I'll let you pick the day and place. I do have one condition."

"Oh. And what's that?"

"No Italian food."

Yeah, we were both burned out on Italian.

"Actually, I've been meaning to talk to you about that business proposition I mentioned the other day. We might be able to kill two birds with one stone as they say."

"What did you have in mind?"

"Well, my friend has a yearly soiree, and she needs food. She wants Italian and of course having had the food at Angelo's I immediately thought of you."

"When is this get-together?"

"Yule."

"Beg pardon?"

"Yule. The winter solstice. It's the twenty-first of December this year."

He sucked in a breath, "That's cutting it close."

"I know. But I already checked the catering calendar. You're free that weekend."

"How many people?"

"Twenty. Twenty-five max. Nothing formal. Buffet style works. No servers needed and she provides her own bartender and clean-up crew. It really will be food delivery. Or you could even cook here. She has a huge kitchen I'm sure you'd love and probably has everything you need."

"And how does this work with our date?"

"Well, the house has a deck, pool, and its lakefront. I figured we could whip up something and have us a private pool party. Watch a couple of movies. She gets great sunset views over the lake."

"Hmm."

I wished I could see his expression. One, to know what he thought of the idea, and two, I could only imagine the naughty thoughts playing over his face. "Well?"

"When should I come by?"

"Early Sunday, if you're free." I knew he was. I'd checked his calendar yesterday in hopes of catching him when he came back into the office.

"How early?"

"Nine-ish. Yaddi flies out Sunday afternoon and I'd like you two to meet. She's already tasted your food and she was impressed."

"Was she?"

I leaned into the conversation, dropping a little sultriness into my voice. "Yes. She was very, very pleased."

"Is that a tease I'm detecting?"

"Maybe?"

Ellis returned the sex-appeal, "Is there anything in particular you'd like me to bring?"

It was my turn to blush, my body warming as the rumble of his voice washed over me, "Chocolate."

"My specialty."

As the call ended, I glanced up to find Yaddi standing in the doorway looking quite pleased with herself.

"It's not polite to eavesdrop." Suddenly parched, I tossed the notepad and pen back onto the nightstand before scooting past Yaddi to grab a glass of water.

"I wasn't eavesdropping. Anyway, was that the mystery man?" Yaddi trailed me through the open living area into the downstairs kitchen. She made herself comfortable lounging in the leather chair next to the theater-seating couch.

"He's not a mystery man."

Yaddi spun in the chair like a kid. "And when will I get to meet him?"

"Weren't you standing there long enough to hear that part of the conversation?"

Yaddi narrowed her gaze, and I dipped my finger into my glass of water, chasing an ice cube around as I stirred before raising the glass to drink. "I told you I wasn't eavesdropping. I only walked up on the last part of your conversation. I came down to tell you the cakes were in the oven."

Though not convinced, I let it go. "He's coming Sunday morning. Early. Plenty of time before you have to head to the airport so you might want to think about the food you want for the party."

"I put you in charge because I trust your judgment."

"And you didn't want to be bothered with the details," I quipped making it clear

I understood her intent to keep me less than idle.

Yaddi rolled her eyes, "Whatever. You assume I had an ulterior motive."

"Don't you always,"

"No, and I'm hurt you think I do. You've never let me down Soliel. I've always trusted you with party planning. You're a pro at it and while you won't admit it, you enjoy it. Or at least you used to. Has this situation with Daniel depleted your confidence?"

I turned, searching the refrigerator to not have to face her. "Not at all. I know you trust me. However, I also know you're picky and while I appreciate the vote of confidence, I'd prefer you to make the final call."

"What are you not telling me?"

"Who says I'm not telling you something."

"Come on Soliel. I've known you too long to play this game. What's wrong?"

I considered my options as I toyed with the idea of a conversation with Yaddi about Ellis. I had a few concerns, but I hadn't said anything to anyone, one because the people at the restaurant would be on his side and also because the situation with Yaddi was still touchy.

"Soliel?" Deep in thought, I hadn't notice Yaddi's approach. She put her hands on my shoulders turning me to finally face her. "What's wrong?"

"Nothing, I mean," I wiggled my way out of her grasp.

"Is our relationship really this strained?"

This time, I saw the tension in her eyes as she tried to hide her pain. I hadn't meant to hurt Yaddi but, I just wasn't ready to talk about everything. It wasn't just the abandonment from Daniel, but I felt she had abandoned me too. I'd gone through so much on my own and now I wasn't sure I could go back to how things were.

"I understand," Yaddi finally said walking away.

Not wanting to wallow in misery I decided to use the time to work on the party arrangements and clear my head. I filled the hours waiting for the cakes to finish with seating and table arrangements. Decorations. Measurements. Any and everything to avoid Yaddi and my own feelings. This wasn't how I'd envisioned the day going.

Baking usually relaxed me. I'd even started the dough to make fresh dinner rolls but the minute I completed a task my mind drifted back to Ellis, Yaddi, and unfortunately Daniel. Only then did I realize how much being at Angelo's offered a reprieve from facing the reality of all I'd lost.

"WELL, WHAT DID SHE say?" Yusef asked as he stood in the office doorway.

Ellis couldn't hide his excitement and relief as he hung up the phone and leaned back in the office chair, "Is that any of your business?"

"Actually, it is. You've been moping around here for weeks since you let her slip through your fingers the first time. I can tell by the way you're cheesing she said yes."

"You're right. She did. And not only that, but she's also throwing business our way."

"Really? What type of business?"

"A catering job." Ellis opened the schedule on the computer, checking the date. Soliel mentioned confirming that they didn't have any bookings for that week. Close to Christmas, he'd been hesitant to commit to any big jobs knowing Linda would be gone and unless he'd found a replacement of her caliber, he'd be spending every extra moment prepping the books for the end of the year.

Then Soliel walked into their door, saving him both work and adding to his income. He'd compensate her of course, but she'd made his life so much easier that he hadn't figured out how as of yet.

"What are you over there plotting?" Yusef asked as he entered, pulling the door up behind him.

"Nothing like what you are thinking. I am relieved she said yes. We had a good talk the other day."

"Did you now? She spill all the details about why she's suddenly not wearing a wedding ring?"

Ellis considered how much he wanted to share with his best friend. He trusted Yusef not to spread his business. They'd been there for one another through good times and the bad, including this last unfortunate bout Ellis found himself in. Yusef had seen Ellis at his worst, needing someone at his beck and call twenty-four seven until he'd relearned how to walk and talk. He still struggled with the hearing loss part, mindful to keep his locks tied back but covering the ear with the hearing aid.

"I don't need the details," Ellis finally said, his heart suddenly aching for Soliel though he wasn't sure what triggered the reaction. From what he'd experienced with her, she was a kind soul, willing to do for others. A rare gem in this chaotic world of every man for himself. And maybe that was the catch. "I know all I need to. She is a woman free to do as she pleases."

"You might want to reconsider," Yusef cautioned, "the crazy you just barely escaped didn't come out of nowhere."

"I'll pay attention this time. You can believe that." Ellis rocked in the executive chair, his mind working to piece together a menu for dinner.

"Speaking of crazy."

"No, she hasn't tried to reach out."

"I wasn't talking about your ex." Ellis stopped rocking as his attention focused squarely on Yusef. "What are you going to do about Marcel?"

He let the frown take hold, annoyance slipping in at the mention of their newly hired pastry chef trainee. Ellis had hired Marcel because she was capable and willing to learn. A friendly addition to their staff, he too noticed as of late the cracks in that overly friendly façade. "I don't need to do anything about Marcel. I don't belong to her."

"You know that. And I know that. But someone needs to remind Marcel."

"I've made it perfectly clear I don't mix business with pleasure."

Yusef crossed the room plopping down on the sofa his gaze locked with Ellis's as he leaned back into the leather. "Do you believe she's gonna see it that way. Soliel suddenly spending all this time in the office, roaming the kitchen, doing inventory. From the staff's perspective, she works here."

"But as she's so eloquently reminded me, she's here on a voluntary basis."

"Sounds like splitting hairs to me. I don't think Marcel is going to take Soliel's new position well."

"Then she's free to leave. Besides, Soliel is already working on an exit strategy."

Surprised, Yusef sat up straight, "she's bailing on us?"

"Us?" An eyebrow rose as Ellis cracked a smile. While he and Yusef weren't legally partners in the business when one was successful everyone shared in the spoils. It was how Mr. Angelo had run the business for thirty years, giving back and pouring into the employees as much as they contributed to their success. It's also why most stayed. He paid well, promoted within as much as possible, and encouraged growth. When an employee moved on it was usually to something bigger and better.

"You know what I meant."

"She's not bailing per se, especially considering the circumstances of her non-employment, but this isn't what she wants to do with her life. I get that. I get the impression her marriage might have stifled her."

"Is that why you're enamored with her? You have always been attracted to free spirited women."

"I am not enamored. And she's a beautiful woman."

"I'll give you that. Her friend was a looker too."

"Hey, hey, now."

Yusef held up a hand, "I'm not going to step on toes. I can admire beauty from afar. Besides, you know I'm already locked down."

"How is that going?"

"It's going."

"Wait, so you get to grill me on my budding relationship and all I get is 'it's going.'"

"Damn straight, You're the one popping off at the mouth and over sharing."

"I'm going to remember that."

"Be sure you do."

Chapter Eighteen

The explosive crack of lightening and booms of rolling thunder shaking the house above woke me around three in the morning. Well, that and the sharp pain radiating through my extremities. Pain I recognized and regretted all in the same thought. I breathed through the excessive aching managing to pop a pain pill and down the half bottle of water I kept on the nightstand.

Laying down only exasperated the condition so I waddled my way into the living room drawing back the edge of the blinds to watch the sway of the trees in the wind. I cracked the door allowing fresh air into the room as I inhaled the soothing aroma of nature's cleanse. Sheets of rain covered the pool, the deck above shielding me from the onslaught.

I welcomed the rumbling of thunder and the flashes of lightening; reminders of the magnificence of creation and of life itself. To bear witness to such beauty even in the dead of night. I eased into the recliner, swiveling to face the storm. My foot moved in a rhythm of its own, slowly rocking my aching body as I thought back over the conversation with Ellis.

"How'd I know you'd be up?"

Yaddi. I didn't know if I was happy to have the company or annoyed that Yaddi was intruding once again. "You know I love the rain," I said, failing to mention the fact my body currently rebelled against me.

"I just came to check on you. If you'd rather be alone, I can go back to bed."

"Lonely?" I asked as the sky lit up.

"You think I miss Dwayne?"

"Not Dwayne specifically." I shivered. The temperature was dropping. As if reading my mind, a warm fleece blanket appeared. I took the offering, curling beneath the red and white blanket as I continued to rock.

"I will say this is strange," Yaddi stepped up to the door sliding the blinds further open but not moving to adjust the door itself. "I'm used to an empty house when my guest leave."

"I won't be in your hair long."

Yaddi's head dropped, her shoulders sagging ever so slightly in defeat. "You can stay as long as you need to."

"That's the thing, I don't need to stay here."

"Then I'm asking you to stay." Yaddi finally conceded, "I miss my friend."

The rain eased, the sheets now a trickle, though thunder continued to rattle the walls. "I don't want to be a burden. Not to you or anyone else."

"Who said you were a burden?" Yaddi turned to face me, her brows furrowed.

Did she think Dwayne had said something to me? "I need my independence. I've been tied to other people over half my life. I want a taste of real freedom."

"And why can't you have that here? It's not like I'm asking for anything but company. And this is a win-win. You have a no cost roof over your head and in return I get a house sitter. I want to do this for you."

Another shudder passed through me as air blew over my face. I pulled the blanket tighter, my limbs growing numb. The meds kicking in left a fog in my brain. "I'll think about it," I managed, not quite stifling the escaping yawn.

Sleep dragged me under, the soothing song of the sandman serenading me into a much-needed slumber. When I finally woke, warm sunlight beamed through the now closed glass door. Yaddi had raised the leg rest and lowered the back of the recliner into the exact position to keep me comfortable.

Savoring the feel of the cozy covers I bunched my hands in the fuzzy cloth drawing it up to my nose as I blew into it to warm up my hands. The perfect scene made me smile. I yearned for a cup of raspberry hot chocolate right about now as I again thought back to the conversation with Ellis.

He'd said he'd enjoyed my company and even though I was warming to the idea, I wasn't afraid to admit that I enjoyed his too. There was still something off about him I couldn't quite place though and it gnawed at the back of my mind. I found his gentlemanly demeanor refreshing. While

Daniel very much played the role of a traditional man, his stay-at-home wifely expectations were smothering. And now as a free woman, I refused to fall into the same pattern of walking behind a man instead of by his side.

I tested my extremities before deciding to take today for me. I called the restaurant leaving a message that I wouldn't be in today and I'd send the address for the consult over later in the day. Then I made that cup of hot chocolate and plugged in for a few hours playing a new game my all-girl team introduced me to before my departure from Baltimore.

The rain returned, forcing me to hunker down in the house when I'd planned to spend time on the patio digging into the history of Angelo's to see if I could provide Ellis assistance with his growing problem with the sons. While my new living digs offered a spacious feel, being cooped up in the house wasn't my style. When the wind eventually died down, I ventured to the dinette beneath the upstairs deck to work.

Chapter Nineteen

Ellis pulled into the driveway of the house at the top of the incline. Immediately the well-manicured lawn and rows of colorful flowers drew his attention. The swing on the front country porch swung lightly in the breeze. As he exited his vehicle, he paused, standing in awe at the simple but elegant beauty of the place. Bright red cardinals flocked to the feeders perched on each side of the porch. Even in the cooler weather they battled with finches for the best seed.

The front door swung open before he could ring the doorbell, Soliel standing before him in an off the shoulder blue and white jumpsuit that clinched in the middle and flared out at the legs.

"Hope you don't mind taking off your shoes," she said, twirling what he suspected was a watermelon flavored Blow Pop. "Yaddi can be funny about tracking the outside in."

Soliel led him to the swing, taking a seat next to him tucking her legs beneath her as he worked to remove his shoes. Ellis couldn't tell if it was the candy or her perfume, but the sweet aroma wrapped around him, making his insides melt. The scent reminding him of his childhood days sneaking down the street to the candy lady's house to by apple Jolly Ranchers and saltwater taffy.

"You look absolutely stunning," he commented before removing the first shoe and leaning over to work on the next. He'd have to remember to bring covers the next time and when they delivered the food for the party.

"This old thing?"

He removed the second shoe.

"Do your socks have little dogs on them?"

Soliel tugged on the leg of his slacks, and he stretched it out to give her a better view. "They sure do. Corgis. We all need a little whimsy in our lives."

'I'd say not professional, but they are too adorable to chastise you about."

"They also make great ice breakers. You'd be surprised how many people notice. When I started wearing them, I got so many compliments that I stocked up. My repertoire now contains characters from the original Peanuts to puppies to holiday sets."

"Wow."

"What?"

"You're just full of surprises now aren't you."

His hand came to rest on hers and when she didn't draw it away, he gave it a little squeeze, "I like to keep people on their toes. Life is full of surprises. You for example."

Her cheeks reddened. The freckles dotting her nose darkening against the warming skin.

"We'd better get started. I think Yaddi still has some packing to do and the sooner we get the menu together the sooner you and I can have our date."

"After you."

Ellis trailed Soliel into the house, his eyes taking in the expensive decor. The framed artwork. Coordinating vases. Mostly neutrals with a pop of accent color to break up the monotony. But it was the kitchen that nearly stole his breath away.

"Wow," he said taking in the open space painted in white and offset by accents of black and gray. He could do some serious damage in a place like this. While an island sat in the center of the kitchen with the appliances in a U shape all around, the size of it alone rivaled his restaurant. "This kitchen is amazing."

"Thank you very much."

Ellis turned at the voice behind him and froze. He recognized the woman with the massive afro and warm smile slipping the longer they stared at one another. He watched her eyes flick between him and Soliel who he felt approaching from behind.

"Ellis, this is Yaddi. Yaddi, Ellis. He owns Angelo's, the restaurant I've been volunteering at."

Yaddi recovered before Ellis, thrusting her hand out. He quickly gathered his wits, shaking the outstretched hand.

"Nice to meet you," he said, glad to have been able to hide the stutter he felt rising.

"Ellis," Yaddi drew her hand away, scooting past them to round the island.

She remembered him. Ellis was sure of it. But the way she looked between him and Soliel he suspected they hadn't discussed the fact that the person potentially providing the food for her party was the same man who'd helped her wasted friend into the car at the club a few weeks back.

"Shall we get started?"

Ellis followed Yaddi's lead retrieving the sample menus from the pocket of the planner he held in his hands. He laid out the pamphlets grabbing a pen to take notes.

"I suppose we should start with a theme."

Yaddi picked up the menu closest to her, scanning over the contents or pretending to.

Ellis watched as she eyed him suspiciously over the edge. At one point, when Soliel moved towards the refrigerator Yaddi mouthed, "what are you doing here?'

"Winter Masquerade," Soliel said as she grabbed a bottle of water. "Can I get you something to drink, Ellis?"

"Actually Soliel, can you do me a favor and grab one of the bottles of cherry wine. I think Ellis might need to see it so that we can pair it properly since I plan to use it as the focal point for the festivities."

"Isn't there a bottle up here?"

"No, we used the last of it to prep the fruit for the test of the Black cakes."

Soliel huffed as she pushed the refrigerator door closed. "I'll be right back."

Ellis fought to hide the smile threatening to crack his professional facade. She was cute when flustered. The moment was short lived, Yaddi turning on him the minute she was sure Soliel was out of ear shot. She stepped right in front of him blocking his view of Soliel as she play-stormed away.

"What are you doing here?" Yaddi whispered, though if Soliel had been by the door, she'd have heard every word.

"Planning a party menu," Ellis said dryly, his attention on the notepad he scribbled on.

Yaddi's hands came to rest on the countertop as she closed the distance between them. At least she remained on the other side of the island.

"That's not what I'm talking about, and you know it. Are you stalking my friend?"

"Excuse me?"

"How did you find her? I don't remember her giving you her number at the club."

Ellis stepped back, reclaiming his space, his arms crossing over his chest as he met her accusations with some of his own, "First of all, I don't appreciate you accusing me of stalking. I have not now, nor have I ever needed to stalk anyone. And second of all, she walked into my restaurant on a bad date that I suspect you set her up on."

That shut her up, or at least for two seconds. She eyed him with disdain, and he almost grabbed his things and walked out. He didn't need this. This woman knew nothing about him and yet he'd maintained his professionalism when he should be cursing her out for potentially endangering her friend's life. Ellis didn't know what kind of relationship the two women shared but they definitely had different definitions of what is and isn't appropriate on a date.

"Does she..."

Ellis quickly shook his head, seeing Soliel approaching. "And I haven't said anything to her about it either." He relaxed his stance, his arms dropping to his sides as he tapped his thigh with the pen he held.

"Here woman." Soliel thrust the unopened bottle of cherry wine at Yaddi.

"Thanks." Yaddi handed it over to Ellis.

He examined the bottle. "I definitely have a few dessert ideas that would pair nicely with this. And if you are doing appetizers then I'd add blue cheese and gruyere. Maybe even a mac and cheese dish." He jotted notes on the pad, his hand furiously scribbling as the ideas poured from within.

"We will need some desserts, but Soliel has graciously agreed to provide us with one of her specialties."

"Oh really?" Ellis looked up from the paper, a curious expression in Soliel's direction as he waited for her to elaborate.

"What my friend means is that she suckered me into making Black cake."

"Black cake? I don't think I've ever had it. Or heard of it for that matter."

"My girl here," Yaddi playfully elbowed Soliel in the side, "has a thing for liquor cakes."

Soliel shot Yaddi a dirty look, "Black cake isn't just any old liquor cake thank you very much." She turned her attention to Ellis, "It is sort of a Caribbean version of a fruit cake. One of the main ingredients is fruit soaked in alcohol. And of course, the cherry wine."

"Sound's intriguing."

The two women shared a chuckle at his expense. "Intriguing isn't exactly the word I'd use," Yaddi bemused.

"Ignore her please. I always do. One of our Trini friends shared her recipe with me. She makes them around the holidays and for weddings."

"But she doesn't let her fruit soak for months on end like Soliel."

"That's on you."

"You know you like it better. Like those Greek party days. Remember, rule number one: never drink anything made in a bathtub or trash can; and rule number two: never ever, under any circumstances eat the fruit."

"Everclear is the devil."

Ellis stood by the sidelines watching the pair travel down memory lane as if he wasn't even there. Eventually, Soliel remembered his presence. She grabbed a brochure and directed the conversation back to business.

"So, think you can come up with something not too heavy," Soliel said, still scanning the paper. Her fingers gripped the sides hard like she was forcing herself to concentrate on the page instead of him. "We don't want our guest falling asleep."

"I've never had this particular wine. I'll need to taste it first. But I'm sure I can come up with something to your taste."

"She kinda picky." Soliel gestured at Yaddi.

"I am not!"

"I call bullshit. Do you know this chick sent back a two-hundred-dollar plate at a charity event because they sprinkled paprika over her salmon."

Yaddi crossed her arms, her lip in a pout. "I specifically requested no paprika."

"Because you were being petty. I've seen you add the exact ingredient to your salmon when you cook at home."

"My paprika is smoked, thank you very much."

Soliel turned to Ellis, her lips pursed in the cutest expression, "See. P.e.t.t.y." She sang each letter of the word in an old cheerleader rhythm.

Ellis could only shake his head. They were cute together, playing off of one another like sisters. "Then I suppose I'll need a list of any particulars once I compile a few dish options. If that works for you ladies?"

They nodded in agreement. "Any preferences or allergies I need to know about?'

"No," Yaddi replied, "We all eat everything."

Ellis added the information to his notes. "Full dairy?"

Yaddi tossed a pamphlet back onto the island as she picked up the bottle of wine and moved to the other side of the kitchen. "The cheesier the better."

"She likes her dairy, too," Soliel added.

Again, Ellis reviewed his notes, making sure he'd documented the name of the brand of cherry wine to make sure he could order a bottle to try. If it wasn't too expensive and he could find a few decent pairings he might even consider ordering it for Valentine's Day to see if it might be a hit.

A glass appeared before him; the bottle next to it.

Yaddi handed him an electric bottle opener. "I'll let you do the honors."

If she thought he didn't know what he was doing she was about to be sorely disappointed. At the least, she confirmed that the wine was corked and probably more on the expensive side. Though after taking in the house and her taste, nothing in this house appeared inexpensive.

Any decent restaurateur would know how to properly uncork good wine. Ellis completed the task with ease, placing the bottle back down to breathe.

"Did I pass?"

Yaddi shot him a nasty look that apparently Soliel caught and gave her an elbow to the side to knock it off.

"I guess," she filled the three glasses she'd set out.

"I don't drink on the clock." Ellis said to the women.

"And I don't deal without a drink. So, I'd suggest you pick up that glass and partake in this offering."

Soliel gave him a half shrug and an expression that said, 'humor her.' He did.

"Cheers to yet another marvelous masquerade."

The women each took a sip.

"Go ahead," Yaddi encouraged. "You're officially off the clock."

Ellis swirled the wine in the glass then inhaled the sweet aroma before following suit and taking a sip. As the cool liquid hit his tongue, he was reminded of what heaven must taste like because it was absolutely divine.

Chapter Twenty

I gave Ellis the lay of the land of Yaddi's in-law suite, providing a quick and not so thorough tour of the full kitchen, living area, bathroom and covered porch while promising we'd venture out to the patio after prepping dinner.

To my surprise, he gathered bags from the back of his catering van after Yaddi officially dismissed him. I assisted in the unpacking of necessities for our meal. He'd even included the necessary spices for his dish along with a plate of cheese, crackers, and fruit for us to snack on.

"You've thought of everything, haven't you?" I mused removing a bag of fresh green beans and a small container of mushrooms.

"Habit, I suppose." He shrugged, his arm brushing over mine as he worked to arrange his cutlery.

"I do have knives you know."

He pointed at the butcher block on the counter behind them. "Sorry to tell you my dear, but those are not knives."

"I beg to differ."

Ellis unrolled the set of sharp, shiny knives in various sizes, and assortment of blades. "These are knives."

I conceded. "Fine."

'You're cute when you pout."

"Oh, so I'm not cute when I'm not pouting?"

He froze, hand hovering over the package of lamb as he studied my face.

I eventually let the seriousness drop from my expression. I'd scared him enough. "I'm kidding." I said bumping him with my hip, "lighten up."

Lips pursed he went back to opening the package. "These should marinade for at least half an hour."

"We have plenty of time. It's still too early and this is supposed to be dinner."

"True. I'm happy I have you to myself today."

"And why is that?" I peered through the window of the bread maker checking the progress of the dough I'd started before the meeting.

"This is supposed to be a date night, right?" I nodded. "It will just be nice to be able to have a private conversation with you without having to worry about an emergency in the kitchen or being called out to deal with an irate patron."

"You do charm them."

Ellis moved to the sink to rinse the meat. "Is that charm working on you?"

"I haven't quite decided."

I refilled our wine glasses, scooping mine up as I watched Ellis work. He'd changed out of the stuffy pressed white shirt into a green and black striped polo. The aroma of fresh chopped garlic for the asparagus filled the space. He moved with precision through the kitchen as if he'd cooked there a thousand times before.

Hip resting against the edge of the counter, a glass of cherry wine in hand I found myself enamored watching Ellis submerged in his natural element. Some men where builders, who spent their days toiling in the hot sun or digging in the dirt. Others, with a knack for the technical, hunkered down behind a wall of screens tapping out the next game release. But the way Ellis handled the knives; the care and artistry of his movements as he chopped vegetables then dipped his pinky into the sauce to dab a bit on the tip of his tongue before washing his hands and adding fresh rosemary and thyme left me utterly speechless. The fluidity of moment warmed my inside like a proud mother standing in the bleachers as her only son made the last game winning touchdown of his high school career.

This man had somehow started to chip away at my barriers and wormed his way into my life and I hadn't even realized when it happened. Yet standing here watching the muscles work in his arms and back as he sliced through the half rack of lamb he'd brought, made my stomach perform somersaults.

He was definitely at home in the kitchen.

The bread maker beeped, signaling the last of the dough cycle. I settled my glass next to it, my back to Ellis as I floured the cutting board and emptied the dough onto it. We'd decided to work on dinner together, using the time to get to know one another.

"You've told me a little of your history," Ellis said over his shoulder as he placed the four portions of lamb onto the lined baking sheet. "But you didn't tell me about what your life was like growing up? Are you an only child?"

"I am now," I said flouring the rolling pin before starting to roll out the dough. "Both of my parents are deceased. And my older brother died in a car wreck four years ago."

"Oh, I'm sorry."

The somber tone made me cringe. The last thing I wanted was pity. "Life happens. My parents lived long full lives. My brother and I weren't really close. We were twelve years apart, so I might as well have been an only child. Needless to say, I think I was a surprise anyway. I'm pretty sure by the time I showed up they thought they were done with kids."

'Do you believe that had an effect on how you were raised?"

"Hadn't really thought about it. My parents were older, about our age when I came along. And I'm sure raising girls is a lot different than boys."

"True."

I worked to round out the edges of the dough into a pie shape to slice for crescents. "What about you?"

"I am an only child. I was raised mostly by my paternal grandmother. My mother worked herself to an early grave and my dad was never in great health. My grandmother did the best she could trying to care for us all. She passed away a few years back."

His voice trailed off and I suspected his thoughts lingered on the memories of his family. "I'd like to think she did a good job. You seem like you have it all together. And so far, I'm liking the person I'm getting to know."

"Is that so?"

The cool air from the refrigerator washed over me as Ellis slid the chops in. I'd almost gotten the top half of the dough to the right consistency when a pair of muscular hands traced down my arms. Warm, firm fingers wrapped around mine on the rolling pin as Ellis's body heat sent blood rushing to my lady parts.

He followed my lead, hands gently resting on mine as we worked the other half of the dough into submission.

"I'm about to go."

We froze at the intrusion, Ellis putting some space between us though he didn't remove his hands from mine or the rolling pin.

I waited for Yaddi to apologize for barging in. Instead, the woman dressed in a powder blue pants suit with fuchsia shirt and heels that made her a taller tower just stood at the foot of the stairs like a disapproving parent waiting for her teenage daughter to act appropriately now that she'd been caught in a compromising position.

"Have a safe trip," I finally said turning back to my rolls. I was glad Ellis hadn't allowed Yaddi to intimidate him into stepping all the way back. The feel of his body pressed into mine, his hands on mine as we worked as a team to prepare the dough, was comforting.

Yaddi entered, her heels clicking on the hardwood as she rounded the island. We continued our tasked, not remotely disturbed by the way she gawked at us.

"Soliel?"

"Yes ma'am?" I responded dismissively.

She nodded towards the stairs. "Can I speak with you?"

"Don't you see we're busy?" Ellis tensed but I continued our rhythm to maintain the edges of the dough. Front to back. Right to center. Left to center. I did look up at Yaddi, though my expression remained non-concerned.

'Are you going to be alright while I'm away?"

"Last time I checked, I was grown. I think I can manage on my own. And if I can't," I teased Ellis with a shimmy of my hips, "I'm sure Ellis would be more than willing to offer a helping hand." I threw that last part in for good measure, just to get under her skin.

This was exactly why I needed my own space. Most would find Yaddi's intrusion endearing. The concerned friend coming to her friend's rescue just in case she'd allowed a psycho in the door. But I knew Yaddi had other motives, even if she wasn't aware of them herself. We'd have to have a talk about this new relationship dynamic. As much as I loved my friend, I refused to return to our college days when Yaddi felt the need to protect me.

I'd come a long way since then. Yes, the transition back into being a single woman in my forties was new territory, but I wanted to explore this new chapter in life my way. And if that meant putting space in the relationship with my best friend, then I'd set that boundary and be prepared to navigate and enforce it as necessary.

Resigned, or possibly defeated, Yaddi turned to leave.

"Make sure you call me when you check into your hotel," I yelled as she stomped up the stairs.

"That was cruel."

Ellis's breath was warm against my ear, and it smelled strangely of cardamom and allspice. Probably the marinade or the sauce for the meat. I'd watched him combine the spices into what I'd initially thought would be a dry rub. Then he added the vegetable oil and Worcestershire and tasted it before dipping each pink cut of meat in.

"You're an outsider looking in. So, maybe it was. But we're navigating new territory and for my sanity I can't let her baby me."

"She's just trying to protect you."

I elbowed my way out of his grasp, and he took the hint. I retrieved the pizza cutter from the drawer on the other side of the kitchen. "You mind handing me the melted butter out of the microwave?"

He slid the glass container over careful to not intrude upon my personal space.

I dipped the brush into the butter. "Can we talk about something else please?"

"As you wish."

Chapter Twenty-One

"Here's a question for you." Ellis reclined in the theater seat watching Soliel surf channels.

"I'm listening," she paused on a station airing a rally race.

He peered at her over the rim of his wine glass. "What's something I wouldn't expect about you?"

"Ooh that is a good one. You have to give me a second to think about that one."

"Take all the time you need. But don't think too hard on it. Usually, the first thing that comes to mind is the most interesting."

"Well, since you put it that way, I can show you better than I can tell you."

His eyes grew wide as he nearly spit out the wine. He managed not to choke on it when she started laughing.

"If you could only see your face."

Ellis took the napkin she held out to him, dabbing the wine he'd splashed over his nose. His gaze never left her as she knelt before the television console and fiddled with the electronics inside. She retrieved a game controller and headsets switching the television to the proper input before tossing a second headset his way.

"What? Don't I get a controller?"

"Sorry. Ladies only. But you're more than welcome to watch us work." As she entered the stream the other ladies greeted her. "We've got a squatter ladies so play nice."

Ellis introduced himself then muted his headset and watched in awe as the women went to town in a game he'd never seen before called Control. Immersed in the comradery, and the bloodshed, Soliel didn't miss a beat when he got up to check the lamb and the bread. He enjoyed the trash talk between the women and a few other players who'd joined their stream.

But all in all, they held their own. Soliel was definitely not like any other woman he'd ever dated. She was focused. Confident. Secure in her abilities and her womanhood. While he didn't believe she'd come out of the other side of her divorce unscathed, she was in a much better place at this stage than he had been when he and his ex-wife split. Of course, their situations were vastly different. His ex-wife had tried to kill him.

Eventually, the aroma from the food could no longer be ignored. Soliel bid her crew adieu just as Ellis removed the rolls from the oven. He'd taken the lamb out ten minutes earlier leaving it covered on the stove to rest.

"I am famished," Soliel said stretching her arms and bending over to loosen the kinks in her back from sitting too long.

"I'm sure you are after all that. You were right, I never would have pegged you for that intense of a gamer."

"I've had a lot of free time on my hands the last year and limited access to the outside world."

"Really?" He passed her one of the two plates she'd set out. She scooped homemade mashed potatoes and bacon wrapped asparagus onto it along with one of the chops.

"Yeah. I got sick a couple of years back."

Ellis prepared his plate. Then, claiming the other from her, he trailed behind as she picked up their wine glasses and led him to the patio. The temperature was dropping rapidly, the sun setting just past the tree line, the rays dancing off the lake as they peaked through the sparse foliage.

Using the remote secured to the side of the house, Soliel powered on the heat lamps so they could keep warm while still enjoying the fresh air.

"I hope your illness isn't anything long-term."

Soliel dug into her food, not commenting. Eventually, Ellis's free hand came to rest over hers.

"Soliel?"

She acknowledged the concern both in his expression and voice. "Unfortunately, it isn't a quick fix. It's not terminal though, so I guess that's a plus."

"That is a bright side," he said squeezing her hand. "Anything I need to know? Or be on the lookout for?"

"Not really. So long as I stay on top of my medication, my health is manageable. And no, I can't pass it on to you. One hundred percent non-contagious. I apparently picked up a parasite on one of my many out of the country excursions. I'd been misdiagnosed multiple times until someone familiar with my symptoms and the areas we traveled suggested a possible cause. By the time I received the proper diagnosis, the infection had already well progressed. I'll admit, I do sometimes have bad days, but now that we have a good combination of meds, they are few and far between."

"And the alcohol."

"Yeah," Soliel swirled the wine in her glass, "I probably shouldn't go overboard. I did the first few nights here and I paid for it dearly."

Ellis wondered if the combination of the medications and her medical condition along with the high volume of alcohol she'd consumed that night at the club was why she'd been so wasted. He'd watched her down at least three margaritas and he knew for a fact the bartender to be particularly heavy handed. He'd dismissed it as the amount of alcohol, especially considering he hadn't known how many drinks she'd had prior to their introduction.

'Do we need to slow down on the wine?" He asked.

"No. I'm good on the wine. It's the hard liquors that do me in. I do miss my White Russians, but I can only tolerate them in small doses now." She cocked her head, cutting her eye at him. "Yusef makes a pretty good one."

"So, my staff is making you drinks now."

"I paid for that drink thank you very much."

"I was just messing with you. Though I do appreciate you not taking advantage."

They chit chatted over minor topics as they ate, everything from their hometowns to favorite foods. Ellis took note of it all, especially Soliel's love of all things chocolate. A woman after his own heart.

"When did you get into gaming?" Ellis asked slicing into his lamb.

Soliel finished chewing before responding, "I've played video games on an off since I was a kid. My dad had a thing for technology, so I grew up with full sized pinball machines, the tabletop sit-down arcade games, eventually graduating to the Bally, Atari, and Commadore 64."

"Wow."

"Yeah, my house was the neighborhood fun house. My brother missed out on some of it. And we had all the accessories: tape deck, external floppy drives, the works. We even had a full-sized jukebox. A Seeburg 222."

"That stuff is probably worth a fortune now."

"Want to hear a secret?"

"Sure"

"I still have them all. In working condition. When I finally get my own place, I'm going to setup a game room. Going all out. I just need to find one of those old Afterburner sit in machines and Dragon's Lair to complete my collection. But as far as getting back into gaming, when I got sick, I spent a lot of time in bed. I didn't have the strength to do much else. My has-been had a PlayStation, so I started with it. I was a beast at Parasite Eve. Eventually I worked my way through the different systems and the Xbox is my latest addition."

"Simply amazing," was all Ellis could say.

"That was absolutely wonderful," Soliel complemented as she slid down in her seat patting her over-filled belly. "I'm not going to be good for anything else for the rest of the day."

"I guess that means you didn't save room for dessert?"

Ellis gathered the dishes taking them back into the house while Soliel stared out into the night. He scraped them clean, washed and dried them before leaving them in the strainer to dry. He removed one silver wrapped chocolate from the box he'd brought placing it in front of Soliel as he reclaimed his chair.

"Since you're full I suppose, the real dessert will have to wait for another time."

She removed the shiny wrapper taking in the white and red ball with lines of dark chocolate swirled over it. Her eyes glittered at the sight; the pleasure undeniable. She bit into the confection, the stiff exterior giving away to a rich creamy center bursting with flavor. A low umm escaped from barely parted lips as she savored the layered flavors.

"This is absolutely orgasmic."

Ellis could only smile as her head tilted back; eyes closed in pure ecstasy. A vision flashed before him; a moment of passion shared between them, the same look of utter pleasure masking her face as he ravished her.

"Is that mango I taste."

"It sure is."

"And," she dipped her tongue into the remaining filling in the other half, "papaya."

"You definitely have a sensitive palette. Yes, that one is a tropical fruit blend."

"OMG, I think I'm in love." Soliel fanned herself with her hand as she popped the other side in her mouth to revel in the complexities of the flavors.

Chapter Twenty-Two

We curled beneath the evening stars, the heaters blaring as we watched *Soul*, *The Photograph*, and *Love Jones* projected on the side of the pool house behind Yaddi's house. I'd drifted off at some point, missing chunks of *The Photograph* only to jerk awake at the beginning of *Love Jones* to find my body curled in Ellis's arms with the green and gold sherpa blanket wrapped around my shoulders and tucked beneath my chin.

I paused the movie long enough to refresh our wine glasses and collect a slice of black cake to share as we settled in. I caught Ellis watching me throughout the movie, just as I'd sneak glimpses of him. Eventually he too relaxed into the seat, his lids growing heavy as the glasses of wine, the good food, and the black cake took hold.

It was long past sunset now. The heat from the propane patio heaters keeping our hideaway nice and toasty. My eyes fluttered open, meeting Ellis's gaze as he'd apparently been watching me sleep.

"Welcome back to the waking world sleeping beauty."

Him watching me sleep could have been creepy, but his smile warmed my heart and the care he took to make sure I remained covered while slumbering only made the gesture more enduring.

"Blame the cake," I said, rolling out of the ball I'd curled into before snuggling into his side.

"If you say so. You missed the end of the movie."

"I've seen it a million times."

"Hmm. And yet you keep coming back for more?"

"Why not. With the way the world is, sometimes we need reminding that Black love still exists."

Ellis dropped his arm from the back of the couch keeping me close. "Have you ever been in love like that?" His eyes flicked to the screen then back to me.

I considered the question, remembering the touching scenes from the movie. Had I ever shared that deep a connection with anyone? With Daniel? With someone before him? I hadn't worked through that part of my marriage falling apart. Or maybe I chose to ignore the possibility that while me and Daniel shared numerous highs, the love depicted in the movies eluded us.

But there was one. Or...yes. I'd felt the connection before, but it was long ago and sadly the details hovered just out of reach taunting me but remaining elusive. I settled on, "I believe so. What about you?"

"On a high level, I'd like to say I'm not convinced love like that exists," he replied without missing a beat. "I mean, it is an ideal and as much as I like the idea of it, I.." he trailed off.

By the pained look in his eyes, I suspected he'd at least tasted that type of connection before. The thought of giving so much of oneself freaked people out. Or maybe he mourned the loss of the idea of an everlasting love. Considering our individual histories, fear of a new partner not living up to the experience of a past ideal wasn't that foreign a concept. "Don't want to get your hopes up trying to attain the unattainable?"

"I think you've hit the nail on the head." Ellis paused the credits before accepting the blanket I handed over. He checked his watch. "Eleven o'clock. Wow. I hadn't expected to spend the entire day and half the night with you. And yet, time seemed to fly when we were having fun."

"I can admit, I've enjoyed myself as well," I sat back down, taking in the beautiful brown Adonis sitting next to me. I could tell he cared for his skin, the flawless canvas of his face only interrupted by the long scar starting at his jawline and jaggedly trailing upwards to where his hair draped over his ear and shoulder. And his lips, though dark in color were plump, smooth and oh so inviting.

Ellis bit the inside of his lip, the flesh rolling under as I watched him contemplate his next move. His eyes, red and hooded from tiredness and the alcohol, harbored an unwavering desire.

He regarded me with quiet intensity as the question "what" fell from his soup cooler lips.

"Nothing." I returned his seductive gaze with one of my own, "Just admiring the view."

He leaned in, a hand cupping my jaw as his thumb brushed across my cheek. I too shifted forward closing the distance between us as our eyes locked moments before our lips. And oh, what a moment it was. I melted into the gentle caress of his hand sliding behind my neck. The warmth of his fingers as he massaged the area, careful to not disturb my hair.

Notes of the bitters from the cake lingered on his lips as the kiss intensified. I hungrily drew Ellis in, hands cupping his face as I straddled him. I moved to slide my fingers into his hair, immediately feeling something shift between us. His fingers quickly moved to encase my wrists as he pulled away, leaving us both panting, the spell now broken, if but temporarily.

Ellis rested his forehead against mine as we each struggled to quell the desire burning within. Eventually, he kissed me on the nose, gazing deeply into my eyes before kissing my forehead and sitting back. Only then did I realize he'd released my wrist, his hands resting on mine in my lap.

"I should go."

I shot him my sweetest pout, but he refused to be deterred. "Are you sure?"

With a pecked on the lips, he wiggled his way from beneath me. He stood, dodging my attempt to seduce him as my fingers grazed his arm. Unfortunately, the upright position didn't last. He wavered, hand reaching out to steady himself using the back of the wrought iron couch.

"Oh no mister, the only place you're going is to the sofa or one of the spare bedrooms."

Ellis eased back into a sitting position, eyes closing in the process, in what I suspected was an attempt to stop the world from spinning. His hand came to rest on his forehead, the fingers massaging the area. "Wine has never affected me like this."

"Not the wine," I chuckled, standing with no problems. "It's the cake." He'd consumed the lion's share and I'd let him without so much as a word of warning, "Yaddi uses the good stuff. Fernandes Black Label. Perfect for a traditional Trinidadian wedding cake. I can guarantee she soaked the fruit for months in it and the cherry wine."

Ellis stilled, his eyes opening as he took in the beauty hovering over him. "I hate to impose."

"Your safety is not an imposition so put it out of your mind. Now," I offered him a hand and while he took it, he only used me to steady himself as he tried to stand again, "if you think you can manage, we'll get you settled for the night."

I WOKE TO AN UNSETTLING feeling. Thoughts of Ellis had invaded my dreams as I'd curled beneath the covers hours ago. I checked the clock, discovering I'd gotten a good five hours sleep. More than I'd suspected, considering the onslaught of horrid images invading my psyche. Donning a plush terry cloth robe and securing it around my waist, my feet slid into my fake fur house shoes.

A chill lingered in the air. I'd forgotten to switch the thermostat from air to heat. The nightly drop in temperature was a norm for this time of year. In late October, Georgia cycled through winter at six in the morning, spring between ten and noon, summer setting in starting at one only for autumn to arrive around seven in the evening. The ever changing and unpredictable weather patterns wreaked havoc on my sinuses and made keeping the inside temperature reasonable nearly impossible.

Padding across the floor, I unlocked the bedroom door quietly slipping out into the living room to adjust the temperature. The bright blue light of the thermostat illuminated the pitch-black area near the kitchen just enough to determine Ellis was no longer stretched out in the seat where I'd left him.

"Where the hell is he?"

Panic set in as flashes of my dream assaulted my mind. The skidding of tires. The catering van wrapped around a light pole. Live wires dancing over wet pavement. A blood curdling scream. I rushed to the other side of the sofa to get a better look only to confirm he wasn't there.

I frantically searched the other rooms, hoping maybe he'd gone to the restroom or camped out on the floor in the room with the workout equipment. Unfortunately, I found both places empty. Thinking he'd taken me up on the suggestion to use one of the spare bedrooms upstairs, my feet carried me to the upper level to peer over the couch in the main living room first then racing her way down the hallway to check the other rooms. He wasn't in any of them.

My heart pounded like the wheels of a locomotive as I ran to the front door releasing a breath when I discovered the van still parked out front undisturbed. The relief was short lived, my mind formulated more not-so-good possibilities. Was he a sleepwalker? Had he gone out the back door thinking it was the way to the bathroom and fallen in the pool, or worse, the lake.

"Ellis!" I bellowed. I took the stairs two at a time nearly sliding to my demise when my ankle twisted in the unsupported shoes the moment I slipped off the edge of the last set of steps. "Ellis!" I yelled again, my fingers clinging to the railing as I hit the bottom and rounded the corner.

Warm air from the cracked door met me as I slid it open enough to slide through, "Ellis?"

He was there, sitting at the table, the soft glow of the blue light backlit phone leaving shadows over his face. "Ellis?" He didn't respond. Relaxing, assuming he'd stepped out to get some air and fallen asleep I touched his shoulder.

His eyes flicked to mine, his hand outstretched encouraging me to sit on his lap. I took it, easing down hoping the chair would support the added weight.

"Look towards the lake," he whispered.

I followed his line of vision. Light from the waning Gibbous moon illuminated the area. At the tree line stood a family of deer, their noses down towards the water as they drank. The buck with the largest set of antlers looked up in their direction before a fawn carefully escaped the brush, his mother a step behind, her ears flicking, head tilted back testing and tasting for danger.

We sat in silence, enjoying the moment watching the beauty of nature until the first light of day sent the family back into the woods. The buck paused just before crossing the threshold turning to face us before appearing to bow as if he'd known they had an audience before trotting off back into the trees.

Ellis shuddered beneath me, and I realized he hadn't brought the blanket back out with him. I gathered his hands in mine sliding them into the pockets of my robe to warm.

"Why didn't you answer when I called?"

"I didn't hear you."

I regarded him disbelievingly. Surely the way I'd been calling his name, even with the music playing right next to him, he would have heard me. Hell, the neighbors had probably heard me. "You had me worried."

"Why?"

"I..." I said sheepishly, head dripping as I looked away, "I had a bad dream. And when you weren't on the couch, I, I thought the worse."

Ellis toyed with one of the twists working its way loose from my colorful headscarf. "First, I'd never drive if I've had too much. Believe me I know my limits. Even if you hadn't offered me refuge for the night, I wouldn't have gotten behind the wheel. I might have slept in the van or called a ride, but I'd never endanger my life or the life of others."

"Good to know."

"Secondly, I wouldn't have left without this," he claimed my lips.

The earnest kiss immediately eased my mind and spirit. It wasn't overly passionate like the one last night, but it assured me he still found me desirable. He ended the kiss, his arms wrapping more securely around me keeping me close to his heart. It was such a beautiful moment I never wanted it to end.

Unfortunately, reality chose to interrupt, the alarm on Ellis's phone reminding us of the responsibilities of the day.

"You should go back to bed." He suggested, "I'll be around for another hour just to be on the safe side."

I eased off his lap, straightening the robe in the process. While I wore satin pajamas beneath, I'd felt the top button come undone when I'd climbed into his arms. "There's coffee and tea in the drawer beneath the coffee maker. And of course, leftovers."

"I'll be sure to partake."

Fingers entwined I allowed Ellis to lead me back to bed. Maybe this time I'd be able to sleep peacefully.

Chapter Twenty-Three

"You've been real upbeat around here lately. I take it things between you and Soliel are doing well," Yusef said as he and Ellis reviewed the two menus he'd decided to present to Yaddi for her all-white winter masquerade.

Ellis didn't make a habit out of bringing work home with him, but the last few days split between Angelo's and The Naughty Chocolatier had him on edge. The first set of chocolate-making and Yule log classes were scheduled to start this weekend. With the height of the holiday season in full swing, he and Yusef arrived on location early to decorate and set up for the holiday themed events over the next few weeks.

It was exhilarating and exhausting all in the same breath. Ellis barely slept a wink, catching a cat nap, when he could, in the hidden loft area on the upstairs floor of Angelo's. At least the mattress he'd stored up there was comfortable enough to quickly lull him into slumber, affording him an hour or so before the kitchen staff arrived, and the clanking of pots and pans made it impossible to sleep.

"So far so good."

"She's been M.I.A. this last week. I was starting to wonder if you'd scared her off." Yusef passed the menu back to Ellis. He pointed out the places he'd marked in red indicating spelling or grammatical errors to be corrected prior to the final mock-up printing for presentation.

Ellis updated the information, adjusting the document font to one he found more aesthetically pleasing. It still wasn't quite right though. He'd have to remember to ask Soliel to see if she found something she liked better. "You sure we haven't just missed her. You know since I gave her a key, she comes in at odd hours. And we've been in and out between the two places. We might just be missing one another. And anyway, why are you concerned about it?"

Yusef held up his hands in surrender, "Not concerned at all. I was just asking. I haven't heard a peep from the staff so I'm assuming we've either been too busy to notice or you two have mastered the art of being inconspicuous."

"I'm surprised Charity hasn't been bugging me about it. I think she'd been eyeing getting Soliel and I together since she discovered that bad date."

"And I'm guessing you still haven't mentioned the night at the club?"

Ellis had toyed with the idea of hinting at the first time he and Soliel had crossed paths. But each time he pondered the potential outcome, he'd ultimately opted to let sleeping dogs lie. "I'll take that night to my grave if I have to. Soliel's friend almost ruined that part of my plan."

"How so?" Yusef picked up his beer bottle only to discover it empty when he tilted the bottle back. He stood, walking the ten paces to the kitchen. "You need another one?"

"No, I'm good." Ellis waited for Yusef to return to explain. "Yaddi recognized me the minute she walked into the kitchen. She found a lame excuse to get us alone and then I suppose she called herself confronting me. The woman had the nerve to accuse me of stalking her friend."

Yusef stopped mid-drink, his hand lowering slowly as he regarded his friend. "Seriously?"

"Seriously. And you know I don't take accusations well."

"You didn't read her for filth, did you?"

"I didn't get the chance. Before I could lay into her, Soliel came back. But I made it clear that I hadn't said anything to Soliel and apparently Soliel didn't remember me from that night. Yaddi seemed to be okay with my decision to keep the night to myself. I don't think she'll say anything."

"And if she does? I mean if that's her best friend and all."

Ellis shrugged, "I'll cross that bridge when I come to it. Speaking of drunken nights, if Soliel asks you to make another white Russian, go light on the liquor."

"Did she say something, or do you think she has a problem?" Yusef asked, a bit appalled.

"No, nothing like that," Ellis didn't want to divulge Soliel's business. He hoped Yusef wouldn't push the subject, "I'm just asking. You know, as a favor to me."

"Why?" Yusef picked up the second menu scanning it for errors, "you've never asked me to go light on the liquor with any of your other women."

Ellis lowered the paper in his hand, regarding his friend with disdain, "don't go there."

"I'm just saying."

"You making it sound like I intentionally bring women into Angelo's for you to get them drunk."

"That is not what I'm saying, and you know it."

Ellis's phone interrupted the exchange. He glanced at the contraption ignoring it before saying, "Your phone is about to ring."

Just as Ellis predicted Yusef's phone rang, rescuing him from descending further into the hole he'd opened. "I gotta take this," Yusef said as he excused himself to the bedroom.

"I'm sure you do. This conversation isn't over."

Ellis sifted through the email box before attaching the final menu mock-ups to an email and shooting it over to Soliel for approval before they were presented to Yaddi. He'd decided on a few combinations that centered around the cherry wine and though he left the door open for tweaking, with the holidays looming, getting a few of the ingredients required him to place orders within a day or so.

Ellis logged off the computer before switching on the game. He propped his feet up on the oval glass top of his living room coffee table, taking another swig of his beer. He could hear Yusef in the other room, the man's voice escalating over the sound of the announcer discussing the review of a call.

The heated conversation continued, eventually forcing Ellis to increase the volume if he wanted to concentrate on the game. He didn't get the chance though. Yusef stormed out the bedroom fuming.

"This some bull."

Ellis only continued to enjoy his beer unfazed. "Who was on the phone?" As if he didn't already know.

"Charity. Apparently, she and Marcel got into it. She's threatening to quit."

Ellis leaned back intertwining his hands behind his head as he rested it against the back of the couch. His eyes remained locked on the screen.

"Aren't you concerned?"

"Nope," Ellis replied propping one foot up on the other. "Not my night."

Yusef released a groan. He swiped his keys from the table. "You lucky I signed up for this."

Ellis half smiled. But he didn't move. "Catch you tomorrow afternoon," he yelled as Yusef made his way to the door. "Don't forget I'll be in late. I need to go to The Naughty Chocolatier to make sure everything goes well with the first class."

Ellis settled in for the night, the exhaustion catching up with him as his eyelids drooped. Sleep threatened to pull him under as his body relaxed into the comforts of the couch. He'd felt his head lull to one side; the sandman's pull irresistible. He should have known it was too good to be true. Just as the voice of the announcer faded into oblivion the ringing of his phone and vibration of his watch reminded him the waking world reigned supreme and it requested his attention.

He almost ignored the incessant ringing, kicking the phone off the table into the plush burgundy rug that drowned out the ringing. Still, the vibrating on his wrist drew his attention. Finger poised to swipe the decline call button, the name on the screen urged him to reconsider his hasty decision to shut out the real world. He did want to speak to the person interrupting his moment of solitude.

With a swipe of a finger on the shiny screen he answered the call, "Well, hello beautiful," he said reaching down to claim the handset. He switched the call to speaker, disconnecting it from the watch to hear better.

"Good evening. I'm not disturbing you, am I?"

"Not at all," Ellis yawned. He stretched as he adjusted into a sitting position.

"Sounds like I am."

He reached for the beer finishing off the bottle. "I'll admit, I might have been drifting off. But just watching the game."

"Charity said you'd taken the night off. She sounded flustered when I spoke with her a few moments ago."

"I think she and one of the kitchen staff had words. Yusef is on his way over there now."

"I hope all is well."

"He'll take care of it."

The line grew quiet, and for a second, Ellis thought the call dropped, "Soliel?"

"I'm here."

"Is something wrong?"

"No. Not at all." Papers ruffled on the other end of the line. "I got the menus. They look great. I think Yaddi will be able to decide fairly quickly."

"I hope so. I'll need an answer as soon as possible to put in the order. A few items needed for recipes on both will require advanced notice."

"I see."

"Are you sure you're alright? You sound," he didn't want to say unwell, especially considering her medical condition and yet, she didn't sound like herself.

"I'm fine. It's just super quiet here without Yaddi. I didn't expect it to be this quiet."

"Ah. I take it you haven't lived alone in a while."

She seemed to consider his observation, a hum echoing from the other end of the line. "You're right. I guess I'll have to get used to it. Especially once I start looking for my own place."

"Would you like some company? It's still early. I can come scoop you up?"

"I don't want to put you out."

"It's no trouble at all. Need me to bring you anything?"

Ellis heard her rambling through the fridge, the sliding of plastic drawers and clanking of glass a clear indication.

"No, I think I'm good."

Her voiced sounded different now. Relieved, like she hadn't wanted to stay in that big ole house alone. He didn't blame her. The first thing he did when the divorce papers were signed was sell his family home and purchase the condo. He'd needed help that first year, so Yusef had moved into the extra bedroom while renting his house out. Ellis had toyed with the idea of finding a smaller single-family home; he did miss having a yard and garden space, he just hadn't gotten around to it yet.

"See you in half an hour or so. It'll take me that long to get to you."

"I'll be here, waiting."

Chapter Twenty-Four

"Welcome to the man cave." Ellis tossed his key into the bowl on the counter by the door as he escorted Soliel into his humble abode. They'd decided to return to his place for the night.

"Nice place. I like the green counter tops."

"We redid the kitchen a few months ago."

"We?" Soliel asked checking out the neatly stacked dishes behind the glass windowed cabinet doors. She found the items neatly arranged, enough pieces for four people. And they all matched. Cups, full sized plates, salad plates, and bowls. She bet he also owned a set of silverware to complete the arrangement, though the place didn't appear big enough to have a formal dining room.

An expresso coffeemaker sat on the counter along with a coffee grinder and a small metal frothing pitcher. And to her surprise, next to the set, near the corner sat an old timing bread box. Like an actual wooden breadbox with a slatted door that rolled up.

"I suppose I should give you the grand tour."

Ellis's hand at her back urged Soliel in the direction opposite the kitchen. He opened the first door on the right flipping the light switch to reveal a modern bathroom decorated in cream, browns, and greens. The tile in the shower carried over to a band around the wall ending as a backdrop to the double sink vanity.

Soliel frowned, "No tub?"

"I gave up the space for the double vanity. The sink used to be in the corner where the shower is now. Besides, the original tub was way too small for me. This was a better use of the space."

"I see."

He led her a few steps down a narrow hall with a door at the end. Instead of opening it, he guided her through the opening to her left which led to the general living area. She caught a whiff of a familiar scent as they passed the closed door. A wall of sliding doors led to a small balcony overlooking the city in the open living area. From this far up, she could see the sunset through the gap between the two buildings on the other side of the balcony.

Soliel found the room cozy, with its chocolate and tan couch, oval table scattered with sports magazines and a couple of books, and burgundy fuzzy rug that made Soliel want to take her shoes off and curl her toes in it. Artwork depicting Black couples watching the sunrise or dancing beneath the night sky hung on either side of the massive flat screen television secured to the wall. A picture of a Caribbean sunset hung above the couch while a five-shelf bookcase sat in the corner by the sliding doors, the books not arranged in any particular way, just haphazardly tossed there she assumed once they were read.

"The other bedroom is there," Ellis pointed to the closed door at the corner of the room on the opposite side, "and of course you can access the kitchen from this side as well. "

"All the comforts of home."

He offered her a seat. "It works."

Soliel tossed her purse on the table, careful to avoid the beer bottles. "How long have you lived here?"

"A couple of years. Though it looks completely different from when I purchased the place. When I finally admitted to myself, I'd be here a while I decided to renovate. One, to increase the value, and two, because, well let's just say I wasn't a fan of the Jacki-O bathroom."

"How old is this place?"

"I think the building itself was built in the thirties or forties. The condo has been renovated a couple of times. In the sixties and maybe the eighties, and I'm gaging that based on the wallpaper I found when I started pulling the layers up. The floors are the original hardwood though. The former owners kept it in good shape. No water damage or anything."

Soliel gave the room the once over, "It suits you. Not entirely masculine. It's nice."

"Thanks. Can I get you a drink?"

"Wine if you have it."

"As you wish. And for future reference, I always keep wine."

INSTEAD OF REMAINING seated, curiosity hooked its sharp talons into me sending me across the room to peruse the books. I found a bit of everything scattered over the shelves. Books on Tibetan Buddhism, astrology and astrophysics, African mythology, thrillers, high fantasy, classics. Even a category romance or two.

"Have you read all of these?" I yelled before a glass appeared to my right. I hadn't heard him approach.

"Most. I had a period in my life when I had a lot of free time on my hands. You took up gaming during your hiatus, I..." His voice trailed off, a heavy sadness hanging in the air, "I sought escape, or at least for a while. Then I fell into the rabbit hole of seeking the meaning of life."

"I'd love to know the answer if you found it."

He took a sip from his glass. "I didn't."

He sounded sad about the revelation. Like, deep inside, he hoped having the answer would make everything right with the world. I understood the feeling. I'd questioned the meaning of it all when I'd faced death. The unknown hadn't scared me like I'd thought it should which also rocked a set of core beliefs I'd reevaluated during those long days and nights alone in the hospital with doctors poking and prodding me but providing no answers.

"Did this free time have anything to do with the scar on the side of your face?" I asked walking back over to the couch. I watched as he struggled to not reach for the jagged scar. "I'm sorry. You don't have to answer that."

"I'd rather not talk about it. Too many bad memories." He joined me, handing the remote over. "I probably don't have nearly as many channels as you're accustomed too. But it's not all sports."

"I don't mind sports."

"But not your preference?"

"I wouldn't say that either. I have my moods. I'm a Super Bowl Sunday kind of woman. And I enjoy petite le mans. I can tolerate basketball in small doses."

"No baseball?"

"Hard pass. My brother played for years and, needless to say, being dragged all across the county then the country my entire childhood wasn't exactly the highlight of my life."

"Got it."

I took another sip of wine, savoring the flavor as the cool liquid's fruity notes played over my palette. "This is good."

"Glad you like it. I get it semi-locally."

"What exactly is semi-locally?"

"Anything within driving distance for me is semi-local. You probably won't find this one in a local package store. The more specialty places would order it, but the trip to Helen gives me a needed break every few months. I've learned I need to take time away from the city for my mental and physical health."

"Oh, I haven't been to Helen in I don't know how many years. When we were in college, Yaddi and I would go up there a couple of times a year. Definitely for Oktoberfest so she could get her drink on. And Christmas. We'd hit up all the Christmas shops to buy specialty ornaments for the obnoxiously large tree she stuffed in the corner of our apartment every year."

"Well then, I guess we'll have to plan a trip."

I peered at Ellis over the rim of my wine glass. "I'd like that." I didn't find petite le mans in the mix of channels and I fought the urge to force Ellis to watch the marathons of cheesy Christmas movies playing between Lifetime and Hallmark channels. We'd done the romantic Black movies before, and I wanted to change things up, so I relinquished the remote. "You choose."

"Nothing to your liking?"

I held on to the remote, playing a light game of tug of war with it while I decided if I wanted to play my hand and make him watch those Christmas movies after all. "I wouldn't necessarily say that. I, however, did choose the last time."

"I didn't mind your choice. I grew up with some those movies. They brought back fond memories."

"Yeah, they were great. Still, I'm not in the mood for sappy and I really don't care." I surrendered the remote, "As long as I'm with you, we can watch whatever."

"Are you tied to the television?"

"Not necessarily. Why?"

"How about a book then? I was just about to start the one on the table."

I reached for the book, admiring the cover. I found the chessboard, glass of what I suspected was scotch, and image of a cigar intriguing. "The Agency: Reviving Resurrection." I said before scanning the blurb on the back. "Thriller?"

"High stakes." Ellis replied. "Charity says there's a bit of a young love story line in it too."

I flipped the book back around, fingers swiping over the cover, "Ah, so she put you on to it."

"You could say that. She's made enjoyable recommendations before. I trust her judgment completely."

I handed the book over to Ellis, "Young love you say? Unlike us?"

"Love stories come in all age ranges."

"Well, I'm game if you are." I climbed into his lap, my back resting against his chest as we shifted to a leg outstretched comfortable position across the couch. He rested one foot on the floor.

The rumble of Ellis's voice against my back and the warmth of his body permeating through mine eventually lulled me to sleep, his voice growing distant until my eyes closed and eventually all grew quiet.

A chill woke me sometime later. That and the buzzing of my watch against my wrist. The gentle tinkling of what sounded like a fountain filling the otherwise quiet space. I curled tighter in a ball to stave off the cool air only for it to click that I no longer felt the warmth of Ellis's body or breath close to me.

It took a moment to realize he must have carried me to his bed and tucked me in. The pillow beneath my head smelled of spice with a hint of sweet chocolate, like no matter how much he bathed or what products he used that richness lingered. The scent was all too familiar. Utterly masculine and all Ellis.

My watch buzzed again, and I realized it was the alarm reminding me to take my meds for the night. I rolled over, patting the other side of the king-sized bed only to discover that side still made and cool to the touch. Ellis hadn't been in it.

I climbed from the bed, using the little light emanating from the salt lamp on the dresser at the foot as a guide to the door. The scent of sandalwood and patchouli wrapped around me as I stepped into the hallway, my foot bumping against the draft blocker which is probably what kept the incense smoke from invading the bedroom. I quickly closed the door to keep the smell out before walking towards the living room.

I was glad he hadn't removed my socks suspecting the hardwood floors would be cold. The little things meant so much and displayed deep rooted character traits I found endearing. Goosebumps formed on my arms, a light breeze in the air. He must have the sliding doors open.

"Ellis?"

He didn't respond. I found him sitting cross-legged on a cushion on the floor in the middle of the living room. Eyes close. He appeared relaxed and I hated to disturb him, so I collected my purse and inched behind the table towards the kitchen.

I rambled through the refrigerator only spotting leftovers I wasn't sure belonged to Ellis or Yusef. Unfortunately, he didn't have any deli meat or fruit I could consume with my medicine. Even the adorable breadbox sat bare. I berated myself for not eating before leaving the house expecting to only stay a little while or at least order something later on.

"Ellis!" I yelled, closing the refrigerator after grabbing a bottle of water. "Ellis?" I leaned into the archway between the rooms. He didn't move. "Ellis," I called again this time moving into the room. I squatted in front him trying to determine if maybe he'd fallen asleep in the position. When my hand touched his cheek, his eyes flew open as he scurried back. "Sorry, sorry," I stood taking a step backwards. "It's just me. I. I'm sorry I had to disturb you."

Recognizing her, Ellis shook the meditative state from his mind. "Is something wrong?" He used the table to balance on as he moved first to a kneeling position and then to stand.

"I need to take meds. And I need to eat with them."

He stared at me for a moment, then the words registered. "Oh. I haven't been grocery shopping."

"I noticed."

An eyebrow rose at the confession. "Give me a second to get my bearings and we can go get something."

I sat on the couch as he headed towards the kitchen then rounded the corner, relaxing when I heard the bathroom door close. The events of a few moments ago nagged at my conscious. That was the second time I'd called his name multiple times and he hadn't answered. Surely, I'd been close enough this time for him to have heard me. The hum of the traffic outside wasn't that loud and there wasn't any music to distract him. I'd dismissed his lack of response the first time as not wanting to scare off the deer, though I'd been loud enough then to do that anyway.

Of course, he might have been deep in meditation. I'd heard of masters blocking out the outside world when they ventured into the deepest states of meditation. It took years of practice and commitment to achieve.

"Have a taste for anything in particular."

Ellis holding out my coat sent my musings out the window. "No. I'm game for whatever."

Chapter Twenty-Five

The pull of the aromas of fresh baked bread competing with the sweet scents of chocolate made a mouthwatering play on my senses as I exited the back of Armond's Genesis. I'd arranged for him to drop me off for my Yule log making class and pick me up a few hours later giving me plenty of time to peruse the bookstore in the same plaza and even catch a cup of tea. I'd briefly considered driving myself. I'd mapped out the location, sure I remembered the city well enough to make it to the all-brick building and back without incident, but upon waking in the morning I'd had a tinge of pain and didn't want to risk driving under the good medication.

"I'll see you in a couple hours?" I confirmed, bundling up against a breeze threatening to chill me to the bone.

"Yes, ma'am."

Armond sent me on my way with a wave, though a quick glance over the shoulder confirmed he didn't drive away until I entered the shop.

"Good morning," a cheerful young lady dressed in khaki pants and a black t-shirt with The Naughty Chocolatier scribbled across the front in elaborate cursive letters. A few other people milled about. An older couple browsing the selection of white chocolate at the end of the counter. A man and a woman hunched over a glowing cell phone in the corner.

"Good morning," I replied as I approached the woman by the display of familiar looking truffles.

"Is there something I can help you with?"

Her name tag read Tiffany, her long blue hair pulled back then pinned up on the top of her head. I appreciated her pleasant demeanor as she smiled a straight-tooth genuine smile at me.

"I'm a little early," I replied checking my watch before giving the place the once over. Shelves of confections lined the walls, some in gold boxes with big red ribbons tied around them. Others in display cases on rotating tiered displays for patrons to peruse. A few Christmas trees sat strategically placed, their decor in red, gold, and white. Ribbons attached to green and gold cloth draped over the walls finished off the holiday decor.

"Ah, here for the Yule log class?"

I nodded.

"Give us a few minutes. They are almost done setting up. In the meantime," she plucked a blue chocolate ball from the stack of trays on the display behind her with a pair of tongs and dropped it onto a square piece of parchment. She handed it to me, "try one of our newest flavors, blueberry white chocolate."

Accepting the morsel, I bit into the confection the middle bursting with sweet blueberry syrup. "This is absolutely delicious. Are they for sale?"

"Sure are. You can grab some after your class. I'm sure we'll still have plenty left."

"Put a half dozen to the side for me, if you don't mind," I checked the sign behind the girl then retrieved a twenty-dollar bill from my purse handing it to Tiffany. "You can keep the change as a tip."

Tiffany's eyes lit up at my generosity. "Thank you," she said excitedly as she worked to fold the box and drop the requested balls of delight into it, "I'll have them at the counter when you come out the class."

"Good morning, everyone," came a voice from the door in the corner. "If you are here for the Yule log class, please follow me."

Tiffany waved me on as she loaded the rest of the order into a white box lined with frosty wax paper. I mouthed thank you as I followed the others through the doorway. Eventually, six more women piled into the room just as the class started.

The group of women, obviously all a part of the same bridal party, gathered around the two tables on the first row and one on the second. The couple who'd been ogling over their phones claimed the vacant table on the second row leaving the older couple at one table on the last row and me, alone at the one closest to the door.

I didn't mind riding solo. I'd learned early on I loved the freedom of doing activities on my own. I attended movies and plays alone. Amusement parks, though that one offered a challenge when it came to proper weight distribution and all. But I didn't mind riding with strangers. If anything, it confirmed that groups typically had one odd person out, or their friends were too chicken to ride up front or at the tail end of a roller coaster.

No. Independence suited me just fine.

After a quick round of introductions and my insistence that I was okay on my own, everyone settled in as the instructor began the class with a corny joke.

THE LIGHTS IN THE ROOM flickering made Ellis look up from pouring chocolate into the last set of molds he'd spread out on the table in the chocolate making room. Tiffany waved him over as she stood on the other side of the closed door. They kept the environment sterile by making sure anyone in and out donned the special suits that covered them from head to toe along with gloves and masks. Or at least they did for the large batch room. Ellis also had a smaller private place employees referred to as 'the closet' where he experimented with new recipes which resulted in piles of discarded slips of paper littering the floors, bottles of oils and flavorings scattered about. For him, it was organized chaos, encouraging the creative juices to flow. To everyone else, it looked like a giant mess.

He scraped the extra chocolate into a little silicone cup, sliding the mold away from the edge in line with the others to solidify, then he entered the tiny dressing room to strip out of the suit and speak with Tiffany.

Ellis handed her the cup with the tiny spoon inside as he unbound his hair, allowing it to drop to his shoulders to cover the scar running up the side of his face. Tiffany danced from one foot to another as she scooped a bit of the chocolate into her mouth.

"I can't quite make out this one," she said licking the back of the spoon. Her nose crinkled, lips in an awkward purse as she worked to identify the different notes in the chocolate.

As a connoisseur of teas, Ellis relied on Tiffany's vast knowledge of flavors and complex layering when he desired to create a new confection to tease multiple areas of the palette. Salty and savory. Sweet and spicy. She'd be the first to identify what worked and what didn't. While she was in her last year of college, she'd taken to learning about the chocolate making process and he hoped she'd stay on once she graduated. He'd even considered adding a line of teas based on her combinations, a sort of partnership for long-term gains benefiting them both.

"Try to separate them."

She dabbed chocolate on the tip of her tongue then tilted the cup a little peering into the smooth chocolate. "Though the coloring is dark, it's definitely sweet like milk chocolate. And I taste a floral, but I can't quite pinpoint which one."

"Go down the list. Think good and good for you."

Ellis watched as Tiffany toyed with the possibilities, the scanning of her list playing over her face as she dismissed each one. "It's earthy and just a little bit bitter. I can barely tell though over the chocolate."

"That's exactly what I was going for."

Hands on hips, though she was careful to not get chocolate on her pants she said, "Okay, I give."

"You're going to kick yourself when I tell you," he teased.

"Well?"

"Dandelion."

"Dammit." Her arm swiped through the air as she berated herself, "I almost said that, too."

"Both good and good for you."

"Yeah. Yeah. Yeah. Anyway, I came to tell you the Yule log class is coming along. All eleven who signed up came."

"Eleven, an odd one out then?" Ellis trailed behind Tiffany as they crossed the building. The larger chocolate making room was located on the side with the bookstore. It was quieter and less heat transfer than the bakery side with its ovens against the wall shared between the businesses.

"Yes. A woman. She's attractive too." Tiffany poked him in the side as she shot him a devilish smile. "And an excellent tipper. She loved the blueberry burst balls. Purchased a half dozen before she went into the class. You should check in..."

"I'm stopping you right there," Ellis said as they passed the main shop heading towards the classroom and his office at the other end of their part of the building. "I'm seeing someone."

"What a shame." Tiffany shrugged as she prepared to go back the other direction.

Ellis froze at the roar of laughter coming from down the hall, his brow furrowing in confusion.

Tiffany must have noticed the change because she asked, "Is something wrong?"

"No," Ellis said without missing a beat. He hoped Tiffany would dismiss his change in demeanor to his concern about their instructor, Donald, telling his bad jokes.

Laughter echoed down the hallway again. "Guess the class likes his horrible jokes," she said as she turned to head back to the sales floor. Tiffany held up the cup with the remaining chocolate, "This would be perfect for a spring release."

Ellis hadn't fully heard Tiffany's last words, his attention focused on the familiar laughter from the room ahead. "It couldn't be," he murmured as he moved closer to the classroom entrance.

"Okay, people." The voice from in the room boomed. "Now that your layer of icing is done, it's time for the most challenging part. The roll."

Hiding behind the door frame, Ellis peaked into the room his eyes widening, jaw dropping as his gaze came to rest on the lone beauty at the table closest to him. She couldn't see him with her back turned and he gaped as she struggled to roll the log alone. Ellis eased into the room giving a quick shake of the head and holding a finger up to his lips indicating to Donald, the instructor, to not give his presence away. The man diverted his path to the older couple as Ellis's arm wrapped around Soliel's waist, his fingers rescuing the outsides of the log threatening to unravel.

"This is much easier to do with an extra set of hands," Ellis whispered in Soliel's ear moments before she nearly elbowed him in the stomach.

She relaxed in his arms, and she melded into him as they worked as a team, she rolling the middle and he the edges until the cake formed the perfect round log.

"What are you doing here?" She asked admiring their work.

"Everyone, can I have your attention?"

Ellis tensed, knowing what his employee was about to do.

"We have a very special visitor today." Again, Ellis gave the man a stern warning, mouthing the word 'no' clearly. Of course, Donald ignored him, "May I introduce to you, our very own naughty master chocolatier."

As much as he didn't want to, Ellis stepped away from Soliel, his arms behind his back to take a bow. She eyed him suspiciously before the realization set in. She'd been had, and she knew it.

Ellis worked the room, speaking with the other attendees, taking pictures, and conversing like this was a regular occurrence. He felt Soliel's gaze on his back the entire time and he longed to expeditiously fulfill his duties so he could return to her side. He'd stay with her to complete the Yule log then sweep her away to the office for what he was sure would be a long explanation.

Pleasant smile still plastered on his face; Ellis addressed the room. 'Thank you all for attending. I hope Donald has been an entertaining instructor," Ellis winked at the man, a silent confirmation that he approved of the unconventional instructing style. If the clients liked the corny jokes, then he was okay with them continuing. "Please do tell your friends and families about The Naughty Chocolatier. And don't forget to consider purchasing additional confections on your way out. I think at least one of your classmates can vouch for the blueberry burst chocolate balls."

Ellis shot a smile in Soliel's direction.

"They are definitely to die for."

Chapter Twenty-Six

"Why didn't you say something," Soliel scolded as she and Ellis entered his private chocolate making quarters. She playfully poked and prodded him but carefully as to not make him drop the boxed Yule log.

He'd initially planned to take her into the office for this discussion but opted for the chocolate lab instead. The soothing aromas would calm her irritation and give him the opportunity to try his hand at wooing her in his natural element.

While the kitchen at Angelo's felt like home, there was still the order of things. The recipes and ingredients consistent. The point was not to surprise the guests. To provide them with the dishes they expected prepared in as close to the traditional recipes to maintain the authentic experience. Ellis had promised Mr. Angelo years ago that so long as he was in the kitchen the highest quality ingredients would remain and the recipes constant, though tweaking was allowed for health and allergy reasons and in case of product shortages. But even then, the years of culinary training kicked in and Ellis personally tended to the substitutions save for the days he found himself engrossed in chocolate making.

"I figured you'd put it together at some point. I mean, the gifts of chocolate. The invoices from The Naughty Chocolatier." Ellis shrugged, placing the box on the back table as he watched Soliel take in his private workspace.

She circled the room, studying the bottles of oils and other liquids. "I thought you might just know the owner. Or it was a company you did business with often enough to receive a significant discount. Not that you owned it." Soliel stopped in front of his favorite place. He hadn't perfected the items yet, so they were just tucked away on the corner shelf; but as soon as he did, he'd make a fortune.

"Are these what I think they are?" She asked, her fingers brushing over green and blue glass bottles on the front of the shelf. She lifted the first, popping the stopper out to take a whiff.

The devil tugged at the corners of Ellis's mouth. His eyes hooded as he rolled his bottom lip under before biting it. Ellis let his eyebrows dance as he gave her a slow seductive nod. "All one hundred percent edible."

She returned the bottle to the shelf, her hand fanning her now flushed face before it came to rest on her chest drawing his gaze there to the soft flesh revealed by the v-cut of the collar of her t-shirt.

"Oh my." Soliel distanced herself, but the blown glass bottles kept drawing her gaze.

"Would you like to taste my latest creation? Tiffany says its perfect for spring."

Soliel met him at the table, staying on the opposite side to maintain a buffer. The edible massage oils and body butters had tempted her. He'd have to remember that. Ellis was close to perfecting the raspberry one and would love to try it out with her. Or rather, on her.

"What are they?" She asked. A finger twirled the tray.

Ellis reached out and stopped the plastic. He flipped it over before popping the six pieces of chocolate out with ease.

"Is that sanitary?"

"The aluminum table is sterile. It's perfect for working with chocolate. I was mixing this batch before Tiffany collected me."

Soliel frowned, "Is that why you showed up to the class?"

"Yes and no. Apparently, she thought you'd be a good match for me. She greatly appreciated the generous tip." He held out a single piece of chocolate. "Taste."

She examined it closely before snapping a piece off between her teeth. "Umm. Dark chocolate?"

"No. Milk."

"Taste like a flower infusion. I can smell it and taste it all the same."

"Wow, you're even better than Tiffany."

"Herbal?"

"Getting warmer." And so was he. His eyes settled on her lips and not just because he enjoyed the way they formed her words when she spoke. The plump flesh drew him in, and he felt himself inching forward across the table to taste the remnants of the confection on her lips.

Soliel stepped back when she realized what he was doing. The movement broke the spell.

"Figured it out yet?" Ellis said regaining his composure.

She shook her head. "I give."

"Dandelion."

He watched as her tongue rolled over her teeth. "Yeh, I can see that. It is sort of spring-like. A little bitter for my tastes."

"Which is why I chose milk chocolate instead of dark. Dark chocolate is bitter by nature, and I didn't want the flavor to lean too far that way. I'm sure I have customers who prefer it. Health benefits and all. I may try a small batch with the loyals. If they enjoy it, I'll add it to the special-order batches."

"Have you considered white chocolate. Maybe make it pop with a little yellow food coloring like the blue berry balls."

He eased onto the stool on his side of the table. "I hadn't considered it. We can try it together if you like. It won't take long to heat a small batch of white. And I have plenty of flavoring left."

"I don't want to impose. You look like you're busy."

Ellis offered his hand and when she took it, he guided her around the side of the table. He tucked her between his legs, his arms encircling her waist as he drew her closer. She responded in kind when his lips brushed hers. They tasted of the sweet cream from the Yule log, remnants of the sugar clinging to the soft pink flesh of her lips. And of course, chocolate.

"At the moment, I wouldn't have it any other way."

WE WORKED FOR WHAT seemed like ages. In reality, only an hour passed. I learned about chocolate as we worked. I found the details fascinating as Ellis educated me on how he layered the flavors.

"How exactly did you get into chocolate?" I asked as his hand guided mine to work the chocolate into the preferred consistency after he added the flavoring to our batch.

"Sweet tooth. I'd baked with my grandmother all my life. She made fudge during the holidays to make extra money to cover any gifts for me. My mother did all she could but caring for my ailing father and trying to keep a roof over our heads meant every dime she made was already designated to bills. My grandmother received a small check she used to cover food but she somehow managed to squirrel away enough to purchase the ingredients for Valentine's Day and Christmas."

"Sounds like your family really loved you." I remembered my parents fondly. I'd only known my maternal grandmother well. My grandfather passed away when my mother was a child. I'd never met my paternal grandfather and by the time I was old enough to get to know my father's mother, the woman had passed on.

"They did. If there was one thing our house was never short on, it was love. But love doesn't always pay the bills."

"The start of life's trouble?" I suspected there were parts of his past Ellis wanted to keep to himself. Still, I wanted to know. No one's life was perfect. The past molded the person, their decisions either damning them or offering redemption. From what I'd observed, Ellis definitely got his act together regardless of his beginnings.

"In a way. When my mom got sick too, everything fell on me. I was still in high school, barely getting by. But my mother was determined I'd graduate if it was the last thing she did. So, I went to class and made enough effort to not flunk out."

"The things we do for our mothers."

"She was so proud. Seeing me walk across the stage." Ellis grew misty eyed, and he turned from me to mask the emotion.

My free hand absentmindedly rubbed his back. "Sometimes the smallest gesture provides the greatest reward."

"By then I'd already had my run-in with Mr. Angelo. Between the two of them I made it through school and home life got better. We didn't have to worry about food anymore. So long as I held up my end of the bargain and came to work at Angelo's after school anything left over from the kitchen was mine."

"Let me guess, there was always plenty of leftovers?"

"At least three times a week. Mr. Angelo packed up trays and dropped me off, so I didn't have to navigate the bus and walk home. Each tray was enough for all of us to eat a couple of meals without getting bored."

"He sounds like a good man."

The light returned to Ellis's eyes. "He was. It's such a shame his boys turned out the way they did."

"Have you heard anything else from them? You know since the last letter?"

"No, which is worrisome. I know they are planning something; I just wish I knew what it was."

Ellis scooped up a little of the chocolate with one of the tasting spoons he'd gathered before we dove into the mixing process. "Taste."

"Yeah," I rolled the chocolate around in my mouth before saying, "I prefer the white. This. This is good."

Ellis leaned in, "You've got a little chocolate, right there."

His lips brushed mine before the tip of his tongue urged my lips apart. I leaned into the kiss, the palette knife dropping from my grasp as my body melded into his. I longed to be close to him, to curl up next to him and let him taste every inch of me as I explored every inch of him.

Unfortunately, we wouldn't get the chance to do any more exploring as Tiffany stuck her head into the room without knocking.

"Oooh...naughty, naughty chocolatier." She smiled awkwardly, catching us sharing more than a professional moment. "Sorry," she said backing out of the room like a kid bursting in on their parents doing the nasty. "I didn't expect anyone else to be back here," she stuttered. Her head dropped, hands wriggling as she contemplated making a mad dash away from the embarrassment.

"It's alright Tiffany. You can come in," Ellis said in a welcoming tone. She hesitated, then stepped across the threshold but stayed near the door. "I supposed introductions are in order. Tiffany, this is Soliel."

Tiffany blushed. "We've met."

"Well now you two have formally met. Soliel has been helping me at Angelo's. Among other things."

The young woman seemed genuinely pleased at the pairing. "Your chocolates are still behind the counter. I was starting to think I'd missed you after the class let out and you'd left without them."

"I could never leave such a divine treat behind. Thank you for keeping them safe." Reluctantly, I allowed Ellis to step away before retrieving the discarded tools and returning to tempering the chocolate the way he'd showed me.

"Is there something you need?"

"Oh, no." Tiffany said without missing a beat. "I was coming to let you know about the chocolates left behind. And Yusef called. He wanted to know if you were delivering the truffle desserts for tonight or if he needed to stop by on his way in."

"How long ago did he call?" Ellis searched his pockets.

"Right before I came back. He said he tried to call your phone..." Her voice trailed off, but in that good way when friends were trying to be inconspicuous, "he thought you might be... busy."

I caught the smile and the nod in my direction, though I was sure the gesture was meant for Ellis's eyes only. Still, I enjoyed the approval from yet another of Ellis's acquaintances. They all seemed to want him to move on with his life, and that meant him finding a Mrs. Right in their eyes.

Ellis checked the time. "Call him back and tell him I'll drop them off. I've already pulled the inventory; I just need to load up."

Tiffany slipped out the door, but not before I caught her giving me one last glance.

"I guess we'll need to cut this short."

"Oh crap!" The tools clanked against the metal table as I dropped them, remembering my arrangement with Armond. He'd probably been delaying his day waiting for my call.

"What's wrong?"

"My ride."

"No worries. I can drop the truffles off at Angelo's and take you wherever you need to go."

"No. I arranged for Yaddi's driver to pick me up after the class. He's probably been waiting for me to call." I fished the phone from the bag I'd discarded in the chair next the table with the Yule log.

"Go make your call. I can finish up here."

I apologized profusely to Armond, but he assured me he'd taken a few close by rides and was just glad to hear I was safe. Relieved I hadn't ruined the man's day, I shot off a generous tip before tucking my phone in my back pocket so I wouldn't forget it. I found everything back in its proper place upon my return to the room. Ellis worked fast. Scraps of paper still littered the floor, but the table shined, and the chocolate trays were stacked on individual shelves in a plexiglass storage box on the corner.

"You must have gotten here after me," I remarked as I followed Ellis down the hallway. We stopped at the front, and he picked up my reserved chocolates.

"No. I've been here since six."

"I didn't see your truck or car."

"I'm parked out back. It's easier to load."

Well, that made sense. I waited with my chocolates balanced on top of my Yule log as Ellis loaded the boxes of Truffles into the back of his truck. When he lowered the cover and waived me out, I allowed him to assist me into the passenger seat.

Before we pulled away, I had one last burning question for him. "So, tell me why they call you the naughty chocolatier."

Chapter Twenty-Seven

It was still early when we arrived at Angelo's. A few patrons sat in the dining area scanning over menus while sipping cocktails. Sunday mornings were slow, the pace not picking up until after church hours and realistically the place wouldn't get packed until well into late afternoon and evening.

I hadn't planned to come into the office today since I'd warned Ellis about my prior engagement. However, since I was here, I saw no reason not to get a head start on designing the job posting for my future replacement. I sifted through the paper and computer files finding the core responsibilities of the business manager position with ease. Then, I set off tweaking the requirements to attract the best candidates for the position.

Thirty minutes of arranging four different possible ads and my stomach reminded me it was time to eat. Well, that and the buzzing of my watch's alarm. I'd committed to timers when I'd missed a dose or two on the new medication and paid for it dearly with hours of agony topped off with a day or two of nausea which made it nearly impossible to keep anything down, including the medicine. I'd relented to hospital visits where they pumped me full of fluid and a liquid version of my meds before sending me on my way and a hefty bill my has-been would be responsible for.

At one point, during the peak of nastiness between us, I contemplated becoming the vindictive person who intentionally ran to the emergency room for every little thing just to drain his pockets. He'd nearly pushed me over the edge a time or two, rubbing his new baby in my face when, for so many years, he'd made every excuse to delay starting our family. Now, I was glad we didn't have any kids. The last thing I wanted was to be tethered to Daniel for anything other than his court ordered alimony and health coverage. No need to talk about anything. No playing nice for the sake of co-parenting. Just a clean cut and we were both back to being single and living our best lives.

I printed the potential listings heading out the office doors intending to locate Ellis to see how long he'd be. I had to eat one way or another and if it meant grabbing something from the kitchen, I could easily find an item to my liking to tide me over until he could drop me off and I could make a meal of my choosing. The sight through the window in the 'in' door to the kitchen stopped me in my tracks. I tried to shake the image from my mind, my fingers balling the papers I held as the betrayal sank heavy into my body.

How could he? Just, how could he. My eyes misted over as I turned and quickly walked away, mindlessly bumping into Charity in my haste to escape the sight now burned into my psyche. Out of sheer habit, the words excuse me and sorry fell from my lips, but they didn't deter me from my mission. To get as far away from this place as I could as quickly as possible.

"Soliel?"

"I'm fine. I just need a minute." I was glad when Charity didn't follow. The last thing I needed was the woman trying to foil my escape.

I left the Yule log and chocolate right where Ellis had put them. The now crumpled ads tossed onto the center of the desk as I gathered my purse and the bag with my tablet in it. I didn't think about food or the buzzing of my watch reminding me I still needed to take my medicine. All I could think of was getting out of Angelo's. I'd work the details through once there was space between me and the place I'd thought was a good fit.

How wrong I'd been. Ellis had fooled me every step of the way. How could I have been so naïve? How could I have let my guard down and trusted him? Why had I once again become another man's fool?

I stormed out the back door. When I turned the corner walking down through the neighborhood, the first tear dared to escape. My feet aimlessly carried me further from the heartache without a second thought as my mind raced to unsee what I'd seen. But it couldn't be erased. Couldn't be unseen.

Eventually, when the threat of my legs giving out had me stumbling, I entered the first store I came across and grabbed a seat. It was a coffee shop blocks away from Angelo's. Away from what I'd thought was a fresh start.

Sinking into the seat I garnered every ounce of strength I could muster to calm my voice and stave off the tears. I couldn't break down here, in public, among strangers. I couldn't go home either. Yaddi would be there and even if I tried to avoid her, I knew my friend's radar would send her to invade and eventually on the warpath to give Ellis a piece of her mind.

No. While I appreciated the temporary home Yaddi provided, it wasn't a safe place for me. I needed a plan B and I had one in mind. I just hoped fate would sprinkle me with favor and make option b a reality.

"DAMMIT!" YUSEF CAUGHT Charity's arm before she burst into the kitchen.

"What's wrong?" he asked, peering over her to see what she was looking at through the door.

"That." She gestured to the window.

"Yeah," he said with a shrug, "what's the problem?"

"The problem is Soliel just saw Ellis like that behind Marcel."

He peered through the window again, getting a much better picture of what Soliel might have seen. "Oh," Yusef got it then. "Yeah, that's probably not going to go over well."

"You damn right it isn't." Charity headed back to the office, her steps calculated but hurried. "Tell him what just happened and have him meet me in the office. Hopefully she hasn't made it out yet."

Charity broke into mall-walker sprint. She didn't want to draw the attention of the customers. They didn't need to know what was going on behind the scenes. However, the nagging feeling in the pit of her stomach told her if she didn't hurry this whole thing could blow up and they'd have to be there to pick up the pieces.

She made it to the office without running into any customers. A plus she thought. But the victory was short lived, her heart sinking into the pit of her stomach as she discovered the office empty. The two boxes from The Naughty Chocolatier still sat perched on the edge of the desk a sign that maybe Soliel hadn't departed for good. Bathroom, Charity thought as she turned on her heel and rushed back the way she'd just come.

"Soliel?" Charity yelled as she popped her head into the restroom. She maintained an even tone like someone looking for a friend who'd had one drink too many. "Soliel are you in here?" She checked for feet beneath the stalls, not the politest action but necessary under the circumstances. "Damn."

She met Yusef and Ellis in the hallway as she exited the bathroom.

"Find her?" Yusef asked obviously more concerned than Ellis which only irritated Charity that much more.

"I'm sure she's fine," Ellis dismissed the pair walking down the hallway. "She probably just stepped out to get some air."

They followed behind, speaking in hushed tones. "What's with him?" Charity said.

"I don't know. He seemed real nonchalant about the situation."

They stopped at the office door, watching as Ellis eased the security door at the back open. Charity suspected Ellis thought he'd find Soliel out in the parking lot stewing. He probably planned to swoop in, give Soliel some lame excuse about showing Marcel the proper way to roll out fondant, and ease her mind with reminders that he only had eyes for her. The concern in his expression only served to confirm what Charity already knew.

"She's not out there," Ellis said.

"No shit." A mega eyeroll followed as Charity entered the office and plopped down on the couch. Yusef trailed behind with Ellis bringing up the rear.

"Her bag is gone," Ellis said as he checked the drawer Soliel normally kept it stashed. He grabbed his keys. "She couldn't have gotten far. And she left her packages."

"That's the point you numbskull. She didn't need them." Charity pointed at the neatly arranged boxes, "She didn't want the reminder. What is wrong with you? Men can be so dense sometimes."

"I don't have time to hash this out." Ellis collected his wallet from the drawer above the one Soliel used, "I need to find her."

"You can try!" Charity yelled at Ellis's back as he dashed out the office.

Yusef plopped into the seat Ellis had vacated. "Now you know you didn't have to do that."

"Soliel is a good one. And you and I both know how Marcel is. Ellis should have known better." Suddenly, Charity found her nails extremely interesting. She'd tried to warn him before. But men didn't listen, and she was getting sick and tired of having to pick up the pieces when the men in her life found themselves in the doghouse.

"I'm not saying I don't agree, but he's freaking out. He's putting on one hell of a show for your sake, but I saw the look in his eyes when I pulled him aside and told him what Soliel saw. It was as if the glass ball he'd started to form around their relationship shattered."

Charity huffed, annoyance reigning supreme as her arms came to rest on her knees. 'None of us want him to lose her. Hell, she's the best thing to happen to him since his son was born."

'Yeah, about that," Yusef rested his arms on the desk. "Do you think he's told her?'

"About Denise and his son?"

"Yeah."

Charity shrugged. "I doubt it. Which, at this juncture, works against him. Soliel hasn't mentioned anything to me, and I think she would have. We've had a few conversations about Ellis. I think she was starting to warm up to her feelings for him."

"She hasn't said anything to me either, "Yusef confirmed. "I actually expected her to. Especially after she came to me to confirm Ellis wasn't seeing anyone. She seems to trust our judgment."

"Which means we're probably going to experience fallout from this too. She'll assume anything we say will be for Ellis's benefit not necessarily because it's the truth."

"I hadn't thought about that." Yusef scratched his beard, "I think we're all screwed."

"That, Yusef," Charity pointed squarely at him, "we are."

PLEASE BE HERE. PLEASE be here. With my sunglasses securely in place, I joined the line of men and women dressed in business attire in the lobby of the downtown hotel. I'd called and left a message for a friend hoping she'd be at work today. Not that I wasn't prepared to fork over the extra cash for a room, but I wanted to make sure I could find something nice. Returning to Yaddi's house was out of the question.

I reached the counter, the young man in a starched white shirt and dark jacket greeted me with a smile.

"Good afternoon. Do you have a reservation?"

"Actually, I was hoping to catch one of your managers. Dawn Rivers. Is she in?"

He gave me the once over. While I wasn't exactly dressed to impress, with the spare jacket I'd donned from the office and the folding flats I always kept stashed in the bottom of my bag, my outfit exuded a modern chic vibe. The over-sized glasses and scarf completed the look.

"Is she expecting you?"

I silently released a breath. He'd confirmed that she was at work. "Probably. Tell her Celestial Soliel Divine is here to see her."

An eyebrow rose at the string of names. I almost thought he didn't believe me, until he proceeded to phonetically write my name on a white scrap of paper before picking up the phone from the counter behind him.

I scanned the lobby, not focusing on anything in particular, just taking in the classic style of the architecture. As many times as Dawn tried to get me to come stay in the hotel she managed, Daniel preferred to be closer to Midtown over downtown Atlanta, and so the opportunity never presented itself. That was until today.

"Ma'am. You can have a seat." The young man gestured towards the gray and white stripped high back chairs in the waiting area. "Ms. Rivers will be with you shortly."

I inched to the side, allowing the woman behind me who frowned disapprovingly as I passed, to reach the counter. I didn't care what the woman thought of me. Whether she deemed the t-shirt and flared black jeans appropriate attire meant little. And not just under the circumstances. While that woman probably stayed in the hotel for work purposes, a perk for her time commitment, I could afford to rent a suite for a month without a second thought or an accompanying expense report.

Claiming the seat closest to the window and furthest from the gathering crowd of individuals in various stages of the checkout process, I tried my best to hold my emotions in check. I couldn't break down. Especially not here, in the middle of the hotel lobby. It had taken all I'd had to plaster on a smile on my way over. My driver, though friendly, seemed to get the hint when I inserted my ear buds and stared into the bright screen of my phone. I'd opted to use a standard ride-share service instead of checking to see if Armond was available to maintain autonomy. I was sure if he'd have detected something wrong, Yaddi would be the first to know.

Though I stared out the hotel window at the passing traffic engrossed in the thoughts swimming through my mind, I felt a presence approaching from behind. My lips donned a cool smile as my former freshman college roommate Dawn approached.

"Well, this is definitely a pleasant surprise." I stood, returning Dawn's hug. "I must say that phone call caught me off guard."

The moment I stepped back out of the grasp I knew I'd been had. Dawn's eyes narrowed as if she could see right through the shades. She clasped me by the wrist and nearly dragged me through the opening next to the front desk where she pointed to the chair before closing the door.

I obliged; glad I'd thought to keep my bag swung across my body lest it be left behind in the haste to get me into a private location.

"What happened?" Dawn asked as she eased into her seat behind the desk. She'd unbuttoned her jacket, her round belly stretching her shirt taught.

"Are you expecting?"

"We're not here to talk about me. And you can lose the glasses. I can already tell you've been crying. Now spill it."

My shoulders slumped, "I really don't want to talk about it. I came here because I didn't know where else to go."

"You and Yaddi finally had it out?"

"No," I shook my head. "But I'm not ready to face her either. You know how she is. I just need a day or so..." My phone rang, this time instead of just ignoring the call I held down the power button and tapped the screen to power the phone down. "To process."

Understanding, Dawn half smiled and started typing. "I think we should have something. Its check out time and fairly quiet in the city. I don't think we have any conferences scheduled so I'm pretty sure I'll have a room."

A weight lifted off my shoulders as I waited for Dawn to find me a hideout for the next couple days. Even if it wasn't in this location, I knew my friend wouldn't stop searching until she found acceptable accommodations.

"There. You're all set. We had an early checkout in one of the suites and it just came back online. I think you'll find it suitable for a couple of days."

My fingers toyed with the strap on my bag, twirling the clasp in one direction before reversing the movement in the other. "How can I ever thank you?"

"Think nothing of it. Did someone already take your luggage."

"I don't have any. This was," I frowned, trying to think of a way to describe my predicament without going into too much detail, "an unexpected detour in my day."

"Hmm. Now where have I heard that before." We shared a laugh. The memory from our college years was still fresh in our minds. "Well, I'm about to head out to lunch. There's a Walgreens down the street. The AmericasMart too. Or we can grab food."

"Food is definitely what I need."

After locking away the bag with my shoes and tablet in it, we made a quick stop at the Walgreens before deciding on Rays in the City for lunch.

"I miss this place," I said after ordering.

"The food's still good. We order in sometimes."

"You never answered my question." Dawn poured over the dessert menu obviously avoiding answering my inquiry. "Was that a faux pas?"

Dawn huffed. "No. I am expecting. But we haven't told anyone yet. And don't you dare mention it to Yaddi."

I rested against the back of my chair, quite pleased with myself. 'Why the sudden secrecy? I mean you'd talked about wanting a family for a long time."

"Yeah, but I hadn't planned on going this route. We've had trouble conceiving and, well, let's just say this," she pointed to her swollen belly, "didn't happen the old fashion way."

"So what? It's the 21st century. We've got all this science and medicine to assist. Why not take advantage."

"You know our circle…"

"Oh please. I know you're not still hung up on that." Our group of friends had made a pact in college to all have our kids together. Five of our crew were married with one or two already in the mix or in the oven. I, Yaddi, and Dawn were the hold outs though no one really expected Yaddi to ever settle down and pop out babies. "We're all grown women. If they have something to say about it, then eff them. You know who your real friends are. You see I couldn't care less about them turning their noses up at me."

"Yeah, but you don't live here. Aside from Yaddi I pretty much don't deal with any of them."

"Ain't nothing wrong with that. And don't let your change in situation suck you back into the toxicity. They've shown their true colors and believe me, that grass ain't necessarily greener."

Dawn leaned in, intrigued. "What have you heard?"

"Enough to know I'm better off shrinking my circle than dealing with the cattiness. I can only imagine what they are saying about me now that Daniel and I have split."

Dawn lowered her gaze.

"See. That's exactly what I thought. Why do you think I had no qualms with being the outsider of that group? Even Yaddi started to see the light when the proposals popped up. I think that's why she took the plunge herself."

"Man, I wish you had been here for that. It was a catastrophe from the jump."

"I'll bet it was," I placed my napkin over my lap as the server brought our appetizers and drinks. "Yaddi has always been unconventional."

"A free spirit," Dawn said.

I detected the hint of jealousy. I knew Dawn wanted to be free like Yaddi, but her strict upbringing challenged her at every juncture, from her chosen profession to settling down with a man I still wasn't sure was right for her. Dawn walked the straight and narrow. I just hoped my friend wouldn't end up in the pits of despair when the dust settled. And even if she did, I would be there to offer a helping hand.

"Free spirit works for Yaddi. That doesn't mean her lifestyle is for everyone. It has down sides too. Don't lose sight of that part."

"I won't."

We chit chatted over the remainder of lunch, sticking to safe topics like our college years. Dawn caught me up on the remainder of our former circle. Who was working where? Who'd up and handed over their career to become stay at home moms. For a moment, I wondered what my life might have been like had Daniel and I decided to have kids immediately instead of traveling. Then Dawn spewed the details of long nights, dirty diapers and suddenly I realized I got the better end of the stick by being utterly kid free.

Chapter Twenty-Eight

"Where are you headed?" Charity asked as she cornered Ellis in the kitchen of Angelo's.

Ellis retrieved the Yule log and berry chocolates from the employee refrigerator where he'd stashed them twenty-four hours ago. Though no one commented on it, he was sure the staff all noticed his sullen mood. As far as he knew, no one had heard from Soliel. Present company included.

"I'm going to her house. The packages are a perfect excuse."

"I'll bet they are. And if she doesn't want to see you?"

His fingers tightened around the smaller box, the sides collapsing as Charity's hand over his encouraged him to loosen his grip before he ruined the contents. "At least I'll know she's safe. That's my primary concern right now. Even if she opts to never speak to me again, I'll at least know I tried and that she..."

"She's fine Ellis."

"I'm not so sure. She has health concerns and I think stress is a trigger. If she didn't go home and hasn't taken her medication, she could be..."

"She's not. Trust me. I feel it. Soliel is fine; she just needs some time."

"I have to try," he said on the edge of defeat.

"I know. Just," Charity fidgeted with a discarded meat tenderizer from the table. "Don't get your hopes up."

"You really think I did it this time?"

"I don't know. I mean, I know what it looked like, and I can only imagine what went through her head when she saw you two."

"But why did she run off? We'd just had a great time at The Naughty Chocolatier. I felt like we were finally connecting."

Charity looked up at him and Ellis couldn't help but notice the pity in her eyes. Was he that naive? Did he not know women like he thought he did? Granted, the whole scenario with his ex-wife had caught him entirely off guard. But as far as he knew, no one saw that level of crazy coming. Denise flipped overnight, going from doting wife and mother to psychopath without so much as a warning.

"Are you sure you read her right?" Charity finally asked.

"Yes. You can even ask Tiffany. She," he lowered his head, blushing, though it probably wasn't obvious with his darker skin, "walked in on us."

Charity raised an eyebrow.

"We were fully clothed," he added assuredly, "but she definitely interrupted an intimate moment."

"All the more reason for Soliel to run out. One minute you two are sharing an intimate moment, the next you're hugged up with Marcel."

"I wasn't hugged up with her." Ellis stopped himself, reigning his anger in. Or maybe it was frustration. If Soliel had confronted him, given him the opportunity to clarify instead of assuming, none of this would be happening. "I was showing her how to properly roll out the fondant."

Charity returned the metal tenderizer to the spot she'd picked it up from, her attention now squarely on Ellis, "Your relationship with Soliel is still in its infancy. And you said it yourself, she's newly divorced. Even the smallest infraction can be amplified by the newness of it all."

'You're right. Even Yusef warned me about Marcel."

"She's still vying for your favor."

"And as I told him," Ellis's gaze flicked to the door as Frederick, their dishwasher, entered. "Not interested. Hell, I'm old enough to be her father."

Charity's hand came to rest on his arm, drawing his attention back to her. "But you're still a handsome eligible bachelor with two thriving businesses and for the most part no drama. You're a good catch for the right woman."

"I don't want to be a good catch for anyone other than Soliel."

Charity smiled a proud motherly smile, "then go fight for your woman."

Ellis did just that, formulating his approach during the cross-town drive to Soliel's place. She'd mentioned that her friend usually traveled during the week which meant she'd probably have the house to herself. He dialed her number again after pulling into the driveway. Again, it went straight to voicemail sending his heart sinking into the pit of his stomach.

He gathered the packages, opting to try the front door before venturing past the side gate to the downstairs entry. To his surprise, a brown skinned beauty with twist down to her behind and a robe that left little to the imagination answered the door. The woman with shiny red lips reeking of alcohol-soaked fruit that she slid from the skewer held between pointy jewel-embellished fingernails drank him in, leaving Ellis feeling almost violated as her tongue swiped across her teeth. She leaned against the door frame, the movement shifting the lay of the shiny barely-there material of her robe revealing she wore nothing underneath.

Ellis adverted his gaze, his free hand sliding behind his back as to not be accused of accidentally encouraging the woman to suspect he wanted to try the goods she flashed his way.

"Angel? Who is it?"

Angel? This woman was definitely no angel. Ellis did recognize Yaddi's voice. She rounded the corner, the bright yellow teddy she wore hugging her curves. To his surprise, Yaddi didn't even try to cover up. Soliel warned him she was a free spirit. However, he'd never expected to see her so fully displayed and nonchalant about it.

"Ellis," Yaddi said stepping behind the woman running the last cherry from her stick over her lips. Yaddi plucked the cherry from the woman's grasp. She plopped it into her mouth before a subtle jerk of the head sent the third wheel further into the living room.

The woman's belt dropped to the floor as Yaddi stared after her, arms crossed beneath her breast giving them a shelf to rest on. Like a kitten seeking attention, the woman crawled on all fours onto the couch, her head coming to rest on folded arms on the back.

Assured her company was far enough out of earshot, Yaddi turned back to face Ellis. Her hands dropped to her sides but again she didn't try to cover up. "I didn't expect to see you."

"I'm actually looking for Soliel." He held the packages with both hands now. For one, it gave him a place to put them; and secondly the boxed provided the perfect buffer. He was sure Yaddi wouldn't try to make a move on him, and by the looks of the woman watching them from the couch, Ellis suspected he wasn't Yaddi's type.

"That's interesting." She stepped to the side encouraging him to enter so she could close the door. "I figured she was with you."

"You haven't seen her?" He trailed Yaddi into the kitchen. "These should be refrigerated." Ellis handed the boxes to her. She opened the larger of the two. Her finger scraped a bit of the creme from one side of the Yule log before she slid it between her lips in an overly seductive manner. Ellis made sure to keep the island between them, just in case.

"No. She left a message yesterday. Something about staying with a friend and not to worry." Yaddi found a place for the boxes in the fridge. She leaned against her side of the island before plucking a chocolate cover strawberry from the cookie sheet in front of her.

Suddenly, Ellis felt extremely uncomfortable and a bit cornered. Like a lion walking into a den of lionesses in heat. He wouldn't cross that line. No matter what tricks they used to tempt him. He'd fallen victim to one manipulative seductress, he wouldn't succumb to the prowess of these two.

"Did you two have a disagreement?"

How much to tell her? Yaddi could be an advocate. Ellis suspected she wanted to see her friend happy and if dating a person of her choice hadn't worked out, supporting a person of Soliel's choosing was the next best option. Ellis settled on, "Not exactly. She left before I got a chance to speak with her. And she left her treats behind."

Yaddi plucked another strawberry from the tray. This time Ellis caught her studying the doorway behind him. "I won't keep you. Just let her know I brought the packages by and to just call me to let me know she's okay."

Ellis turned, expecting to exit without incident. He'd gotten what he came here for, even if laying eyes on Soliel directly wasn't in the cards. Instead, Yaddi's companion blocked his exit, her arms above her head, hands gripping the door frame on each side. She leaned forward with everything from the waist up exposed in all of its smoothed skinned glory. Only her hair created a peekaboo effect to provide a pretend front of modesty.

Ellis maintained his position, though he glanced at Yaddi over his shoulder. His expression clearly indicating he refused to play this game and they could stand here all night like this if his only option required him to touch the woman blocking his path.

Yaddi eventually smiled, apparently pleased with his lack of submission. "Let him by. And no funny business."

Angel purred as Ellis passed on his way to the front door. He caught a glimpse of Yaddi's hands sliding over the woman's exposed breasts as he turned to pull the door closed behind him. He'd escaped this time, but he still had no clue where to find Soliel.

Disappointed and feeling a bit defeated, Ellis returned to Angelo's and threw himself into work. The staff avoided him as much as possible, almost anticipating his needs. Warm chocolates appeared before he asked. Chocolate shot glasses in need of mousse fillings made their way to the dessert station before he could turn around and retrieve them from the cooler. It was as if every cook and server knew he needed to focus on something he could control.

The phone in his pocket buzzed as he applied the finishing touches on the last pastries for the night. If they ran out, then they'd just be out. Between the lack of sleep and the trying moments at Yaddi's place, Ellis was on the verge of passing out where he stood. He pulled his hair out of the ponytail when he exited the kitchen on the way to the office. He hadn't recognized the phone number on the call, but the person had left a voicemail, so he decided to check it just as he stepped into the office.

Like fresh salt and lemons poured into a festering wound Ellis nearly dropped the phone as bile rose into his mouth. He managed to close the door collapsing in the chair as the voice on the other end stole his breath away. He lowered his head between his knees taking deep, slow, calculated breaths as he fought not to lose it right there. He was glad no one had seen him come down this way and he only hoped he could escape before someone realized he was missing.

Chapter Twenty-Nine

Though the hotel bed cradled me softly, I uncurled from my ball of sorrow. After the hours of saving face with Dawn my first night, I hadn't been able to do much other than wallow in the reality of the mess of my life. I'd finally opened up to someone. Allowed the wall erected around my heart to weaken, only to have hope snatched from beneath me. I should have known better.

This was it. No more. Three days was enough of shutting out the world and reflecting. I knew heartache all too well. I'd become intimate with betrayal. But I also knew how to overcome the adversity of both. And hiding out in a hotel room stuffing my face with cookies and candy and soaking in a tub until my skinned pruned only delayed the inevitable.

I abandoned the bed, stripping out of the sheets as I turned the shower water to as hot as I could stand it. Then, I stepped beneath the spray to wash away the abandonment and reclaim my power. When images of the past no longer plagued me, I dressed in my laundered clothing and sat at the desk in my room.

The electronics beaconed me, yet I quieted my mind in preparation. I needed to focus before diving back int to the shark infested pool that was reality. Eventually, the nagging in the recesses of my mind forced my hand and I relented. I finally powered up the phone; my first official task of returning to the outside world. To my surprise, I discovered a full voicemail.

I ignored the messages from Ellis, deleting them without a second thought. I even skipped over the one from Yaddi assuming he'd reached out to her to advocate on his behalf. It was the message from a number I didn't initially recognize that changed everything. The words 'we need to talk; you've assumed and you're wrong' caught me utterly off guard. For one, the voice was female and vaguely familiar. But there was something else, not just the words themselves but an underlying sadness in the tone that planted a seed of doubt in my conscious.

While my finger hovered over the skip button, I couldn't bring myself to dismiss this one. I listened to the short message to the end, scribbling the number the woman rattled off before announcing that Ellis didn't know she was calling, and she hoped to have our conversation in confidence.

"Charity."

So, he'd put her up to this. Or maybe not. Of all the people who'd called, Charity was the least likely to leave this type of message. I actually considered the woman a friend. In the short time we'd known each other, Charity presented herself as she was. Straight. No chaser. A woman secure in herself even at such a young age. Charity reminded me of Yaddi around that same age, rebelling against societal norms when it came to attire, hairstyles, and her sexuality. Many found Yaddi loud, brash, and overbearing. And even when she attempted to be tactful in her presentation, she was who she was and if you weren't on board, you were free to move along.

I dialed the number, not sure if Charity was at work or not, but hoping she answered. The last thing I wanted to do was get all the way back to Yaddi's only to have Charity call and ask to meet in person.

Luckily, Charity answered on the third ring. The clanking of plates in the background indicating that she was probably at Angelo's.

Dismissing traditional formalities Charity plowed into a speech I suspected she'd rehearsed hundreds of times waiting for this call. "We've been worried sick. I'm glad to at least know you're okay."

"You said you wanted to talk. So," I plucked the nail file from the side pocket of the bag next to my meds. Even if I wanted to hide longer, I'd have to make a medication run which I'd ultimately decided was a waste of time, "Talk."

"This isn't the kind of conversation to have over the phone. Do you mind coming to Angelo's? Or we can meet somewhere close. I'm acting manager on duty, but I'm allowed lunch just like everyone else."

I checked the time; ten till noon. Though Dawn assured me a later checkout time if I needed it, I did need to tie up loose ends at Angelo's so I could move on with my life.

"I can be there in twenty."

"THANK GOD." CHARITY slumped against the walk-in freezer, her fingers gripping the phone so tight they ached. Voicemail immediately answering calls had meant one of two things. A powered down phone or, well she dismissed the other option now that she'd spoken with Soliel directly. No need to entertain worst case scenarios.

"What are you over here thanking God for," Marcel said stopping short of the end of the table to gawk at Charity.

"Don't you have work to do? Those desserts aren't going to prep themselves."

Marcel rolled her eyes, not making a move, "I think I'll wait for Ellis. I might need another lesson on rolling out dough."

The old Charity would have snatched Marcel up and made it perfectly clear she needed to leave Ellis be or there would be hell to pay. Instead, Charity allowed the woman to think she had the upper hand. That's what little girls did. They played games. But Charity knew when people played stupid games, they received stupid prizes. Marcel's days here were numbered, she just didn't know it yet.

"Get to work."

Marcel sucked her teeth in response, but she complied like a good little worker bee. With no additional comments from the peanut gallery, Charity decided to wait for Soliel in the office. They didn't need to know she was on her way.

Charity checked the clock over the door, circling the space as she admired the photos on the walls. She barely noticed them now, and not just because she spent more time in the office pulling her weight as an acting assistant manager. The past seemed surreal, the faces in the photos a mere shadow of the way things once were. Even the smiling faces of Mr. Angelo's children appeared forced and ghost like. They'd pasted on fake smiles and pretended to be the doting sons until they reached the age of escape, then they abandoned their father and family business and only now returned to try to get their slimy claws into profits not due to them.

Ellis contended with so much, and now, with Marcel throwing a huge curve ball into his budding relationship, he needed his small circle to be his backbone. If that meant they had to work their magic behind his back, then Charity was content with doing just that. And if he found out, well, she'd cross that bridge if she ever got to it.

A tapping at the door sent Charity crossing the office unsure who'd be knocking. To her surprise. Soliel stood on the other side; in the same clothes she'd raced out of Angelo's in days ago. "Hey," Charity said opening the door wider to allow Soliel to enter. "You didn't have to knock."

"Habit," Soliel dismissed. She took a seat at the little dinette.

Charity noticed Soliel's stiff back and adverted gaze. She was trying to remain detached. Had she already decided to make a hasty exit? Would she even see out the new hire and on-boarding of her replacement?

Soliel folded her hands across the bag she'd placed on the table. "I'm here and I'm listening."

Charity considered claiming the other seat. Instead, she rolled the more comfortable chair from behind the desk still giving Soliel her space but not wanting to have both the desk and the table between them. "First of all, how are you?"

"Well." The word came out short and matter-of-factly.

So much for breaking the ice. "I meant what I said over the phone. We've all been worried about you." Soliel just stared at her, leg bobbing as if she wanted this conversation to be over so she could bolt before Ellis showed up. Fine, if she wanted the blow by blow, then Charity would give her the condensed version of the real events as they'd transpired that day. "You know, my mother used to always say, what happens when we assume? We make an ass out of u and me. Have you ever heard that saying?"

"No."

"Well, the gist of the adage is one cannot always believe what they think they see. Thine eyes will deceive thee."

Soliel leaned forward, her lips twisting in an unpleasant sneer, "I know what I saw."

"Do you?" Charity maintained her composure her body remaining relaxed and open, contrary to the vibes from the woman sitting a few paces away. Before Soliel formulated her response she continued, "Have you ever hand-rolled pastry dough?"

Crossing her arms, Soliel leaned back. "I have not. I'm a baker but alcohol cakes are my specialty."

"Then you have no idea what it takes to teach someone the proper technique. The appropriate bodily posture and skill necessary to maintain the integrity of dough, especially when it needed to be paper thin. The sheer pressure needed to even start to flatten it from a ball state." The sneer fell away to thoughtful curiosity as Soliel chewed on her bottom lip. Maybe there was a chance Charity could pull this off. "What you think you saw was a teachable moment."

"He didn't have to be standing behind her like that. She was enjoying more than just a lesson."

"Marcel is a manipulative little...well, you know the word I'd use here. I'll leave it at that. And yes, Ellis might be naive when it comes to some of her tactics. But believe me, he sees through her games when necessary. He doesn't want her. And as much as she attempts to hook him, he'd stay single before entertaining even a play date with her. Marcel played you. You reacted just as planned. She wants you out of the picture and what better way than to parade around here like she has a chance with him."

Charity waited for Soliel to process her words hoping with all hope that her message got through. Ellis needed her in his life. Probably more now than he ever had. She'd walked in right on time and Charity hated to think of something potentially magnificent being ruined by the petty likes of Marcel.

The office door swung open, Yusef stepping through before he realized Charity was in conference. He paused when his gaze came to rest on Soliel. Both women witnessed the relief as his features softened.

"See," Charity chided, "told you we were all concerned."

"Welcome back," Yusef said quickly closing the door behind him. Charity nodded her approval. They'd agreed that if Soliel returned, they'd allow her to decide if she wanted the rest of the staff to know.

"Thanks. But I'm not a hundred percent sure I'm back."

Yusef moved to stand next to Charity. Not necessarily a united front or anything like that, but just a friendly gesture that whatever Soliel decided, they were prepared to deal with the consequences.

"I think we both understand that," Charity said.

"We do. And I'm sure Ellis will too. "

"Speaking of Ellis," Soliel said, "Where is he? I suppose we need to have a conversation."

Sliding to sit on the corner of the desk Yusef responded, "That's actually why I came in here." He directed his next statement at Charity, "Have you heard from him?"

Charity's eyes narrowed. "Not today. Come to think of it, he snuck out some time yesterday, Early, too. I remember because," she frowned, trying to decide if she wanted to share her next thought with Soliel sitting right there. Eventually, she decided it needed to be said. She would, however, tiptoe around some details. "Well, because a couple of people asked about him."

"That doesn't sound like Ellis," Yusef said. He retrieved his phone from his pocket, dialing.

The office fell silent, only the ringing of the phone on speaker interrupted. The phone rang four times before the voicemail picked up. Sourness churned in the pit of Charity's stomach as her intuition screamed something wasn't right. She pressed the speaker button on the office phone using the speed dial feature to try again. Same results.

"Let me try." Soliel pulled her phone from her bag, "Maybe he's still worried sick and isn't answering because he hasn't heard from me."

The air sucked out of the room as again the phone rang and rang until the voicemail answered.

"This isn't right. Something isn't right," Charity said turning to Yusef. "How was he this morning?"

"I don't know. I haven't been to the condo in a couple of days. I figured he'd want to be alone, so I went home."

The date on the desk calendar caught Charity's attention. She pointed, "Oh crap. Oh crap. Oh crap. Oh crap!"

Yusef's eyes bulged as he too took in the date. He snatched the calendar up flipping through it to confirm it reflected the correct date. He looked at Charity, a silent conversation passing between them as Yusef dug for his keys. "We forgot."

"Forgot what?" Soliel asked. Neither responded, they just collected their belongings and headed for the door. "Forgot what?" Soliel asked again as she trailed them out the office. Her fingers grasped Charity's arm and the woman paused realizing they'd all but forgotten about Soliel.

"We need you to stay here," Charity said as they headed down the hallway.

"No. If something is wrong with Ellis, I'm coming with you."

Charity caught up with Yusef seeking an intervention. He was Ellis's best friend. If anyone could discourage Soliel from this trip it would be him. Instead, Yusef only shrugged and held the door open for both women to pass. Charity instinctively headed to Yusef's truck. Like the one Ellis drove, it was an extended cab version, allowing them all to pile in comfortably.

"I'll call and let Aundre know we're both out and he's in charge."

"IS SOMEONE GOING TO tell me what's going on?" I asked as Yusef tore through city streets. A truck laid on its horn as he cut the driver off, barely missing the box truck by inches. He drove like a bat out of hell as my mother used to say, skirting through yellow lights, and bobbing around slower moving vehicles in their wake.

Still, no one answered the question, and I decided pressing the point might be a distraction, so I let it be as they continued out of Midtown to the downtown area. Yusef circled the block of one-way streets pulling into the gated parking area of a high rise before following a blue SUV into the resident parking beneath the building.

He rolled to a stop in the parking spot next to where Ellis's truck sat. At least he was here, we hoped. Yusef tapped an electronic key card he'd grabbed from the truck against the black box at the elevators and we piled in, the doors painstakingly slow to close.

'Are you all really not going to answer my question."

Between the two, I expected Charity to give in. To my surprise Yusef offered a partial explanation. "This time of year is touchy for Ellis. A lot has happened over the years around this time, and he doesn't always handle the memories of the past productively."

I watched as Charity punched Yusef in the arm in warning.

"Not our place," she said to him, her back to me in avoidance.

He dismissed Charity's warning with a question directed at me, "How much of his past have you two talked about?"

The elevator dinged before I could answer, and Charity made a point to push her way out before either of us could exit. She clearly didn't approve of the conversation, and her actions showed she didn't want any part of it.

"Not much. Every time I scratch the surface, he changes the subject. I know the past can be painful to relive so I haven't tried to pry. We talk a lot about the future, and he always has a million questions for me."

"Figures." We met Charity at the door, she shuffled from one foot to another, impatient. Yusef waited for her to move out of the way before inserting his key. He inhaled, mentally preparing himself for what they might find on the other side. "You two wait here."

"I'm coming in," Charity said over his shoulder.

"So am I." I wanted to push past him, but fear kept me a step or so behind.

The smell hit us first, my hand slapping over my nose as I tried to breathe through my mouth. It was putrid; reeking of alcohol and what I was sure was spoiled food or something. My stomach knotted as I slid the scarf from around my neck to use as a filter.

Charity coughed and gagged beside me. She swallowed hard as she hung close to the door. Yusef didn't appear to be bothered by the smell as he waved us back. He made a round to the right towards the bathroom and Ellis's bedroom. To my surprise instead of entering the main living area from the other side, Yusef circled back. That couldn't be a good thing.

'Stay here," he demanded as he walked into the kitchen to access the living room from our side.

I concentrated on breathing. Reminding myself to keep my mouth open to lessen the impact of the stench. Seconds ticked by, then minutes, worry setting in when Yusef didn't immediately return. No longer able to fight the urge to know what lay on the other side of the kitchen, I closed my eyes and said a prayer before pushing past Charity.

"Vindictive bitch!"

I kept a step or two ahead of Charity the scarf still pressed firmly against my nose as I rounded the corner to see Yusef about to chuck a phone into the wall.

"Don't!" I coughed as I accidentally inhaled through my nose after yelling. I'd caught Yusef in time though, his fingers tightening around the device he held before it careened into the wall and shattered. It tumbled from his grasp as he lowered his head, my eyes following the phone's decent in slow motion as it fell to the floor.

The room appeared ransacked. The table tossed on its side. Shattered bottles scattered about with two new holes in the wall where the television still hung. At least it, the bookshelf, and fountain had been spared. "What the hell happened?"

"Don't come in here, there's glass and vomit everywhere," Yusef warned through gritted teeth. He shifted not so carefully but his foot hit an open bottle of pills sending it sliding under the couch. I wondered if the smell was finally getting to him. It was absolutely awful in here.

As I continued to inventory the damage, two empty bottles of liquor, one brown and one white caught my attention. This was bad. Mixing liquor was not the move. Even I knew that. My heart dropped to the pit of my stomach when I noticed Ellis's limp arm draped over the edge of the couch above those empty discarded bottles.

I almost screamed, but a hand gripping my arm and tearing me away from the scene distracted me enough to stave it off. My mind shut down; my legs threatening to give way as my brain struggle to process what I'd just seen. I jerked out of Charity's grasp, racing back the way we'd come, barreling into the bathroom to expel the little food I'd managed before leaving the hotel.

Glad to have tied my hair back, I heaved into the porcelain throne until nothing else came up. Then I dry-heaved even more, until a cool rag came to rest on the back of my neck.

"He's alive," Charity whispered as she slid down to the pristine white tile floor.

My stomach released, the vice squeezing my heart loosening as genuine tears dropped from my eyes. I rolled back into a seated position, my back and head resting against the wall. Charity had rolled up a towel and stuffed it under the door blocking the smell from the vomit in the living room. She'd used the air freshener as well. It was pleasant. Neutralizing. Not at all overbearing in the small space.

Charity reached up to turn on the fan. It felt good to be able to breathe normally. The little victories in life.

"I've never seen him like that," I said, closing my eyes before moving the cooling cloth from the back of my neck to my forehead. The world swam, even behind closed eyes, and the nausea forced me to slide my knees up to rest my head on them.

"I'm sure he never intended for you to."

Panic setting in, I buried my face in my hands. "I don't understand. Did he do that because of me?"

"No. And don't you even start to think you had anything to do with this. We all have our demons to fight. Sometimes we deal with them in a healthy way. And sometimes..."

'I need to help."

A knock on the door interrupted the conversation. "Charity. You guys need to go. I need to get him cleaned up and situated."

"I'm not leaving him," I demanded, though the words came out weak. Even if I wanted to stay, I wasn't sure how much good I'd be to Ellis.

"Yes. You are." Charity stood. She eased the towel away from the door slipping out to speak with Yusef.

I heard them arguing through the door. Yusef was adamant that we leave. That Ellis wouldn't want me to see him like this, and it seemed eventually they both agreed. I pulled myself together, slowly standing to stave off a bout of vertigo as I used the wall and shower to walk my way to the door. I swung it open, holding my breath expecting the previous smell to assault my senses. To my surprise, when I took a shallow breath, only an undertone of the previous smell remained.

"I'm not leaving."

"Yes, you are." The pair said in unison.

"Look, the best thing you can do for Ellis right now, is to let me take care of him. And if I have to sling you over my shoulder, carry you to the door, and lock you out, I am prepared to do just that."

Surprised in the authority of Yusef's position, I stepped back. I pondered the idea of locking myself in the bathroom, but sooner or later I needed to eat, and I still hadn't replenished my stash of meds which meant I needed to get home, and soon.

"He's going to be fine," Yusef assured us. He faced Charity before tossing her the keys. "Use my truck. Take Soliel home and then hold down the fort. Call The Naughty Chocolatier and tell them Ellis will be out a couple of days. Let everyone at Angelo's know that we'll both be scarce. But you know if you need me, you can always call."

Charity nodded.

"And don't fire the staff while you're in charge."

Just like that, the mood in the room lightened. "Oh, can't I?" Charity pleaded, "I just need to downsize one."

I barely believed the banter between the two. But I reminded myself that I was new to this scenario. I got the distinct impression they'd been down this road with Ellis before, which made me feel a little better. I was leaving him in good hands and Yusef would do everything in his power to make sure his friend came out on the mend.

Chapter Thirty

Ellis wasn't sure which burning hurt worse. The stringent smell of hospital grade disinfectant, the burning in his throat, or that behind his eyes. Everything ached. His head. His body. Yet the pain was nothing compared to the aching of his heart.

The voicemail from his ex-wife played on repeat in his mind, the reminder of what she'd taken from them. When it had all fallen apart. He'd almost forgotten the anniversary, the concern over Soliel and her well-being sitting front and center in his mind. But that message brought it all back, the anguish flooding into his being until all he could do was drink himself into a stupor and hoped the alcohol numbed him enough to sleep.

Ellis's thought circled back to the beginning. The happy times. The day when she'd told him he was going to be a father. When they found out they'd be having a son. His first, third, sixth and last birthday. The first tear escaped; rolling down his cheek. He wanted to wipe it away, but he couldn't move his arms.

Ellis finally opened his eyes to the bright light shining into the room. Hushed voices from around the corner drew his attention. Hospital was the first thought as he tried to move his arms again. Damn. They'd restrained him. The cold seeped into his veins, the beeping of the blood pressure machine activating made Ellis look up to see an IV bag hung from a metal pole, the liquid dripping gradually sliding through the tube that disappeared beneath the white sheets and blankets haphazardly tossed over his body.

He'd never hear the end of this. Recognizing Yusef's voice, Ellis tried to call the man's name. But it hurt to talk and only a whisper escaped. He moved his legs, realizing they weren't restrained he managed to bump the sliding table enough to knock over the plastic cup sitting on it.

Yusef immediately rounded the corner, a young nurse with burgundy hair and fake eyelashes following behind. Ellis saw the disappointment in his friend's expression, but Yusef remained silent, and the nurse approached.

"Welcome back to the waking world Mr. Mason. You gave your friend here quite a scare." Ellis only stared at the woman. "If you promise to play nice, I'll remove the restraints.' When she was assured he was coherent enough to understand, she removed the restraint on her side. Yusef stepped out the way so the woman could reach the other side. She plucked the empty pitcher from the rolling table indicating she'd bring in water, her way of giving the men a moment alone.

When the door clicked closed, Ellis expected Yusef to lay into him. He wouldn't blame the man. What he'd done was stupid. He should have at least told someone he was leaving. This could have ended differently. Hell, this stunt could have ended him.

"Say something," Ellis finally said. But Yusef remained silent. He just stood at the foot of the bed; arms crossed, fury raging beneath an otherwise cool exterior.

The nurse returned, the stalemate still in full effect as she dropped off the water and a clean cup before, mumbling something about the doctor would be making rounds in an hour or so, she made a hasty retreat.

This time, when the door closed, Yusef moved to stare out the window, his back to Ellis. "Yusef."

'I should kick your ass right now in this damn hospital," Yusef said. His fingers balled into fist, though he kept his arms at his side.

"I'm sorry."

"Are you? I recall that being the same thing you said a few years back. Yet here we are," Yusef's hand cut through the air as he turned on his so-called friend, "on repeat with the same bullshit. You promised us. Not just me, but Charity too. You promised if you ever felt like you were going back down to that bottomless pit of despair that you would find one of us."

"I..."

"Save it. You don't have to explain it to me. Hell, you don't even have to explain it to Charity. We saw the messages and I played the voicemail for her. We know the trigger. However," Yusef closed the distance between them, He claimed the chair next to the bed, "you will have to explain this to Soliel."

"How," Ellis managed before is throat ceased on him. Yusef must have noticed the anguish because he filled a cup with water and handed it to him. Ellis drank slowly at first, the water cool against the burning inside of his throat. It still hurt to swallow, and Ellis suspected they'd put a tube in to pump his stomach. When he was sure he could finally speak, he continued, "how did she find out?"

"She doesn't know the details. We basically told her it wasn't our place to reveal your demons. But she refused to let us check on you without her. She came back to Angelo's to talk to Charity. I went into the office to see if Charity had heard from you and that's when we realized what day it was."

"The condo?"

"You don't remember?"

"Nothing past the first bottle," Ellis admitted.

Yusef sighed. He pinched the bridge of his nose, annoyance setting in, "I cleaned up all the vomit. You owe me for that one. I think I got most of the glass too though I'd suggest we remove everything from the living room and do an extra sweep with the vacuum. There are two new holes in the walls, and I don't think the table is salvageable. I left it for you to decide though."

Ellis scanned the room, "Wait, how long have I been here?"

"Almost forty-eight hours. Your breathing worried me after the first hour. And I couldn't get you to wake up. I found a few white pills as I cleaned and then discovered the empty sleeping pill bottle. With that and the realization you'd probably finished off more than two whole bottles I didn't want to risk it, so I called an ambulance."

"This bill is going to be a bitch," Ellis said, refilling the cup with water and slowly sipping.

"Oh, they are just getting started. I'm guessing they gonna send the shrink down to have a conversation with you. I was real vague on the details but anyone who drank as much alcohol as they pumped out of your stomach is either a hard-core alcoholic hitting rock bottom or needs to be on suicide watch."

"You don't have to hang around. I'm sure Charity could use your help."

"Charity is fine. Soliel is pitching in to make sure the schedule is covered and any orders that need to be made for the weekend are handled. And don't change the subject."

"I'm not." But Ellis looked away, the words weak in delivery.

Yusef leaned on the side of the bed, waiting for Ellis to look at him. "I need to know. Were you trying to ..."?

"What? Off myself? Because of Denise?" Ellis's brow furrowed as he stared at his comrade. Yusef had been there when he'd woken up from the car accident. He'd been the one to tell him that his son hadn't survived. "Do you really think that's what I was trying to do?"

"I don't know what to think at this point. I mean, I get it. You had a lot going on. With Soliel walking out and then the anniversary. Not to mention Denise's messages. You'd just started to hope for the future. Looking past the restaurant and The Naughty Chocolatier; towards stepping out on faith and pursuing a real connection with another woman."

"I messed up, okay? I should have said something. But I'm not suicidal. I wouldn't give Denise that level of satisfaction."

"And Soliel."

"I'll admit I'm frustrated. But it's my own fault. You tried to warn me about Marcel, but I didn't listen then."

"So, you're listening now?"

"Definitely."

Chapter Thirty-One

I celebrated the four hours of sleep I'd managed before the thoughts racing through my mind again tore me from dreamland. It was nice to know at least I wasn't alone in the house. This being Yaddi's week to work with local clients I'd heard my friend return from work earlier in the day. Another female voice indicated that she wasn't alone, which was fine by me. The longer Yaddi stayed occupied with her company, the less time she had to venture downstairs and catch me in a moment of weakness.

Unable to succumb back to slumber, I gathered the items to perform a burning bowl ceremony. I'd learned the process from a friend who attended a Unitarian Universalist church in Montana years earlier. The ritual had helped me come to terms with my illness and divorce. Now I hoped it eased my mind from the stress of my current life struggles, including what to do about Ellis.

I plucked two half pieces of parchment, a pot of 'dragon's blood' ink, and a quill from my travel alter, carrying them all outside. The knee-length wrap I donned kept me toasty, the temperature dropping rapidly now that the sun had set. With the items organized neatly on the silver tray next to a copper bowl filled with sand with an incense cone perched in the middle, a book of matches, and a tea-light candle I carried my supplied down to the water's edge to a spot with a folding table where Yaddi and I sometimes came to meditate. The soft grass ticked my legs as I sat and crossed them. I draped the wrap around me to stave off a chill before I set to work pouring my frustrations out onto the paper.

"Don't tell me you already trying to burn this man out of your life."

I dotted the end of the last sentence on the parchment before responding. "I am not."

"Then what are you doing?"

That was actually a good question. The original intent when I made my way out to the edge of the lake was to write anything that came to mind. Ellis. Daniel. Hell, even the stressful situation with Marcel trying to stake a claim on a man I knew carried no such torch for her . Yet when I dipped the tip of the quill into the ink, semi-familiar emotions flowed through me. Like a dam I'd erected around a piece of my psyche suddenly gave way.

I stared out over the lake, half expecting to see the ducks or deer return but only the silhouettes of the line of trees reflected in the water. "I've been having dreams." The words fell from my lips in an almost detached fashion, like I'd said them, but it wasn't me speaking. I expected Yaddi to move closer, even join me on the grass. It wasn't like we hadn't sat out here for hours at a time since my arrival reminiscing.

When I finally looked up at my friend, Yaddi had made herself comfortable on one of the sliding chairs. Her foot rocked the contraption as she stared up into the night sky.

"Did you hear me?" I asked.

"I heard ya. It's this place you know. That's the thing about the quiet of the semi-country. Plenty of time to contemplate the present. And the past."

"The past is what I find so frustrating."

"How so?"

The last of the incense smoke drifted out over the water fading into a light haze before disappearing all together. It was quiet here. Almost too quiet. No crickets. No leaves rustling. Just that eerie serial killer in the woods silence that made the hair on my arms stand at attention. My fingers gripped the insides of the wrap burying into the plush lining to stave off an unnatural chill.

"I keep having these dreams about me and a man."

"Well, it has been a minute. I've tried to help you out with that..."

"Not that kind of dream; thank you very much."

"Oh. Well," Yaddi suddenly found the sleeves on her jacket interesting. "Continue."

"I think the dreams are memories." I waited for Yaddi to offer...what? What did I think she could offer in this situation?

As if understanding the unspoken, Yaddi said, "The doctors said you might remember eventually."

"But that's what's so frustrating. I don't really see the man's face, but I can feel the emotions. Like what I'm feeling now with Ellis I've felt before."

'Maybe you're getting those first butterflies with the new relationship. Like with Daniel."

"This is nothing like Daniel," I vehemently responded which caught me off guard as well. If I felt this way now, and my mind related these feeling with Ellis and someone in my past, did it mean I never felt this connected to Daniel. Had that all been a mistake from the start? Did I get with him and stay so long because he was the safe option? Had I ever really loved him?

"Soliel?"

"Huh? Oh, sorry. Were you saying something?"

Yaddi swung her legs to the side, standing to ignite the propane heater next to the swing. "I was asking if something happened between you and Ellis. And before you shut down and go off on a tangent about boundaries, I am respecting the ones you've established. However, in order to discuss these newfound dreams of yours, context on my side might be helpful."

She had a point. These dreams manifested after the initial fallout with Marcel. I spent much of my time cooped up in the hotel evaluating the circumstances between me and Ellis. The pros and cons of our budding relationship. What I felt after the Naughty Chocolatier revelation. It all came down to I still knew so little about his past relationships. We'd discussed his upbringing in terms of how Angelo's became his. The struggles as a young man and guidance he received not just as a restaurateur but as a man from the person who'd been all but a surrogate father to him.

Still, whenever I broached the subject of past relationships, Ellis erected a wall. What was he hiding? And is the secret so devastating that it could spell the end of our relationship before it even started.

I settled on, "Do you want the short or the long version?"

"I'll leave that up to you. The heat will kick in in a second. You should come up here before you catch your death."

I provided the condensed version of the buildup of our relationship. And as we partook of the bottle of Moscato Yaddi had brought down with her I realized I wanted to share this with Yaddi. As much as I wanted to set boundaries, the fact that Yaddi left the door open for me to decide how much to share confirmed that flexible boundaries was really what I'd been seeking all along. I love my girl. Yaddi was the sister I never had, and being a real ride or die, she took my words to heart.

I took another drink from the bottle, giggling as more of it than I intended poured into my mouth nearly shooting out my nose. I was tipsy.

"I guess what I was feeling for him didn't set in with me until the other day. It was such a good day too. I had a great time at the Yule log class. I was just trying to do something different and then to discover Ellis owned the place, and all these chocolate treats he slipped my way were made by him. It only made the torch I suppose I carried for him burn brighter."

That was it. I finally admitted to myself that even after everything, this was the answer I'd been avoiding as I wallowed in sorrow in the hotel. I hadn't been ready to admit that I was falling for Ellis and fast. The thought freaked me out. Dare I consider the idea of love again. And finding it so quickly after the ink dried on my divorce papers?

"What are you thinking?" Yaddi asked after the silence stretched between us.

I handed the bottle over after taking one more drink of liquid courage. "Tell me about Tyler." I blurted out of nowhere. Yaddi lowered the bottle, gawking at me before she took another drink. Suddenly serious, I eyed her in anticipation. "I'm sure the dreams are about our time together." I shrugged. "Maybe Ellis is Tyler reincarnated."

Yaddi stifled a laugh, but not very well, "Ellis is a little old to be a reincarnation."

"Guess you're right. But maybe Tyler sent Ellis to me. Maybe he loathed Daniel as much as I do now."

"You and Tyler were definitely soul mates. Most would call you two twin flames which isn't always the easiest relationship to maintain. It also doesn't necessarily make you soul mates, but I'm sure you two were both."

"We brought out the worst of one another huh?"

"In many ways. But you two also brought out the best in each other. You both learned from each other, getting through to one another when you'd shut down to any outside intervention. Watching you two play off one another freaked the hell out of most of our social group."

"Is that why they stopped inviting us to hang out?"

"Maybe. They couldn't understand the intensity between you two, but I always knew he was the one for you. I used to watch him staring lovingly at you when you crossed paths on campus."

"You mean stalking me?"

Yaddi finished off the bottle placing it in the grass beneath her chair. "He didn't stalk you. But he definitely paid attention, waited for just the right moment, then he made his move."

I felt a smile tugging at my lips, but it never fully formed as the memory I struggled to retrieve from the dark place in my mind refused the bait. "I wish I could remember."

"You know, maybe its best you don't," Yaddi stretched. A yawn followed as she prepared to retreat into the house. "Maybe you are getting enough glimpses to confirm that you and Ellis have something special. Maybe not in the same way as you and Tyler, but just as deep and just as meaningful."

Chapter Thirty-Two

Ellis reveled in the feel of what he deemed to be 'real clothes;' not like the thin, over-washed, open-back strip of worn cloth this place passed off as a hospital gown. The green sweater he now donned fit him perfectly, the sleeves hitting just below his watch. He'd found this perfect pair of jeans on one of his wine retrieval trips. The outlet mall beckoned as he drove towards his destination. Giving in to the silent summons on the return trek, he stumbled upon the hidden treasure as he perused the gathering of stores. With two pair just the right size in black and dark blue but not quite navy dark tucked safely away in a bag, he'd returned to his regularly scheduled mission of driving back to Atlanta to make his delivery.

Although the current goal involved exiting the hospital as quickly as possible so he could have a much needed and long overdue conversation with Soliel, Ellis still took his time dressing, running through what he planned to say to the woman who made him want to share his deepest darkest secrets. She'd invested her time and care in him over these last few weeks and he'd only shut the door tighter each time she tried to venture over the prison wall he'd erected around his heart. Well, that all ended today. Ellis decided he was done letting the past dictate his present.

The hospital room door opened, Yusef entering before it closed again.

"I am so ready to get out of this place," Ellis muttered. He worked to slide on his socks as Yusef rounded the bed to plop down in the chair again.

"The nurse said she'll have your discharge paperwork in a few. Including the therapy referral," Yusef said peering at the booklets still sitting on the rolling bedside table. "You're not taking your pamphlets?" He slid the suicide prevention one closer to Ellis.

"No." Short. Simple. Flat out to the point.

Yusef gathered the brochures tucking them into the outside pocket of the duffel bag he'd brought with clothes for Ellis. He plucked a small black plastic case from the other pocket, placing it on the table.

"Thought you might want this."

Ellis glanced over his shoulder, brow furrowing at the case. "Where'd you find it?" He asked, reaching for the case.

"Under the couch."

"Seriously?"

"Yeah. You're lucky it didn't get stepped on or crushed when I moved the couch to clean the floors."

"Thanks again. I owe you big time for this."

"Damn right you do. I got to think long and hard on a repayment."

Unfortunately, or maybe fortunately, a knock on the door saved Ellis as the nurse entered. She pushed the door all the way open, the magnetic stopper at the top clicking into place as she rolled a wheelchair into the room.

"Well, Mr. Mason, you are all set."

"Um, I can walk on my own," Ellis said as he made one last quick round of the room to make sure he hadn't forgotten anything. He accepted the bag Yusef handed to him.

"Hospital rules." She handed him the paperwork as he sighed but reluctantly agreed. "Any questions before we let you go?"

Ellis flipped through the paperwork, frowning at the follow-up instructions but understanding the necessity under the circumstances. The last thing a doctor wanted to be liable for was not providing the appropriate resources to a patient they deemed in need of a counselor. When the social worker first visited, he'd considered being an ass to the woman. But she was only doing her job, and from their perspective, it appeared he'd attempted to end it all. Still, he had no plan to follow through with the appointment. He just played nice, explained the situation, and accepted the literature so he could be released without too much fuss.

"Do you know where the patient pickup area is?" The nurse said to Yusef.

"Yep. I'll see you both in a few minutes."

They found Yusef exactly where they expected him, in the turnaround at the patient retrieval area. As the only vehicle picking up at the time, he'd parked right in front of the doors. The rush of cold air woke Ellis all the way up as the woman rolled him to the outside. Yusef leaned against the front panel like a slacking valet.

At least he'd opened the door. "You need some help there buddy?"

Ellis glared. He briefly considered feigning weakness but didn't want to alarm the nurse. "No. I think I can handle it." He thanked the nurse as he stood. She shot him a smile then turned to get back to her other patients.

"Why are you driving my truck?" Ellis asked, tossing the bag in the back seat before climbing into the front. Yusef closed his door donning the seatbelt before starting the vehicle.

"Because gas is expensive. You did this to yourself, so you need to pay for transportation as well. I should send you a bill for my cleaning and chauffeuring service."

"Fine. Do whatever you like. I'm just glad Linda convinced me to get health coverage. The bill for this stay would have eaten me alive."

"Hmm. Do you think you needed that wakeup call?"

"No. Believe me, I got the message loud and clear. Never again. No way. No how. Not going to happen."

Before they pulled off, Yusef handed Ellis a clear square bottle he grabbed from a bag on the floor behind the seats. "Here. The doctor said to make sure you stay hydrated."

Ellis read the label. "Are you seriously giving me Pedialyte?"

"You're lucky they only had the store brand." Yusef chided as he merged into traffic.

They rode in silence, Ellis toying with the radio stations before conceding to the lack of inspiration. He stared out the window, drinking from his electrolyte beverage while Yusef battled with bumper-to-bumper traffic.

"Why didn't you take the highway?" Ellis finally asked as they stopped at yet another red light.

"I need to make a stop by Angelo's."

"Really?" Ellis caught the concern in his tone and hoped Yusef didn't notice.

"Charity has been successfully holding down the fort; but today is payroll and she isn't authorized to sign paychecks."

Ellis adjusted in the see to glare at his friend, "putting me back to work already?"

"No," Yusef changed lanes to get around a car parked illegally in the already narrow streets. "You heard the doctor. You still need to rest a couple of days."

"For what? And who is going to make me?" Ellis heard the pout in his voice quickly adjusting his posture and tone to no longer sound like a toddler justifying not going to bed at a designated time, "Not like there's a boss I report to." Yusef raised an eyebrow splitting his attention between the still stopped traffic and Ellis. "Fine."

A half smile and Yusef went back to concentrating on driving.

"Speaking of Angelo's. Mind if I run something by you?" Ellis said.

"I don't like the sound of that."

"It's nothing bad. Quite the opposite."

"Shoot."

"Well, you know Soliel and I have been seeking a replacement for Linda." Ellis waited for Yusef to respond but when he didn't Ellis continued, "Charity has been with us a long time. And she is more than capable. I mean, if Soliel doesn't mind training a new person, then why not offer the position to Charity? She's been hinting at more money, and we've pretty much dumped the responsibility in her lap on more than one occasion."

"She's definitely proven she can handle it."

"Ten times over. So, you agree? I mean, you'll still have seniority but giving her an official assistant manager title with Linda's responsibility and the occasional coverage in case we have a big catering job or you're on vacation and I'm needed over at The Naughty Chocolatier seems reasonable."

Yusef squeezed between a semi and a tiny red car that looked like it might blow away with one hefty gust of wind. He turned onto the side street, pulling into the parking lot and into Ellis's designated spot at the back of Angelo's.

"I think it's a good move. But..."

"Here it comes."

"See now who's jumping to conclusions?"

Hands raised in surrender, Ellis said. "Okay. Okay. You were about to say?"

"I was about to say what about Marcel?"

Ellis frowned. "I've thought about that too. I know Charity can handle her. Still, it will be a touchy transition."

"Are you prepared for that?" Yusef said unbuckling his seatbelt.

"I think I am," Ellis replied, doing the same.

"Um, where are you going?"

"In with you. What does it look like?"

Yusef's lips tightened into a thin line. Ellis waited for the man to challenge him and slowly released the breath he'd been holding when Yusef reached over to turn off the truck and remove the keys from the ignition. One battle won. But he was sure the war waited just on the other side of the door.

Chapter Thirty-Three

I checked the clock at the corner of the computer as I verified the last set of employee hours to run payroll. Yusef should be here any minute now. He'd assured me he'd arrive before opening to make sure checks were ready for the staff before the start of their shifts. I stretched, rolling my head in one direction before repeating the same motion in the other to loosen the tension from my neck. I needed to move around and the moment the thought formed my bladder nudged me to the bathroom.

Marcel entered the ladies' room just as I prepared to wash my hands. We'd successfully avoided one another since Ellis's departure as I completed my tasks each day and exited hours before Marcel's scheduled arrival. I wasn't exactly avoiding the woman, but I was sure Marcel took my initial disappearance and Ellis's subsequent one as a sign that something was amiss.

From the corner of my eye, I caught Marcel pausing in front of the door. Ignoring her disdain, I lathered and washed my hands.

"I wasn't sure you were still employed here," she said, while blocking the exit. She stood with her arms crossed over her less than ample chest.

Unbothered, I continued my routine waiving my hands beneath the faucet to activate the water. "I don't work here, thank you very much."

"Then why are you always here? Up under my man."

I tried to stifle the laugh. I failed. Miserably. "Is that what he is? Let me give you a little advice." I plucked two paper towels from the electric dispenser allowing the whir of the contraption to fill the intentional pause in my warning, I dried my hands as I spoke, baring down on the woman half my size and probably half my age. When I stood close enough to see the fear starting to inch into Marcel's eyes, I spoke, "first of all, when a man wants you, he clearly lets you know. I have yet to hear Ellis stake a claim to you. Secondly, you might think you know me but let me tell you like my mother used to tell me, don't let your mouth write a check your behind can't cover. Now, you might want to run along little girl. Your shift starts in ten."

Unfazed, I reached around Marcel to open the door. Any intimidation the woman may have presented upon entering the ladies' room now lay shattered on the black and white tile floor. I, on the other hand, made sure Marcel understood that as a grown woman who held her own through more than Marcel had seen in her young life, I knew how to manage mine. Marcel stepped away and I left her to her thoughts.

The kitchen was a buzz, the early arriving staff members setting up for the lunch crowd. Bread plates and silverware clanked as they were stacked on the cart to complete the initial table settings. Bundles of fresh lettuce hit the vegetable wash station as pots filled with water simmered on the stove waiting for their share of the first batches of pasta. The table in the center of the room held everything from paring knives and cleavers to those solid meat tenderizers; all waiting to be collected and utilized by the expert chefs.

My fingers brushed over the jacket with the name Ellis embroidered on the left breast. It was all so busy. Not wanting to get in anyone's way, I collected the clipboard from its designated spot on the wall and crossed through the kitchen to the table at the back between the two sets of doors. One leading to the massive walk-in freezer and the other to a storage closet where they kept the cases of sauces, spices, and miscellaneous dry items necessary for their variety of Italian dishes and desserts.

Leaning on the table, minding my own business I sorted the inventory list into my preferred order. The hair on the back of my neck stood at attention. The buzz in the room continued, so I tried to ignore the inkling of danger approaching from behind. I rarely ignored the warning, years living in a sketchy part of town during my stint in college kept me on high alert. Yet, my mind couldn't fathom danger coming from anyone in the kitchen.

I got along with the staff well. They appeared to appreciate the efficiency I'd brought to Angelo's after the short stretch of chaos with Linda's sudden exit. I'd even implemented a couple of their ideas, rearranging the pantry to make finding and tracking what they needed a seamless task.

Still, alarms rang in my mind, my eyes flicking up to see a dark figure approaching in the shiny metal backsplash of the table.

"Look out!"

I reacted before my mind registered the warning. One of the female servers screamed just as my elbow slammed into the stomach of the frail body behind me. I turned, instinct kicking in as I thrust the butt of my hand upwards snapping my adversary's head backward. I only saw red as someone lifted Marcel's body upward swinging her away in the same motion as her arms flailed in an attempt to assault me.

My eyes widened when Marcel head butted Ellis in the midst of her attempt to finish the job she hadn't even gotten a chance to start. I caught sight of something small fall from what I assumed was Ellis's hair as he hurried to remove Marcel. Still in a bit of a daze, I took the three steps across the now empty kitchen, retrieving what I discovered to be some sort of electronic device from where it sat as a vast contrast against the light-colored floor. My fingers curled around the tiny contraption as Yusef re-entered the kitchen.

"Are you alright?" he asked, his hand grasping my arms as he gave me a once over.

"Yeah. I'm fine. Go help Ellis. Marcel head butted him, and I think he was losing his grip."

Yusef dashed away in the direction I indicated as the sound of a person scooping ice drew my attention.

"Let me see your hand," Charity said.

"Where'd you come from?"

"I heard the scream and came running. I'd ask you what happened, but I think I know." She examined my hand, wiping away the blood there with one of the ice cubes. "Are you cut?"

"No. That's Marcel's blood. I suspect she either has a busted lip or possibly a broken nose. I didn't mean to hurt her."

"Not your fault. And don't even think about blaming yourself. She attacked you." Charity retrieved the now discarded meat tenderizer. "She tried to hit you in the head with this."

The adrenaline now but a memory, my hand reached out for the table. I used it to steady myself, the realization setting in nearly stealing my breath away.

"Can you make it to the office?" Charity asked, concern forcing her eyes to narrow as she took me in.

"Yeah. You might want to get some ice on Marcel. Especially if it's her nose."

Charity nodded. "You have plenty of witnesses. Don't worry about this. We'll be in as soon as we can."

She was gone before I gathered my wits enough to exit the kitchen. I'd expected to find the staff milling about, trying to get a glimpse of the remaining events as they transpired. Instead, the area around the doors was empty, the narrow hallway leading to the office as well, which pleased me. I wasn't quite done processing the events and didn't know if I had it in me or even was supposed to discuss it with anyone.

An eerie quiet met me in the office. In the entire building. Everyone must be in shock. Who'd have thought on a regular day like this that an employee would attempt to assault another? I slid into the office chair, my head resting in my hands as I stared down at the tiny electronic device I'd dropped on the desk. My eyes refused to focus on it as they filled with tears. The emotions set in as the rage dissipated. Anger still pulled at my heart and mind and that was really what the tears represented.

I quickly wiped those tears away with the back of my hand as the door eased open and Ellis slipped through. He paused and I saw the worry in his eyes.

He pressed his back to the door, maintaining distance. "There was blood. Are you hurt?" He asked with quiet anticipation.

"Ha." I chuckled. "That bitch lucky I ain't t cut her ass." Ellis shot me a quizzical look I understood all too well. "Just because I opt not to use bad words, doesn't mean I don't know any."

"Oh."

I sniffed. "But I'm okay. Really."

He dragged one of the chairs from the dinette table over, placing it before me. His hands wrapped around mine, his fingers rubbing over my knuckles as he sat. "Are you sure?"

I nodded, my eyes darting from him to the tiny device I'd collected off the floor. I watched as his gaze followed mine, his shoulders tensing before releasing. A sigh followed. A sigh of what? Relief?

"Guess the cat's out the bag?" He half smiled at me like he'd been trying to figure out how to broach the subject but found the answer now presented itself.

"You're..."

"Eighty percent deaf in one ear. Yes." He picked up the hearing aid checking it over for damage before retrieving the case from his pocket and tucking it away.

"How? I mean you speak so well."

He gave my hand a reassuring squeeze. "It only happened a couple of years ago, so it hasn't affected my speech. It's one of the few lasting effects of the car accident."

"Car accident?"

"Yeah, we should talk about that too. But not here. And not now. I need to deal with the paperwork about this incident."

"Do you think she's going to press charges?"

"Not if she has any sense." He stood, and with the slight tug he gave my arm I did as well. "You have plenty of witnesses on your side who saw her attack you. Not to mention the camera footage."

I'd forgotten about the cameras all over the place. "Self-defense it is."

We settled into working on the paperwork. I hovered over his shoulder as he walked me through the legalities and the proper documentation, just in case.

"I don't foresee you having to do this. Especially since we are working on your exit strategy," Ellis said. He leaned back in the chair; fingers perched in a triangle as he admired the thoroughness of the report.

I too reviewed my statement. We'd spent the last thirty minutes going over the events. "I haven't run out yet. And if this incident didn't immediately send me packing, you should know I'll stay as long as you need me. But don't think I'm looking for a permanent position. I don't mind filling my time here right now, but once I decide what my next long-term move is I'll be striving harder to bail."

"I'm glad Marcel hasn't scared you off. She's been a handful for a while."

"Then why was she still here?"

"You sound like Yusef and Charity. I suppose, initially I saw a lot of myself in her. She was driven. Quick and willing to learn. My running between the two businesses meant limited direct interaction and Linda mentioned a time or two her concern about Marcel's constant badgering of the male employees but I guess I thought once she realized no one was interested she'd let it go."

"I grew up with women like Marcel. Her behavior can't be dismissed as youth. They've been groomed to find a man to complete their lives. I knew when she tried to confront me in the ladies' room, I hadn't seen the last of her trying to mark her territory. I just never expected her to resort to violence."

Ellis pressed the print button, the printer clicking as it turned on to warm up. "You handled yourself well, according to every staff member in the kitchen. Where'd you learn moves like that?'

"Wouldn't you like to know," I said with a grin.

"Truth be told, I would." He leaned closer to me staring up as I hovered. "I find it quite sexy that my woman knows how to defend herself. I must say you have been full of surprises, and I've enjoyed the process of discovering each and every one of them." Ellis plucked my hand from his shoulder, his lips brushing over my knuckles.

Our gazes locked and I moved in for a kiss. Unfortunately, someone clearing their throat shattered the moment before it even got started. We turned to find Yusef and Charity looking quite pleased as they stood in the doorway.

"Time for you two to go," Yusef said, handing the keys over to me. "He's supposed to be resting."

"And we can handle things around here." Charity said as she popped the top on the bottle of water she picked out of the mini office refrigerator.

Ellis retrieved the printed paperwork, pointing to the signature line. Once signed, he handed them to Yusef who scanned them before nodding his approval.

"I don't want to see either of you for at least two days. Do I make myself clear?"

I collected my purse and slid out the way so Yusef could take the seat Ellis vacated, "Payroll is ready for you."

Yusef shoo-ed us away. "Yeah yeah. Now, get out of here you love birds."

Chapter Thirty-Four

"I'd love to know when I became your woman," I said as I unpacked the grocery bag lining the items up on the kitchen counter for Ellis to put away in their designated spots.

After two pit stops on the way to his place, one for me to pack an overnight bag and the other to grab groceries, we'd decided to hold up in is condo until Yusef deemed us released from mandatory rest.

"I don't believe I can pinpoint an exact day or time."

"Try."

Ellis feigned deep thought as he gathered the newly purchased spices and moved to the other side of the kitchen to store them in the cabinet at the far end.

"Come up with an answer yet?" I shouted behind the open refrigerator door.

I piled the shelves with the Mediterranean salmon, shrimp, scallops, fresh greens, avocados, and herbs we'd purchased before tucking the juices onto the shelf. When I moved to close the door, strong arms encircled my waist drawing me back to the solidity of Ellis's chest. He was still soft around the middle, a man who indulged and enjoyed the rich dishes he prepared. Not to mention the sweet delicacies. But I liked him like that, just as he appeared to enjoy my layer of fluff.

The fullness of my hips and thighs were exactly why I refused to fear Marcel. The way Ellis watched me for the corner of his eye when I walked away. He was a man who appreciated a woman with a little meat on her bones. Marcel was but a drop in the bucket compared to the fountain of overflowing I offered.

With a shimmy of my hips Ellis loosened his grip enough for me to turn to face him. I cradled his face and for the first time I realized he didn't flinch or try to pull away. He'd pulled his hair all the way back this time revealing his ears, confirming that he'd used his hair to mask the hearing aid since the first time we'd met.

"Well?" I purred as he drew me close again. He wanted me; I could feel it. Hooded eyes stared down, drinking in the curiosity I sent his way with a raised eyebrow. There was something sexy about a man gazing into your eyes as he chewed on his bottom lip.

Ellis leaned closer, his lips but a breath from mine, before answering. "If I had to put a time to it." A quick peck, enough to send butterflies fluttering in my stomach. "I'd have to say," Another kiss, this time on the side of my mouth, "probably," and yet another peck on the other side. "The first time I kissed you."

No longer able to deny the burning desire between us, or tolerate his teasing, I drew Ellis into a kiss. My escaping moan reverberated through my body as my hands slid behind his neck. I wanted to crawl over him, to have him sate me until I whimpered like an over-indulged kitten. When his hands traveled lower cupping my behind, I took full advantage.

He lifted me with ease. I half expected him to utilize the now empty counter space. Instead, he walked us through the living room eventually depositing me on the bed.

Ellis never broke the kiss, instead deepening it as his hands explored my curves. He didn't rush the process and I enjoyed every gentle caress from the kisses he trailed down my neck to the way his fingers tiptoed over my thighs. I matched his level of exploration, my hands roaming over his back, nails raking over the taught muscle. While Ellis might be soft in the middle, his arms and back reflected the hours spent kneading dough and tending to fondant.

A growl reverberated over my body as I caressed a spot Ellis obviously enjoyed. He tensed, but in that good way and I felt other parts of him react which only encouraged me to play there even longer. He shuddered before tearing out of our kiss when he hit is breaking point. An audible growl followed as his hands raced to remove my top. I reciprocated, dragging his sweater over his head. Our hands entangled in the mix of cloth above my head.

I saw the desire in his eyes. The way he studied me, his chest heaving as he tried to catch his breath. Eventually he tossed our discarded clothes aside and reclaimed my lips, his hunger apparent in the way he nibbled on my upper lip before our tongues played in a mating dance.

Ellis rolled us onto our side giving one of his hands-free reign without having to bear his weight on one arm. It roamed from my back over my side. Then time froze and so did I. I knew the minute Ellis noticed, his body heat pulling away as he did too.

"Did I do something wrong?" He asked.

I struggled to answer. This was my hang-up; not his. As I'd done many times before while staring in the mirror, my hand slid over my stomach. They were still there, the reminders of what my body had been through the last year as I fought the will to die. My eyes closed, the burning behind them giving way to tears that streamed down onto the pillow beneath my head.

Warm fingers brushed the tears away before coming to rest on mine. Ellis slowly eased my hand away and I let him, allowing myself this moment to be vulnerable with him. He'd finally shared a secret with me and now it was time I did the same.

"We all have scars you know," Ellis said quietly, drawing our intertwined hands up to scar stretching up his jaw line to his ear. He held them there so I could feel that he too carried imperfections. "They are a part of our story. A part of our experience in this world. I want to know all of your stories. Especially the ones that have left the deepest scars."

The words melted my heart. Any doubt I'd harbored about the authenticity of this man's character wiped away in one clean swoop.

"Say something Soliel. Please? If I've done something wrong, tell me. If I've hurt you tell me. We're both consenting adults here, right? If this isn't what you want, then..."

I steeled myself, not wanting my voice to crack when I spoke, "It is what I want."

His features soften, "then what stopped you?"

"I," I turned from him, but he wouldn't let me retreat. Ellis released the hand he held at his jaw the fingers brushing away my tears as he encouraged me to look at him.

"Talk to me."

I relaxed, sinking into the feel of his other hand caressing my back. I snuggled closer, missing the feel of his warmth against my skin. "I've never let anyone see the scars. Let alone touch them." I didn't want to admit that I'd been starved of intimacy for far too long. It wasn't just that I hadn't had sex, but I missed the caresses of a partner who genuinely cared about my feelings and needs."

"I can try to avoid them if that's what you want."

"No," determined to sate the desire I'd ignored for far too long, I decided it was time for me to stop waiting on others and go after what I wanted. With a little nudge of my hips, Ellis rolled onto his back, allowing me to straddle his waist. The position was far from lady like with the skirt I wore but acting like a sophisticated lady in this moment didn't register anywhere on the radar.

Dropping any inhibitions drilled into me from childhood, I gave Ellis the most seductive smile I could manage. I grasped both of his hands placing each palm down on my thighs as I guided them upwards then beneath the cloth jacked up to my stomach. The time for talking had long passed. Now was the time for action.

Chapter Thirty-Five

As much as I tried, I couldn't ignore the buzzing on my wrist any longer. Not that I should. The alarmed signaled the ever-looming medication time. The bane of my existence, but a necessary evil to not end up strapped to a hospital bed writhing in pain until some white coat determined sedation was best and I slipped into a never-ending slumber.

I stretched, the sliver of retreating light daring to penetrate the folds between the wooden floor-length blinds indicating I hadn't made it entirely to nightfall. An interesting light in the shape of a bonsai tree sat in the corner, the tiny optics on the ends of the wired strands casting just enough of a glow to chase away the fear of the dark.

The soft bubbling of a streaming fountain added a layer of auditory ambience while a constant mist from a humidifier kept the room cool, or close to the perfect temperature to cuddle up with a loved one in bed and read a good book or wind down from a hectic day. A perfect place for meditation. And seduction. I buried my face in the pillow, inhaling the traces of orange and spice that always seemed to linger on Ellis's skin. I'd chalked it up to the layered flavors of the dishes and chocolate and yet he hadn't cooked anything.

The alarm buzzed again. Reluctant, yet resigned, I peeled myself from the comfort of Ellis's bed donning the shirt I'd nearly torn from his body. I was glad he'd taken the sweater off himself. The undershirt fared well but I'd have hated to accidentally damage the sweater in my haste to get my hands on the bare skin of his chest.

A soft blue glow illuminating the floor beneath the bed as I stood granted me enough light to not stumble into the shelf of plants near the door. When I finally broke the seal, the scent of the Mediterranean salmon engulfed me. It smelled absolutely divine. Like the imaginary coaxing hand from the cartoons of my childhood, the aroma hooked me drawing me through the living room to stop at the archway to the kitchen.

I found Ellis there, pinky finger poised to swipe chocolate off the spoon he held in the other hand. He'd donned a pair of gray sweatpants and a green t-shirt that covered the imprint of, well, I didn't want to think about what the shirt covered at the moment. Couldn't get distracted. I needed to take my medicine.

He cut his eye in my direction, "Are you going to make it a habit of sneaking up on me now that you know I probably won't hear you coming on that side?" Ellis made a production of tasting the chocolate, slowly drawing his finger through his lips.

"I wasn't trying to sneak up on you." I entered the kitchen, my arms carefully circling his waist. I rested my head between his shoulder blades, smiling up at him as he peered at me over his shoulder.

He swiped the pinky over the spoon again holding it out to me, "taste."

I slowly drew the digit into my mouth, my tongue swiping over it more than necessary. Had the watch not buzzed again I was sure we wouldn't make it to food quite yet. I allowed an umm to escape as I drew away from the enticing appendage and the man before me.

"Running?" He asked.

The rumble of his voice and his hooded eyes set my lady parts ablaze, but the watch again reminded me of the current priority. Thank goodness for one minute reminders. Good thing I hadn't shut the alarm off.

Ellis turned to draw me to him, but I stopped him with a hand to the chest. And what a chest, firm and...I shook the intruding thoughts from my mind focusing on the task. "I need to take my meds. And I need to eat."

He nodded his understanding. "Can you give me five minutes to finish the potatoes? I wanted to wait until you got up to whip them."

I plucked a stalk of asparagus from the pan next to the double boiler with the chocolate. Ellis shifted the potatoes from their spot on the stove pouring them into the glass bowl before securing it on the mixing stand.

"What happened to the wine?" I yelled over the sound of the mixer. I moved a few items around in the refrigerator but didn't see the bottle we'd purchased.

"Bottom cabinet in the corner." He pointed to the cabinet.

To my surprise, when I drew the door back, I found a wine cooler. "Now that was unexpected." I squatted, sliding a couple of bottles out to read the labels. "Any preferences?"

"Sauvignon Blac is traditional."

I slid the bottle of Riesling back into its slot and happily took the hand offered to me. "Thanks." Ellis handed over an electric bottle opener then went back to check his potatoes. "What? You're not going to ask if I know how to use it?"

"Do you?"

I gave the contraption a once over, "Well, yeah, but..."

"No buts. I've made enough assumptions." He scooped a portion of potatoes on each of the plates lined up on the counter, "I'm learning."

His confession warmed my heart. He'd just earned a long lustful good night kiss. With the wine open, I gathered two glasses and followed Ellis into the living room. He'd turned the television to one of those virtual fireplace stations and I realized he'd strategically placed candles around the space as well.

"Setting a mood?" I placed the glasses on the table, glad it was salvageable as Ellis held out a knife and fork.

He poured while I dug through my bag. Triumphantly retrieving the package of medicine at the bottom I ripped it open at the seam as I picked up my glass.

"Should you be drinking with those?" Ellis gestured to the handful of pills I held.

"Hard liquor, probably not. But since I'm eating, wine is fine."

"And so are you." Ellis quickly stuffed his mouth with potatoes as he watched me down the five pills one at a time. "Floaters huh," he commented, swiping his fork through my salmon, and holding it up for me to eat.

"What do you mean?"

"The pills. Most people tilt their heads back to swallow. With floaters, you do the opposite, tilt your head forward and the pills float to the back of the throat to swallow."

I considered his observation, "I never even thought about it." I shrugged. "Guess you're right. They are floaters." I concentrated on my food, enjoying the burst of flavor from the potatoes.

"So," Ellis said.

I stiffened, hand stopping mid scoop as I prepared to have the conversation about my health. Instead, Ellis surprised me.

"Care to tell me about how you learned to defend yourself so well."

I released a breath, leaning back as I chewed the last of the asparagus I'd just eaten. "I could say that's a funny story. I don't know why people assume because I'm cute, I can't fight."

"Oh, from what my employees said, there wasn't any fight necessary. You pretty much took Marcel out without batting an eye."

"Well, I spent three of my college years with Yaddi living in a hole in the wall apartment in the bluff. The guys below us weren't exactly on the up and up."

"Sounds like you had to learn to defend yourself?"

"On the contrary. They were the least of our concerns. Yaddi's cooking saved us the hassle. She'd keep their bellies stuffed which afforded us some level of protection. It also meant we never had to pay for food. At first, they'd send the kids upstairs with bags of meat, fruits, and vegetables and she'd throw something together. It was always plenty for us and them."

"Ah, Bribery?"

"I suppose. They were getting the trash stuff first. But we'd sit out on the stoop with them. Smoke. Play cards. Get drunk."

Ellis's brow furrowed, "You smoke?"

"Every once in a blue moon. But it's been a minute."

"I wouldn't take you for a smoker. Now your girl."

"You hit the nail on the head. I was pretty much the straight and narrow one of our crew. The dependable one."

Ellis finished off his potatoes, "the designated driver, huh."

"Yeah, where the hell were the ride shares back in my college days. Anyway, Eventually, Yaddi started giving them list of ingredients. She said If they wanted to keep getting fed, they'd bring her what she really needed."

"Did they comply?"

"Yep. Then word got around. She started slinging plates on the side which sometimes brought undue attention to our block."

"Bad for your neighbor's business huh?"

"Yeah. I think their rivals assumed we were their girls since we used to all hang out. They were cool people. Not necessarily my type but we knew if anything went down, they had our backs."

"Don't cutoff the hand that feeds you."

"Exactly. One night it got ugly around the spot. Somebody tried, well did, break into our apartment. I think they thought the guys downstairs lived up there. I was home that day, but Yaddi had made a run. They got the door open and were coming for me. I was holed up in the bathroom. Somebody must have heard me scream because the intruder turned tail and ran, I heard shots, but I didn't dare open the door. Next thing I know Yaddi was banging on the door and when I opened it, she was standing there, pistol in hand, the guys from downstairs at her back."

"I could definitely see her as a shooter."

"Most definitely. Shoot first, ask questions later. She was legal though. Can't say the same for our neighbors. Anyway, I was pretty shook-up. It took me a long time to feel comfortable there again. But the guys downstairs wanted to make sure if we needed to defend ourselves, we could. I'm sure they were more concerned about me than Yaddi. She proved that night that she didn't take no shit. Hell, I didn't even know we had a gun in the house."

"Did you learn to use it?"

"Reluctantly. But she made arrangements with the campus police and some of the sororities on campus to host a few self-defense courses. I learned a lot, not just the physical attack defense part, but other ways of protecting myself."

"Wait," Ellis paused with his glass inches away from his lips, "is that what you meant by Marcel was lucky you didn't cut her?"

"Yep. I ain't no fool. I always walk with knives or razor blades. Save for the airport, government offices, the police station of course, but the minute I cross that threshold its back where I need it."

Chapter Thirty-Six

The newly bound couple opted to save the remaining heavier conversations between them until the next day. With the weight of the food setting in, and another rump in the hay, they'd both slipped into a comforting slumber, a plan in place to do a little swimming and cooking at her place for a change of scenery.

The eight AM buzzing of Soliel's watch broke the spell of their quiet slumber. Ellis groaned at the interruption, his arms tightening around the comforting beauty in his arms. He didn't want to let her go and he made sure she knew this as well as he squeezed tighter each time she tried to wiggle out of his grasp.

Soliel's hand tapped his wrist. "Okay, I know you don't want to let me go, and believe me I'm in no rush to climb out the bed myself, but I need to take my meds and you're pressing on my bladder."

He quickly released the hold allowing Soliel to slide from the bed. She made a mad dash for the door as he rolled over into the now vacant spot. It smelled like her perfume, the refreshing undertones of cucumber and some sort of melon. It was cool and sweet all wrapped up in one with just a hint of cocoa he was sure originated from the oil she used in her hair.

Ellis reveled in the familiarity, the desire to have the scent always linger in his bed and on his skin drawing the corners of his lips up in a smile. He hadn't meant to fall for the beauty on the other side of the door. Hell, the last thing he'd been looking for was a steady woman in his life. He'd been down this road once, only for it to end in catastrophe.

The sun creeping through the blackout curtains tempted him from the comfort of the covers. He wrapped the green bamboo sheets around his waist gathering the long t-shirt he'd rolled Soliel's body out of only hours before. When she didn't return, he assumed she'd made a detour to take her meds.

He found her in the kitchen, glass of juice in hand as she popped yet another of the pills into her mouth. She appeared unconcerned with her nudity, batting his hand away when he offered her the shirt.

"I could get use to this view," Ellis said, taking in every ounce of her. He expected she'd change her mind at his scrutiny, or at least turn away. Instead, she popped the last pill into her mouth, took a swallow of the juice then wrapped the now free hand around the sheets tearing them away.

"Clothes are overrated."

Ellis forced himself not to reach for the cloth resting in a crumpled pile at his feet. However, he had little control over his body's reaction as she closed the distance between them planting a kiss on each cheek before she nibbled on his lower lip.

He pulled away, the stiffie between them a clear indication that if she wanted to finish what she started, he was both ready and willing to do just that. "You know if we keep this up, we'll never make it to your place."

Soliel shot him a devilish grin, her fingers claiming the prize she planned to work into submission. "We have plenty of time. A whole day ahead of us. What's an extra hour between lovers?"

With an inevitable detour to the bedroom at hand, a quick roll in the hay later they agreed no more touching until they made it to their next destination. Both held to their end of the bargain, at least until a short pursuit over the keys ended in a kiss that gave Soliel enough of an advantage to pluck them from where he'd stashed them in his pants in an attempt to keep her from finding them.

"You are supposed to be resting, remember?"

"Then I don't think a doctor would approve of sex and swimming. Hmm," he considered that combination, finding it amusing that the thought of swimming with Soliel might lead to another round of sex encouraging him to drop the idea of fighting her to drive, "I actually don't think I've been this relaxed in years. You are definitely good for my spirit,"

She regarded him coolly, collecting her purse and waiting by the door as he checked to make sure the fountains and lights were all off. "There is always the jacuzzi too. Nice and relaxing. It will help with those sudden aching muscles of yours."

Ellis attempted to elbow Soliel in the side, but she scooted out the way before he made contact. He'd complained about his shoulders being stiff as a way to get a massage out of her; not that he thought she wouldn't have given him one if he'd flat out asked. Still, she seemed to like the lightheartedness of his hints, and she played along, boosting his ego with comments about the definition of the muscles in his back and shoulders.

They made it to Yaddi's house in record time. Soliel whipped through the traffic with ease in his little car. He was still upset with himself for assuming she wouldn't be able to handle it.

"Looks like the rest of my stuff is here," Soliel said. She pulled into the driveway, stopping in front of the set of garage doors furthest from the main part of the house.

"You had your things shipped?"

"A friend of mine closed out my storage unit. I flew down and didn't want to be bothered with the packages at the airport. I did bring a trunk with my most valuable items and the electronics were brought down by another friend who was driving this way anyway."

"Wow."

"Yes, I love it when a grand plan comes together." She verified the car was in neutral and the parking brake set before she turned the ignition off. "Do you mind helping me..."

"I got them."

"We can drive them down if it's easier."

"How so?"

"This garage has double doors. I suspect the previous owners must have had a boat or maybe a trailer. You can pull straight through. Yaddi leaves this side open when the landscapers come so they drive the lawnmower through without having to unlock the gates."

"Convenient."

"Yep."

"Good to know, too. So, we don't have to trample through the house for the party."

Soliel exited the car, her arms resting on the roof. "I hadn't even considered that. I guess you can pull the catering van through." She peered at the garage, "Should be enough clearance."

After testing the weight of the boxes, Ellis opted to just carry them in. When they sat in a pile in the corner of the room Soliel designated as the workout space, Ellis plopped down on the couch.

"You look tired." Soliel commented. "Are you okay?"

He rolled his shoulders before stretching out his mid-section. "Yeah, just a little slow. The doctor said pumping my stomach would make me sore. Well, that and the restraints. I guess I hadn't thought much of it until moving those boxes."

She handed him a bottle of orange juice, concern furrowing her brow. "Pumping your stomach?"

Damn. He'd forgotten they hadn't talked about the details of his hospital stay. She probably thought Yusef had just taken him to a doctor to get checked out just to be safe. He'd cut the id band off in the truck before going into Angelo's.

"Yeah," he conceded, using the juice as an excuse to gather his thoughts. He slowly downed the liquid, his head back to not meet her glare.

The silence lingered, seconds ticking by. Soliel gave in before he finished. "You're stalling."

Busted. "It's no big deal."

"You did not just say that."

"Alright, it might be a big deal and maybe I should be taking the doctor's orders more seriously."

"No swimming for you." Ellis narrowed his eyes at her before feigning a pout. "Fine, I give, you can swim. But I'll be watching you like a hawk."

"Feel free. I love it when you watch me."

She stood at that, again putting space between them. While they agreed on no touching, the contract was now void since they'd reached the final destination.

"If you're up to it, you can help me get these cakes started. The party is only a couple of weeks away and the longer they sit the better they get."

"You mean to tell me you're going to show me your secrets?"

"I don't mind."

Together, they gathered the ingredients, ultimately deciding to work in Yaddi's kitchen which afforded them much more space to maneuver without being on top of each other.

Ellis stood on the side of the island opposite Soliel watching as she carefully measured out the ingredients one by one starting with flour, butter, and sugar. She gathered the six eggs she'd removed from the refrigerator upon their arrival and brought them to the counter in a bowl.

"This is more than I expected," Ellis said taking inventory of the rows of bowls and measuring cups.

"Black cake is a process. You missed the fun part, cutting up the fruit to soak. We started that weeks ago."

Gathering a cast iron Dutch oven and placing it over the burner Soliel measured out brown sugar. "You know, this cake is actually dangerous to make."

"Dangerous how?"

"Well," she poured the brown sugar into the pot turning the heat on medium before filling the electric kettle on the counter with water from the filtered dispenser and setting it to boil. "I'll show you in a minute. In the meantime, can you grab those two bottles of rum off the top shelf. I don't know why she always puts them up there. Yaddi knows I'm vertically challenged."

Ellis retrieved the two bottles. He placed them on the counter next to two jars Soliel placed with the gathering of the other items for the cake. The jars contained a murky liquid with chunks of something floating inside. He turned the jars around picking them up and peering closer to determine the contents. "What is this?"

Soliel looked up from the glass jar of mixed peel she was pouring out. "The fruit. Like the cake, the longer it sits the better it gets."

"Now this sounds dangerous."

"Not as dangerous as the fruit at a Greek party. Rule number one, never ever drink anything made in a metal trash can or a bathtub. Rule number two don't eat the fruit. Everclear is the Devil, and it will come for you."

"This fruit has been soaking in Everclear."

"No, rum and cherry wine. Still, the logic is the same. Some of the alcohol cooks out, but part of the traditional Trinidadian black cake is fruit soaked in alcohol."

ELLIS JOINED ME AT the stove, watching over my shoulder while I constantly stirred the cooking sugar.

With my attention split between the task at hand and the heat pulsing off of the man hovering behind me I asked, "Are you going to tell me more about what triggered you the other day?"

He stiffened, though he quickly stepped away to mask the reaction. The looming conversation made him uncomfortable, and I couldn't blame him. But we needed to have this talk. I needed to know of anything I should be on the lookout for just in case he felt the need to repeat the events of the other night. We'd tip-toed around this conversation all yesterday and vowed to hash it out today. Still, I felt if I didn't broach the subject, he'd be content to let it drift away into obscurity.

"My ex-wife tried to kill me and ended up killing our son in the process."

My hand stilled at the confession, the shock rocking any sense of confidence in my mind that while the events might have been traumatic, they couldn't have been that bad. His admission unseated me. I almost dropped the spoon. Unable to form words I went back to stirring.

A heavy silence hung between us as a plethora of questions vying for answers flooded my mind. Yet, I couldn't bring myself to utter one word. How, I asked myself, how could he be with a woman capable of trying to kill him. And then his son. Their son. To put the life of an innocent in danger. It was definitely a lot to take in.

"Say something Soliel."

I failed horribly at steadying my shaking voice. "I...I don't know what to say."

Ellis leaned against the opposite counter. "I'm sure you have questions."

The sugar darkened, the smell of it burning permeating from the cast iron. The kettle boiled as well, both offering distractions. I'd thought I was prepared for this conversation but after his revelation, I wasn't sure I could stomach the details.

"Hand me the kettle please."

My words came out slow. Calculated. I was trying to hold it together. He complied and while I'd removed the pot from the heat to a cold burner, the minute the boiling water hit the sugar it bubbled and popped like a lava spewing volcano.

"Dammit!" I snatched my hand away as some of the sugar popped onto my arm. Out of it, I barely noticed as Ellis guided me to the sink turning on the cool water and holding my arm beneath it. "Keep stirring that," I said shooing him away.

Ellis complied; the wooden spoon clasped tightly in his hand. "You don't have to worry about her coming after you. She's in jail and will be for a long time." He looked away embarrassedly, like the words sort of found their way out of their own accord.

Giving the now blistering burns the once over but deciding there wasn't much I could do about it right now, I plucked the spoon from his fingers, reclaiming my spot at the stove. I could tell he wanted to say more. Yet, with his constant shuffling of the measured-out bowls of ingredients on the counter, I suspected this wasn't going as he'd played it over in his mind.

"You don't have to talk about it if..."

"I'm fine with talking about it. I feel like I need to talk to you about it. But only if you're okay with it as well. The entire fiasco is a lot to take in."

So, he considered his previous marriage a fiasco. Would he feel the same if we reach the marriage level only to have it fall apart? I pondered my approach to this delicate conversation wanting to tread carefully. I didn't want him to feel like I was accusing him of the downfall of the marriage.

"How did you end up with a woman wanting you dead?"

"She wasn't always that way. I don't even recall when it started falling apart. All I know is, she turned into a stalker when I opened The Naughty Chocolatier." He toyed with an apple plucked from the basket of fruit in the center of the island. "New businesses take a lot of time. I supposed she felt neglected, though she shouldn't have." He said the last part under his breath, but I heard the disdain. "I don't know. Maybe me being away and her being left with our son sent her off the deep end."

"Did she just not want you to have the other business?"

"Maybe. Our finances took an initial hit. She was not pleased at all when I reminded her to ease off the spending for a while. I knew the place would be a success. The customers at Angelo's were the reason I dared to work on the venture. They raved about my chocolate confections and a few even offered to invest. I tried to talk to Denise about it, but she kept saying she was fine. That everything was fine."

"Fine is definitely a dangerous word in a woman's vocabulary."

"I've known that for a long time, but I didn't know what else to do. She wouldn't talk to me and like I said getting the business up and running took every spare moment I wasn't spending with our son or at Angelo's."

"How long were you two married?"

"Nine years."

He grew distant, his eyes roaming the room as he remembered.

"Was it ever happy?" I joined him at the island adding a little more water to the pot. The popping had ceased now that the sugar had cooled. The added water only thinned the burnt sugar.

"Early on. We dated for two years before getting married. She was there when my mother and grandmother died. She was there when Mr. Angelo passed. I thought she had my back through thick and thin."

"And you really think the new business led to the downfall?"

Ellis sighed. His mind wandering along with his gaze.

I stood by quietly as he deliberated. Emotions passing over his face furrowing his brow and turning his lips down at the corners. Was he blaming his wife for everything or was he considering his role in the downturn of the relationship?

"Ellis?" I finally said after the silence lingered longer than expected.

"I overlooked a few red flags. I mean, no one's perfect. She made mistakes. I made mistakes."

"Did you cheat on her?"

"No. No, I would never. I loved her. She was my wife. My confidant. The mother of my only child."

He responded quickly and a bit defensively, but his earlier comment made me believe him that much more. "Yet, you still seem to feel responsible for the way the marriage ended."

"I don't know. I think in her own way she was asking for more time from me. She needed constant confirmation. Early on she made it clear she was emotionally high maintenance. We worked through her abandonment trauma, or at least I thought we had. But Denise always needed to be the center of everything. Even with the time commitment to the other business she was still the center of my world. Her and our son. If she had just given me more time to get the business up and running, I could have spent more time with them both."

I heard the emotion rising in his voice, so I changed direction. "Tell me about the accident."

"It wasn't an accident," he snapped, and I almost stepped back at the harsh declaration. "She meant to hit me." He turned, rounding the island before starting to pace. "She meant to send me over the edge of that embankment to my death."

"Are you sure?" I kept my gaze transfixed on the ingredients. I added them a little at a time to the mixing bowl alternating between wet and dry items folding them in before adding more.

"She knew exactly where I would be and when I'd be there. When the police checked her phone, they discovered a tracking app. The forensic team found a tracking device beneath the license plate on my truck. She waited till I got to just the right spot to ram me."

That got my attention. I looked up, staring at his back when he stopped. Stunned.

"I didn't want to believe it. I refused too even after Yusef repeated the information a second time. I just couldn't wrap my head around the idea of her resorting to...." The words fell away, silence thickening until his shoulder's rolled forward in defeat. "The officer who came to question me about what I remembered confirmed it and I couldn't do anything but accept the facts. My wife had tried to kill me."

"I don't see how you trying to get a new business off the ground would push her to the point of trying to kill you." The words came out dismissive. I regretted the delivery, though not the comment itself.

"It wasn't just the business." Ellis replaced the apple before staring out the window over the sink into the back yard.

"Tell me."

He sighed heavily; eyes narrowed before he spoke. "She found out I had filed for divorce and for custody of our son. I kept my confirmations to myself, but I knew she was cheating on me. I even had a DNA test done on our son because she'd been messing with the guy for years."

"Oh wow." I absorbed the remainder of the story as Ellis purged it.

"Truth be told, her infidelity made me start the second business. The Naughty Chocolatier gave me an excuse to pull away from her. Give me time to think on what I wanted to do. I still loved her, but I just wasn't sure I wanted to stay. Of course, I didn't think about it that way at first, but while in rehab and therapy it all started to make sense to me. I wasn't ready to confront her about the cheating, so I avoided the conversation by finding something, anything to occupy every minute of my time."

"And Angelo's wasn't enough?"

"Too many people around. I didn't want to talk about what was going on at home. I knew either Yusef or Charity would get suspicious if I started hanging around more than usual. It was easier to put my hurt and frustration into the physical aspect of getting The Naughty Chocolatier together than to face them."

"And your son?" My fingers tightened on the edge of the counter, heart aching and sinking with each word.

"She brought him with her. He'd undone the seatbelt to grab something he'd dropped. The cops suspected she'd been sitting in that parking lot for hours watching. Waiting. He didn't stand a chance."

Ellis's words cut me to the core, my stomach twisting in knots as I caught a flash of memory that retreated before my brain processed it. I doubled over, hands on my thighs as emotion threatened to overwhelm me. Stumbling back, the counter kept me from tipping backwards as I sniffed. I buried my face in my hands, mouth contorting as I fought with everything inside to not completely collapse.

My sniffling must have alerted Ellis. He drew near, face blurring as tears pooled in my eyes before sliding down my cheeks.

"What's wrong?" He asked, pulling me into a hug.

I shook against him, almost violently as he held on to me. The ache inside the depths of my spirit refused to release as I inhaled the sweet lingering of the soap against his skin. I tried to relax, my lungs struggling to catch a breath. I heard the oven buzz before the image of light barreling down on me clouded my mind. My fist buried in the shirt of the man holding me tight, I submitted to the intense wave of emotion and wailed.

Chapter Thirty-Seven

When the agony of loss abated, I curled further into Ellis as he cradled me in his lap. He'd carried me to Yaddi's couch keeping me close to his heart as years of trapped emotion poured out of me. Though the initial tears were for me, the latter were for him. For the loss of his son. The loss of all he'd known before the incident that changed everything.

Though I didn't know why, I connected with his loss and the pain he must have felt. It rang true in a way that made my soul ache. I wanted to take the pain and sorrow from him even though I had no idea what I'd do with it. I just wanted to make everything better.

A warm thumb swiped at drying tears as I concentrated on breathing. Ellis held me close, the consistent cadence of his heartbeat soothing my aching soul. He sighed, as if a tightly wound knot between us slowly unraveled. Only then did I look up to see the remnants of tears on his cheeks.

I loosened my grip on his shirt. Reaching up, I cradled his face. No words needed to be spoken. We'd bonded in a way I didn't think either of us had expected and yet we'd needed. Eventually his solemn expression broke, a smile tugging at the corners of his lips as he leaned over and kissed my forehead.

"I'm sorry," I said when he pulled me into hug. "I didn't mean to fall apart like that."

"You're soft-hearted," he replied, the rumble of his voice echoing through my body. "I need a soft-hearted woman in my life."

I drew back, just enough to be able to look him in the eye, "Just because I'm soft-hearted doesn't mean you can take advantage."

"Believe me. I know that all too well. Soft-hearted people are some of the strongest people in the world. Though soft-hearted probably isn't the best description."

I drew circles on his arm until he wrapped his larger hands around mine crossing my arms. It was an endearing gesture, a hug from behind. "Compassionate?"

"Yes. I think that's what it is. This world has so little left. I'm glad I've found you."

"You say that now. Until I start to work your nerves." My watch buzzed. Medicine time. I expected Ellis to release my arms so I could dismiss the alarm. Instead, he held me that much closer. "Ellis?" I asked, concerned when his grip tightened. His breathing grew deeper, heavier, and more intent. Instead of pulling away I ignored the vibrating and allowed him to hold me close as he processed his thoughts.

The moment passed quickly, the buzzing ending after its two-minute interval. Ellis granted my reprieve allowing me to climb from the couch.

"I'll be right back."

He offered a smile and shifted from the stretched-out position to sitting upright. He didn't move to stand though as his hands worked to gather his locs and tie them back. I gave him one last quick glance over my shoulder before descending the stairs to the lower level.

Instead of gathering one of the pre-made packs of meds from the nightstand, I opted to gather the pills directly from the bottles. I needed to check my stash anyway, a refill due in the next couple of weeks. I also added a reminder in my phone to setup a follow-up appointment. I'd yet to find a doctor in Atlanta since the move and would have to make a trip north in the coming weeks to avoid too much of a hassle.

Bloodshot eyes stared back at me in the mirror, the tell-tale sign of ugly crying. I looked a hot mess. Yet, I felt light as a feather. Purging pent up emotion did that to the soul and I needed to be free. To feel safe enough with someone to be vulnerable. For the first time in a long time, I felt I'd found that person.

Still, I vowed to remain cautious. My relationship with Daniel started with a level of comfort I hadn't known and look how that turned out. No, I'd remain vigilant, giving some of myself but keeping an eye out for red flags on the horizon before falling hopelessly down the love abyss.

Three pills popped and a warm rag to wipe away the remnants of my emotional submission, I ascended the stairs to find Ellis at the island, a piece of Yaddi's aloe vera plant in hand as he scooped the contents out with a spoon.

Our eyes locked. "Come, let me get a look at those burns."

I'd forgotten all about them between the shock of his words and the bursting of the damn around my emotions. I studied the welts on my arm as I crossed the kitchen. He took considerable care rubbing each of the four areas with contents of the cold spoon slathered in aloe.

"That feels wonderful."

"Nature's healer."

I reached around him plucking a snack sized zipper topped bag from one of the drawers. I held it out and he slid the remainder of the plant and the gel he'd collected into the bag before placing it on a shelf in the fridge.

"Now where were we?" He asked, his hand gesturing to the half-completed cakes.

We worked in unison, him handing the appropriate ingredients when I requested them. I could have dumped everything in at once and used the electric mixer, but I needed the process of mixing by hand as a distraction to keep from crawling back into his arms. I desired to be close to Ellis, to curl up with him until the sun set then make love until sunrise. But I also didn't want to get lost in the shared physical passion. There was still more I wanted to learn about his past and things I needed to share about mine.

With the lost time from my breakdown, the sun's descent met us by the time we popped the cakes into the oven. It wasn't late per se, sixish by the clock on the microwave. Still, night crept in, the solar lamps lining the pool bursting to life with the escape of the last light of day. "How about a dip while these bake?"

"Are you trying to get me out of my clothes?" Ellis chided, behind a devilish grin.

"Why," I feigned my most Southern-belle accent possible, "I'd never." I dashed for the stairs, bits of clothing flying off in my wake as I made a b-line for the heated pool. Not that it needed to be heated at this point. End of November or not the upside to the south was the surprise warm evening and tonight Mother Nature blessed us with balmy high sixties.

I dove in the deep end making a lap reminiscing on how much I'd missed warm winter nights during the last few years above the Mason Dixon. While I enjoyed my indoor heated pool at my former home, there was nothing like swimming beneath the stars. Ellis soon joined me, though he eased in instead of diving in headfirst.

"Perfect temperature," he commented going all the way under before reemerging behind me.

"It has some sort of regulator on it. I checked it before I came back upstairs."

"Does it run all the time. I mean," he backstroked away resting on the side of the pool where he could stand on the bottom, "isn't that a waste of energy?"

"Solar. The whole freaking house is. She even has a cistern system even though the house is hooked up to the city water. The people who lived here before she bought the place had all kinds of nifty apocalyptic, off the grid systems installed. When the house was built, it was on well water. The first thing Yaddi did was cap it off when she found out city hookups were available."

"Bet that wasn't cheap."

I relaxed floating in the warm salt water. "Look around. Money only half registers for Yaddi. I think the house is actually paid off. She's good at what she does but she manages her finances like she still living in that house in the trap."

"Interesting. What about you?" He swam away from the wall making a round across the pool before settling on floating next to me. "Have you figured out what's next on your life path?"

"I have a few ideas. Of course, I want to make sure Charity is up to speed before I make any sudden moves. I promised you that much."

"I hope you don't feel obligated. I can train her."

"I want to. I like Charity and she seems more than capable. I think she'll pick up everything quickly."

"She will. I should have offered her the position in the first place. I mean, after Linda left. Besides it's not all foreign to her. She helped a lot while I was," he paused.

I assumed he didn't want to upset me, so I finished the statement myself. "Indisposed?"

"Yeah. I don't know what I would have done without she and Yusef. Between the two, Angelo's continued to run smoothly until I returned. They kept me up to speed but didn't rush my recovery. I was able to heal at my own pace both physically and mentally."

"Do you think you've healed? I mean entirely?"

"I won't ever be the man I was before the accident. I can't get any of that back. But I can continue to build forward. It still hurts to think about Devon sometimes though."

"That was your son's name?"

"Yeah. He was such a vibrant kid. He loved soccer. We'd spend hours early in the morning before I had to go to work, or he had to go to school going over drills. He was good at it too. His coaches even said so."

"I hate he was stolen from you."

Ellis's fingers tightened around mine, "Me too. I suppose the silver lining in all of this is you being sent to me."

I didn't know what to say, so I chose to focus on the feel of his fingers against mine. The sense of weightlessness as I concentrated on letting my body relax so I could continue to float in utter contentment with my man beneath the twinkling of the stars. Crickets, nature's nighttime musicians, filled the silence with their melodies as a light breeze rustled the last of the leaves clinging to the trees.

"Do you want children?"

The question startled me out of my musings bringing me back to the present. I shrugged, which shifted my weight enough that I had to adjust to keep my head from going under. The spell of relaxation broken, I encouraged Ellis to follow me to the edge of the pool where I effortlessly lifted myself up to perch on the edge and immediately regretted it as the concrete scraped my bare bottom. I quickly dropped back into the water wading over to the stairs to properly climb out.

Ellis followed a step behind accepting the towel I held out to him and wrapping it around his waist. I hated to lose the view, but I didn't want to have this conversation in the buff in case he got any ideas. Besides, I needed to check the other 'cakes.'

Chapter Thirty-Eight

I appreciated Ellis not pressing for an immediate answer as we set the cakes to cool and made dinner. I pondered the question while we worked, music from the television filling the silence as we danced around one another in the confines of the kitchen. Did I still want children?

We gathered the plates. Ellis tucked a bottle of Bellini peach under his arm. He managed two wine glasses between his fingers while balancing plates on the same arm.

"Show off," I said plucking the covered tray of confections he'd brought for dessert.

"It took me years to master this. I'll take room temperature plates over steaming hot ones fresh from the kitchen any day."

A thought caught me and before considering it any further I blurted out, "wait, is that why the wait staff always wear long sleeves?" He only shook his head in disbelief. "Well duh."

I retrieved the blanket from one of the lawn chairs, a discard from a couple of days earlier when I'd performed another burning bowl and convening with the ancestors ritual. Luckily it remained dry thanks to the rain holding off until the coming days. We'd enjoy this last night before showers graced our doorstep.

With the citronella torches lit around the area we laid, we dug into dinner. I toyed with the mushrooms in my salad, mind distracted, contemplating the answer to the question about children.

"Penny for your thoughts?"

I took a long sip of wine watching him over the rim of the narrow glass. "I don't know."

His fork froze midair, brow furrowing as he watched me. "You don't know what?"

"The answer to your question." I looked away, my gaze intent on the plate instead of the man sitting next to me, "About children. I don't know."

Understanding, he ate the fork full of food dabbing the remnants of the homemade salad dressing from his lips before speaking. "You don't know the answer to the question?"

"I don't know if I want children. I mean, I hadn't even thought about it."

"You've never tried?"

"I haven't tried not to, if that's what you're getting at. I guess I've always been in the camp of if it's meant to be it will. And if not, well, it is what it is."

"But you've never actively tried to have a family?"

"No, I wasn't out sowing my wild oats at any point in my life with the specific intent to procreate." I wanted to retract the jab immediately after the last word tumbled recklessly from my mouth. While I meant what I said, the delivery cut deep even to my own ears. "Sorry. That didn't come out right."

"Your truth is your truth. I hope you don't think I was implying that you were," he chewed on his bottom lip, searching for the right word.

I rescued him from the torture, "I understood. I actually don't know why that touched a nerve."

"Regret?"

"Possibly. But I also look at the world today and," my heart grew heavy, I both appreciated the wonderful life I'd lived thus far while still feeling for those on the other end of the spectrum trying to keep a roof over their head or having to decide between food and medicine. 'I don't know. I mean, I think I would have been a great mother. And under the circumstances my kids would have had a stable home."

"You mean up until it all fell apart?"

That snapped me back to reality sending me down the path of would've, could've, and what might have been. I sighed heavily as I stared out over the still water of the pond.

"Don't get me wrong, neither of us is a spring chicken. But we don't exactly have one foot in the grave either. Plenty of couples our age are just embarking on the journey of starting a family. Especially for women. If it something you think you still want, it's not exactly a lost cause."

His response caught me of guard. Surely, he wasn't thinking of having another child now. "Is that a deal breaker for you?"

"What?"

"Kids."

"No. Like you said, if it is meant to be it will be. And if not, there are plenty of children looking for good homes with people who can love, care, and guide them."

"You've considered adoption then?" I finished my salad, turning to the next course on the plate. I fought the urge to skip straight to dessert though the scents of the decadent chocolate truffles tugged at my senses.

"I have. Even as a single parent. I'd choose an older child though. Everyone wants babies and while I'd be open to doing the diaper and sleepless nights thing with my own children, I think I could offer a better opportunity to an older child who might be overlooked because, again, everyone wants babies." He turned to me, all serious as if my answer to the next question determined if our relationship fizzled out right now. "Would that be a deal breaker for you?"

Instead of beating around the bush or taking too much time to think, I listened to my gut. "No, children either way aren't a deal breaker for me. If anything, I think I can look back at my life, the freedoms I've had from financial stability to traveling the world and be okay with the shift to motherhood."

"Could you see having a family with me?"

"Is there a reason you're asking me these questions? I mean, I know, if I want to have a baby my clock is winding down and all."

"I'm not trying to rush anything. But I also don't want to waste time. Yours or mine. I don't have my heart set on a family."

"Been there done that huh?"

"Yeah. Don't get me wrong I do want to settle down. Get married again if, or when, I find the right person. Children are an open topic but if you were dead set on having babies and wanted to start right now, I'd definitely have to reconsider."

My fingers found his, my eyes never wavering from his. "I'm open to it either way. And I'm in no rush. Should we reach that threshold, we'll let the chips fall where they may." I leaned in for a kiss to seal the deal. "Agreed?"

With a quick peck on the lips, Ellis responded, "agreed."

"Speaking of settling down..." I waited for Ellis to give me his full attention again.

"Uh oh. That doesn't sound good."

I plopped a shrimp into my mouth chewing slowly, devilishly watching the tension growing beneath his gaze. I eventually granted him a reprieve. "Are you dead set on city living."

"Oh heaven's no. The condo was a quick compromise. The market was good. It was a place I knew I could flip with minimal upgrades. It was affordable. Convenient to the restaurant and therapy. Since I needed someone to stay with me Yusef and Charity tag-teamed and it was perfect for everyone. After all that happened, I, well I just couldn't go back to that house."

"Family comes in many forms. Biology is not a requirement. Those two are definitely family."

"Agreed. What about you? Do you love the flashing lights of the city?"

"Hard pass. I'm a country girl. Or citified country if you will. As much as I love this place, this is a little far away from civilization even for me." Leaves rustled to their right, the glowing eyes of a ground foraging critter flashing in the glow of the moonlight as it moved along the line of the trees. "I do need greenery in my life. I miss my gardens immensely. I've been looking for a place closer to the city that still has a decent amount of land. But I'm not going to pay an arm and a leg for it. I need another project, something to occupy my time when I'm done at Angelo's."

"You don't have to be done. You are more than welcome to stay."

"No. I do."

We lightened the conversation for the rest of our picnic by the pond, sticking to safer topics like our most embarrassing childhood moments and most beloved holiday experiences. By the time we finished dinner and dessert the temperature waned. Even the crickets retreated, the silence in our slice of paradise unnerving.

I stretched rolling the tension from my neck and flexing my fingers to get the circulation going again. I'd been on my side too long, but I hadn't been able to look away from the man meticulously splitting each chocolate truffle before feeding it to me. I'd sucked on his fingers in the process, and we'd stolen kisses, feigning the need to remove a rogue drop of chocolate from the lips of the other.

Eventually, we returned to the house, packing the cakes away in separate tins and tucking them into the pantry for safe keeping until the party.

I reveled in the feel of Ellis against my back as we stopped at the bottom of the stairs. While he'd thrown on a pair of sweatpants before dinner, he'd chosen to remain shirtless. His skin was warm where it touched mine, the dip in the back of the housedress I'd donned offering no barrier for skin-to-skin contact as his arms circled my waist. He propped his chin on my shoulder before nuzzling my neck.

"Are you going to be able to sleep here tonight?" I asked. My hands came to rest on top of his as I sank into the comfort of his embrace.

"Why do you ask?"

"Well, your bedroom is conducive to sleep. Between the white noise and plants. The fountains. Best I can offer is a bit of aroma therapy. There aren't any windows in my bedroom so light isn't an issue."

"Oh, are you saying I've been upgraded? I'm not relegated to the theater seating anymore."

"Um, after last night," I bit my lip trying to hide my smile and failing miserably, "I think I'm the one getting an upgrade."

He gave me a squeeze before turning me to face him. "I should be fine. Besides, if I can't sleep, I don't mind so long as you're next to me."

"I do have something that can help you sleep,"

"Do you now?"

I playfully pushed his shoulder slipping from his grasp as I crossed the living area and stopped in front of a glass doored cabinet. I rambled through the bottles plucking one from the rear and holding it out for him.

"What's this?" He asked, examining the label.

"Magnesium oil. If for some reason I'm unsuccessful at putting you to sleep," his eyebrow rose at my insinuation, "or you can't stay asleep, rub a few drops into the bottom of your feet. Now, let's see if we can get the sandman to visit tonight."

ELLIS TIGHTENED HIS grip around the body lying in the bed with him. Another nightmare he mumbled still half under the spell of the sandman.

"Ellis. Ellis wake up. What is that noise?"

The violent shaking of his shoulder tore Ellis from dreamland sending him sitting up in bed. Only then did he hear the muffled but still loud alarm. He'd been sleeping on his good side, Soliel preferring the wall side of the bed. He'd thought the flailing was his son having another nightmare.

"Shit." He scurried from the bed hitting his foot on something hard that sent him plopping back down before reaching his destination. The room was pitch black save for the sliver of light from the corner of the bedroom door daring to peak around the pile of clothes they'd left there.

A moment later, the ceiling lit up with images of the night sky. Planets circled in waves of colorful nebula, dancing over the canvas of white paint to offer enough light to retrieve the phone from the pocket of his discarded pants by the bedroom door. He silenced the alarm, scrolling through the alerts from the security company monitoring Angelo's.

"Something wrong?" Came a soft voice from behind.

Ellis glanced over his shoulder at the Goddess propped up on one arm watching him from the other side of the room. She hadn't tried to hide her nudity, but he forced himself not to get distracted. Luckily, the phone rang, pulling him back to the emergency.

"I need to take this. It's probably the alarm company. I'll be right back."

He stepped out, hoping Soliel didn't dress or follow. While he needed to tend to this business, there was no need for her to interrupt her night to tag along. With a swipe of a finger, Ellis answered the call without even looking at the number.

"Don't even think about leaving," Yusef said on the other end of the line.

"What's going on?"

"Not sure. The window sensor went off first. I thought it was just a fluke. But then the office door alarm activated. Someone must have broken in."

"I'm at Soliel's place. I can be there in an hour."

"I figured. And I can be there in twenty minutes." The line rustled, like clothing rubbing against a headset. "Let me handle this. Besides, you're still on rest."

"Yusef."

"I got this Ellis. I'll call if the place has miraculously burned to ashes. Other than that, it can wait until morning. It's probably just some kids. They won't find much unless they have an inkling for high end cooking equipment. Charity and I have the laptops, I made the bank drop before getting here and of course the liquor is locked up."

"Fine," Ellis relented. He wasn't happy about the situation, but Yusef was right. They didn't both need to be there, and he was closer. Still, an uneasiness crept in. Like this had been the next brink waiting to drop.

"Now go back to bed. I'll catch up with you in the morning."

The call ended, Yusef hanging up to not give Ellis the opportunity to protest further. He glanced at the clock, discovering it was five in the morning. He'd never get back to sleep at this point. Meandering back into the bedroom he found Soliel stretched out, eyes closed. The quiet rhythmic pattern of her breathing told him she'd fallen back to sleep.

Not wanting to disturb her slumber, Ellis donned his pants and slipped from the room.

Chapter Thirty-Nine

The sweet aroma of waffles enticed me from slumber. Immediately my arm swung over to the side of the bed Ellis vacated. Cold. So, he hadn't come back to bed after the call last night. I understood his anxiety, the not knowing if everything was okay at Angelo's. The fact that I smelled breakfast meant he hadn't snuck out to check on the place without me.

I tossed on the discarded dress not wanting to distract Ellis as he worked around a hot stove. The smell of bacon greeted me, my stomach happily approving of the potential meal. I didn't immediately approach, my gaze lingering on the muscles in Ellis's back as he added more milk to the waffle mix before pouring the next one.

"Good morning," I said claiming a seat at the island opposite to him. He'd already set out two proper place settings: a creme and gold filigree placemat, spoon, knife, and fork in the appropriate formal left to right order for each of them. Seeing the meal was almost complete, I filled our glasses with juice, contemplating mimosas before deciding we'd had enough last night.

Ellis turned at my greeting, his eyes roaming over my face. A smile followed, "Good morning beautiful. I assume since I found a waffle iron in the cabinet you like waffles?"

"Waffles are fine."

"I can't promise they'll be perfect. I must admit this is my first time making them with sesame milk."

"They look like they are turning out just fine." I watched him flip the bacon in the pan before removing the last waffle. "They smell divine."

"I'm going to take that compliment. Hope they taste as good as they look."

Bacon drained; blueberries sprinkled on the pancakes; Ellis joined me at the counter to eat. I slathered my waffle in syrup.

"Hiding the taste already? You haven't even tried it."

"I know they're good. Everything you make turns out perfectly. Plus, I usually use sesame milk, so I expect the underlying nut flavor."

He bit into a slice of bacon, brittle pieces falling to his plate in the process. "And the syrup?"

"Habit," I admitted. "I'm a southerner and I likes my sugar."

"One day it's going to catch up with you."

"I know. I need to do better. Of course, dating a chocolatier isn't exactly making that decision any easier."

Ellis cut his eye in my direction. He plopped a blueberry in his mouth then proceeded to do exactly what I had done and slather his waffle with more syrup than necessary. "I do make sugar-free confections."

"Oh really? Well then, my waistline might be safe after all." I dug in, finishing half my waffle before coming up for air. "These are perfect. I bet they'd sell like hotcakes with a scoop of ice cream and chocolate syrup."

"Possibly, I do like the nutty flavor, add a dash of cinnamon. Maybe some spiced apples or peaches. I can taste it now, a crepe with caramel and a rich whipped chocolate mousse. I'll have to try it out and see if the staff like it first though."

"Speaking of staff," I cut the remaining half of my waffle into wedges, breaking up and sprinkling the crispy bacon over the top. "Is everything alright? I mean, the alarm last night."

Ellis shrugged as he studied his plate. "Considering Yusef didn't ring me back, I can only assume the building is still standing."

"Let me guess, he strongly suggested you let him handle it."

"Oh, you can use the word forbade."

"He only has your best interest at heart."

"He knows I love that place."

How to make him see that being away can be just as productive as working in the trenches. I'd met men like Ellis before. Good men who used work as an escape for life. The entrepreneurial spirit ruling their very existence until one day they look up and they're old and tired and alone. I didn't want that for Ellis. I didn't want that for us.

"I get that you've put your all-in keeping Mr. Angelo's dream alive. And a fool can see the dream has become an extension of you as well. But, in order for it to continue to thrive, you need to loosen the reigns and allow others to sometimes shoulder the responsibilities. You do pay them for that; don't you."

"It's hard."

"I know." I'd run a couple of business over the years and had to remind myself from time to time that the businesses didn't define me. I cradled his hand between mine, "But you need to rest. You need to know who you are outside of the restaurant. Outside of The Naughty Chocolatier."

"You're right," he conceded. "I've been kind of lost since my personal life fell apart. I can admit I found an escape in the businesses."

"Typical avoidance."

"Now you sound like my therapist."

"What? Then your therapist sounds like they know what they're talking about. Now," I released his hands and worked to sop up the last of the syrup with the lone triangle of waffle, "once we finish breakfast, we can head over to Angelo's."

"I thought you wanted me to let my managers handle work."

"I didn't say you were going to work. But I feel like seeing the place still standing without you running at the drop of a hat will do you some good."

IT WAS STILL EARLY when they arrived at Angelo's, a flurry of activity already in progress as they rounded the building and Ellis parked in his designated spot out back. A light mist coated the windshield, just enough to be annoying but not enough to warrant rain gear or an umbrella.

Instead of entering from the rear, the couple circled to the front to get a better look at the shattered window. Two work trucks sat out on the street, one with a replacement window fitted for the gaping hole near the front door and the second from a handyman repair company. The police were long gone.

Though residential houses stretched down the side streets, the houses on the main side here had all been converted to businesses. Restaurants and coffee shops lined the strip, offering a variety from Italian, to Greek, to Indian cuisine. Most were high end restaurants requiring a formal attire including jackets and ties. They catered more to special occasion patrons: prom, weddings, socialite girl's night out. An art gallery with a studio, co-op workspace, and a hand full of boutiques rounded out the possibilities for this thriving but unique community.

"Damn," Ellis said preceding Soliel up the two steps leading to the front entrance. He recognized the men removing the remainder of the glass on the ground before working to replace the shattered pane. He gave a curt nod to the company owner, a man he'd gotten to know after the last rash of break-ins in on the strip. At the time, Ellis felt lucky to be spared, the one night his establishment was targeted he'd hung around on a hunch. When the band of kids discovered a pistol pointed at them, they'd moved along and not come back.

Of course, that was seven years ago. The world was much different now. He would only draw when he planned to fire. These trifling thieves nowadays wouldn't think twice about shooting back; so, instead of confrontation, Ellis opted for high quality cameras everywhere with off-site recording and monitoring.

"Look on the bright side. You can use the salary savings from Linda's departure to cover the insurance deductible."

Ellis felt his head shake at Soliel's observation. Not in disbelief per se, but more of an actuality he should have predicted. "Leave it to you to find a silver lining."

"It's what I do."

They made a quick round of the restaurant and kitchen, Ellis noting the hidden door to the loft above had been disturbed. Yusef would have noticed but he was sure the other staff were unaware of its existence. They checked the pantry and found everything in order. The equipment was all accounted for. The damaged hinges on the office door indicated forced entry. That and the crushed knob.

Soaked papers lay scattered over the floor. The rug hastily folded to one side revealing the door to the wine cellar. The painting concealing the original wall safe sat on the couch intact.

"Interesting," Ellis said as he studied the safe. His hand ran over the edges checking for any indication of a crowbar or tool used to damage the lock or casing.

Soliel stepped up next to him. "What?"

"It wasn't forced."

"You think whoever did this came looking for something specific?" She asked.

"You think it was the Angelo boys, don't you?"

The couple's heads turned simultaneously as Yusef entered the office.

"Yep," Ellis responded turning his back to the open safe. He crossed the office, retrieving the keys he'd dropped on the desk before waving an object in front of what appeared to be a shelf that once held books. The books themselves had been tossed to the floor during the ransack process. The shelving popped forward and with a tug the shelf gave way to the secret compartment behind. "Guess they didn't think I'd have a new safe installed."

"Of course, they didn't," Yusef responded. "But are you sure it was them. I mean, with the way you escorted Marcel off the property, she has motive. I'm pretty sure she knew about the original safe, the way she used to bust in here without knocking. I guarantee she saw the picture off the wall."

"I don't think she knows about the cellar though. And she surely wouldn't have known the safe combination."

Not wanting to distract the men, Soliel had taken to gathering the papers from the floor. She did, however, provide her two cents, "Even so. Anyone could guess there was a stash of alcohol in here. And if I was planning to ransack the office, I'd turn over everything."

"My sentiments exactly," Yusef confirmed. "Actually, we found everything but the couch and desk out of place. They were too heavy to tip over. Whoever was in here was looking for something. Probably the computers."

"They weren't looking for computers," Ellis said. Assured the insurance papers hadn't been disturbed and the petty cash was in order he secure the safe and returned the shelf to the appropriate place.

Soliel rested a stack of papers on top of the desk, "How can you be sure?"

Ellis glanced at Yusef, the man staring back as if trying to read his mind. "Did you check the loft?" He asked his friend. Yusef shook his head. "Then we need to go up. I noticed the shelving in front of the door was pulled forward."

"I didn't think to look. The police had already secured the premises by the time I arrived," Yusef said as they exited the office.

To his surprise, Soliel didn't follow. Once in the kitchen they rolled the shelf forward. The door was barely ajar, probably pushed closed with the shelf instead of secured first. The old lock didn't always catch, so Ellis made sure to secure the exterior hook and latch before returning the shelf to its proper place.

"Only someone who worked with Mr. Angelo knows this door is even here."

"You sure?"

The door wasn't actually a door but a removable panel sitting flush with the rest of the paneled wall. It didn't have a handle. Pushing on the panel released an old magnetic latch. A space no bigger than a person stood behind the panel with a ladder leading up to the loft. "Positive. I'm going up. Roll the shelf back but leave enough space so I can see out. I'll let you know when I'm back down."

Ellis used the flashlight feature on his cell phone as he climbed the ladder, Yusef keeping watch by the door to make sure no one barged in to discover the secret room. He flipped the switch at the top and the inset LED fixture he'd installed a couple years back illuminated the open space. The ceiling felt low, the walls closed in, as he hunched to enter the space.

As an early teen, he and Angelo's boys spent hours up here during regular restaurant hours. After striking the initial deal to keep him out of juvi Ellis spent his time helping with prep and cleaning on the weekends. After school, he'd check to make sure the restrooms stayed clean during dinner hours between homework. With Mr. Angelo knowing his story, the man wanted him to still enjoy his youth, so he allowed Ellis time with his boys to do what boys do. They hung in the loft playing games and eventually talking about girls.

Ellis scanned the room. While on the surface all appeared to be in order, he'd spent enough time here playing with the Angelo boys to know all the hiding spots. He checked each one, a loose floorboard, the panel in the wood on the wall. Even behind the crate used as a nightstand for the lamp next to the memory foam mattress on the floor. They'd all been disturbed, confirming his suspicions.

He knew the item they sought, his heart growing full of confirmation that his gut led him down the right path when it told him not to leave the tin organizer in the restaurant. He'd considered just finding a separate hiding place for the treasure. Or creating a new one. The old, converted house still possessed plenty of nooks and crannies perfect as a hiding place. Even the dirt floor of the wine cellar offered potential. But the nagging in his gut and mind told him the safest place was off the premises.

Even more convinced of their suspects, Ellis descended the ladder and called Yusef over. The pair walked in silence, passing workers headed towards the office hauling tools to replace the lock on the door. Five neatly arranged piles lined the couch, Soliel standing over them sorting the papers in her arms.

"I'll check the wine inventory," Yusef announced before he descended the staircase to the cellar. He dragged the rug over the half-closed cover to keep the prying eyes of the workers at bay.

Ellis joined Soliel, his hand outreached for her to relinquish part of the stack to him. "This wasn't Marcel's handiwork he whispered in her ear." The concentration on her face told him she was worried the woman might be out for revenge. He suspected Soliel thought Marcel was coming after his business and would eventually come after her on a personal level either as retribution or just out of sheer embarrassment that she'd been bested by and older woman.

Soliel visually relaxed. Ellis was glad his words eased her mind. Unfortunately, the true culprits were just as, if not more dangerous than the jilted former employee.

"If it wasn't Marcel, then who was it?"

Soliel's phone rang before he could answer. She stepped away and he watched as she glanced at the screen. Her brow furrowed like she was trying to determine if she should answer the call or not. She swiped, then pocketed the device before starting back to sorting.

"Everything alright?"

"Yeah. I think it's a spam call. I've had a rash of them in the last week."

"Welcome to the club. Ever since the housing market changed, I've been getting a boat load of them too. People offering to buy the condo."

"Well, that is prime real estate."

"True."

"But I don't own any property. Nothing in my name since I sold my townhouse before moving down here. They are barking up the wrong tree if they think I have anything to offer."

She continued the sorting process, their hands bumping as they both reached to place a page on the same pile. Ellis's hand caught hers. His fingers wrapped around hers as he caught her watching him from the corner of her eye. Unfortunately, her phone rang again breaking the moment. This time she checked her watch and swiped the hang up icon. She slowly drew her hand from his and he reluctantly allowed her to draw away.

"You were about to tell me who your intruders were," Soliel said, her attention focused on the next page.

"It's not much better news. I suspect it was Angelo's sons."

"Why would they break in?"

"The recipes."

"They didn't get them, did they?"

Ellis found her genuine panic endearing. "Don't worry your pretty head about it." Hmm where had that come from. He was starting to sound like the men who used to visit his mother and Ellis didn't like it one bit. He'd have to ponder on that when he got a moment to himself. "I mean, no they didn't. On a hunch I removed them from the restaurant."

"What makes you so sure it was them?"

"The way the office was left. The old safe open. The wine cellar." He decided not to mention the details he discovered in the loft. "Only someone with intimate knowledge of this place knew about the cellar. While Marcel might know about the safe because of her barging in unannounced, I lock the door before entering the cellar. Only Yusef, Charity, you, and I know about it."

"And since you and I were together and Yusef and Charity have keys..."

"Process of elimination."

"What about former employees. People who worked for Mr. Angelo over the years."

"Same story. They wouldn't know about the cellar." *Though they might know about the loft space but not the hide-y-holes there.* "I'll know for sure once I get the footage. Even if they'd have destroyed the cameras, the footage is kept off site and," he gestured to the three cameras mounted on the ceiling, "the cameras appear untouched. Since the potential thieves pulled books from the top shelves, they probably stared right up into one."

Soliel dropped another sheet on the second pile. "They might have worn masks and gloves."

"True. We'll cross that bridge when we get to it. But Angelo's boys aren't that bright. And the cameras are past their time."

"Let's hope they are as sloppy as you think they are."

Chapter Forty

"Heard I missed all the excitement."

I looked up to find Charity leaning against the door frame, arms crossed over her chest her lips twisted up in annoyance. Instead of her usual hostess attire, she donned a black cotton dress with three quarter length sleeves. And heels. Real high heels.

"You look amazing."

"Thanks," she entered, pulling the now repaired door closed behind her.

"Why are you so dressed up? Hot date?"

"I wish. Management duty. I don't know if I'm cut out for this stiff attire."

I giggled. "You do look uncomfortable. Did Ellis tell you pants were unacceptable?"

"No. I just did a search on what managers should wear and grabbed the first appropriate item from my closet. I guess I'll need to go shopping."

"Pay raise will help with that right?"

"I suppose. Still."

"Girl, find you some nice dress pants and blouses and call it a day. And while heels are cute and all, if you think you're going to be on your feet then a pair or two of black flats will work just as well."

"Thanks for the tip. So, are you going to dish on the break-in?"

"Not much to tell. Ellis thinks Angelo's boys broke in."

"Looking for the lucrative recipes?"

"Yeah." I scooted over, allowing Charity to roll the spare chair behind the desk.

"Do you think it was them?" She asked.

"It makes sense. Though my gut still thinks Marcel might be involved."

"She is vindictive. And she's met them before."

"Really?" Leaning back in the chair, I gave Charity my undivided attention.

Charity, on the other hand, scurried to make sure the door was secured before reclaiming her seat. She leaned in, whispering to me, "They came to the restaurant a couple of times after the accident. I don't know how they found out, but it seems word got back to them."

My eyes narrowed as I processed the implication. "If they'd been watching the restaurant, they might have gotten suspicious when he stopped showing up."

"Possibly," Charity responded after a moment of contemplation.

"You think they've been talking to the other employees?"

"I wouldn't put anything past those two. Or Marcel."

I rested my head on the back of the chair, staring at the ceiling, deep in thought. If they'd been watching the restaurant then, they were probably still doing so. Or had a spy inside. "Think Marcel was working with them. Maybe trying to figure a way to use her to get to Ellis and the recipes?"

"Marcel is a smart one. And manipulative."

"In other words, you wouldn't put it past her?"

Charity shrugged. "Your arrival would have put a kink in their plan. And her dismissal, the nail in the coffin."

"Have you informed Ellis of your suspicions?"

"Not yet. I figured I'd wait until he received the footage from the alarm company. Marcel is a long stretch. She might not have anything to do with it."

"Or she might have everything to do with it." My phone rang again. The same unfamiliar number with the 410-area code. I almost answered just to tell the person to stop calling but dismissed the call yet again. "I hate span calls."

"Thank goodness for carriers marking them as spam likely."

Interesting enough the number on the screen read verified. Which meant while the number was unknown to me, it belonged to a semi-legitimate organization or person. Back to the business at hand, I slid the computer in front of Charity. "I guess today's lesson is gathering insurance paperwork and policy information."

"Sounds boring."

"Believe me, it is. A necessary evil." I retrieved Linda's notebook from the cabinet handing it over to Charity. "There's a section in there about it. I'll let you follow the instructions and if something is unclear, ask. That way we can update or add notes to the documentation as we go."

An hour of step-by-step tutorial and we were both spent.

"Lunch?" Charity asked. Her fingers rubbed her temples before pinching the bridge of her nose.

As if on cue, my phone rang again. I nodded shouting, "bring me back a salad" as Charity exited the office. Two minutes after ignoring the 410 number yet again, a text from Yaddi reading *call me ASAP. Emergency*' flashed across my phone's screen. I paced as I dialed the number. Yaddi's first words sent me sinking down onto the couch.

"Put me on speaker and check your email."

Yaddi's calm demeanor sent up alarms in my mind. Yaddi was never this calm. Something was wrong. I complied, opening my email to a message from a hospital in Baltimore. There was a message from a nurse requesting I call as soon as possible. I didn't recognize the nurse's name and it wasn't a hospital I'd ever gone to, so it couldn't have been about my medical condition. Or could it? At my last visit, I'd given permission for my doctor to forward my test results to another specialist. Had they found something? Was I sicker than my body let on?

"What's going on Yaddi?"

"You haven't checked your voicemail? I gave the nurse your number. She's been trying to reach you for a few days now. She just called me saying you haven't responded, and time is running out."

"Time is running out. I don't understand."

"Listen to me Soliel. Call the nurse. She wouldn't give me details, but she was adamant that you contact them immediately."

"I...I..."

"Is there someone there with you? I can't get back for a day or so. Even if I wanted to catch a flight, there isn't anything available. I can do a standby..."

"No. No I'll be okay. I'll call the nurse, then call you back."

"Are you sure?"

"Yeah," I lied. "I'm sure. I'm at the restaurant. I'll, I'll be alright. I mean, the worst thing she could say is I'm dying." It was a joke. Or maybe not a joke. My doctors said early on I was the exception to everything they'd seen in other patients with Changas disease. And death was always a possibility. I lived with the reality that any moment could be my last. But this felt different. Like the final coffin nail teetering beneath the hammer's head. "I'll let you know what she says."

The call with the nurse lasted five excruciating minutes. Five minutes that changed everything I thought I knew about where I stood in life. I couldn't bring myself to wipe the tears running down my cheeks. The heaviness in my heart and spirit made my limbs numb. My eyes barely focused on Charity, the fog in my head not allowing me to understand the words the woman spoke.

It wasn't until Ellis eased down on the sofa next to me did, I succumb to the all-consuming sadness. The ugly cry eluded me, which was something to hold on to. That and my man. The new rock in my life that I needed at the moment. Questions and possibilities swam through my mind sending my stomach twisting in summersaults as I worked through the implications. What did I need to do? What was my responsibility? Do I listen to my head or listen to my heart?

Time passed in a blur; a bottle of water covered in condensation appearing before me. Shaking fingers wrapped around the ice-cold plastic before a set of warm hands covered mine as I brought the bottle to my lips and managed a few sips.

I didn't have time for this. I needed to move, and I needed to do it now before the war between head and heart forced me into a place of inaction and regret.

"I have to go," I managed in a squeaky voice. I tried to sound self-assured, but I knew I failed when Ellis tried to pry the phone from my hand.

"Soliel?"

"I have to go. I have to do this." I stood, then crossed the office, methodically gathering my things. I shoved my tablet into my bag, scanning the desk before grabbing the notebook and pen I kept notes in. Ellis cornered me and I froze.

"Talk to me Soliel. Please."

My gaze darted to the closed door, then back to Ellis. "I have to go."

"Okay. You've already said that. Go where, hun?"

"I have to go. He's dying. And...and he doesn't have any family...and the nurse said...I..." I gathered the bag and my purse giving the desk one last look before rounding it on the opposite side.

"Are you serious?"

The seething in Ellis's voice stopped me in my tracks. I turned to face him and for half a second my resolve faltered. "I'm sorry Ellis but I..."

"You're seriously going to be with him? After what he did to you?"

Taken aback, I took a precious moment to gather my thoughts. "Are you questioning my judgement?"

"I don't know. Should I be?"

"Why do you have a problem with me going? If I feel like this is something I have to do, why are you doubting me?"

"Let's be clear, this isn't exactly something you have to do," Ellis made sure to emphasize the 'have to' part. "You have to breathe. You have to pay taxes, though even that can be negotiable. But what you don't have to do is run back to a man who threw you away. Who cheated on you and had a baby with another woman while you were knocking at heaven's door?"

"That's not what I'm doing."

"It's exactly what you're doing... And let's be clear, this is a choice."

"He's dying," I pleaded.

"And so were you. But did he offer the same courtesy?"

His words hung heavy between us. Ellis didn't understand and I was at a loss of how to make him see it from my perspective. Yes, I'd been in my ex-husband's shoes. At that place of regret and wanting to say the things I'd been too scared to say for years because I didn't want to hurt him. But me going to be by my ex's side had nothing to do with the man on his death bed. Nothing to do with him speaking his peace and everything about me speaking mine.

"You really don't understand," I whimpered.

"Oh, I understand perfectly. He's dying and all of a sudden you drop everything to be by his side."

"It's not like that," I again pleaded, and I hated myself for having to. I hadn't meant to raise my voice either, but I loathed the underlying accusation in his response.

"Save it Soliel. I see now."

Neither moved a muscle squaring off to see who'd give in first. Well, I didn't have the luxury of wasting time trying to justify why I needed see my ex-husband before he died. And truth be told, I was glad I was seeing this side of Ellis. Maybe I'd been wrong all along. Maybe my belief that he'd support me no matter what, was wrong. It wouldn't be the first time, but it would be the last.

With a deep breath to steel my voice I spoke the last words I was sure I'd ever say to the man I'd begun to actually love. "I guess you do. You know, I thought you'd learned about who I was, who I am over this time we've been seeing each other. Guess I was mistaken. If you think me going to see my ex on his deathbed is me choosing him over you, then you don't know me at all."

"You made your choice."

"I have. I'll see myself out." I grabbed my jacket sliding it on and pausing, my hand hovering over the doorknob. I kept my back to him, no longer feeling the need to address him face to face. "One more thing. You might be right about the choice part. I'll give you that much. However, it's the why you are sorely mistaking."

Chapter Forty-One

Between the free-flowing shots and Tupac blaring in my headphones, I managed to hold my emotions in check during the flight. The flight attendant, a bright smiling young woman named Kendra checked on me, making sure I ate as I downed an exorbitant amount of alcohol. Private planes came with perks. I silently berated myself for the overindulgence. I'd pay for it later tonight, the thought too little too late.

With only the small bag I'd crammed my tablet and purse into slung over my shoulder, I made my way to the pickup area at the small airport. At least I'd had the forethought to call a friend to pick me up. Not that a quick call to a car service wouldn't have worked. I did after all still keep in contact with the has-been's circle.

I hunkered in the thin jacket I donned as I dashed out the door to the waiting vehicle. Two months in the warm temperatures of the A and I'd lost my love of snowy winters. I'd been solely unprepared for the blast of cold wind slicing across my face as I raced to the warmth I knew awaited on the other side of the Cadillac SUV doors.

"I owe you big time girl," I said slamming the door shut while rubbing my hands together over the vent to warm them. A pair of faux fur-lined leather gloves dropped into my lap, and I quickly donned them reveling in the immediate comfort of the familiar accessories.

"Guess it's a good thing you gave me some of your things," the woman said pulling out into traffic. "Your coat's back there and I packed a couple of sweaters and pants. Wasn't sure how long you planned to stay but figured a couple of days' worth would tide you over until you could shop."

"Thanks Donna." My girl wore oversize sunglasses and a headwrap intricately crowned her head. The beautiful fabric, layered with pink, blue, and gold added a burst of color to offset the black sweater and jacket she wore. "I appreciate you picking me up on short notice. And the foresight on the clothes."

"I hope the clothes still fit. You looking a little healthy over there."

I snickered. The same thought crossed my mind. I'd put on a few pounds since dating Ellis. Between the rich sauces at the restaurant and the sweets he delivered weekly my waistline inched outward. "I have put on a few pounds. Is it that noticeable?"

"The weight looks good on you. Happiness looks good on you. Don't let anyone tell you otherwise."

"Thanks." I appreciated the compliment, especially since so many of my associates had marveled at how much weight I'd lost over the last year. They hadn't known about the stress at home. Or my illness. That the weight loss wasn't something I'd strived for to meet societal standards of beauty but a result of the trauma I faced daily.

"You mind if I ask what this sudden trip is about?" Donna merged into the lane to exit the airport speeding to keep up with the flow of traffic. When I didn't respond, Donna said, "Its Danny isn't it."

I offered neither confirmation nor denial, just stared out the window watching the world go by. I struggled to maintain my composure battling with my conscience and empathy to keep the tears at bay. What was I doing here? An ache deep within stole my breath as a flash of memory refusing to fully surface made me question if my returning to Baltimore had been an act of fate or mercy.

"Are you alright?"

With a heavy sigh, I responded, "Yeah. And it is Daniel. The nurse I spoke with said he's on his deathbed." I waited for Donna to say something; anything. Instead, silence hung in the air. Only the occasional horn from a passing vehicle broke through.

"He's been looking bad for weeks now," Donna finally admitted.

"What?"

This time, Donna released a labored breath, "Girl yeah. We've crossed paths a couple of time since your departure. The last one at the grocery store."

"Daniel? At the grocery store?"

"I guess he felt the need to get out. I don't think his happy home was all that happy. Rumor has it the new chick has been MIA for two weeks. I figured karma was kicking his behind for what he did to you. God don't like ugly."

"Wow."

"My sentiment exactly. Word around our circle is he's been trying to find you for weeks. He's been calling everyone to see if we knew where you'd gone. Of course, none of us gave up your whereabouts."

While I'd given Donna Yaddi's address to send out the last of my belongings, the other women in our circle didn't know I'd settled in Atlanta. Donna was the most trustworthy, the others willing to sell their souls to the highest bidder if it meant moving further up the social ladder. They'd married for money and status, wives of doctors and lawyers who rubbed elbows with bankers and politicians at five hundred dollar a plate events. Donna and I had lucked up on our men, locking them in before they rose in the ranks.

Donna's husband was a heart surgeon who catered to the elite. He did, however, consult and volunteer at a children's hospital to keep up on new developments in the field of pediatrics, where his true interest rested. We'd met at a hospital event, neither feeling the need to work the room like the trophy wives. We spent the night hunkered in a corner discussing creative endeavors discovering we preferred to have our own careers and identities outside of being a doctor's wife.

"It's his own damn fault." I muttered. "He cut the phone off after he signed the divorce papers. Didn't even tell me. I found out when I reached the airport and tried to call Yaddi."

"Trifling."

"That's putting it lightly."

"Any idea what he has?"

"Not a clue. I was surprised the nurses have been trying to hunt me down. I thought he'd moved the woman he was cheating on me with into the house."

"Oh, he did. Her and the baby."

I had forgotten about that part. Or maybe I'd intentionally pushed the information out of my head after closing that chapter. "Any ideas why they were pressing me to come then?"

"Can't really say. I don't think he married that chick. Maybe he hadn't changed the emergency contact information since the divorce."

"I suppose it's possible."

"You think it's something else. Don't you."

She couldn't hide her smugness. "The grass ain't always greener."

"True that, girl. True that. So, you think he wants you back?"

"If he knew what was good for him. But I meant what I said. I'm done. Hell, I'm not even sure why I'm here."

"Why are you here?"

"I don't know how to explain it. You know, how, sometimes you just know you are called to do something. You don't know the rhyme or reason you just know your spirit and the universe are telling you to move and you have to obey."

"No. I can't say I can relate. But on an intellectual level I guess I get it. Still, you better than me. I would have shut that voice up with a bottle of bourbon quick."

Donna turned into the hospital driveway rolling to a stop in front of the visitor's entrance. I reached over the back of the seat grabbing the coat and worked my way into it. "Thanks again."

"You know you're my girl. If you need me just call."

We hugged one of those long I haven't seen you in way too long hugs that reminded a person they had at least one friend in their corner in their time of need. I gathered my things, swinging the bag of clothes over my shoulder before waving goodbye as Donna drove away. I popped a mint from my purse into my mouth before entering the hospital. The scents of chicken and bacon hit me before I reached the visitor's information desk. The cafeteria must be nearby.

The woman with silver streaks in her black hair directed me to the appropriate bank of elevators and begrudgingly I made my way to the third floor. The distinctive smell of hospital grade disinfectant greeted me when the doors opened, and it took a moment for me to saved off the urge to gag. According to the sign on the wall, the nurses' station was to the right, so I followed the directions stopping at the round desk in the center of an area surrounded by seating and hallways.

When the woman at the desk looked up, her features softened.

"You must be Mrs. Brodie."

I considered correcting her, since technically speaking, I'd reverted to Boudreaux when I filed the paperwork the day after the divorce was finalized. But it was a formality at this point. If Daniel told them to expect Mrs. Brodie, then I'd play along. For now. I nodded and the woman stood.

"We're so glad you made it."

We? I scanned the space for another nurse. Who was this 'we' she spoke of?

"I'm sorry you all had such a difficult time reaching me. I've recently relocated." The woman gestured for me to follow, and I did. We took the hallway directly behind the desk passing two occupied rooms before rounding a corner.

"We've heard. Mr. Brodie was adamant we find you. Said he wasn't going to die in this place before speaking with you."

Now that sounded like Daniel. Spewing orders and decrees even when his time was running thin. "How is he?"

"As good as can be expected under the circumstances. He's been stable the last few days. His mood improved significantly when his nurse told him she'd found a good contact number for you, and we were just waiting for you to return the call."

I got the impression she wanted to ask why I hadn't been here sooner. With the same last name and Daniel not clarifying otherwise, I guessed the hospital staff assumed we were still married. The thought also made me question why Daniel chose this hospital instead of the one he worked in. Was he avoiding his colleagues? Their stares and scrutiny. Especially if what Donna said was true and his new woman abandoned him the minute she found out he was dying. Serves him right. Nothing like a taste of one's own medicine to see the error of their ways.

Stopping in front of the last room on the hallway, a corner room with what I assumed was the best view on the floor, the woman gave me a saddened look. "He sleeps a lot now. And doesn't eat much. That's usually the signs of the bodily functions shutting down."

"In other words, he doesn't have much time left." I understood the eventuality of the situation having been by my mother's side when she transitioned. "Thanks."

The nurse nodded instead of offering a blank apology. "I'll send his nurse down. She has the paperwork you need to sign for him to go home."

"Go home?"

"Yes. He doesn't want to die in the hospital. From my understanding all of the details have been taken care of. He's spoken with a social worker and authorized home hospice care. We just need you to sign some papers before they can transport him."

So that's what this was about. Use me as his nurse so he didn't have to die in the hospital. Unbelievable. The nurse retreated, leaving me standing at the closed-door seething. I considered walking away, leaving him to rot in the hell he'd created for himself. Yet my feet refused to move. My conscience telling me that this wasn't about him. That my being here was all for me.

Chapter Forty-Two

I didn't think it was possible, but this room felt colder than the rest of the hospital. Like death camped out waiting for the last grain of sand to fall to collect its due. The room was spacious, not quite large enough to fit two patients but with enough space to have more than one visitor chair with ample room to circle the bed. I was sure Daniel footed the bill for the amenity.

The head of the frail body in the bed turned as the door clicked closed behind me. Daniel spoke before I got the chance to take in the full sight of him.

"You came." He said it like he couldn't believe I stood before him. Like he believed my presence was a hallucination brought on by his mind slipping away.

The anger amassed on the other side of the door drifted away, a sense of sorrow and understanding taking up residence. Daniel was definitely knocking on death's door, no inkling of a reprieve in site. I'd expected him to look sickly, but not ashen like life had dragged him through the dirt and spit him back out here.

"Hi Danny." I fought the urge to correct myself. I hadn't used the nickname since finalizing the divorce when the man I once knew and loved became a stranger not deserving of the familiar moniker reserved for lover and trusted friend. His hand waved weakly, barely lifting from the bed as he gestured for me to come closer.

I moved into the room, setting my bags down next to the chair as I lowered myself into it. When he rolled his hand over palm side up, I rested my hand in his.

"You look good," he said, a bit of a gleam in his eye.

I only squeezed his hand, not knowing how to respond.

"Guess I look like shit huh?" Daniel said chuckling before it turned into a cough that had him doubling over. He reached for the pink plastic up on the table. I beat him to it. I helped him drink before he plopped back against the bed.

An uncomfortable silence lingered as I took in the man I'd once fallen head over heels for. His once well-defined physique now but a memory, the muscle mass wasted away leaving pockets of fat gravity pulled downward. The yellow eyes staring back at me spoke of his sickness. Splotches of red dotted a once vibrant complexion.

"I came up with an entire spiel of what I planned to say to you when I saw you again," Daniel said, "But it all seems pointless now. I'm so sorry Soliel. I was a fool and let the best thing that ever happened to me walk out of my life. Can you ever forgive me?"

Apology aside, I'd already forgiven him. And myself for staying so long in a place that no longer served me. Forgiveness for me wasn't about absolving a person of wrongdoing, but my way of acknowledging the events, working through any attachments to the past, then letting them go. His actions were his own and I'd resolved to allow him to be the fool he chose to be as I moved on with my life.

"I do."

His body relaxed, his expression filled with relief, "I don't have much time. There is so much I want to tell you. Will you stay?"

The nurse entered, interrupting the conversation, and giving me time to decide if I wanted to give this undeserving man a minute more of my time or walk away.

I BEAT THE TRANSPORT ambulance to the house. Daniel insisting, I get settled before his arrival. We only spoke a few minutes, the first of his two dying wishes fulfilled upon laying eyes on me. As far as he was concerned, everything else would wait. He wanted out of the hospital asap. Daniel Brodie wasn't going to die in a hospital.

Daniel's call to the nurse prevented us from diving into any deep conversations and I appreciated his kind gesture, needing time to go through the items Donna packed to determine my needs and make arrangements for fulfillment. I also wanted to take a quiet moment to process the events, not just the visit to the hospital and seeing Daniel in such a dire state, but the events that transpired prior to my departure from Atlanta.

Was this how it ended? Was I officially single again? Had Ellis meant what he said about me making a choice? Did he really believe I'd chosen being by Daniel's side over standing with my new man?

The questions rolled through my mind as I stared up at the two-story house with well-manicured lawns I used to call home. The brown stone front reminded me of the years of joy I'd experienced in this place. A fresh dusting of snow covered the bushes around the entrance, but the three stone staircases had been swept clean.

The wind cut through the warmth of my coat and gloves sending me forward up the stairs to escape the wrath of jack frost. The door swung open before I pressed the bell, a warm smile and open arms greeting me as I stepped into the comforting embrace of Mari, the housekeeper.

"I thought I heard a car door close," the woman said squeezing me.

I reciprocated, "it's been too long."

"Very much so." We parted, Mari ushering me out the cold. "I didn't know you were coming. I would have prepared something to eat."

I smiled at the clipped words in Mari's native Dominican accent. She'd come to us as a once-a-week housecleaner transitioning into her own business as she completed her studies to become a chef. We liked her so much, when she graduated, we offered her a steady job, more cooking than cleaning and eventually she'd taken over the task of running the household when Daniel and I were away.

"I didn't know I was coming," I said giving the entry the once over. It was just as I remembered, though the spot on the wall where our portrait once hung sat bare.

"Mr. Brodie?" Mari asked, genuinely concerned.

I handed Mari my gloves and coat as I stripped them off, "On his way. He's being transported by ambulance."

"He wasn't doing well," Mari said. She stashed the gloves in the drawer of the table by the front door, hanging the coat in the closet on the other side.

"He's still not. He doesn't have much time left."

"Are you staying?" Mari asked gesturing at the bag sitting at my feet.

"Yes."

"I can..."

I stopped the woman mid-sentence with a pat on the shoulder. "Don't go to any trouble. We can work out the details once Daniel is situated." Mari nodded.

"How about tea then? I think I still have a stash of your special brew."

"That would be lovely."

I sat at the kitchen island watching Mari buzz around in her natural element, the kitchen. The fashion forward fit young woman hummed a tune as she filled the electric kettle and set it to boil before gathering the tin of tea, cups, sugar, and honey. By the time the items sat neatly arranged on the counter-top between them, the water was ready. Mari joined me at the island adding the dried tea leaves and fruit to the diffuser before dropping it into the pot and covering it with water.

"What kind is it?" I asked inhaling the aroma as the pot seeped.

"My own special blend of peach and mango with a white tea base. Very close to your blend but not quite the same. The company that used to mix it went out of business, so I've done my best to duplicate it since I enjoyed it too. I thought I had a little of the original left, but it's gone."

"Keeping the caffeine low, huh."

"Yes ma'am. Perfect before bedtime."

Mari prepped both cups, adding two teaspoons of honey to mine while pouring sugar into her own. Just like old times.

I took a sip, "Umm. Absolutely divine."

"Pun intended?"

We shared a laugh. "Pun intended. Thanks."

I appreciated the momentary distraction from the impending doom and gloom encroaching upon my temporary doorstep. Though the joke reminded me of my time with Daniel, I thought of happier times where he used the Divine part of my middle name to butter me up before dropping the news of an event requiring my attendance. As much as I hated mingling with the snobs at those formal dinners, at least the food made my presence tolerable.

I blew over my piping hot tea, daring another sip before I spoke. "You know, you don't have to worry about rushing to find a new place and job."

"Actually," Mari lowered her cup to the saucer, "you're the one who doesn't have to worry. A lot has happened in your absence."

"Really? Do tell."

"Well, I should probably start from the beginning. See, I saw the writing on the wall when you started to get sick. I've always considered you to be a strong woman who gave people a chance to do the right thing. But everyone has a breaking point. I watched how Mr. Brodie treated you. I also watched that little hussy start to spend more time here on your stints in the hospital."

I frowned. "Guess the rumors were true."

"I didn't say anything to you because you already had enough on your plate. Besides, like you said, I wasn't the only one to notice. I figured you'd heard and were just biding your time; getting your house in order as they say. At any rate, I was plotting my exit strategy."

"Were we that bad?" I said.

"My goodness no. I loved it here. At least I did before 'she' moved in and tried to take over."

"So, the new mistress was a handful?"

"To say the least. And couldn't cook worth a lick. I'd actually threatened to quit when she barged into my kitchen one evening demanding I drop what I was doing and make her this obnoxiously complicated dish that we probably didn't even have the ingredients for. All the while ranting about how I was supposed to be a chef, yet I was basically a glorified housekeeper like this some *Fact of Life* remake and I'm Mrs. Garrett. Hangry pregnant or not, that heifer had no business speaking to me that way."

I almost spit out my tea. I stifled my laugh though, my hand covering my mouth. Luckily, when I drew it back it was still dry. "Wow."

"Mr. Brodie thought the same thing. Needless to say, I reminded him about the terms negotiated in my employment; the part about unless a prior arrangement exists in writing, my evenings were my own. And I was finishing off meals for a catering gig that night. I had neither the time nor the patience to deal with foolishness."

"Good for you. Standing your ground. Not that you've ever had a problem speaking your mind." I smiled when Mari eyed me suspiciously. "Oh, come on. You know I have seen you on the warpath a time or two when Daniel hosted dinner parties and his guest over stepped."

Mari self-consciously looked away but not before I caught the edges of her lips twitching as she struggled not to return the smile.

"Good times," Mari said.

"Definitely good times. So, you got your catering business off the ground?"

"Yes."

"Glad to hear it. I know food is your passion. Believe me, I have enjoyed every lick of it. I can admit, it is one of the few things I miss about being here." My mood turned somber, but I quickly reminded myself that this too shall pass. "I learned a lot from you. I'm glad you've found a way to make it work outside of being our personal chef."

"I love it here. Or did. And I will be sad that our time together has come to an end, but I have to thank you all for everything you've done. You paid well. I never felt mistreated. It's been a joy to work here. Not to mention with room and board included I have been able to pay off my debt and save a boatload of cash since my other expenses were low. I even purchased a couple of properties I'm renting."

I refilled my cup, having finished off the first one while we chatted, "Please don't feel obligated to hurry out of here. I am in no rush to sell this place."

"Thanks. But I'm good. Like I said, I saw the ax preparing to fall. Last year I warned the tenants in my smaller unit that I wouldn't be renewing their lease. I figured a year gave them plenty of time to make other arrangements and they've already notified me they do have a new place lined up and will be vacating on time. They just had a baby and needed a larger home anyway, so it is all falling into place."

"And employment? If you need references or..."

"All covered as well. The upside to Mr. Brodie's parties was that I could try out my recipes and build my client list.' Mari held up a hand to stop my next words, "and I know, it might not have been the most ethical thing to do."

"No worries. Truth be told I sent them your way anyway. Like you said, you held no obligations to us after hours and neither Daniel nor I wanted to stifle your creativity in the kitchen or kill your passion. I'm proud of your success. And utterly happy for you."

"Thanks."

"Can I ask you something?" I added more honey to my tea, my gaze locked on the cup as I stirred.

"Um. Sure."

"What happened with the other woman?"

Mari leaned in, not that there was anyone else in the house to overhear the conversation, "I actually don't know for sure. They started arguing. A lot. About a week later Mr. Brodie got real sick. Or maybe that's not right. He hasn't been right for a couple of months now. I didn't say anything, but I could tell he was off. He asked me to change his diet a couple of times and I didn't ask questions, just did my job and tried to avoid them both."

"What was wrong?"

"Don't know. He started dropping weight. I'd prepare full meals and end up with plates of leftovers. I even halved the recipes to lessen the waste."

"Hmm."

"And not only that, between you and me, I saw that baby. No way Mr. Brodie is the daddy."

Taken aback I said, "Really now?"

"And get this." Mari leaned back, cup in hand as she watched me over the rim. Not one to entertain gossip, I still found myself drawn into the conversation, "the first time he was admitted to the hospital she brought another man to the house. I'd gone out to get groceries but realized I'd left my card. Let's just say she was more than surprised to see me. She tried to pass him off as a handyman, but I know this house like the back of my hand. He might have been a handy man, but he wasn't here to work on the house."

Chapter Forty-Three

It was still early when Daniel finally arrived. While I had made a round of the house venturing down memory lane, I avoided the library on the first floor near the entry. When I lived in the home, I only entered to select a book or two from the stocked shelves quickly retreating while Daniel held conference calls or poured over mounds of medical journals and paperwork. I'd take my treasure to the garden and camp out on the swing, enjoying the tall tales woven together by the craftsmanship of a writer committed to telling their story to the world.

Ms. Langly, the social worker, spoke with me in the living room while the medics situated Daniel in the office. It made sense to leave him on the first floor, the room spacious enough for the rolling bed and comfortable enough with the plush chaise and view of the gardens that spending an extended amount of time there wouldn't be awful.

"How long do you expect before he transitions?" I asked as I sipped yet another cup of tea.

"The nurses said a few days. He's already in decline, unable to stomach solid foods. The body begins to break down near the end."

I stared at the woman dressed in a royal blue blouse and black skirt. She sat straight-backed in the chair; legs tucked demurely to one side. A clipboard rested on her lap, the pen hanging down the side from the metal ball chain. I found her utterly business like, exactly the type of person I expected Daniel to select to make sure his final days were orderly.

"Will he be in pain?"

"No," she replied in a clipped tone. "If he complains of or shows signs of pain, please let the nurse know so his medication can be adjusted. I've spoken at length with Mr. Brodie and understand his wishes. We will make sure to do all in our power to insure a smooth and pain-free transition."

Ms. Langly was all business and no compassion. I supposed in her job she had to maintain a professional level of disconnect. Working with the dying wasn't for everyone. I finished my tea, placing the cup and saucer onto the silver tray sitting on the table. "Is there anything you need from me? Or anything you think I should know?"

"I understand your concern. I can assure you we've taking care of every detail so that you and Mr., Brodie can spend his final days as you see fit. A nurse will be here at all times, one for the day and one for night should you need them. They will stay out of your way if you wish. As for any other questions," she removed a stack of papers and handed them to me, "This should cover everything."

I skimmed the text. "And when the time..." my voice trailed off, my mouth not able to form the words.

"Just let the nurse know."

Ms. Langly returned her teacup to the tray before standing. She straightened her skirt, grasping the clipboard close to her chest. "I do understand this is a somber time for you and your husband." Again, I opted not to correct someone referring to Daniel as my husband. He'd apparently gone to great lengths to make sure the people he dealt with believed we were still married. "Should you need further assistance with anything," she thrust a business card out to me, "feel free to give me a call."

I took the card, Mari appearing before I could stand and escort the woman to the door. "Thank you," was all I could say before watching Mari guide Ms. Langly toward the entryway.

I poured another cup of tea, glad Mari thought to leave the teapot with the cups when she served. The warm liquid eased my mind, offering comfort in the familiar during such a tumultuous time. All I could do now was wait. And be there for Daniel in his last days. I still struggled with the sense of urgency that sent me here. The need to be present when this chapter of my life closed permanently. It just didn't make sense.

Mari popped back into the room, her face solemn. "He's asking for you."

I nodded, quickly finishing the tea before gathering courage to walk down the hall to see my ex-husband possibly for the last time. No one knew for sure when their time was up, yet Daniel assured me his time was drawing to a close.

As I'd suspected, I found Daniel setup in the study. He appeared comfortable; the bed positioned near the fireplace but facing towards the double doors leading to the back yard garden.

"Have you been to the gardens yet?" He asked, his gaze locked on the scenery.

"No."

"You should. Tonight." His head lulled to the side his hand gesturing for me to sit on the chaise next to him. "I wouldn't let her ruin it."

I eased onto the plush lining of the chaise, opting to sit instead of stretching out. I needed to focus. Answers wouldn't come without hard questions and time wasn't on our side. "I appreciate that. I must say, I was surprised you were looking for me. I mean, you obviously had moved on." The words tasted bitter as I spoke them, though I kept the venom of discontent in check. "So, why am I here and not her? And why does everyone seem to think you and I are still husband and wife."

"I suppose you deserve the truth," he said.

"Suppose?"

"Okay. You, of all people deserve the unbated truth. First, to answer your question about why I've implied to everyone we're still married. It was just easier. Especially as far as the hospital was concerned. You're still listed as my next of kin on all legal documents and you know I tried my best not to mix home and hospital life aside from the mandatory engagements and my small circle of associates. Many of them are unaware of our change in circumstance."

Wonder how he pulled that off. Instead of venturing down that path, I asked, "why didn't you update the records?"

"Bear with me." The words came out slow, like he struggled to finish. "I'm getting to that."

"Sorry." I slid back into the corner of the chair, my feet still flat on the floor. But I leaned against the side in a more comfortable position.

"I," he paused, sadness stirring beneath his withering gaze, "I'd planned to update everything after I proposed." Daniel waited for me to respond. I just stared at him un-fazed. "I wanted to wait until after the baby was born; just to make sure."

"Then why did you change your mind?" I didn't let on about the rumored suspicions. He'd made the deal, now he needed to pay the piper.

Daniel's gaze flicked away, finally settling on the lit fireplace over my shoulder. He couldn't even look me in the eye when he told me he'd been had, and he'd thrown away their time together on a lie. Eventually though, he conceded his fate. "I took one look at the baby and..." He inhaled, mouth bunching in utter disgust, "I knew."

"Babies don't always look like their fathers. Especially newborns."

"Don't. Please, don't try to defend her."

"Oh, believe me," I suddenly found my nails quite interesting, "I wasn't."

"Unbeknown to her, I got a test done..."

"Not yours, huh?" Aside from the snide remark, of which he deserved much more, I kept my feelings to myself even though an 'I told you so' teetered on the tip of my tongue.

"No Soliel, he is not my son."

It wasn't the words themselves, but the way he said them, that gave me pause. And for the first time since his arrival, I witnessed his hurt and it clicked. "I'm sorry."

"Don't be. Not everyone is meant to leave a legacy. My work will live on. I have that much. Which brings me to the topic of my wishes after I'm gone."

"We don't have to talk about..."

He cut me off, "Yes, we do. And time, well time is slipping away. I only have a few things I want to tell you. First and foremost is that you won't need to fret over arrangements or anything like that. Everything is already in place. Once I've transitioned the nurse will contact the social worker. I've already signed the necessary paperwork to immediately donate my body. If my organs are viable then they will go to needing recipients."

"And if not?"

"Either way, what's left of me is to go to a body farm. I dedicated my life to science and medicine. Only makes sense to do the same in death."

"Funeral?"

Again, he stopped me before I tumbled down a slippery slope of questions, "No. I don't want a funeral or memorial or anything. Please."

I offered a half smile and nod, accepting and committing to his wishes.

"I've put you through enough. The only reason I want you to know all of this is because, of all people, aside from Mari, you're the one I trust. You should also know that everything is still in your name. My attorney's card is on the desk over there." He raised a weary finger pointing at the desk.

"You don't."

"It's already done. I need you to do me a favor if you can?"

"What?"

"On the bookshelf, bring me *The Burning Queen* from the third shelf. The author's name is Aziza Sphinx."

I rose to fulfill the request. My fingers ambled over the rows of first editions all filed alphabetically in their proper place. "I don't see it." I said, scanning the shelves where the S authors were filed.

"Check the new book section."

I moved to the other bookcase, the one by the desk where he usually kept books when he started them but hadn't finished. The book sat with two others by the author, *A Licentious Storm* and *A Moment Before Midnight*. I plucked the paperback from its place scanning the back cover text as I crossed the room.

"Where'd you discover this author?"

"Our old book club. I stopped attending after our separation, but I still get the emails. They finally took your advice and broadened the reading selection. They chose Black indie authors in science fiction and fantasy this month.

"Hmm." I moved to place the book on his lap, but he stopped me.

"There should be an envelope in the back."

I found the tiny white envelope, my thumb tracing over the impression of what I determine to be a key. Before you leave this room, I want you to take the business card and key. I updated the safe in our bedroom. I...I mean the master bedroom. You'll need the key to open the door and the combination is your mother's birth month and day."

I sat stunned. And speechless.

"There's roughly fifteen thousand dollars in cash..."

"What!" The sheer amount of cash in the house put me on edge.

"I know how you feel about large sums of money. But I didn't put it all in there at once. It was my insurance in case old girl tried to freeze my assets. No one is going to try to extort it from you. You're the only other person who knows how much it is. Use the money for immediate needs. House payments. Travel expenses. Whatever."

"Daniel."

"Please Soliel. I need to make sure you're taken care of in the short term until you can get the death certificate and gain access to the bank accounts and insurance money."

The shock dissipating as his explanation sank in, I relaxed. "Okay."

"Good. Now, my attorney knows about the baby situation. No one else is entitled to a dime since I proved the child's not mine. And she and I never married. I want to do this for you my dear Divine. The house. The insurance. The investments. All of it, save for a trust setup for Mari to make sure she's covered for at least the next six months, is yours. Not like I can take it with me. Right?"

Tears welled in my eyes, not just for the final gifts Daniel bestowed upon me meaning if I didn't lose my mind or fall victim to an unscrupulous scheme, I'd never have to work again, but that he really was waiting at death's door for the moment he was due.

"I know it doesn't make up for the pain I put you through, but it's the right thing to do. And, at the very least, I can do the right thing before I leave this Earth."

In that moment, the encasing around my heart shattered, the tears trailing down my cheeks as I wrapped my fingers around his and wept for all that had been and what would soon be.

Chapter Forty-Four

"HOW LONG HAS HE BEEN like this?" Charity stood in the Angelo's kitchen in doorway staring at Ellis's back as he drew a knife from the butcher block on the back table and just stared down at the chocolate on the wax paper. He didn't move to chop, didn't even start to break it up, he just stood there, staring at the unprocessed confection before returning the knife to the block and folding the edges of the paper over the chocolate again.

"Two days," Yusef responded over her shoulder. "He's been drinking again too." She whipped around, eyes wide in concern. "Not overindulging. But I did find a new bottle of Crown on the counter when I stopped through. Looks like he'd only had a couple of shots before calling it a night."

The pair stood in silence; the place empty save for the three of them. Charity had called Yusef in when she'd found Ellis in the kitchen alone with the knives. He seemed out of sort, like he couldn't make up his mind what he should be doing. He hadn't spoken a word to her when he'd passed her in the hallway. Just circled back, as if in a daze. Back to the kitchen. The pantry. The knives.

"Have you heard anything from Soliel?" Yusef asked.

"No. Which worries me."

He frowned, "Have you tried to call?"

"Yes. Her phone goes straight to voicemail."

"Think this has something to do with her?" Yusef gestured towards Ellis who'd again unfolded the paper from around the chocolate. Though, he hadn't retrieved the knife yet,

"Definitely. I didn't catch the entire conversation but before she left, I could tell they'd argued."

"Any ideas about what?"

"None. And he's not talking."

"I might be half deaf, but I can hear you two."

The pair exchanged glances, Yusef gesturing for Charity to engage. When he stepped away, she joined Ellis at the table near the back of the kitchen. "Talking might help."

He shrugged. "Nothing to talk about."

Charity leaned against the table, her arms crossed as she caught his eye, "You've never been a good liar."

"It's none of your business."

"Oh really?" Her finger wound in circles in the air. Not directly accusatorily pointing at him, but posturing in his general direction, "Like the phone calls and text from your ex weren't any of our business. You see where that landed you. Listen Ellis, we're more than just employees. We're your friends. And don't think everyone hasn't noticed. While they may not approach you, we've been questioned about Soliel's abrupt absence."

"Well get used to it."

The words knocked the wind out of Charity's sails so to speak. "She isn't coming back?"

"Probably not."

The response rendered her momentarily speechless. She eventually recovered, diving right into the most pressing question. "What happened?"

"I told you. Its none of your business." He turned from her, fingers tightening around the knife he'd just retrieved, the muscles taught with frustration.

Charity inched away as her gaze narrowed in on him. She saw no point in pushing. He'd shut down, which only frustrated her more. The last thing she wanted to see was a repeat of a few weeks ago but she'd be damned if she continued to talk to a brick wall. "Fine," she spat at him pushing away from the table. "I'm done with this. Do whatever the fuck you want. Just know, I won't be the one explaining to Soliel when you unintentionally off yourself on some self-sabotaging bender."

She pushed through the 'in' door, going the wrong way and inadvertently slamming into Yusef as he carried the bin with napkin-rolled silverware.

"You need to talk to your boy, 'cause I'm done with this." Charity stormed past, shouldering him in the process as fury consumed each step. If he didn't care, then she didn't care. Her anger escalated as she entered the office, the reminder of the training session she was supposed to have today with Soliel staring her in the face in bright red on the calendar.

Charity retrieved the open bottle of wine from the shelf not caring that technically she was on the clock. Hell, as far as she was concerned, Ellis could fire her now. She could find another job, but she couldn't find another friend like Soliel. Glass only a fourth full, Charity plopped down on the couch. She dialed Soliel's number again, disappointment settling in as it once again diverted directly to voicemail. This wasn't like her. They'd been down this road before when the Marcel incident occurred. Soliel was intentionally avoiding them yet again. She downed the last of the drink sliding the glass onto the counter behind her head as voices from the hallway approached,

"Have you at least tried to call?" Yusef said as the men rounded the doorway.

Neither seemed to notice Charity hunkered in the corner of the couch, her gaze locked on her phone, though she did watch them over the top.

"She made her choice."

"Have you seriously become that much of an ass? After all she's done for you. For the restaurant."

Ellis claimed the seat behind the desk, but he gave no indication of seeing her, so while eavesdropping wasn't the politest thing to do, Charity saw no reason to bring attention to herself. She jumped when Ellis slammed his hand into the desk.

"I told you. Leave it alone. She's moved on and so will I."

The gasp escaped before she could stop it, and both men turned. Well, so much for hiding out.

"Get out. Both of you. I don't want to hear another word about this. And you can tell the staff what you want, but I expect any dealing with Soliel to be done. Do you understand?"

Charity stood, inching towards the door leaving Yusef as a buffer. To her surprise he didn't say a word, just followed her out the door and pulled it closed behind them.

"What the hell?" Charity said as they walked the hallway.

"I don't know. But it must have been some argument. I know you two have become friends. Any luck reaching Soliel?"

"None. Her phone keeps going straight to voicemail. I sent her another text telling her to at least call to let me know she's ok. I'm starting to worry."

"Me too. Though Ellis doesn't seem to be as worried. Or at least not about her safety. He wouldn't be putting up such a fight about discussing what happened if he thought she might be in harm's way."

"What did he mean about her making a choice?"

"I wish I knew." The clanking of dishes and the hostess bellowing "show time people' signaled it was opening time. "Unfortunately, we don't have time to worry about it. We both need to get to work."

"CIRCLE THE BLOCK OR find a parking spot. I'll call when I'm ready to leave." Yaddi slid Armond a fifty as she exited the vehicle. He pulled away, turning the corner as she reached the landing to the front porch of Angelo's. While the sprinkle of tables outside sat quiet and empty, the hostess just on the other side of the door spoke with three women in business casual attire catching a late lunch.

Yaddi struggled to maintain her composure, the voice in her head nudging her to elbow past the group. However, her professionalism capped the thought as she focused on the purpose of her unannounced visit. The group lingered, the hostess stepping away to speak to the bartender, a man Yaddi recognized from the night at the club where she and Soliel first met Ellis.

Her mind reeled, trying to remember the man's name. To no avail. Her gaze scanned the interior as the hostess returned, searching the scatter of faces hoping to find her target.

"Can I help you?"

Engrossed in her search, Yaddi failed to realize the women had claimed their seats and the hostess waited for her to approach. She plastered on her poker face, the one she used when her clients tried to convince her that they were following her suggestions knowing good and well she'd spoken with the staff and knew they'd implemented the items she deemed minimal, only to gloss over the meat of her recommendations.

"Actually, I think I'll go to the bar." Her eyes locked with the bartender. Yaddi sneered the moment she realized he recognized her. With each step, that sneer grew more mischievous as she watched his panic escalate. He'd grabbed the phone by the time she reached the halfway point, but his gaze never diverted from hers. "Where is he?" she spoke through gritted teeth when she reached her destination.

"Long time no see."

"Don't patronize me. I will burn this bitch down, light a cigarette, and drive myself to the police station."

"Your anger is misdirected."

"Yaddi."

Yaddi turned at the sound of her name, seeing Ellis standing at the other end of the bar watching her intently. He appeared disheveled, like he hadn't slept in days, which formed a kink in her angry armor. Instead of making a scene, she joined him, much to the bartender's relief as he made a b-line for the kitchen door. "We need to talk."

Ellis hesitated, his brow rising as he gauged her mood. She reigned in madam fury, forcing her features to relax into a more suitable reaction to get him to take her to a place where she could lay into him without prying eyes.

After a moment more of scrutiny, he said, "we can talk in the office," before abruptly turning his back and walking down the hallway.

Well, that was rude.

She followed, her anger in check as she watched the way his shoulders slumped, the slow pace grating against her nerves. He walked like the world weighed on his shoulders. Still, she refused to be deterred. They entered the office and when the door closed behind her, she dropped the gates.

"What the hell did you do?"

Ellis eased into the chair behind the desk, rolling his shoulders in the process as his hand rubbed over his face. "Excuse me?"

"You heard what I said. What the fuck did you do?"

"First of all," he leaned forward, eyes narrowing as they locked with hers. The weariness long gone. "Don't come into my establishment making accusations."

"Huh. Like I told your boy, I don't give a rat's ass about this place." She remained standing, matching his glare with one of her own. They gawked at each other, an ominous silence lingering between them.

Ellis was the first to give in. "Are you going to tell me what you think I've done?"

Instead of remaining standing like a tower of power designed to intimidate, Yaddi claimed the seat across from Ellis. "Have you spoken to Soliel?"

"Have you?" He retorted with a bit of an uncomfortable edge.

"I asked you first."

He frowned, lips drawing into a thin line, "I have not. Not in a few days."

"And you're not worried?"

"Didn't know I should be."

"She hasn't been home or answered her phone in three days. It just goes to voicemail. I thought she might be here but if you haven't seen her..." Yaddi's voice trailed off as she looked away.

"And?"

"What do you mean? And?" The fury returned with a vengeance; her worry now thrust to the side as this man acted as if her friend meant nothing to him. "And I'm worried about her. The last time I heard from her I told her she needed to call the hospital. She said she was here. Then nothing. It's been days. I checked the cameras and alarm at home. She hasn't been home, so she obviously didn't have any clothes when she disappeared. And she's not answering the phone. I don't even know if she has her meds."

"Are you saying she left to go see her ex-husband and didn't go home to pack a bag?"

"Wait. She went to see Danny?" His words held deep concern and surprise, the first indicator that they'd both been left in the dark. "Hello, I haven't spoken to her. Why was she going to see Danny?"

"Seriously? You two haven't talked about this?" Ellis grabbed the phone, dialing Soliel's number. "It's going straight to voicemail."

"No shit Sherlock. I just told you that. It's been doing that for days."

"Maybe she doesn't want to talk to anyone."

"Obviously she's avoiding you," Yaddi didn't hamper her accusation. Not answering the phone is one thing. Turning it off was another. Something had happened and she needed to know what.

"You can accuse me all you want, but if she hasn't reached out to you then I'm not the only one she's avoiding."

"I don't have time for this. This isn't like her. She usually at least checks in, but at this point she's not answering, and her voicemail is full. She hasn't responded to emails or text messages and I'm beyond just worried. None of our regular circle has seen or heard from her and I'm afraid without her meds she might..." Yaddi didn't finish the thought, unsure how much Ellis knew about Soliel's medical conditions, and it wasn't her place to tell him. "Can you at least tell me why she was going to see Danny?"

"If she didn't call to tell you, she didn't want you to know."

Yaddi stood. "Forget it. But if she is dead in a ditch somewhere I'm blaming you." She moved to exit.

"He's on his deathbed."

Yaddi froze at the declaration, her blood running cold. "Come again?"

"Her husband. Ex-husband. The call from the hospital was to inform her that he was dying and wanted to see her."

"Dammit," Yaddi held onto the doorframe for balance. "It's the Tyler thing all over." She whispered the last part, more to herself than anything else.

"What did you say?"

Damn. Yaddi maintained her silence. Mind racing.

"Yaddi?"

She felt him move closer, the walls seemingly closing in.

"Who is Tyler?"

He was right behind her now. She considered running, but he was too close. He'd grab her before she managed two steps. With a sigh, resignation sinking in, Yaddi lowered her head, "Tyler was Soliel's first husband."

"So, she's been divorced twice?"

Ellis moved away, the heat from his body retreating with him. The disappointment in his voice confirmed Soliel hadn't told him about Tyler. "No." Yaddi managed, keeping her voice calm as the anticipation of the impending conversation settled around her. "Divorced once. She's also a widow." When the quiet stretched on for too long, Yaddi faced Ellis only to witness the weight of the world again falling upon his shoulders. "She didn't tell you?"

He just stared at her, wide eyed, shaking his head in disbelief. "I shouldn't have said..."

So, they'd had an argument, which explained the phone being off. Still, Soliel should have checked in by now, and this new development only deepened Yaddi's concern of her friend's mental state and whereabouts. Should she ask about their disagreement? Would it help?

"Why didn't she tell me?"

Yaddi sat again. She chewed her bottom lip, the ramifications of this conversation gnawing at her gut like her teeth gnawed at her lip. But he needed to know. And while Soliel might have had her reasons for not mentioning Tyler, this was one truth Yaddi felt she couldn't withhold. "This really isn't my place, but the entire situation with Soliel and Tyler is complex. He was her first love. The love of her life. When she lost him, I wasn't sure she'd ever recover."

"What happened?"

"They'd just gotten married. Had planned this big honeymoon trip that they were supposed to leave for right after the wedding. The weather turned, so they delayed the trip. It was actually fortuitous, since the extra time allowed them to file the marriage certificate and update legalities. That was Tyler, forever dotting the I's and crossing the T's." Yaddi's mind wandered back to that day, the happy couple basking in the fresh glow of matrimony. "I think it was the happiest day of her life."

"How long were they married?"

"They dated for years, both wanting to finish school before settling down. Though, to answer your question, legally, fourteen days."

"Wow, she lost him that soon?"

"Yeah. On their way back from the honeymoon they were hit by a drunk driver. The doctors prepared us for both of them not to make it. Soliel was in a coma for five months. Tyler tried to hold on, but he took the brunt of the impact. His airbag didn't deploy."

"My God."

Yaddi shuddered, the memories of watching as the nurses turn off the machines keeping him alive invading her mind. "He died four weeks after the accident. We had the funeral. He was buried all while Soliel remained oblivious." The office fell quiet again, neither knowing what to say to the other under the circumstances.

"Did she ever visit his grave?"

"No."

"This doesn't make sense. I told her about my ex-wife, how she tried to kill me and ended up killing our son. Why wouldn't Soliel tell me about this?"

"Probably because she doesn't remember."

Eyebrows raised, Yaddi held up a hand to stop the onslaught of questions she predicted, "she had a bad head injury. I mean, having to relearn basics like language and walking head injury. The doctors said she might not ever remember the accident. That it could be the physical injury she sustained or a psychological one. Sometimes people who experience that level of trauma block things out."

"Did they tell her? I mean, about her husband?"

"I tried," Yaddi responded. Her fingers pinched the bridge of her nose, a headache brewing as she struggled to maintain her composure. She shouldn't be telling him this. "We didn't want to push. You have to understand, she had so much else to worry about. I got her settled into my place. She didn't have any family and Tyler's family thought it best she be with someone she remembered."

"Must have been hard seeing her like that."

"It was. The money made it easier. Between the sale of their house, the life insurance policies, settlement checks, and disability payments I was able to focus on being her full-time caregiver. When she recovered enough to regain her independence, I tried again to talk to her about Tyler. Eventually I think she understood what happened on a high level, but a disconnect remained between her mind and heart. I left it up to her if she wanted to talk about him or not."

Ellis stood, rounded the desk as he retrieved the half bottle of wine from the shelf. He collected two glasses before returning to his seat. "You think she remembers, don't you," he said sliding a half full glass in Yaddi's direction before filling the second for himself.

"I do. She brought him up a few weeks ago. I let her talk, didn't push. She asked about him and I answered her question."

"And you think she needed to go see her ex-husband as a form of closure."

"It makes sense. She didn't get to say goodbye to Tyler. I don't think she wants a repeat. If she has the chance for closure, nothing could stand in her way."

AFTER FINISHING THE last of the bottle, the pair parted ways with an agreement to reach out to the other should they hear from Soliel. Ellis barely sat back down when Charity slid through the door. He suspected either she or Yusef would question the visit, he just wished he'd had a moment to process everything before having to explain the visit to someone else .

"I'm guessing that woman is a friend of Soliel's."

Ellis nodded. He rubbed his eyes, staving off a headache. Maybe that last glass of wine was a mistake. The bottle beaconed, if he topped off, he might hit the sober/drunk plateau.

"Don't even think about it."

Charity scooted into his line of vision, forcing him to look at her instead of dreaming about drinking his sorrows away. "Did you need something?" He said dryly, beyond the point of frustrated.

"Has she heard from Soliel?"

"No. That's why she showed up here. Hoping she'd find her."

"So, what are we going to do?"

"Not much we can at this point. Hope when she's ready she'll turn her phone on and reach out to someone." Charity frowned, toying with the envelope in her hand. "What you got there."

"What? Oh. Yusef asked me to bring it back. Said he had to sign for it."

Ellis took the envelop she slid his way, his head dropping as he read the names of the attorneys on the return address section. "Dammit."

"Bad news huh. The Angelo brothers?'

Ellis huffed. "In all likelihood." He tore open the side of the envelope retrieving the folded pages inside. A deep breath to prepare, his head cocked to the side as he read.

"What is it?" Charity asked, leaning over the desk.

He flipped through the pages again, shaking his head in disbelief.

"Ellis?"

"It's, it's a cease-and-desist order."

"They're shutting us down?"

Ellis retrieved the envelope checking the address. Baltimore. "You said Yusef had to sign for this?"

"Yes. I was in the kitchen when it arrived. It's addressed to the restaurant even though it came certified."

"This doesn't make sense."

"What's wrong?"

He finally looked up at her, "Its a copy of a cease-and-desist order sent to the Angelo brothers on behalf of my attorney. They've been instructed to stop harassing us about the restaurant and the recipes. With Mr. Angelo's will already completing probate and found to be valid, they have no claim."

"When did you hire an attorney?"

"I didn't."

Ellis dropped the papers and Charity immediately scooped them up and scanned over them. "Baltimore? Isn't that where Soliel was from?" He nodded. "You think she?"

He didn't know whether to jump for joy or berate himself. Yet again, Soliel proved her loyalty which only reminded him of his horrible treatment.

Charity waved the papers in front of him, "Still going to wait around for her to pick up the phone?"

"You have an idea?"

A devilish smile crept across her lips, "Maybe one or two."

Chapter Forty-Five

I took Danny's suggested walk in the garden, the early evening still bearable so long as I donned a long coat, hat, and gloves. Mari provided a scarf along with a steaming travel mug of Mexican hot chocolate to keep me nice and toasty during my garden tour. With his eyes closed, I assumed Daniel slept, yet I felt him watching as I slipped through the double doors out into the chill of the night.

Refusing to be deterred, I roamed the gardens, my fingers brushing over the bare vines woven through the arches and trellis. I was glad the garden remained, unsure if the new mistress of the house appreciated its beauty or opted to wipe any memory of the first wife from the premises.

The mini greenhouse, barely big enough for two, greeted her with sweet scents, the tables covered in spring and summer vegetables: tomatoes, squash, and beans still blooming in the temperature-controlled environment. I'd find the winter selection: kale, kohlrabi, and cabbage thriving in the crisp cool air outside.

I sighed, wondering what would become of my beloved garden once I sold the place off. Would the new owners appreciate the care? The hours committed to tending to the seedlings before transplanting them after the last frost. I plucked a cherry tomato from the potted plant near the back before circling the worktable littered with herb trays and exiting into the night garden.

I perched on the bench, chocolate in hand as the sweet floral scents enveloped me, sending my mind wandering in the direction of what lay on the horizon. I could stay here a while, no real obligations in my new home except Yaddi's party and it only required an overnight trip to coordinate the setup and a little packing before riding back off into the sunset if I so chose. Maybe it was a good thing I hadn't found a house yet.

The people at Angelo's would miss me; but, like other employees, people came and went when they found better prospects or sought a change of scenery. Being back here brought back good memories. I could easily dive back into gardening. Help Mari when she needed an extra set of hands. Catch up with my sprinkle of friends and still do calligraphy on the side. Mari might appreciate my skills when catering, handwritten place cards an added touch.

Yet, as quickly as they formed, I dismissed the fleeting plans knowing I couldn't stay in this house. While the walls held plenty of good memories, they'd been stained with the bad, the hurt too fresh to subject myself to the constant reminder. And when Daniel transitioned, in my heart I wouldn't be able to stomach the house any longer than necessary.

Besides, I needed to at least try to see if Ellis and I had a chance. As the day slipped by, I'd considered his perspective on my sudden departure. And I understood. I'd question my partner's motive to drop everything and run back to the person who'd destroyed their life too, if in his shoes. For a split second I considered calling but squashed the inkling deciding that conversation required face-to-face interaction.

Eventually, I made my way back to the house, quietly entering the library hoping to not wake Daniel. I settled into my spot on the chaise, book in hand as the fire roared strong in the hearth. My gaze lingered on the garden on the other side of the window by the fireplace still reminiscing.

The uneventful day stretched into evening. Daniel only took a couple of sips of water, and I expected tonight might be his last night on the physical plane. We hadn't chatted much during the day, I just sat in the chaise reading a book to him as he conserved his little remaining energy. With no signs of pain, the nurse left them to their quiet time together until I too slipped off to sleep.

As the sun began its descent, I found myself drawn to the double door to watch.

"Does he love you? And I mean, the way you deserve to be loved?"

"What?" I continued to stare out the window admiring the night garden now in bloom beneath the light of the full moon. I would miss the gardens most of all. They beaconed to my soul; still, I chose to remain close, wanting to be there when the clock finally ran out on Daniel. The gardens brought years of enjoyment. Late evening strolls enjoying the scents of pink evening primrose, moonflower and Japanese wisteria enveloping me as I wound my way down the lit paths.

Daniel's light chuckle drew my attention away from the beauty of the night. "I might be dying, but I'm not blind Divine."

"Don't call me that."

"Fine. Celestial." I cringed at the use of my first name. "Now answer the question."

His smug attitude grated on my nerves. "I don't know what you're talking about," I finally muttered, my gaze still locked on the twinkling lights hanging from the pergola over the herb section.

"Are you sure? Or are you in denial about your feelings?"

"I'm not in love."

"Oh, my dear Divine."

"Don't," I turned to face Daniel, "call me that." I bit each word in warning.

He held up his hands in surrender as best he could, in his weakened state. They barely reached above the sheets, but I got it. "I apologize. But it doesn't change the fact that you are in love. Whether you admit it to yourself or not. I'm actually happy for you. You deserve someone who will love you the right way. And it eases my mind that you've moved on and found happiness."

"Why are you saying this?"

"Because it's true. You have that glow again. The spark I extinguished with my neglect. You know, if you'll humor a dying man, tell me about him."

"I don't think that's appropriate."

"Come on. What do you have to lose? Not like I'm his competition at this point. And by the looks of it, at the very least he has you eating again."

I narrowed my gaze, sharp eyes focused, "Are you calling me fat?"

"I would never. But I will say that I can see you've regained some of the weight you lost when you got sick. You look good. You look healthy."

I glanced away, self-conscious. "I didn't think you'd noticed."

"I have. I noticed before, but..." his voice trailed off, then he doubled down on his request, "so, are you going to tell me about him?"

"What do you want to know?"

"Well, I'm guessing you aren't missing any meals."

"That could be Yaddi," I retorted.

"True. But I have a hunch it isn't."

"You're right. He owns a restaurant and a chocolate shop."

"Entrepreneur. A man after your own heart."

I thought about his words, and they made sense. My love for seeing others succeed. The time I spent working behind the scenes in the food industry, and not because I needed the money. I did it for the love of helping others. And of course, the free food. "I guess he is."

"And?"

"And you're right. He is a good man. Compassionate and caring." *And a great lay.* "He has his demons, but don't we all. He's good to me and I do think he loves me."

"You know, you were the best thing to ever happened to me, the light of my life, and I couldn't see it. I was a fool Soliel, and I want you to know that I want you to be happy above all else."

I shrugged, not knowing what to say to the declaration. It wasn't like I wanted to talk to him about my love life. It wasn't any of his business. Yet, I needed to process what happened and it wasn't like Daniel would be around to use the words against me. Resigned to my need to purge, I moved from the window to the chaise next to Daniel's bed.

"What if I am in love?" I murmured more to myself than Daniel, "how I feel might not even matter." The words stung, like I'd finally admitted to myself my choice to come here might be the end of a blooming relationship.

"What happened?" Daniel said, urging her to continue.

"You. Hell," I waved at the bed and machines, "this."

"I don't understand."

I sighed. Annoyed and a bit betrayed I said, "he thinks I chose you over him. That my coming here means that you mean more to me than he does. I couldn't get him to understand that a nagging within sent me here."

"You aren't obligated to me Soliel. If I had known it would cause you this much grief, I never would have asked you to come."

"No. I need to be here. And not because of obligation. I haven't said anything to anyone, but I think I knew you were dying. Or that I was going to face someone close to me transitioning."

"You had a premonition?"

I shuttered at the word. As much as doctors, preachers, or science in general warned that we never know when someone's time was up, I sometimes knew. Maybe not the specific date or time but an intuition inside gave me clues to pay attention, be vigilant, and check in with those closest to me. I saw it happen a time or two, even worked to warn those who's spirit visited in the waking hours to prepare me for what might come.

"Not a premonition per se. But an inkling. And..." my voice trailed off, my mind wrapping around the words my mouth wanted to say but my heart wanted to hold close in secrecy.

"Soliel?"

Daniel's hand came to rest on mine to draw me back to the present. I stared back at him with blurry vision, the tears threatening to spill over. "I...I think I remember. Or I'm starting to." I couldn't hide the tremble in my voice. The aching in my heart. Daniel knew me well enough to see the pain I tried to lock away.

He squeezed my hand, "Tyler." The tears fell with the slight nod of my head. "Do you want to talk about it?"

I shrugged.

"You don't have to," he said, "the decision is yours."

"I don't know. It's like, I've been getting these flashes. They're becoming more frequent. I dream about him sometimes. I dream about our honeymoon and how in love I was then."

Daniel glanced away for a moment as if it hurt to see me like this. Or maybe my words cut deep that instead of bringing beauty and love into my life he only contributed to the pain and sorrow I'd tried to avoid after the accident.

"Do you think your current situation is triggering your memory? Yaddi told me you didn't recall much of your time with Tyler, but that it was one of the happiest times of your life. She hates the fact you don't remember any of it."

"I suppose anything is possible. I've always felt a presence with me. Nothing out to torment me or make life more difficult. But that unfinished business kind of presence. I used to think it was my mother looking out for me. Maybe it was really Tyler protecting me from the memories until I came to a place in life where they wouldn't send me down a path of no return."

"How do you feel about it?"

"This does help. The talking I mean. I do think he's with me, preparing me for your transition and to fully be present for what lies on the horizon."

Again, he squeezed my hand, "And love?" This time, I looked away. "Listen to me Soliel. Don't shy away from it. You have such a kind heart and loving spirit. Don't let my foolish actions sway you. Accept love again."

I pulled away, "I can't deal with anymore hurt."

"And yet you're here. Whether you still love me or not you hold compassion for your fellow human and that will always lead to happiness for a while and hurt when those things come to an end. Even if that end is death."

I leaned forward, elbows resting on the side of the bed as my hands rubbed over my face. He was right. At least this time. "I'll think about it. It might not be my decision to make though."

"If he has even a lick of sense, he'll come around. And if he's made it past Yaddi's radar, he's a good one."

"What's that supposed to mean?"

"It means you have a friend looking out for you. Truth be told, she cornered me on our wedding day. Threatened to castrate me if I ever hurt you. I've actually been looking over my shoulder since you filed for divorce expecting her to make good on her promise."

"You know Yaddi is all talk."

"I'll agree to disagree with you on that. If Yaddi isn't anything else, she's patient. The kind of woman to enact revenge years after her victim forgets the wrongdoing. I think she'll be sorely disappointed to learn karma beat her to the punch." Daniel smiled when I chuckled. "But back to your conundrum. Have you spoken to him since you arrived?"

"No. I haven't spoken to anyone and I'm not in the head space to."

"You think that wise? The last thing I need is Yaddi at my doorstep raising hell. What will the neighbors think?"

We shared a laugh. Or rather, I laughed. Daniel's attempts were met with a coughing fit. "She'll be fine. I left her a message that I had business to tend to."

"You and I both know such a lame explanation isn't going to fly."

"Its fine. I'll catch her this evening. She should be back in Atlanta tonight. Probably hasn't checked her messages yet. She was the one who told me to call the nurse back. I'm sure, if she has checked her messages, she's put two and two together by now."

"I wondered how they found you." My eyebrows rose. "I know. I know. Asshole move shutting your phone off."

"I'd say. Who knew you could be so cruel?"

"And so much of a fool."

Chapter Forty-Six

At Daniel's insistence, and against my better judgment, I spent a tumultuous night in one of the guest rooms upstairs. After assuring the night nurse Daniel was resting, I'd retired for the evening, only to find my mind immersed in a web of memories refusing to be ignored. Memories of how good it felt to trust someone with my heart.

A wet pillow woke me at sunrise, my heart full. My memory of the joy my first husband brought into my life fully intact. Daniel was right. Letting go of control. The hurt. All of it acted as the key. My time in the land of the Sandman allowed the flood gates to open, the emotions and memories to flow freely, giving me back a part of myself I hadn't known I'd lost.

With a sense of renewal, I slipped the plush purple robe from the bathroom over a fresh set of pajamas from a box of my belongings I'd apparently left behind and bound down the stairs to tell Daniel about my revelations. Not bothering to knock, I eased into the library, pulling the door closed behind me.

The machines were quiet. The bag with the pain medicine empty. I'd left him scribbling away on a notepad now strewn across the floor, the pen, nowhere in sight. I reached for Daniel's limp arm hanging off the bed to move it to his stomach assuming he'd fallen asleep and dropped it by his side. Yet, the moment my fingers brushed his cold ones I staggered back, hand slapping over my mouth as I backed away from the body.

He was gone. Though I knew any of these moments I spent with Daniel might be our last together, inside I was still unprepared to find his cold body in the bed at sunrise. It took a moment for my mind to process the sight, to accept the idea that I'd never hear his voice again. He'd spoken his peace, told me his truth, and sent me away because he wanted to leave on his own terms.

I garnered the strength and frame of mind to summon the nurse who first ushered me out of the room into the waiting arms of Mari before entering the library and quietly closing the door behind her. He'll never know how his words healed me. And yet, in my heart, I was sure he already did. That's why he'd sent me to the comforts of another room. His final act of kindness, granting me the peace of mind he too sought.

A cup of chamomile tea appeared on the counter before me. I blinked, my mind processing the fact that I sat at the island in the kitchen, Mari at my side.

"I shouldn't have left him." I turned tear-filled eyes up to Mari, "I should have stayed. I was supposed to be there when it...when he."

"Shh. Don't do this. You gave him what he asked for. What he needed. He wanted you here. Close. That doesn't mean he wanted to burden you with his final moments. You did good Soliel," Mari said.

The warmth of the mug and Mari's hands guiding them around the cup kept me grounded. "He did good." I lost the battle, tears streaming down my cheeks as I stared into the depths of the steaming liquid.

True to his word, we didn't have to do anything. The nurse made the calls and within a couple of hours Daniel's body was headed to its final resting place and the bed was removed. I remained transfixed to my seat; my body numb. When the tears ceased, Mari slid a card in front of me.

"Ms. Langly left this for you. There's a 24-hour hotline on the back if you need to speak to someone. Otherwise, you can make an appointment with a grief counselor at your convenience."

I continued to stare at the cup, the tea long cold. "Is this real?"

Mari's arms wrapped around me. "I'm afraid so. How about something to eat? You need to keep your strength up."

I nodded, words failing to form as my mind raced. I relinquished the hold on the cold cup of tea before resting my head on folded arms on the countertop. This was real. All of it. A salad appeared before me, Mari placing a fork next to two dressing options as the doorbell rang. We exchanged a glance before Mari indicated she'd answer it.

Word traveled fast. A steady stream of visitors stopping by to pay their respect. While I hid in the kitchen, I gave Mari sole discretion to handle guests as she saw fit. I recognized many of the voices. Mostly men and women from the hospital. People I'd conversed with at charity events and fund-raising dinners. A few of Daniel's friends who traveled with us stopped by as well. I kept waiting for Daniel's voice to boom over them all as he always did when his buddies dropped by. Yet, it wasn't meant to be. He was gone, and I needed to get used to the idea.

It quieted down for a while, and I found solace in the quiet of the house too big for just the two of us. Daniel had purchased it for me because of the garden. I'd fallen in love the first time I walked over the cobblestone paths. He would have given it to me in the divorce if I'd asked. And now, once again it was mine.

Raised voices from the hallway drew me out of my funk. An argument ensuing, the raised voices speaking over one another made it difficult to make out the words, but I definitely heard a heated exchange between Mari and another woman. Then, a baby started to cry.

How dare she? Of all times, how dare she intrude upon this moment of mourning. I slid a meat cleaver from the butcher's block as I exited the kitchen and headed toward the foyer.

The woman momentarily ceased her rant when I rounded the corner.

"Get out." I articulated each word, my fury directed at the woman who'd been a thorn in my side and attributed to the downfall of my marriage.

"And who are you?" She demanded, hands on hips like I couldn't knock her on her behind with a mere thump.

"I'd think you'd recognize me. I'm sure before you called yourself redecorating, my face was plastered all over this place." My thumb rubbed over the metal handle of the knife. I held it behind my back out of sight but if this trifling piece of trash even thought to put her hands on either me or Mari, she'd draw back a nub.

"You have no right to be in my house!" She declared.

"Your house?" I countered, in an eerily calm tone. The change was enough to have Mari glancing over her shoulder. The woman didn't move though, maintaining her spot as a buffer. The knife would be last resort. I was sure this hussy didn't know about Mari's years in a boxing ring. She was sorely out gunned.

"Damn right. Danny is dead and this place is mine."

"Tsk tsk. I'm sorry to inform you, or, well, maybe sorry isn't the right word. However, you have no claims here. So, I suggest you collect your things and go find your real baby daddy."

The woman froze, unsure what to say. Her eyes darted between me and Mari as she tried to determine how much of the truth we knew. "Run along now," I said drawing the cleaver from behind my back. My knuckles whitened as burning rage tightened my grip, "before someone gets more than their feelings hurt."

Their uninvited guest made a hasty retreat and Mari slammed the door shut behind her. "Wow," she said turning to face me.

The facade of strength fell away as my resolve withered with the danger now past. The knife dropped from my grasp clanking against the floor as I reached for the wall to keep from collapsing.

Mari rested a hand on my back, allowing me to shift my weight from the wall to her, "Come on, you need to finish your food and another cup of tea will do you good."

"Bump that tea. I need a drink."

Chapter Forty-Seven

By the third day after Danial's transition, the steady stream of visitors turned to a trickle of one or two people a day. Most came to find out about his funeral or memorial service. They left disappointed when I informed them I planned to adhere to his wishes and forgo both. Besides, with his body already donated to the hospital, a funeral was out of the question.

"Have you decided if you're staying here or going back to Atlanta?" Mari asked as she prepared yet another meal for two.

I retrieved a bottle of water from the fridge before closing the door and leaning against it. "Yeah. I think it's time to head home. Yaddi's party is in a couple of days, and I need to be there to make sure nothing falls through the cracks."

"It's good you have something to go back to. I mean, to occupy your time."

A thought crossed my mind. One I should have considered a while ago. Mari spent so much time with them, catering to their needs. On her off time, she worked on getting her business off the ground. The woman's life revolved around doing for and caring for others. "I can stay a little longer if you want company. I can handle details from here."

"No. I'll be fine." Mari's gaze longingly scanned the room. "This is going to be a big adjustment."

"I know. Back-to-back too. With my initial departure, the arrival of the mistress, and now Daniel's death, you've experienced a lot of upheaval in a short period of time."

"Well, that would be three."

"True. I know we've talked about my plans, and I meant what I said. There's no rush for you to vacate. And while I'm going back to Atlanta, I'll be back after the new year. I need to go through the books, inventory, and pack things up." I dreaded the task awaiting me after the new year. Unfortunately,

291

there was no avoiding it, "which reminds me. Go through the house. If there's anything you want, furniture or decor wise just make a list. Just," I hesitated, studying my hands, "just leave the office, I'd like to go through it myself first."

"I couldn't."

"Please. Aside from the books, there's nothing here I want. Maybe I'll do an estate sale? Or just donate it all. I suppose I can auction the artwork, but I don't know that I have it in me to even be bothered." I trudged across the kitchen, plopping down in the chair at the island and Mari piled two plates high with lasagna. "I do have a favor to ask."

Mari looked at me after settling into her seat. "Anything."

As we ate, I explained about the cash Daniel had left. I wanted to make deposits in multiple banks but didn't trust a ride share. "I don't trust myself driving right now."

"Believe me, I understand. Anything you need I'm here. We can leave after lunch if that works for you."

"It does."

I settled into the passenger seat as Mari drove to our first stop. Guess it was time to open the lines of communication. I powered the phone on for the first time since stepping foot in hospital and found over fifty missed text messages and a slew of voicemails. Maybe falling off the face of the Earth hadn't been the best idea.

"Wow. I don't think I've ever heard anyone's phone ding that much," Mari commented.

"This is my first time turning this phone on in days."

"Seriously?"

"Yep." I scrolled through the text messages, checking for the confirmations from the party vendors. "Unlike most, I'm not attached to my phone." I returned confirmations after each stop, strategically ignoring personal messages. I'd deal with them once I arranged my return flight.

We returned to the house, and I made my travel plans dismissing the slew of notifications popping up on the side of the computer screen while I filtered through flight options. I lucked up and grabbed the last seat on the last flight out for the night. With little to pack, I booked a ride to the airport and gathered my measly belongings.

"Soliel!" Mari yelled from the front door, "I'm guessing this car is here to take you to the airport."

I met Mari at the bottom of the stairs, my bag in one hand and an envelope in the other. I held the envelope out to Mari. "This is for you. From Daniel and me. It should cover any incidentals until I can get back."

Mari flipped through the stack of bills in the envelope, "I can't accept this." She tried to give it back. I flatly refused.

"And just so you know, he set up a trust for you to ease your transition into your next opportunity. I know you said you have everything covered and you're in a good place."

"I am."

"Once the estate is settled, the money will be there for you to do with as you please. Danny really did try to make things right."

Mari's eyes misted over, and I pulled her into a comforting embrace. "I'll see you in a couple of weeks. Okay?" The woman nodded into my shoulder. "Take care of yourself."

She pulled away before wiping her tears with the back of her hand. "You too."

"And call if you need anything."

With a smile, Mari gave a thumbs up as I turned and walked out the door.

I made it Yaddi's house without incident, my decision to use a ride share instead of calling Armond allowed for a stealthy return. I collected the box of flowers at the door, before quietly descending the stairs to my current humble abode. The house was quiet, and while I dared not check the garage for fear of waking Yaddi, making it downstairs without confrontation about my disappearing act meant I was likely home alone.

After arranging the flowers in a vase, I took a moment to admire the spray of peach, yellow, and green roses. I understood the significance: peach for sincerity and gratitude, yellow for friendship and new beginnings, and green signifying peace and harmony. What I didn't understand was why Ellis would send me this color combination.

I plucked the envelope from the box carrying it with me to the bathroom. Between the errands, packing, and the flight, I only wanted to take a long bubble bath and crawl into the comfort of my own bed. Candles lit, with classical music playing low in the background, I eased into the warmth of the lavender scented water. A nagging in my gut forced me to read the message on the card and once again my world took an unexpected turn.

My dearest Divine,

I know you weren't expecting these, which is why you need and deserve them most. If you feel the need to mourn, make it short and move on with your life. My dying wish is for you is to consider these roses as my final gift to you. May they serve as a reminder of our last conversation. I cannot thank you enough for being my light in the dark, and now that our chapter has come to a close, I wish you peace and harmony in your new beginnings. This is your new beginning. Embrace the journey ahead and always remember, my love and Tyler's love will always be with you. The world needs more people like you. Don't ever change and don't let your new blessing slip through your fingers. Go after it with all you have. And once it's yours, don't ever let it go.

Forever yours. With all my love.

Danny

My tears flowed freely. The coffin now sealed as this chapter of my life finally closed. I expected the sadness and allowed it to run its course. I wailed until the aching of my heart stole my breath away, my chest tightening with each inhalation. When I felt strong enough, I climbed from the tub, dried off, and crawled into bed. Exhaustion settling, in I succumbed to weight of the world and the enticing song of the Sandman.

Chapter Forty-Eight

After a day in bed to recover, I welcomed the rumble of lawnmowers at dawn. My to-do list beaconed, the party of the year starting on just over twelve hours. I climbed from bed, tossing on jeans and a tee shirt with a cartoon grim reaper holding a cup of coffee the tagline 'I feel like death' plastered across the front. To my surprise. I found Yaddi sitting at my kitchen island two cups and a carafe of coffee in front of her.

"Welcome back," Yaddi said, her fingers plucking a wilting petal from a yellow rose.

I rounded the island scooping up the empty cup. I filled it with coffee adding two tablespoons of sugar before searching the fridge for creamer.

"You're out."

So much for stalling. What did Yaddi expect me to say? I barely held my emotions in check at the moment. If she started talking about Daniel...well, I didn't have time to talk about Daniel. If the landscapers were here, then we needed to start folding napkins and preparing the centerpieces.

"Have the flowers arrived?" There, focus on the to-do list.

"They're upstairs."

"Then we should get to work." I tried to scurry past, but Yaddi caught my arm. As much as I wanted to run, at the very least, I owed Yaddi an explanation. Taking the seat at the end of the island to give myself space, I admitted, "he's gone and I'm trying to hold it together."

"Oh, Soliel."

I stopped Yaddi from moving closer. "Please. Don't. I just need to get through today."

"Are you sure? I can handle..."

I held up a hand, "No. I need to do this. I need the distraction." Yaddi reluctantly agreed and we headed upstairs to work.

We prepped the napkins in silence, each focusing on the folds to make the ten perfectly symmetrical origami swans. The center pieces took a little more planning with Yaddi allowing me to design the first one before she dove into the task of duplicating the arrangement. The landscapers pulled her away and she returned with two vases of red roses.

"You ordered roses too?" I asked as she added the last section of baby's breath to her project.

"No. The guy said these were just delivered. They're addressed to you."

I froze. The last set of roses I'd received came from Daniel. Had he scheduled another delivery for today as well?

As if anticipating my next question, Yaddi said, "They're from Ellis."

A breath I hadn't realized I held escaped. "I'll take them downstairs. We still have two more of these before we can call it a day."

"I can handle them. The rental people should be here soon with the tables."

"Are you going to have them put up the tent too?"

"No. It's supposed to be clear skies. I will have the heaters though just in case."

Gathering the vases of flowers, I descended the stairs. I left one vase on the counter next to the ones from Daniel and set the other on the bathroom counter where they'd get plenty of light. The message on the card was short and simple. *Thinking of you, Love, Ellis.*

My heart softened. Maybe there was still a chance for us to work things out. Still, not wanting to get my hopes up, I decided not to get ahead of myself. I'd take it moment by moment, without placing too much stock in resolving anything today. Right now, I needed to focus on the party. When the dust settled, I'd contemplate my next move.

Like clockwork, the rental company arrived. As each table was placed. Yaddi and I worked on the settings. We danced around one another like professionals expediting the process until only two tables remained. Yaddi disappeared with the crew, I assumed to walk them out. By the time I placed the last tablecloths, centerpieces, and dishes Yaddi returned.

"You are planning to attend? Aren't you?'

And there it was. "I don't think so." I straightened a misaligned swan before stepping back to admire my handy work. "I'm tired, and I don't want to be in the way."

"You mean you don't want to run into Ellis," Yaddi said. She crossed her arms over that ample bosom of hers, making a point to track my gaze as I tried to avoid her scrutiny.

"Tonight's not the night."

"And why not? You've obviously been avoiding him. And you best believe, he was worried when I showed up at the restaurant."

"You did what?"

"Don't act surprised. It's your own damn fault. If you'd have returned my calls or answered your phone, I wouldn't have had to try to track you down."

With no defense, I conceded. "Well, that's neither here nor there. I'm not in the mood to party."

"I'm not asking you to party. I am suggesting the business potential this gathering has for you. Not just for your calligraphy and stationery, but should you decide to go into party planning, rubbing elbows with my crew will definitely get you noticed. You know my associates are highbrow. One or two parties from them and you'll have high society knocking down your door."

"You're right."

"I know. I'm not asking you to stay all night, but at least make an appearance."

"I'll think about it," was all I could give. While the business potential was enticing, the matter of crossing paths with Ellis still weighed heavy on my heart. I needed to have a clear head before facing him again. "I'm going to rest. I'm sure you can handle things from here." Without giving her a chance to rebut, I made a b-line for the sliding doors and headed for a much-needed nap.

"YOU READY FOR THIS?" Yusef asked as Ellis pulled into Yaddi's driveway.

"Um, why wouldn't I. We've done this hundreds of times." Ellis rolled to a stop, leaving the back end of the catering van perfectly positioned by the front door.

"I'm not talking about the catering, and you know it."

"You know I've perfected the art of not mixing business with pleasure."

Yusef leaned up taking in the lay of the land. "Yet here we are."

"Tonight will be fine." He turned off the ignition, "Besides, she might not even attend."

"You two still avoiding each other huh."

"Can we not do this?" Annoyed and needing a moment to himself, Ellis climbed from the vehicle. He rounded the back before heading towards the front door. A light breeze brushed across his face carrying the scent of azaleas and fresh cut grass as he waited for someone to answer the doorbell. While her yard always appeared well manicured, he could tell the landscapers took extra care today.

"Right on time," Yaddi said when she swung the door open.

Ellis followed her through to the kitchen. "Where is everything being setup?"

"You have full use of the upstairs kitchen," she said giving her best Vanna White presentation wave. "We have two tables setup on the deck with 8-quart roll-top chafing dishes. I hope that works for you."

"Perfect." He trailed behind, eyes taking in the all-white decor suspecting she'd made the changes in case the party needed to be moved inside. White tablecloths decorated with silver bells and crystals sat on the deck. Wide white ribbon wrapped around the banister, silver and crystal wind chimes offering a sweet melody as the wind danced among them.

"The bar is on the main level. The bartender has his own waitresses who are responsible for keeping the liquor flowing."

Ellis peaked over the side, admiring the flow of the setup impressed with the wooden floor covering the pool. A scattering of heaters left no spot without warmth and a giant screen with curtains draped on each side strategically acted as a divider to keep guest from roaming past the designated party area. Unless a guest over indulged, they should have no trouble navigating the area. Ellis turned back to the patio setup, inspecting each chafing dish while calculating the necessary portions.

"Is it just the two of you?" Yaddi asked as they returned to the kitchen.

"Yes."

"Good. If you need extra hands, feel free to commandeer one of the drink servers."

"Got it."

"Also, I need to speak with you both about tonight." The men exchanged worried glances. "I'll let you get acclimated first. I'm not expecting the first guest to arrive for at least another hour. They will be on time though so please take that into account when deciding when to transition the food to the chafing dishes. I won't be far."

Instead of elaborating, Yaddi excused herself sauntering away, her hips swaying in the free-flowing purple dress. When she was out of earshot, Yusef asked, "What do you think she wants to talk to us about?"

"I'm assuming she wants this to remain strictly professional."

"Yeah, I'm not so sure. I think she knows you well enough to not let your emotions cloud your judgment and interfere. Otherwise, I don't think she would have agreed to you catering the event with just Soliel's word."

"Yaddi is a bit eccentric. One thing I won't expect from tonight is a boring evening. Now let's get this food unloaded."

Ellis took in the lay of the land while Yusef made multiple trips to the van. To his surprise, Yaddi had emptied the refrigerator giving them full access to the wide shelves where they loaded the trays of salads and decanters of homemade dressing. He set the two ovens to keep warm before sliding in two of each tray of pasta.

"This is a nice kitchen," Yusef commented when he finally took a second to take it in.

"You telling me. I swear I'm gonna have one like this in my next house."

"You're more than welcome to use mine whenever you like." Yaddi said, startling the men as she stealthily re-entered. "So, has he told you about my guest?" She directed the question at Yusef who seemed surprised. "By the look on your face, I'm guessing that's a no. Here are the ground rules," she tore a gold strip from the hand full of wristbands making her way towards Ellis. She secured it to his wrist before focusing on Yusef. "As the nondisclosure agreement states, the identities of my guest are strictly confidential. Understood?"

"Understood," Ellis responded.

"And you?" She waited for verbal confirmation from Yusef before continuing.

"Understood."

"Good. However, I'm not entirely a party-pooper, so I'll let you choose." Crossing the kitchen, she stopped in front of Yusef. "I'm sure Ellis already knows this, but my annual soirée is for me to select my 'special' friend or friends for the next year. However, we are a group that doesn't necessarily mind sharing if you catch my drift."

When Yusef stared at her like a deer in headlights, Ellis filled in the blanks, "They're swingers."

Yaddi turned, her gaze narrowed and pinpointed on Ellis, "We are not swingers. We're more into polyfidelity thank you very much."

He shrugged. If that's how she saw it, then so be it. As an outsider looking in, well, Yaddi's personal life wasn't any of his concern, so he opted not to engage.

"At any rate." She focused on Yusef again, "you're a nice-looking man and from what I've heard, you'd mesh will with the group. I can see some of my associates taking notice; so, I'll leave it up to you. Red means you're free and open to anything. Green indicates you prefer the opposite sex. And Orange indicates a preference for the same sex."

"And the gold?" Yusef asked gesturing towards Ellis.

"Off limits."

Ellis glanced at the golden band on his wrist. He suspected it identified him as a staff member and not a party participant, but he hadn't considered a meaning beyond that.

"Think I'd better stick with gold."

Yaddi pursed her lips, "Pity." She obliged, tearing one more gold strip from the bands, and securing it around his wrist. "Let me know if you change your mind. It's just a piece of plastic. Like so many other things in life," she paused, making a point to step away and give him a thorough once over, "it can easily be replaced."

Chapter Forty-Nine

Ellis and Yusef worked side by side through the evening, tending to the food to make sure nothing overheated and burned. They stole glimpses of the partygoers dressed to the T in white from the sparkling adornments in the classic updo's to the dangerously high heels the women sported. On more than one occasion Ellis witnessed a couple or threesome sneak off to a corner, their conversations intense, hands not so secretly sliding up the open slit of a high cut dress or beneath the billow of flowing cloth. And the women weren't the only ones on the receiving end of pleasurable petting. The men enjoyed the not-so-innocent brush over their chests or salacious hands testing the merchandise as they leaned into whisper into the women's ears.

"They are wild."

Ellis moved to the side, the empty pasta tray in hand as Yusef dropped the full one into the chafer. "Yaddi did warn us."

"That she did. But damn, I never expected them to be this open. She might not like the term swingers, but I've been in one of those parties and it was pretty much just like this."

"Wait, what?"

"Hey," Yusef took the empty pan off Ellis, "we all have a past."

Ellis followed the man as he walked away, not answering the question. "So, you used to go to swinger parties?"

"I didn't say that."

"Yeah, you kinda did."

"I said I've been in one before. I should have known something was up with the girl I was dating. I mean, we weren't exclusive or anything, but whenever we hung out with her friends there was always this feeling that her girlfriends were eyeing me. She didn't seem bothered about it at all, so I thought they might just be into sharing."

"Well, obviously they were."

"Yeah, their boyfriends too. Not my scene."

Ellis understood. Like himself, Yusef felt no urge to dabble in the other side. "How long did that last?"

"A couple of weeks more. Then one of the men propositioned me and wouldn't take no for an answer. It didn't end well."

"Is that the night I had to bail you out of jail?"

Yusef nodded. "Enough about me and memory lane. Have you seen her?"

"Who?"

"Don't play. You know exactly who I'm talking about."

"No," Ellis responded. He scraped the remnants of food from the tray before adding it to the discard pan by the sink.

"Think she's avoiding you?"

"I don't know. I have no idea what she's thinking. I messed up and I'm trying to give her space to come to me."

"Might not be the best plan. One of you is going to have to make the first move."

"I know. If I don't see her tonight, I'll reach out tomorrow." Ellis crossed the kitchen gathering the two boxes of The Naughty Chocolatier treats he planned to add to the pre-approved dessert.

Yusef busied himself with preparing dessert, slicing through the first tray of tiramisu. "These are perfect," he commented as he started to plate.

"Homemade ladyfingers."

"I thought you always made them yourself."

"When I make desserts, I do. However..."

"Never mind. I know where you're going with this and there's no need. Speaking of going somewhere, I saw you packed a change of clothes. You planning to join the party?"

"He sure is," Yaddi burst through the kitchen, eyes bright with excitement, "That is if you can spare him."

"Oh, he can be spared," Yusef responded a little too quickly for Ellis's taste.

"Did you do as I asked and bring a white suit?" Yaddi leaned against the island peeking into the window of one of the boxes of chocolate.

Seeing her interest piqued, Ellis opened the lid. Using tongs, he placed each of the four chocolate balls onto a white porcelain plate and slid it over to Yaddi. He waited for her to pop the first one, the black cake covered in cherry dark chocolate, into her mouth before responding. "I did."

"Oh, my Goddess these are utterly orgasmic."

Ellis beamed as Yaddi reached for the second one on the plate, this one a puree of the extra alcohol infused fruit and mixed peel Soliel gave him covered in an orange milk chocolate. She released a moan that obviously distracted Yusef enough to cause him to drop the cold silver serving spatula he used to transfer the slices of cake to their respective plates.

"Slow down," Ellis said. Those are full of alcohol.

"And absolutely divine. Are these on the menu?"

"They can be. I have enough for your guest, and an extra box for you. We can add them to be served or the guest can take them home as goodie boxes."

"Do they have your information on them?"

He slid one of the labeled boxes in her direction, the beautifully lettered silver logo for The Naughty Chocolatier scribed over the top of the box. He'd embezzled the date and event name on the front and contact information for The Naughty Chocolatier on the back side.

"You've thought of everything."

"Actually, the gift box was Soliel's idea. The calligraphy is her doing. We already had the boxes, just had date and event stickers printed up just in case."

"I see. Well, I'll have to thank her later. In the meantime, you should change. The bedrooms are down the hall that way." Yaddi pointed towards the living room. "I hope you brought plenty of business cards. I'll formally introduce you in a few minutes. They've all been raving about the food, and I am sure dessert won't disappoint."

Before Yaddi sauntered too far away, Ellis managed to catch up with her. She slowed, as if expecting him to question her.

"I haven't seen Soliel at the party," he finally muttered looking away.

"She opted not to attend."

"So, she is avoiding me? I don't want to cause any..." Yaddi's hand resting on his arm stopped him.

"These are my friends. They aren't exactly her type. But that's not what's important. One of you needs to make the first move."

"I don't want to overstep."

"Reaching out to let her know you're thinking of her and checking to make sure she is doing well is far from overstepping. Now, go get changed, and make sure to keep that band on. The vultures are circling, and you don't want to become prey." With a chuckle and a devilish grin, Yaddi made her exit as only Yaddi could do, leaving Ellis staring behind the woman who knew she walked at the top of the world tonight.

"YOU'RE NOT DRESSED yet woman?"

Annoyed beyond comprehension, I ignored Yaddi as I continued to behead fantastical enemies with my online teammates. I'd already made it clear, with the party planning done, anything party-related that needed to be handled from this point forward, Yaddi would have to figure out on her own.

"I know you hear me!"

I shrugged but didn't move, my eyes still fixated on the blood dripping horned creatures barreling down on me on the screen. I didn't hesitate, fingers moving across the controller button and knobs with ease. Another head flew to the right, sprays of red following as yet another creature jumped from the grouping of trees ready to attack. No matter all the huffing Yaddi performed, I didn't stop playing.

When Yaddi stepped in front of the television, I leaned to one side to see around the woman only to have her shift into that spot. We danced like this for a few moments, though I continued in my combat without an additional care in the world.

"Don't make me pull the plug. You know I'll do it."

With a huff, I gave in. I told my crew I had to bail, and I'd catch them tomorrow at our regularly scheduled time. I glared up at Yaddi, headset flying to the next seat landing with a thunk. "I told you," I said with a sneer, "I'm not going to the party."

"Why are you being like this?"

I stood, rounding the couch on the side opposite Yaddi taking the long way around to the kitchen. I filled my glass with Bellini before taking a long refreshing sip.

"Say something?" Yaddi demanded, her hands sitting firmly on her hips like a mother preparing to scold her disobedient child.

"I'm tired. I'm annoyed. And frankly I've done my job. I see no reason to spend my night being hit on by your entourage."

"They won't hit on you."

"Yeah, I've heard that song and dance before. This isn't my first rodeo. Remember."

Yaddi joined me in the kitchen, though she remained on the other side of the island, "You two need to talk."

"We'll talk when I'm good and ready. I... I just can't right now."

"And why not?"

"Why are you even pushing this?"

Instead of immediately answering, Yaddi pulled out one of the chairs and took a seat. She stared out the window into the night. "You know, I've lived vicariously through you for years."

"Excuse me?"

"You heard what I said. As much as I enjoy my freedom and poly lifestyle, I do sometimes feel like I'm missing out."

"On what?"

"Married life. Settling down with one person. Starting a family."

I stared at her for a moment, my mind struggling to wrap around this sudden confession. I moved closer, leaning on the island but leaving it as a divider. "I don't understand. Didn't we have a conversation a few weeks ago about your annulled marriage."

"I know."

"Then where is all of this coming from?" The music outside changed, the beat picking up. A head passed the window and for a moment, I thought someone might knock on the door. But the sound never came, and I turned back to Yaddi who'd been sitting quietly twiddling her fingers. "Yaddi?"

"I guess, I feel like maybe I didn't give monogamy a fair chance. Or that I should have given it another chance after my first marriage fell apart. But now, seeing what you and Ellis are building. How you were able to come back after the fiasco with Danny. It...it just made me think that maybe all hope isn't lost."

"You said it yourself, monogamy isn't for everyone. Have you looked at your friends out there? Legally married couples who still live a poly lifestyle. We've always viewed the world differently; why shouldn't this be the same way. If you think you've found someone to settle down with who understands your lifestyle and can accept you and it, then there is still hope."

"It sounds easy."

"Yet it's not. Marriage isn't easy. It's the bumps in the road and how they are handled as a couple that can make or break the marriage. But both parties have to be all in. That means accepting one another as they are and working to grow and understand each other as you grow as people." I looked away, the words sinking in. I'd grown as a person while Daniel remained stagnant, stuck in his younger ways until it was too late. I understood now why he wanted me to move on.

"I suppose. But this is a conversation for another time." Yaddi slid the chair back as she stood. "Are you really going to leave money on the table like this just to avoid Ellis?"

"Give me fifteen and I'll see you outside. No funny business though. I'll play along with your formal introduction, then I'm out."

Yaddi's smart-alecky smug wasn't lost on me, but I didn't let it get to me. Instead, I decided to play along. I had just the outfit in mind to entice the crowd and garner a reaction from the friend who thought me a party pooper. I planned to teach Yaddi a lesson. Careful what you ask for, you just might get it.

Chapter Fifty

Ellis stood at the top of the balcony stairs, again scanning the crowd for any sight of Soliel. He'd taken longer to dress than anticipated, fussing over the fact, no matter how much he tried, braiding, and tying his locs back on his own proved to be a daunting task on a good day. Add heightened nervousness and the mix made for stiff fingers that refused to cooperate. Eventually, he gave up the task, opting to pull them back and secure them with a loc wrapped around the middle. Luckily, they were long enough to achieve the desired effect, still providing enough give to cover the ear with the hearing aid.

By the time he completed the ordeal, what should have been a ten-minute wardrobe change had lingered past the twenty-minute mark. Or maybe it wasn't the hair and wardrobe that delayed his entrance to the party, but the plethora of scenarios dancing through his mind. Most ending with Soliel turning her back and walking away.

Eventually, Ellis decided to step out on faith. He'd never have the answer if he forever avoided the situation. Sooner or later, he needed to know if he could at least speak his peace. If she rejected him, so be it. If not, well he hoped she'd at least hear him out and they could talk.

Ellis adjusted the jacket; the custom tailored all white double breasted suit fitting him to a T even with the few pounds he'd shed worrying about the state of his restaurant affairs and his relationship. Living in limbo didn't sit well with his constitution, his love of food waning. At least the sorrow and uncertainty hadn't tainted his cooking. Forks scraped across plates; smiles of enjoyment plastered across the faces of those indulging in the fruits of his labor.

"Looks like dessert is a hit too."

He jumped, nearly losing his footing as Yusef pulled him out of the way to allow the waitress with the last tray of plated tiramisu to ease around him and descend the stairs.

"You look nervous," Yusef chided, elbowing Ellis in the side. "See her yet?"

Before Ellis could respond, he caught the glimpse of a beauty dressed in a sparkling skin-tight all-white body suit and high heels that would make even the baddest drag queen question their ability to strut across the stage. Yet her confident stride garnered the attention of every man, and a few of the women, as she flitted from table to table greeting those with mouths stuffed full of tantalizing tiramisu.

Soliel hadn't looked his way, her back to the house the entire time as she conversed with each set of party goers. She stopped at a table of women and even from this vantage point he could see the interest in their eyes as they took in every adorned curve of his woman. A man joined the group, sliding up to Soliel from behind, his hand resting at her back as he bent over to whisper something in her ear. Ellis felt his anger rising as the man twirled Soliel around holding her at arm's length as he took all of her in, from the scarf wrapped around her hair to the solid band of the sparkling white belt cinching her waist. They wanted her. And so did he.

"Down boy," Yaddi said as she shimmied her way between them, her back to the events transpiring below. Her hand brushed over Ellis's bald fists. "Dwayne is harmless. But I suggest you go claim your prize. She isn't wearing a wrist band." Yaddi waved a golden wristband in front of him, and he plucked it from her grasp with ease.

Ellis relaxed, reigning in his fury as he straightened his jacket sleeves making sure the golden band hung low enough for everyone to see he was off limits. He descended the stairs, Yaddi a few steps behind. No one appeared to notice their arrival, their attention still on Soliel laughing at something Dwayne said.

Her eyes flicked his way, her shoulders and expression tensing at his approach. Dwayne must have noticed the change because he cocked his head to the side glaring at Ellis over his shoulder. While Dwayne might have had Ellis by a few inches in height and carried a much more muscular build, the man didn't seem to want a fight as he drew Soliel's hand to his lips, quickly pecked her knuckles, then casually continued on his way.

Soliel stole Ellis's breath away as he, like everyone else, took in the full outfit from the high neckline halter style top with the oval cut out in the front revealing the swell of her breast to the fact that aside from some strategically placed full cloth patches, the rest of the bodysuit was not just sparkling but utterly see through. Ellis quickly claimed Soliel's hand, securing the yellow band around her wrist before he forgot the thing and scooped her up in his arms to whisk her away from the ogling eyes of the crowd.

Yaddi tapped the microphone, "Can I have everyone's attention?"

Ellis half expected Soliel to reclaim her hand as they waited for Yaddi to complete her introductions and spiel. Instead, she intertwined her fingers with his, giving a gentle squeeze as she smiled up at him. So, all wasn't lost. And he relaxed.

Unfortunately, after the introductions the couple spent the next half hour passing out cards and fielding questions. They hovered near the back of the grouping of tables, stealing glances and sharing smiles while performing the networking duties thrust upon them. By the time Yaddi pulled her guest away for her final announcement of the night, Ellis could tell Soliel had had her fill of people.

He inched closer to her, careful to not draw attention as he leaned over and whispered, "is there somewhere we can talk?"

Soliel grabbed his hand, tugging the edge of the curtain back before pulling him through the opening behind her.

They walked hand in hand down the familiar path, stopping at the water's edge. Soliel shivered, and Ellis immediately removed his jacket and draped it over her bare shoulders. He stood behind her, his arms wrapped around her waist, his head resting on her shoulder as they watched the stillness of the water. She nuzzled into the warmth of his body, and he smiled at the feel of her against his chest.

Even with the party only feet away, it felt like they were the only two people in the world. "This is nice," he finally said, arms tightening around her waist as if to convince himself she was actually here.

"It is."

Unable to stand not gazing down into those big beautiful brown eyes of hers, Ellis turned Soliel around to face him. The lone tear trailing down her cheek surprised him. "Are you alright?" he asked as he cradled her hands in his. His thumbs drew circles over the back of her hands as she smiled up at him.

"I am now."

"I am so sorry." Ellis blurted out. "I was wrong on so many levels. Can you ever forgive me?"

Soliel pulled a hand free from his grasp as she raised it to cradle his cheek. She bit the bottom of her lip as she drew him down to her and with an urgency he hadn't expected, she poured her confirmation into a kiss sweeter than any chocolate he'd ever tasted.

THE END

Don't miss out!

Visit the website below and you can sign up to receive emails whenever Ana'Gia Wright publishes a new book. There's no charge and no obligation.

https://books2read.com/r/B-A-LCXE-PLMBC

BOOKS 2 READ

Connecting independent readers to independent writers.

About the Author

Ana'Gia Wright is a firm believer that reading and writing go hand and hand. A Southerner through and through, she loves her peaches and pecans while curling up with a good book. A master of resourcefulness, her love of research leads her down paths of discovery that touch every aspect of her writing. Her love of reading ignited her passion for writing resulting in her frequently fill page after page with tales of her beloved characters' adventures. An influence and an adversary, she loves to sprinkle facts about her beloved Georgia throughout her fictional worlds.

Read more at www.anagiawright.com.

www.ingramcontent.com/pod-product-compliance
Lightning Source LLC
Chambersburg PA
CBHW071105250626
47159CB00002B/611